Form and Love in the Poetry of Jacques Roubaud

Modern French Identities

Edited by Jean Khalfa

Volume 148

PETER LANG
Oxford - Berlin - Bruxelles - Chennai - Lausanne - New York

Thea Petrou

Form and Love in the Poetry of Jacques Roubaud

PETER LANG
Oxford - Berlin - Bruxelles - Chennai - Lausanne - New York

Bibliographic information published by the Deutsche Nationalbibliothek.
The German National Library lists this publication in the German National Bibliography; detailed bibliographic data is available on the Internet at http://dnb.d-nb.de.

A catalogue record for this book is available from the British Library.

Names: Petrou, Thea, 1984- author.
Title: Form and love in the poetry of Jacques Roubaud / Thea Petrou.
Description: Oxford ; New York : Peter Lang, 2024. | Series: Modern French identities, 1422-9005 ; volume 148 | Includes bibliographical references and index.
Identifiers: LCCN 2023042984 (print) | LCCN 2023042985 (ebook) | ISBN 9781800792654 (paperback) | ISBN 9781800792661 (ebook) | ISBN 9781800792678 (epub)
Subjects: LCSH: Roubaud, Jacques–Criticism and interpretation. | Love poetry, French–20th century–History and criticism.
Classification: LCC PQ2678.O77 Z75 2024 (print) | LCC PQ2678.O77 (ebook) | DDC 841/.914–dc23/eng/20231124
LC record available at https://lccn.loc.gov/2023042984
LC ebook record available at https://lccn.loc.gov/2023042985

Cover design by Peter Lang Group AG

ISSN 1422-9005
ISBN 978-1-80079-265-4 (print)
ISBN 978-1-80079-266-1 (ePDF)
ISBN 978-1-80079-267-8 (ePub)
DOI 10.3726/b18083

Published by Peter Lang Ltd, Oxford, United Kingdom
info@peterlang.com – www.peterlang.com

This publication has been peer reviewed.

Contents

Acknowledgements

I would like to thank Timothy Mathews for his guidance, encouragement and advice throughout the time I have known him. Tim inspired a love of poetry in me some years ago, when I was an undergraduate student, and it was a privilege to have him as my supervisor and mentor while working on my thesis. Now I am grateful to have him as a friend. I would also like to say thank you to Jane Gilbert for the practical tips and approaches to staying sane while researching and writing, which I still rely on. Thank you, Stefano Rossoni, for reading my writing over the years, but most of all, for your friendship. And thank you, Laurel Plapp, for guiding me through the publishing process with patience. I would also like to thank Gallimard for their permission to quote from Jacques Roubaud's collections *Trente et un au cube, Dors* précédé de *Dire la poésie, Autobiographie, Chapitre dix* and *Quelque chose noir*. And I would like to thank The Josef and Anni Albers Foundation for the use of the front cover image, *Angular*, by Josef Albers.

I will always be grateful to Jacques Roubaud, composer of mathematics and poetry, for his kindness, the memories and the stories he shared with me during an interview in London shortly before I began my PhD. They say never to meet your heroes, but I am very glad that I have.

Finally, I thank my parents, Maria and Michael, and my partner, Stuart, for their love (which I regularly put to the test) and their unwavering support, and for always inspiring me to be better.

Note to the Reader

In citations, I have endeavoured to reproduce Roubaud's poetry as it appears in the original text. The wide landscape format of the poems in *Trente et un au cube* and also in Roubaud's 'Poème de présentation composé pour une lecture de *Trente et un au cube* à Shakespeare et C°' means this has not always been possible. I have chosen to represent the particular layout of the poems in *Trente et un au cube* using a single dash to represent a space between fragments (|), two dashes to represent a line break (||) and three dashes to signal a new stanza (|||).

Where original citations occur in French, I have generally chosen to provide my own translations into English. These translations are a way of sharing my readings of the various texts that have shaped this monograph, in particular the poetry that forms the core of the study, which it could be argued is often interpreted more subjectively than other genres of writing. I have used published translations for the citations taken from the more technical psychoanalytic texts. Where I have used published translations, they are referenced in the footnotes.

Introduction

This book is rooted in a love of poetry, and especially the poetry of Jacques Roubaud. A full-length study on any topic should be inspired by at least a sense of curiosity, but with poetry some might argue that the commitment is greater. Poetry's apparently waning readership has been put down to its difficulty by Roubaud himself. In his *Poésie, etcetera: ménage* [*Poetry, etcetera: Housekeeping*] the poet speaks of doing 'le ménage dans [sa] tête' [mental housekeeping] with regard to a number of questions he feels poets are faced with today, including 'La poésie contemporaine, pourquoi si difficile?' [Contemporary poetry, why so difficult?], to which he dedicates an entire section of this pocket-sized theoretical treatise.[1] He suggests several reasons for the perceived difficulty of poetry, including our lack of understanding as to why the genre should exist in the first place, the challenge of tackling a new metre and the barrier that is our lack of patience when confronted with a text we cannot penetrate.[2]

The obstacle perhaps most likely to intervene in a reading of Jacques Roubaud's own poems is that of 'l'ignorance de la poésie qui se fait' [not knowing about the poetry that is being written], or a non-familiarity which functions on two levels.[3] Roubaud explains: 'la poésie est liée à la mémoire, elle l'est à la mémoire de chacun; si elle n'est pas, ou plus, dans votre mémoire, alors vous ne connaissez plus ce qu'est la poésie' [poetry is linked to memory, it is linked to each person's memory; if it isn't in your memory, or it was but no longer is now, then you don't know what poetry is any more].[4] When we are not in the habit of reading poetry, we lose the

1 Jacques Roubaud, *Poésie, etcetera: ménage* (Paris: Stock, 1995), p. 7. See also in the volume 'Section L – La poésie est difficile', pp. 263–75. All translations are my own, unless otherwise noted.

2 Roubaud, *Poésie, etcetera*, pp. 263–70.

3 Roubaud, *Poésie, etcetera*, p. 266.

4 Roubaud, *Poésie, etcetera*, p. 266.

very sense of how to read it: it is traditionally something which is memorized, or recited, gaining additional meaning through its gradual absorption into our mind, and also through its constant comparison there with other poems. Immersion will be more difficult for someone not already familiar with poetry and its techniques. The problem with contemporary poetry then is one of change, or rather our reluctance to accept change. When poems no longer sound like those we used to know, the patterns we have memorized, whether the difference is one of 'vocabulaire, constructions, formes, présentation, idées, …' [vocabulary, constructions, form, arrangement, ideas, …], their language comes across as 'insolite' [unusual], 'étrange' [strange] or 'difficile' [difficult].[5]

Critic Alain Bosquet singles out Roubaud's *Trente et un au cube* [*Thirty-One Cubed*] for its lack of penetrability for the average reader: 'le malheur est que, pour le lecteur de bonne volonté moyenne, Jacques Roubaud se barricade dans ses livres et en interdit l'accès' [the unfortunate thing is that, for the average reader, Jacques Roubaud barricades himself in his books and forbids anyone else from entering].[6] The volume Bosquet criticizes, true to its title, is described by Roubaud as 'un livre composé d'un poème qui est trente et un poèmes, dont chacun est trente et une lignes (ou vers), chaque ligne comptée trente et un (suivant le décompte que voici: chaque voyelle non élidée est 1, chaque e muet (élidé ou non) est 1 ou 0 au choix)' [a book that is a poem of thirty-one poems, each of which is thirty-one lines long, and every line made up of thirty-one syllables (according to the following count: each non-elided vowel is 1, each mute e (elided or not) can be 1 or 0)].[7] The implications of this description for an analysis of the form of *Trente et un au cube* will be discussed in more detail elsewhere in this study, but a superficial glance is enough to identify the difficulties of 'ignorance' or 'non-familiarity', which a reader might experience. The emphasis on the syllable count, in particular the reference to the *e caduc* [mute e], implies an

5 Roubaud, *Poésie, etcetera*, pp. 267–68.

6 Alain Bosquet, 'Jacques Roubaud, ou la technique ennemie du poème', *Le Monde des livres*, 22 February 1974, p. 16. I consider Bosquet's criticism in greater detail in the third chapter of this study.

7 Jacques Roubaud, *Description du projet*, intro. by Jean-Jacques Poucel (Caen: Nous, 2014), p. 78.

assumed knowledge of traditional methods of counting French verse. An ear trained in conventional metres will also pick up on Roubaud's radical break here, since his lines of thirty-one syllables are divided into counts of 5-7-5-7-7 after the Japanese *tanka*, an unexpected sequence in French verse. A reader of *Trente et un au cube* might also be struck by the prominence of its intertextuality. This operates visually throughout the book, as the poems are interspersed with nearly blank pages dedicated to single quotations from other texts, sometimes poetic, but also mathematical and scientific ones. A final page of credits at the end of the volume attributes some of the intertextual extracts to their respective authors, but not all are identified.

A reader of the book should then be sufficiently familiar with the rhythms of traditional French metres; her memory should know the patterns of poetry, if only to be able to notice the contrast made with the deviating scansions employed here. Through this play with the poems' metrical features and the proliferation of intertextual references, Roubaud places his poetry within a series of interconnecting relationships with the writings of others. Perhaps Jacques Roubaud's poems are 'difficult' then, but an intricate, concentrated, repeated reading yields greater rewards: an awareness of the links extending beyond his texts brings to light a network of allusions and associations that might otherwise have remained hidden.

Other readers of Roubaud have responded more sensitively than Bosquet to the dense quality of his poetry. Jean-François Puff writes of the demands made on a reader of *Trente et un au cube* as 'un investissement, intense, dans une complexité que le désir seul peut soutenir, le désir ou l'amour de la poésie' [an intense investment in a complexity that only desire can maintain, desire or a love of poetry].[8] Here the reader's love of poetry takes the form of perseverance through the sheer complexity of the poem itself. For Puff, the challenge lies in the layers of meaning that constitute the text:

> Il faudrait notamment considérer quel usage conjointement formel et expressif Jacques Roubaud fait de la théorie du rythme qu'il a contribué à développer [...].

8 Jean-François Puff, 'Le Déploiement du nouveau chez Roubaud', *Formes Poétiques Contemporaines*, 1 (2003), 99–119 (p. 100).

> Consubstantielle à la forme du poème, cette théorie en soutient aussi le sens. Cela exige une vraie lecture de la théorie *et* de la poésie.[9]
>
> [In particular, the reader should consider Jacques Roubaud's jointly formal and expressive use of the theory of rhythm that he had a hand in developing [...]. An integral part of the poem's form, this theory also underpins its meaning. This requires a committed reading of the theory *and* the poetry.]

To know the poem is also to know the theory of rhythm that it speaks of and through, the theory that is both subject matter and form of the poem. There are echoes of this approach in Jean-Jacques Poucel's reading of *Trente et un au cube*. Like Puff, Poucel recognizes the overlap of content and form in the book as key to its understanding: 'Roubaud's poetic "cube" foregrounds how formal constraints engender textual meaning.'[10] Poucel also explains that the theoretical value of the work is articulated through the poetry itself: 'Reading the work as a poetic treatise on the art of poetry is fundamental to understanding how Roubaud turns literary self-referentiality into a study of poetic rhythm and memory.'[11] What is common to both arguments is not only the self-reflexivity of *Trente et un au cube* but also its particular way of engaging the reader, inviting her to participate in her own relationship with the text. That idea has been central to the impetus behind my study of Roubaud's poetry.

The self-reflexivity of his writing and a beckoning to the reader come together at a particular moment in Roubaud's poem of poems:

> le chant | se perd qui circule | seulement contre soi-même | rouille gèle se dissout ||| s'altère cède se | complique. voilà ce que | je lis pour toi sous | ces quatre vers de Bernart | Marti '*lo pintor*' (ainsi || s'est-il nommé lui- | même dans une chanson) | ensuite je lis | ce vers d'un poème de | lui, perdu avec le chan || sonnier de Sault (pillé par Jehan de Nostredame) | '*tant es ma donna* | *endurmyda*' (car ma dame | est si profondément en- || dormie) j'écris silencieusement sur ma feuille | 21 × 27 | dans la jaune lumière *endurmyda* qui vient de droite || le déclic du radiateur stimulé par son | rhéostat envoie | une lueur rouge dans | le verre laiteux de la ||| télévision;

9 Puff, 'Le Déploiement du nouveau chez Roubaud', p. 100.

10 Jean-Jacques Poucel, *Jacques Roubaud and the Invention of Memory* (Chapel Hill: University of North Carolina Press, 2006), p. 118.

11 Poucel, *Jacques Roubaud and the Invention of Memory*, p. 118.

> je le | note aussi. je te regarde | dormir. tu dors nue | tranquillement appliquée | tranquillement arrondie.[12]

> [the song | is lost when it meets | nothing but itself | it rusts freezes dissolves ||| falters gives in gets | tangled. this is what | I read to you in | these four lines by Bernart | Marti '*lo pintor*' (so || he called him- | self in a song) | then I read | this line from a poem by | him, lost with the song- || book of Sault (plundered by Jehan de Nostredame) | '*tant es ma donna* | *endurmyda*' (for my lady | sleeps so | deeply) I write silently on my page | 21 x 27 | in the yellow light *endurmyda* that comes from the right || the clicking on of the radiator triggered by its | rheostat sends | a red glow into | the milky glass of the ||| television; I note | that too. I watch you | sleeping. you sleep naked | quietly applied | quietly curved.]

These words and the visual components of the setting that they evoke have worked their way into my memory; I am drawn to this moment in time captured in poetry for a multiplicity of reasons. I am initially intrigued by its self-referential quality. Roubaud writes the details of the act of composition into the poem itself: '"*tant es ma donna* | *endurmyda*" (car ma dame | est si profondément en- || dormie) j'écris silencieusement sur ma feuille' ['*tant es ma donna* | *endurmyda*' (for my lady | sleeps so | deeply) I write silently on my page], then 'le verre laiteux de la ||| télévision; je le | note aussi' [the milky glass of the ||| television; I note | that too]. It is as though the reader is given a privileged position presiding over the creation of the text as it comes into being. The time of composition, the poet's writing and noting, merges with the moment in which the reader's eyes scan the words on the printed page of the published volume. The poet also states that the poem needs a listener, a reader, an addressee of some sort, in order to survive. Without someone to respond to it, to activate it, 'le chant [...] | rouille gèle se dissout ||| s'altère cède se | complique' [the song [...] | rusts freezes dissolves ||| falters gives in gets | tangled]. The sense of movement which derives from the enumeration and accumulation of verbs comes up against notions of decay, immobility and confused entanglement in the semantic value of the words. While the 'chant' then still exists and remains dynamic in some monstrous form, it only ends in ruin when not directed towards someone in particular.

12 Jacques Roubaud, *Trente et un au cube* (Paris: Gallimard, 1973), p. 21.

The markers of contemporaneity in the piece also captivate the reader. Roubaud's situation watching his lover as she sleeps reminds him of a line of poetry from the past: '"*tant es ma donna* | *endurmyda*" (car ma dame | est si profondément en- || dormie)' [(for my lady | sleeps so | deeply)]. The scene brings the line out in his memory, giving it new relevance in the present moment. The effect is one of a *mise en abyme*, like viewing a window through a window. I cannot help but wonder at the surprising juxtaposition of a verse of troubadour love poetry with 'le déclic du radiateur' [the clicking on of the radiator] and 'le verre laiteux de la ||| télévision' [the milky glass of the ||| television]. The conspicuousness of the radiator's click, and the unnatural light of the television come to life in the poem, functioning quite literally as distractions to the reader, perhaps to make her feel self-conscious, as reader. As I become aware of myself reading the lines of the verse and of being drawn into this intimacy with the poet and his lover, I realize that in some ways I am replicating the scene in the poem, for Roubaud too is reading another poet, Bernart Marti. Somehow the windows multiply, extending out towards me and creating a web of links between my present and the different pasts represented in the writing.

This book is rooted in a love of poetry in more ways than one. For Jacques Roubaud, there is necessarily love in reading poetry and the process of reading it is inextricably linked with the act of writing. As the poet composes these lines of *Trente et un au cube*, he reads both to his lover and to his reader who, addressed as 'toi', become one and the same at various points in the text: 'voilà ce que | je lis pour toi sous | ces quatre vers de Bernart | Marti "*lo pintor*"' [this is what | I read for you in | these four lines by Bernart | Marti '*lo pintor*']. If 'toi' [you] encompasses both the lover and reader as addressee, in 'je lis' [I read] the poet's announcement of reading becomes confused with the act of composing the text for our eyes; he writes those words in his poetry, but the first-person present tense seems to simultaneously perform the action of the verb in 'je lis pour toi' [I read for you]. Writing poetry is in part formed of reading it and the words of the poem emanate from this act of reading, that is, from 'these four lines' that Roubaud reads-writes for his lover and reader.

The four lines by Bernart Marti to which Roubaud refers are printed on the left-hand leaf of the book, parallel to the poem which unfolds to the right on the facing page:

aisi vauc entrebescant
los motz e'l so afinant
    lengu'entrebescada
    es en la baizada

ainsi je vais enlaçant
les mots et affinant la mélodie
    comme la langue est enlacée
    à la langue dans le baiser.[13]

[so I go interweaving
the words and refining the melody
    like one tongue is intertwined
    with the other in a kiss]

The excerpt by Marti is both part of and separated from the book's fourth poem. The body of the text unfolds, as do all the poems in the book, on an extended page that opens out to the right-hand side in landscape format. The Marti extract, on the facing page, to the left of the poem, follows the title page printed with the number '4', thus enclosed within the fourth 'section', but simultaneously isolated in its own blank space opposite the poem itself. The liminal position of the troubadour verse gives it a certain prominence and it soon becomes clear that this is the seed from which Roubaud's own poem grows. Marti writes of the action *entrebescar*, translated as *enlacer* by Roubaud, to liken the intertwining of words in interwoven troubadour rhymes to that of tongues in a kiss. Roubaud's repetition of 'langue' [tongue / language] in the modern French translation, while 'lengu'entrebescada' appears only once in the original Provençal, emphasizes that double meaning. Poetry composition and physical passion are tied together in the verse: like the kiss, the act of writing poetry is motivated by love.

13 Roubaud, *Trente et un au cube*, p. 20.

In the opening lines of the poem proper, Roubaud's own words are crafted according to this reading of Marti:

> LA BOUCHE EST DOUBLE et | la langue est double dans la | bouche et dans la double | bouche naît l'unique langue | langue des baisers et du || chant, la langue du | chant dans la bouche est double et | dans la bouche la | langue s'enlace à la langue | double langue d'une bouche, || un instant, unique; | bouche qui n'est rien sans autre | bouche; langue qui | n'est langue vraiment que double | à la naissance du chant.[14]
>
> [THE MOUTH IS DOUBLE and | the tongue is doubled in the | mouth and in the double | mouth the unique language is born | language of kisses and of || song, the language of the | song in the mouth is double and | in the mouth the | tongue intertwines with the tongue | doubled tongue in a mouth, || a single moment; | mouth which is nothing without another | mouth; tongue which is only truly a tongue when doubled | at the birth of the song.]

The 'chant' [song] is constructed through the repetitive doubling, the enlacing of 'bouche' [mouth] and 'langue' [tongue / language], the love that drives both the kiss and language towards the beloved. The enjambment that occurs line after line, or rather fragment after fragment, with 'bouche' [mouth], 'langue' [tongue / language] and 'chant' [song] often falling in the prominent first position of each segment, creates the effect of an overflowing. All boundaries between the 'langue' [tongue / language] of the 'baisers' [kisses] and that of the 'chant' [song] fade and the two lose any individual sense they might have had, finally merging. Through the coaxing interactions of the repeated rhyme words in the technique that is *entrebescar*, mouth and tongue, initially doubled in their actions of kissing and speaking to and of their lover, end in the 'fusion' of love and language that is 'un instant, unique […] la naissance du chant' [a single moment […] the birth of the song].

In *Trente et un au cube*, love of poetry is also a poetry of love. Coaxing the reader into the text, intriguing her with the possibility of interaction, Roubaud then merges the reading of poetry with its writing. This crafted fusion suggests that the reader participates in the creation of the text, or at least fashions her own relationship with it. Jacques Roubaud himself further

14 Roubaud, *Trente et un au cube*, p. 21.

constructs the poem with his own readings in mind, situating his writing in a web of intertextual links, so much so that the reader is never certain where the poet's own words begin or end. In this poem, love in reading and writing poetry converge in the self-reflexivity of the poem, as the poet entices the reader into a sense of intimacy with the text, addressing her and giving her a privileged relationship with its words. He lets me into the quiet space he shares with his lover, trusts me with this private, sensual moment.

The reader, along with the poet, watches the beloved. It is the perfect voyeur's gaze, unchallenged, taking in the naked woman who is asleep and unaware. The power of the gaze appears to be further confirmed when the poet repeatedly addresses his lover in terms of her silence: 'la | nuit avançante ta tranquillité ensommeillée || m'engourdissent, surtout ta tranquillité engourdie et chaude, le | sérieux, l'application de | ton silence' [the | night coming in your stillness heavy with sleep || make me sleep, your drowsing and warm quiet, the | gravity, the application of | your silence].[15] In my translation of Roubaud's words I am torn between 'quiet' and 'stillness' for 'tranquillité'. She does not respond, instead characterized as a blank space onto which the viewer projects his or her own image. She is the perfect muse, inspires the poet-lover, features in his lines as a reflection of his desires, her own unaccounted for. Yet something of the lover herself remains independent and elusive; as the poet writes silently on his sheet of paper so as not to wake her, there is the sense that as readers we cannot reach her. Her silence is not passive, described in terms of its 'application', which connotes decision and concentration, and introduces tension into the atmosphere of quiet and tranquillity that prevails. The same term appears earlier in the description in adjective form: 'tu dors nue | tranquillement appliquée | tranquillement arrondie' [you sleep naked | quietly applied | quietly curved].[16] The adjectives 'appliquée' [applied] and 'arrondie' [curved] have an enigmatic quality and are not immediately comprehensible in their denotation of the sleeping woman, but they are subtly linked: they may both be used to describe handwriting, the careful, rounded lettering of his poetry. The woman is not only the purpose of Roubaud's poetry, the

15 Roubaud, *Trente et un au cube*, p. 21.
16 Roubaud, *Trente et un au cube*, p. 21.

person to whom it is addressed, but like language, love and the passionate kiss, she is woven into the words on the page: 'j'écris en travers, de très | longues lignes qui | t'enlacent (ou le prétendent)' [I write across, in very | long lines that | embrace you (or claim to)].[17] At least, the poet attempts to capture her in his writing, even as his parenthetical aside to the reader expresses an element of doubt.

It is this moment of *Trente et un au cube* that has drawn me into Roubaud's poetry. I am intrigued by this privileging of the reader: I stand in the poet's position, made aware of the quiet intimacy of the moment by the jolt of those distractions that echo out from the lovers' bedroom into my present. Then I am outside the scene again, self-conscious as reader of the poem. Roubaud's use of *mise en abyme* creates a series of parallels to be explored: between reader and poet, reader and beloved, reading and writing, and between love and poetic form. I am carried along by the wordplay that twists and turns around definitions of love and poetry, and love poetry. I take up the role of observer offered, and in doing so cannot help but think that there is something about this vision of the woman who sleeps that resists an understanding of the muse in poetry as simply one who silently inspires.

*

Like the studies conducted by Puff and Poucel, my interest lies in the self-reflexivity of Roubaud's poetry and the privileged role he provides for the reader. My own focus is created in the points at which these aspects of his writing coincide with the poet's portrayals of the lover, on the one hand, and his use of form on the other – the poem's shape and structure, and the effects of sound and rhythm produced by these. With this introductory reading of *Trente et un au cube*, I hope to demonstrate that through his focus on the feminine, and the imagery used to convey the nature of the relationship that she forms with the male narrator, Roubaud comments on poetry both as a genre and as a mode of self-expression. Roubaud's accounts of love in poetry are often characterized by the absence of his lover, and the poetic relationship between his male narrator

17 Roubaud, *Trente et un au cube*, p. 21.

and the woman he loves comes to be structured through separation or a struggle to assert feminine presence. This sometimes results in alienation, even oppression, for the narrator; I have chosen to explore how it might also function as a source of creativity. The woman who is his muse comes to stand for the ambition and purpose itself of poetry, always through a concern with form.

Trente et un au cube contextualizes my enquiry and is central to it, taking up the largest part of my readings. Written shortly after a well-documented shift in Roubaud's approach to poetry composition, following which he endeavours to prioritize form and sustained metrical shaping over free verse structures, this volume of love poems is well placed to provide an insight into the poet's ideas on the expression of love through poetic form. I explore the ways in which poetic form opens out the poems to an interaction with the memory of the reader. The poet's beloved addressee is woven into this relation and her position in the poems creates the space through which the reader enters into a deeply personal engagement with them.

My exploration of *Trente et un au cube* is centrally positioned in the chronology of my study; I begin with a consideration of Roubaud's texts which relate to his earliest composition processes, including *Autobiographie, chapitre dix* (1977) [*Autobiography, Chapter Ten*], *Poésie:* (2000) [*Poetry:*] and *La Vieillesse d'Alexandre* (2000) [*The Ageing of Alexander*]. These texts reveal something of the poet's engagement with Surrealism, and provide commentary on his decision to move away from the influence of the writing practices associated with the movement. They also give an account of Roubaud's early conception of love poetry, rooted in his own memories of first love. Entangled in these accounts of love and poetic form is the poet's struggle with the particular influence of Paul Éluard; while expressing the need to distance himself from the composition practices of the Surrealist poet, Roubaud simultaneously uses an Eluardian formula (*L'amour la poésie*) [*Love, Poetry*] to inscribe himself in the tradition of love poetry. What is the place of Éluard in Roubaud's own conception of poetic language? How does Roubaud respond to the crisis in his creativity and what role does his feminine addressee have in his formal solutions?

After exploring the ways in which Roubaud finds his autonomy as a love poet in *Trente et un au cube* through the institution of form at the heart of his poetic practice, my reading focuses on texts written after the death of Roubaud's wife, Alix Cléo. Looking in particular at *Du noir tombe* (1985) [*Darkness Falls*] and *Quelque chose noir* (1986) [*Some Thing Black*], I reflect on the shifts in form that occur from Roubaud's earlier texts as he now addresses his grief in poetry. While in my first three chapters I build an understanding of Roubaud's approach to form and the ways in which it is used in poetry to represent the lovers' relation, in my fourth chapter I encounter an unravelling of the poet's methods. Memory has a central role in the network bringing together poet, reader and beloved in *Trente et un au cube*, but it emerges as the source of formal expressions of inadequacy in the later texts, as the poet grapples with the reminders of his life shared with Alix Cléo. We have seen how love is woven into the metre itself of Roubaud's love poetry, in a gesture reaching out to the beloved. When love is lost, rhythm is unthinkable and the two-dimensional space of the page on which poetry is composed becomes irreconcilable with the poet's memory of love.

Alix Cléo was a photographer as well as a writer, and it is through a web of intertextual connections drawing together her photographs, the writings of her *Journal (1979–1983)* and his own poetry that Roubaud seeks out a solution to the failure of poetic structure to hold onto her memory. Directing the reader beyond his own texts to those of Alix Cléo, Roubaud seeks to extend her presence in collective memory, but does the poet's posthumous engagement with her work constitute an appropriation, or some form of collaboration? What does it mean for a poet to establish a dialogue through poetry with a beloved after she is gone?

In each stage of this book, I focus on the position of the beloved addressee in relation to the formal construction of Roubaud's poetry. I trace the chronological development of the poet, from his ambivalent engagement with conceptions of the poetic muse in Surrealism, to his own reformulation of what it means to address the beloved in poetry, especially in *Trente et un au cube*. Finally, I reflect on what it means for the poet to mourn his loss of love in poetry, from the impossible articulation of grief in poetic form, to the hope for some form of collaboration, or dialogue with the beloved.

Form and Love

The title of this volume would be at home among the 'form and' constructions Angela Leighton identifies 'in a multitude of book and essay titles':

> form and feeling, form and intent, form and authority, form and contentment, form and meaning, form and time, form and format, form and poetry. It is as if there were something unfinished, even unformed, about form. It hangs on its other half, needing that support or relief. At some level an old soul-body dualism underpins these constructions, reminding us that form, without its shaping partner, might be so disembodied as to mean nothing at all. But that suggestion too is complicated by the fact that form, by itself, can also mean body, shape, or matter.[18]

Leighton's articulation of the two-way interaction in the notional partnerships described in this passage is an apt model for my own enquiry, although I came across her description after completing this project in its first guise as a doctoral thesis. I am looking into the way form 'hangs on' love, its 'shaping partner', in a deliberate selection of Roubaud's poetry that brings together formal innovation or experiment and an expression of love, either through the themes of the poetry or in its mode of address. As Leighton writes, however, the matter is 'complicated' by the fact that 'form' too can refer to 'body' or 'shape' and, in the same vein, 'love' can also be a reference to the lover: my love, *mon amour*.

The 'form and' construction is itself a relationship in which its terms find mutual 'support' and 'relief' and, like in any relationship, the parties involved are continually shifting in their relation, reacting to one another, adjusting, accommodating, conflicting. Love shapes form, it drives form in some of Roubaud's poetry, as we have seen in my initial readings from parts of *Trente et un au cube*, where the troubadour *chant* malfunctions and corrodes in the absence of the poet's reader-lover, and the entwinement of rhythm and language is an expression of desire and the wish to attract the attention of the loved woman. Yet form in itself is also an intention

18 Angela Leighton, *On Form: Poetry, Aestheticism, and the Legacy of a Word* (Oxford: Oxford University Press, 2007), loc. 54–62/4122.

in Roubaud's poetry composition, following his decision to place it at the centre of his practice, inspired by his studies in mathematics at the time – he later became a professor of mathematics – and an interest in poetry tradition. The question naturally arises as to whether or how 'form' is in turn given to 'love'.

Against the backdrop of discussions around mathematics and formal constraint that frequently accompany critical readings of Jacques Roubaud, who is one of the longest-standing members of the Oulipo, the theme of 'love' might seem at first like an uneasy fit in this pairing. Yet the young poet's obsessive interest in poetic form stems from the original love poets, the troubadours, and an affinity the poet has suggested can be explained by his own Provençal roots. A reader of Roubaud's bilingual anthology *Les Troubadours* [*The Troubadours*], whose poems have been introduced, selected and translated by the poet himself, is given an insight into this personal passion. The poet's lengthy introduction to the anthology (57 pages) outlines the shaping of the *canso* by its constituent parts – the *cobla* and, within the *cobla*, the *vers* – and explains key themes held within it, for example, *printemps*, or spring, *la dona*, the beloved lady, and *regard*, or the beholding of the lady. He also sets out three modes of analysis that the poems may be subjected to: *la formule métrique*, the syllabic count of each line, whose variations and repetitions make up the rhythmical pattern of the *canso*; *la formule de rimes*, the rhyme scheme(s) of the poem; finally, *la formule mélodique*, which gives the music against which the texts were performed.[19] Over the following pages, Roubaud offers example readings of metre and rhyme, summarizing the former in lines of numbers (of syllables) and the latter in configurations of letters representing repeated and interweaving rhymes at the end of lines, and in his accompanying text he elaborates on types of rhyme, caesuras and stressed syllables. And all this for the love of *la dona* and the desire to sing her beauty far and wide in a manner that is worthy of her.[20] Love's expression in intricately formal poetry is clearly not a new concept.

19 Jacques Roubaud, *Les Troubadours: Anthologie bilingue* (Paris: Seghers, 1971), p. 27.
20 Roubaud, *Les Troubadours*, p. 10.

Jean-François Puff gives a comprehensive and immersive reading of this troubadour influence on Roubaud's poetry in *Mémoire de la mémoire*, and in Chapter 3 of this book I touch on his analysis of the love relation in *Trente et un au cube* according to those troubadour concepts. In his study, *Jacques Roubaud and the Invention of Memory*, Jean-Jacques Poucel also offers troubadour poetry and its concepts as a valuable intertext for a Roubaldian poetics, beginning with Roubaud as reader and positing the methodology of literary analysis developed in the poet's volume on troubadour craft, *La Fleur inverse* [*The Inverse Flower*], as a 'blueprint for Roubaud's creative agenda'.[21] Although I explore troubadour concepts in my readings of Roubaud's love poetry, together with the influences of other intertexts such as medieval Japanese poetry anthologies, and mathematical and scientific texts, central to my inquiry is the woman at the centre of these writings, the woman who has not yet been the main focus of a full-length study on Roubaud. What, specifically, are the implications of the poetic forms imposed on the love(r) addressed in the poems that make up my core reading, poems that span Roubaud's life as a poet, from his early links to the Surrealist writers to the texts he wrote after the death of his wife, Alix Cléo? And, to use Angela Leighton's imagery, if love, or the lover, is form's 'shaping partner', its 'support' or 'relief' in Roubaud's poetry, what are the particular terms of the relation? Is it true to say that without her, form 'might be so disembodied as to mean nothing at all'?

Musing on Psychoanalysis: A Lover's Discourse

In the opening of his *Fragments d'un discours amoureux* [*Fragments of a Lover's Discourse*], Roland Barthes writes of the '*extrême solitude*' [*extreme solitude*] of the lover's discourse:

> Ce discours est peut-être parlé par des milliers de sujets (qui le sait?), mais il n'est soutenu par personne; il est complètement abandonné des langages environnants: ou

21 Poucel, *Jacques Roubaud and the Invention of Memory*, p. 21.

> ignoré, ou déprécié, ou moqué par eux, coupé non seulement du pouvoir, mais aussi de ses mécanismes (sciences, savoirs, arts).[22]
>
> [This discourse is spoken maybe by thousands of subjects (who knows?), but it is not supported by anyone; it is completely abandoned by the languages around it: or ignored, disparaged, or mocked by them, cut off not only from power but also its mechanisms (sciences, knowledge, arts).]

While love can touch anyone, Barthes points out the lack of serious critical or analytical attention that is paid to its discourse. Love does not feature on the current agenda preoccupying what he calls 'les discours objectifs – scientifiques ou moralistes' [the objective discourses – scientific or moralistic].[23] Barthes takes Freudian and Lacanian theory as his own point of departure in his study of a lover's discourse, pointing to psychoanalysis as the only framework available through which love and the love relation have been extensively explored: 'c'est le seul discours qui se tienne aujourd'hui sur le sentiment amoureux, toutes les autres *épistèmè* dédaignant d'en parler' [it is the only discourse today that accounts for the lover's experience, all the other *épistèmè* do not deign to speak of it].[24]

The love relation, and its position at the core of the interaction between the poet and his muse in Surrealism, forms my starting point, and psychoanalysis is certainly the dominant point of reference. Seminal studies of woman's role in Surrealist literature and art, such as Xavière Gauthier's *Surréalisme et sexualité* (1971) [*Surrealism and Sexuality*] and more recently, Katharine Conley's *Automatic Woman* (1996), have frequently turned to Lacan to exemplify the relation between the male poet and his feminine muse. The structures representing their interaction in Surrealism have been often aligned with the Lacanian teaching: 'il n'y a pas *la* femme, la femme n'est *pas toute*' [*woman* does not exist, woman is *not whole*].[25] Commentators on Lacan agree that the empty status he attributes to woman as a universal

22 Roland Barthes, *Fragments d'un discours amoureux* (Paris: Seuil, 1977), p. 5.

23 Roland Barthes, *Le Discours amoureux: Séminaire à l'École pratique des hautes études 1974–1976* suivi de *Fragments d'un discours amoureux: inédits*, ed. by Claude Coste (Paris: Seuil, 2007), p. 688.

24 Barthes, *Le Discours amoureux*, p. 696.

25 Jacques Lacan, *Le Séminaire, Livre XX: Encore* (Paris: Seuil, 1975), p. 13. In English translation as Jacques Lacan, *The Seminar of Jacques Lacan, Book XX: On Feminine*

category designates her position as defined purely in relation to the masculine position, existing as the 'not all' and thus the 'vanishing point' in a system of gender representation that is phallically orientated.[26] As such, devoid of an identity specific to herself, she becomes that 'fantasmatic place' or receptacle for the projections of male fantasy, for which she, nonetheless, cannot fulfil the role of 'guarantor'.[27]

Luce Irigaray reverses the analogy, describing what she perceives to be the stifling of the feminine in predominant psychoanalytic structural accounts of the masculine-feminine relation in terms that evoke woman's position as muse to the male writer:

> Mais encore faut-il interroger [les mots] comme revêtements dont le 'sujet' habille, pudiquement, le 'féminin'. Lequel, enfoui sous toutes ces métaphores, survalorisantes ou dénigrantes, ne sait plus comment (s')en découdre de ces déguisements, y trouvant d'ailleurs un certain plaisir, en rajoutant même dans le genre plaqué or. Mais, de plus en plus investie de tropes, comment pourrait-elle articuler quelque son – quelque 'mon' – de sous ces chevaleresques oripeaux? Comment trouver une voie, une voix, assez forte ou assez fine, pour retraverser

---

Sexuality, The Limits of Love and Knowledge, trans. by Bruce Fink (New York: W.W. Norton & Company, 1999), p. 7. Emphasis in the original texts.

26 Elisabeth Bronfen, 'Fatal Conjunctions: Gendering Representations of Death', in *Lacan, Politics, Aesthetics*, ed. by Willy Apollon and Richard Feldstein (New York: SUNY Press, 1996), p. 250. Early commentators have disagreed, however, on whether Lacan's theory is to be interpreted as prescriptive, or simply descriptive of the history of gender relations in Western society. Luce Irigaray as well as Hélène Cixous react against the structural prioritization of the male term in psychoanalytic practice in their early works: *Speculum de l'autre femme* (Paris: Éditions de Minuit, 1974) and *Ce sexe qui n'est pas un* (Paris: Éditions de Minuit, 1977) by Irigaray; *La Jeune Née* (Paris: Union générale d'éditions, 1975) and *Le Rire de la Méduse* (Paris: Galilée, 2010) by Cixous, with Catherine Clément in the case of the former. However, other responses to Lacan explore the possibilities for feminist theory in his teaching: see, for example, Jane Gallop's *Reading Lacan* (New York: Cornell University Press, 1987), Jacqueline Rose's *Sexuality in the Field of Vision* (London: Verso, 2005), and Elizabeth Grosz's *Jacques Lacan: A Feminist Introduction* (London: Routledge, 1990).

27 Rose, *Sexuality in the Field of Vision*, p. 72.

> ces couches de style ornemental, cette sépulture décorative, où elle perd jusqu'à son souffle? Étouffée sous tous ces/ses airs.[28]
>
> [But we must go on questioning words as the wrappings with which the 'subject', modestly, clothes the 'female'. Stifled beneath all those eulogistic or denigratory metaphors, she is unable to unpick the seams of her disguise and indeed takes a certain pleasure in them, even gilding the lily further at times. Yet, ever more hemmed in, cathected by tropes, how could she articulate any sound from beneath this cheap chivalric finery? How to find a voice, make a choice strong enough, subtle enough to cut through those layers of ornamental style, that decorative sepulcher, where even her breath is lost. Stifled under all those airs.]

Irigaray's woman is one that has been written into the story by men, 'stifled' beneath 'eulogistic metaphors' and 'chivalric finery', and 'layers of ornamental style'. Here patriarchal discourse, even (or particularly) when it appears in the form of adulatory descriptions of the feminine, is likened to artificial garb that conceals the true nature of femininity: she becomes the muse to male subjectivity. Irigaray's criticism of what she sees as dominant patriarchal psychoanalytic theories of the subject, elaborated by and for the male term which remains central, overlaps with the world and vocabulary of literature; it is the muse shackled into the story by her male author that needs to break free. Is Roubaud's addressee too hemmed in and cathected by tropes? Irigaray alludes to disguises of decorative clothing, likening their artificial veiling to the ornamental flourish of the lyric poet. Roubaud's poetry speaks both of and to his feminine love; are we to see her as this muse adorned with his own lexical embroideries? Does the reader glimpse her own presence beneath the poet's elaborations, or is she silenced by his poetry, as Irigaray believes the feminine is stifled by her place in the structures of psychoanalytic theory? Where should the reader look for her in the lines of Roubaud's poetry?

28 Irigaray, *Speculum de l'autre femme*, p. 177. In English translation as Luce Irigaray, *Speculum of the Other Woman*, trans. by Gillian C. Gill (New York: Cornell University Press, 1985), pp. 142–43.

Lacan, Irigaray and Roubaud

There are several voices woven into this project. In addition to the full-length studies by Poucel and Puff which I have already mentioned, a number of other critical works on the significance of love and its loss in the poetry of Jacques Roubaud have inspired and helped to clarify my own insights into his writing. I bring these readings and arguments into play throughout the four chapters of my own main body of research, when they support and interact with my thoughts on Roubaud's texts, as well as when they open up paths that run slant or that diverge. Perhaps I can say that mine broadly differs from the critical studies on Roubaud that have come before in taking an approach that is nurtured by psychoanalytic theory. It is a risky endeavour: while psychoanalysis has been said to dominate modern investigations into love, it has been suggested that Roubaud distances himself from psychoanalytic theory, rejecting the Freudian unconscious.[29] By aligning elements of Roubaud's poetry with Lacanian, and in turn Freudian and Irigarayan representations of the sexual relation, however, I do not suggest that the poet may be classified as subscribing to any of their ideas.[30] Neither do I claim or wish to provide a psychoanalytic reading of the poet's life or his work. Just as Irigaray

29 Elisabeth Roudinesco, 'Écrire d'amour: hommage à *Action poétique*', *Mezura*, 49 (2001), 359–67 (p. 367).

30 In his little book *Ma vie avec le docteur Lacan*, made up of eleven chapters, each just one or two sentences long, Roubaud briefly outlines two biographical 'non-encounters' with the psychoanalyst, one being the connection of friendship with Roubaud's father-in-law, Paul Bénichou, recounted through a 'discreetly ironic' anecdote referring to the 'colourful cardigans' Lacan would wear in his younger days, and the other a memory of Lacan discharging Roubaud from a hospital and accounting for him and his mental health following the suicide of the poet's younger brother. The two threads of the story provide a rather charming picture of Lacan, who is portrayed as slightly eccentric but kind. In the book, Roubaud demonstrates his engagement – or at least his familiarity – with Lacan's ideas when he mentions trying to get to grips with the psychoanalyst's famous lecture on 'The Purloined Letter'. Of course, this does not equal any kind of endorsement. See pages 23, 31 and 35 of *Ma vie avec le docteur Lacan* (Bordeaux: Éditions de l'Attente, 2004).

describes the sexual relation in Lacan's work with metaphors evoking the male poet, I read Roubaud's poetry and its presentation(s) of the love relation through the lens of selected texts by Lacan and Irigaray. I engage with these texts as a way of illuminating the structures of loving and reading in Roubaud's poetry, allowing me conversely to explore Irigaray's poet-theorist analogy in relation to the effects of Roubaud's poems and my close readings of them.

I find that the Lacanian articulation of the love relation in terms of the numbers 'one' and 'two', and Irigaray's interpretation of it together reveal ways Roubaud's poetry revolves around the absence and presence in love of the feminine. If Lacan proposes the impossibility of the sexual relation in *Encore*, as a deconstruction of the mythical two-become-one, what does this mean for the disparate 'two' which still remains? Irigaray draws on Lacanian thought while forming her own interpretations of this notion of a disjunction at the heart of the sexual relation and her readings lead me to ask whether the impossibility of the 'union' can be the site of creative conceptions of love. Poetry has often posited the muse as the mirror image of the poet: the 'other' through which he gains insight into his own soul.[31] Through the structures of loving set out by Lacan and Irigaray in turn, I consider the extent to which, or whether at all, Roubaud moves away from this conception of the poetic muse, somewhat aligned with the Surrealist muse, and towards a more collaborative, interactive relationship in poetry, centred on the articulation of love in poetic form.

31 Daniel Rivas, 'Éluard's "L'Amoureuse": Mimesis and Semiosis', *The French Review*, 55 (1982), 489–96 (p. 491).

CHAPTER 1

Young Love, *Amour fou*

A study of Jacques Roubaud's poetry necessarily begins with a consideration of form. Described as 'formalist' by some, others who look more favourably on his work have focused on a range of structures as eclectic as the Japanese *tanka* in *Trente et un au cube*; collage and pastiche in *Autobiographie, chapitre dix*; innovative sonnet forms, including prose sonnets, long and short versions of the structure and even sonnets of sonnets, in *Signe d'appartenance* (1967) [*Sign of Belonging*]; and more recently the spiralling, intertwining branches of his prose cycle.[1] An exploration of form is at the beginning of things for several reasons. It is demonstrably at the heart of Jacques Roubaud's approach to poetry in general, but it also has a particular relationship with content when it comes to the representation of love in many of his works.

In this chapter the interface between form and the feminine presence will be considered in the context of Roubaud's early years as a poet. A comparative reading of selected poems from *Autobiographie, chapitre dix* and passages from Roubaud's autobiographical volume *Poésie:* draws together some of the commentary on poetic form in these texts and the life experiences that shaped them. These readings are illuminated by the poet's theoretical reflections on the status of the *vers* in modern and contemporary French poetry in *La Vieillesse d'Alexandre*. These elements are

1 Roubaud himself writes 'je suis un poète qu'on dit formaliste' [I have been called a formalist poet], in *Poésie, etcetera: ménage*, p. 58, while warning against 'une position formaliste qui consiste à avoir une idée simplificatrice du formel' [a formalist position which consists in having a simplistic idea of the formal], in 'Le rythme, le formel et le formalisme' ['Rhythm, Form and Formalism'], an interview with Pierre Lusson and Mitsou Ronat, *Action Poétique*, 62 (1975), 61–75 (p. 61). The significance of the formal and criticism of Roubaud's 'formalism' will be discussed further in Chapters 2 and 3.

brought together by a definitive, contemporaneous decision made by the poet to establish the activity of form at the centre of his writing. This decision is to be made operative at the level of the poems themselves, which will in turn contribute to a structured volume, finally to be part of the greater architecture known as the *Projet* [*Project*]. Form becomes central to Roubaud's texts through the prioritization of a certain 'rigueur' [rigour] henceforth in his work routine.[2] This establishment of a definitive writing process is simultaneously a rejection of another way of writing: a less structured, supposedly 'freer' *vers libre* associated with the Surrealist movement, embodied, it would seem for Roubaud by the work of Paul Éluard, whose influence is described by Roubaud as 'particulièrement débilitant' [particularly debilitating].[3] Éluard is therefore a key figure in this part of the analysis, featuring as he does centrally in Roubaud's autobiographical writing on the poetry project in *Poésie:*, as well as in poetry pastiche, *Autobiographie, chapitre dix,* and treatise on form, *La Vieillesse d'Alexandre.*

I gather a selection of Éluard's poems which are particularly pertinent to my understanding of Roubaud's decision to distance his own poetic output from the work of the Surrealist writer. The poems foreground the feminine beloved as muse to the poet's creativity: a binary relation that can be illuminated with readings of Freudian and subsequent Lacanian theories of the sexual relation. I turn, in particular, to Irigaray's deconstruction of these perspectives, and her unpicking of the Freudian principles that underpin Lacan's work. A reading of some of Éluard's poems through the lens of these theories and a comparison with Roubaud's reaction to those poems show the limits of such binary structures as a basis for our understanding of the relation between poet and beloved, or muse.

2 Jacques Roubaud, *Poésie:* (Paris: Seuil, 2000), p. 104.

3 Roubaud, *Poésie:*, p. 104.

Beginnings: *Vers*, or Worms and Verses in the Enchanted Forest of Childhood

The Surrealist movement and its poetry form the backdrop to Roubaud's youth, first loves and his beginnings as a poetry writer, and the poet's autobiographical accounts of episodes from the time are inextricably linked with arguments for his decision on poetic form. Of Roubaud's six autobiographical prose volumes charting the failure of his *Project*, collectively known as *'le grand incendie de londres'* [*'the great fire of London'*], *Poésie:* is most closely concerned with his early poetic influences.[4] In the chapter entitled 'Forêt racine et labyrinthe' ['Forest, Root and Labyrinth'], the reader is transported to the magical forest which is the setting for Roubaud's earliest encounter with poetry. The forest seemed to have a certain power over the young poet. In a curious passage, Roubaud describes the noises that would arise from the usually very quiet forest beyond his bedroom window: 'les après-midi ensoleillés, un bruissement continu se faisait entendre, un murmure de mastication appliqué, par des milliers de mandibules. Alors les feuilles étaient dévorées de vers minuscules' [on sunny afternoons, a continuous rustling could be heard, a murmur of careful chewing, by thousands of sets of jaws. The leaves were being devoured by tiny worms].[5] The chomping worms working with a manic intensity reappear throughout the chapter: 'Les petits vers du parc et de la forêt murmuraient des mandibules dans les hêtres' [The little worms in the park and forest murmured through their jaws in the beech trees].[6] Some pages later, the poet writes of 'le murmure des petits vers dans les feuilles des hêtres' [the murmuring of the little worms in the beech trees], and finally he adds: 'Dans la forêt, le travail des petits vers dévoreurs me

4 Roubaud distinguishes between the title in lowercase letters and single quotation marks, which is representative of his six-volume prose cycle, and the same words capitalized and italicized without quotation marks, to designate the novel which would have accompanied his original conception of the project, as a 'telling' of that project: see Roubaud's *Poésie:*, p. 235 and p. 239.

5 Roubaud, *Poésie:*, p. 184.

6 Roubaud, *Poésie:*, p. 197.

fascinait' [In the forest, the work of the little devouring worms fascinated me].[7] The cumulative effect of this is a forest that appears to be calling out to him; Roubaud observes with fascination the murmuring worms and the intensifying of their noisy consumption through the pages of the chapter.

Vers assumes its double meaning when we discover that his forest excursions coincided with a retreat into poetry: 'Alors je partais en forêt avec un livre de poésie, avec un cahier à poèmes' [In those days I would head into the forest with a book of poetry, with a notebook of poems].[8] The land of the rustling, murmuring creatures calling Roubaud away from his everyday studies becomes a new territory of poetry for him to explore: 'je venais de voir s'ouvrir devant moi tout un territoire entièrement nouveau, inimaginable auparavant, de poésie' [I saw a completely new territory opening up before me that had been previously unimaginable, a land of poetry].[9] Roubaud is absorbed into this land of poetry. Just as the forest 'vers' chomp through the beech leaves, so too the young poet becomes an avid consumer of poetry: 'Je rongeais des pages-feuilles mentales de poèmes, en murmurant' [I chewed my way through mental leaves-pages of poems, murmuring as I went].[10] He is one of the murmuring worms of the forest, greedily consuming, absorbing and spewing out poetry. He writes of 'une orgie de lecture, [...] une mise en mémoire ou composition de poésies mollement inspirées' [an orgy of reading, [...] the learning by heart or composition of idly inspired poetry], he also expresses the process in terms of 'l'incessante et boulimique lecture' [incessant and bulimic reading], absorbing poetry 'telle une éponge métrique' [like a metric sponge].[11]

The adult narrator lists poets he had become familiar with during his earlier childhood, such as La Fontaine and Victor Hugo, progressing through Baudelaire, Rimbaud and eventually coming to Mallarmé, describing the renewed effects of discovering each one anew in terms of shocks absorbed by his body:

7 Roubaud, *Poésie:*, p, 199 and p. 212.
8 Roubaud, *Poésie:*, p. 213.
9 Roubaud, *Poésie:*, p. 199.
10 Roubaud, *Poésie:*, p. 214.
11 Roubaud, *Poésie:*, p. 197, p. 199 and p. 214.

> Chaque fois, à chaque nouvelle irruption d'une voix nouvelle de poésie encore insoupçonnée, j'absorbais un nouveau choc sonore intérieur, mental, qui était composé à la fois d'émerveillement, de jalousie, de désir, d'émulation, de découverte de recettes versificatoires, d'efforts de nouvelles mises en mémoire.[12]
>
> [Each time, on each fresh emergence of a new voice in poetry until then undreamed of, I absorbed a new resounding shock to the innermost recesses of my mind. These shocks were made up of wonder, jealousy, desire, emulation, the discovery of new formulae of versification, and the efforts to commit my reading to memory.]

The poet is changed by these experiences, they mould him into the poet he will become, forming elements of the work he will produce, without him always being conscious of it: 'J'absorbais et apprenais et me récitais et copiais explicitement sur des pages, involontairement dans les vers que j'écrivais' [I absorbed and learned and recited to myself and copied directly into my notebook, involuntarily in the lines of poetry that I wrote].[13] His young memory, the memory of a poet, works much like that of poetry itself, soaking up poetic traditions and leaving traces of them in works to come. The influence of poetic history and tradition is incorporated into his own progression, becoming part of his being and also his own poetic production.

The young Roubaud's emergence from this enchanted forest of poetry is marked by a rather sudden discovery, which he describes as 'ma dernière influence de ce genre' [my last influence of this kind].[14] It is a coming of age of sorts, the last youthful influence in the stages of his evolution as poet:

> Mon professeur de première, Mr Espiand […], me conseilla la lecture d'autres modernes que Rimbaud […]: il énuméra ces poètes bien loin du 'programme du bac' – Lautréamont, Corbière, Germain Nouveau, Guillaume Apollinaire, Blaise Cendrars et 'quelque chose que vous devrez connaître aussi si vous voulez écrire de la poésie'. – 'Quoi ?' ai-je dû dire. – 'Le surréalisme'.[15]
>
> [My sixth-form teacher, Mr Espiand […], recommended that I read modern poets other than Rimbaud […]: he gave me a list of poets who did not feature on our 'study

12 Roubaud, *Poésie:*, p. 214.
13 Roubaud, *Poésie:*, p. 215.
14 Roubaud, *Poésie:*, p. 215.
15 Roubaud, *Poésie:*, p. 216.

curriculum' – Lautréamont, Corbière, Germain Nouveau, Guillaume Apollinaire, Blaise Cendrars and 'something you should also know about if you want to write poetry'. 'What?', I must have replied. 'Surrealism'.]

His teacher mentions key figures Breton, Éluard and Aragon to clarify, explaining that their writing was less 'classique' [classical] than pre-war poetry. The simplicity of the teenager's unquestioning acceptance of his teacher's suggestion, expressed in 'Je l'écoutai. Je lus' [I listened to him. I read], only emphasizes the violence of the reaction that ensues: 'Mettre certains textes de ce genre […] entre les mains d'un élève de première nourri de Victor Hugo ne peut que provoquer en lui une conflagration intérieure' [Putting certain texts of this kind […] into the hands of a sixth-form student brought up on Victor Hugo can only start a fire burning inside him].[16] For the young poet, embarking on this new reading represented an irreversible fissure between poetry and schooling:

> À la suite de cette rencontre changea du tout au tout le rapport que j'établissais entre la poésie et le lycée […]. Je peux dire que dès que j'ai lu <u>Capitale de la douleur</u>, <u>Persécuté persécuteur</u> et <u>Nadja</u> (dans la même journée), j'ai cessé de considérer qu'il pouvait y avoir le moindre rapport entre la poésie et les institutions d'enseignement.[17]
>
> [Following this encounter the links I had established between poetry and school changed completely […]. I can say that after reading <u>Capital of Pain</u>, <u>Persecuted Persecutor</u> and <u>Nadja</u> (all on the same day), I stopped thinking that there could be the slightest connection between poetry and institutes of education.]

The ardour provoked by these Surrealist texts stems in part from the allusions to an adulthood not yet within reach, their subject matter extending beyond the familiar framework of his secondary school reading experience. Equally, the formal arrangement of these poems was a significant departure from the poetic structure Roubaud had come across as a school pupil. While the undermining of regular rhythm and innovation in traditional metres had begun long before the Surrealist movement, for example, in the work of Hugo and Baudelaire, in what Roubaud terms 'un geste de destruction-libération' [a gesture of destruction-liberation] with

16 Roubaud, *Poésie:*, p. 216.

17 Roubaud, *Poésie:*, p. 217. Typography reproduced from the original.

regards to tradition, the Surrealists largely did away with metric regularity and recognizable rhythms, opting instead for a *tabula rasa* in verse: *vers libre.*[18]

Through his adolescence, Roubaud's ardour for this new discovery in poetry grows ever stronger, reaching a climax of sorts in the later chapter 'LamourLapoésieLamour' [LovePoetryLove]. This part of Roubaud's account in *Poésie:* is climactic in more ways than one, exploring memories of fragments of poetry, his own and that of other poets, which are tied in with reminiscences of increasingly passionate sexual encounters. The autobiographical episodes recounted are not without relevance for a reflection on Roubaud's poetic practice, since the writer himself explains that as its title suggests, this 'branche' [branch] of his prose series 'nécessite un débordement de ma vie en prose sur ma vie en non-prose' [requires a spilling over of my life in prose into my life in non-prose].[19] Roubaud's intertwining of life and poetry – and love and poetry – encourages the reader of *Poésie:* to explore these tales of his love encounters for their influence on form in his writing.

First Loves

The chapter 'LamourLapoésieLamour' ['LovePoetryLove'] begins with all the optimism and energy of youth, looking back to the summer of 1950, at the 'Festival international de la jeunesse' [International Youth Festival] in Nice: 'C'était l'été. J'avais dix-sept ans. Pas de parents, pas de connaissances. Tout changeait. Tout finissait. Tout commençait' [It was summer. I was seventeen. No parents, no aquaintances. Everything was changing. Everything was ending. Everything was beginning].[20] The repetition, throughout the segment, of very brief sentence structures listing single actions creates an accumulation of activities and, in turn, a sense

18 Roubaud, *Poésie, etcetera*, p. 170.

19 Roubaud, *Poésie:*, p. 249.

20 Roubaud, *Poésie:*, p. 374.

of growing possibilities. A sense of nostalgia also pervades the opening of the chapter, as Roubaud captures the joy of early friendships forming in a newly experienced freedom away from home: 'On riait. On discutait. On parlait de la paix. On parlait d'amour. On racontait' [We laughed. We debated. We spoke about peace. We spoke about love. We told stories].[21] The cumulative use of collective pronoun 'on' [we / one] and the imperfect tense sweep the reader along on a wave of joyful reminiscence. The scene is set for Roubaud's first love, a summer love, Michelle, who somehow merges into the surroundings and seems to be as much a part of the setting as the sea and the stars: 'C'était la plus jolie (je trouvais); petite, plutôt silencieuse, plutôt timide. On parlait tard le soir. C'était l'été. Sable, étoiles, mer' [She was the prettiest (I thought); small, rather quiet, rather shy. We spoke late into the evening. It was summer. Sand, stars, sea].[22]

It is not long before Roubaud's attraction to Michelle is swept up in his other great passions of the time: politics and poetry. The two were not unrelated: Roubaud writes that he was a member of the 'Groupe des Jeunes Poètes' [Young Poets Group] as well as the 'Parti communiste' [Communist Party].[23] Through a volley of exclamatory phrases, Roubaud ecstatically connects Michelle's mixed Chinese and Spanish heritage with Communist revolutionary ideals: 'L'Espagne! la Chine! la guerre perdue par la République! Guernica! la Longue Marche! la guerre gagnée hier (en 1949) par la Révolution! mon amoureuse chinoise! mon amoureuse espagnole! comment aurais-je pu ne pas l'aimer?' [Spain! China! The war lost by the Republic! Guernica! The Long March! The war won by the Revolution (1949)! My Chinese love! My Spanish love! How could I not have loved her?].[24] Poetry merges with life as the young Roubaud embraces Surrealist ideals of revolution and love, that is, revolution through love, as Xavière Gauthier puts it: 'la révolution sera sexuelle ou ne sera pas. La liberté sexuelle passe par la révolution sociale' [the revolution will be sexual,

21 Roubaud, *Poésie:*, p. 374.
22 Roubaud, *Poésie:*, p. 375.
23 Roubaud, *Poésie:*, p. 374.
24 Roubaud, *Poésie:*, p. 378.

or it will not take place at all. Sexual freedom comes through social revolution].[25] Sexual freedom was a step in social revolution.

For Surrealists such as Breton and Éluard, love was a positive and transformative force. Gauthier describes both the Bretonian and Eluardian conceptions of love as 'un *amour heureux* [...] *partagé, vivant, formateur, conciliateur et conciliant*' [a *love which was happy,* [...] *shared, living, formative, conciliatory and conciliating*].[26] While it must be conceded that there are moments when love fades or conflict arises in its representation in the work of both writers, love remains at the root of the transformation of everyday experience for these Surrealists. Breton, for example, describes the restorative impact of the lover on his existence: 'Avant de te connaître, j'avais rencontré le malheur, le désespoir. Avant de te connaître, allons donc, ces mots n'ont pas de sens' [Before knowing you, I had encountered misery, desperation. Before knowing you, come now, those words have no meaning].[27] For Éluard, the sexual revolution frequently takes the form of the feminine as a pathway between the individual and the community beyond. Of his lover, the poet writes: 'Cette main double la mienne | Pour tout lier pour tout délivrer' [This hand doubles mine | To connect all deliver all].[28] The couple is the site where difference and the bonds between individuals in love can flourish and extend towards wider society: 'La première femme étrangère | Et le premier homme inconnu' [The first foreign woman | And the first unknown man] become at once 'Et la première différence | Entre des êtres fraternels' [And the first difference | between fraternal beings] and 'Et la première ressemblance | Entre des êtres différents' [And the first resemblance | Between different beings].[29] Nevertheless, while Roubaud's own revolutionary love for Michelle appears to reach similarly euphoric heights in this passage, the series of exclamations with which he describes her gradually takes on an unreal, unconvincing quality. Of course, the links he establishes between his lover and his political agenda are rather tenuous, an admission Roubaud confirms through his humorous rhetorical

25 Xavière Gauthier, *Surréalisme et sexualité* (Paris: Éditions Gallimard, 1971), p. 36.

26 Gauthier, *Surréalisme et sexualité*, p. 157.

27 André Breton, *Arcane 17* (Paris: Pauvert, 1971), p. 26.

28 Paul Éluard, *Poésie ininterrompue* (Paris: Gallimard, 1946; repr. 1953), p. 25.

29 Éluard, *Poésie ininterrompue*, pp. 21–22.

question in the finale of the extract: 'comment aurais-je pu ne pas l'aimer?' [how could I not have loved her?]. Rather than presenting his experience of love as a transformative force according to Surrealist ideals, Roubaud's attraction to Michelle seems itself to be driven by his involvement in the cultural movement and a youthful desire to be swept up in the feeling of possibility it opened out.

These traces of doubt in the relationship grow in the account of the couple's return to ordinary life in Paris following the summer festival, where the writer nonetheless comes to establish the link between love and poetry that will become integral to his poetic practice. Roubaud takes Michelle to meet friends at the Saturday meetings for members of the 'Groupe des Jeunes Poètes' [Young Poets Group]. Here, love comes together with both politics and poetry: 'Elle y rencontra mes amis de poésie. Nous étions ensemble. J'étais fier. J'étais deux. Tous mes amis d'alors étaient deux' [She met my poet friends. We were together. I was proud. I was two. All my friends then were in couples].[30] The narrator's description of being in a relationship is upbeat and proud, but Michelle herself fades into Roubaud's sense of self, here elided in the personal pronoun *je* [*I*] that represents Roubaud in 'J'étais deux' [I was two]. Their relation is, for Roubaud, a part of being caught up in the revolutionary movement that Surrealism represented, expressed resolutely as his own experience.

After listing the names of couples whom they met regularly at these gatherings, he elaborates further on the inextricable ties linking love and poetry:

> Être deux était une condition nécessaire et suffisante de la poésie. Être deux était une condition nécessaire de la révolution. <u>L'amour la poésie</u> était un titre d'Éluard (Éluard surréaliste); qu'on peut comprendre comme un génitif de la vieille langue: l'amour de la poésie. Alors il vaudrait mieux dire: l'amour la poésie l'amour. L'amour de la poésie de l'amour.
>
> soudain je fus amoureux: l'amour la poésie lamour
> lamour lapoésie lamour lamourlapoésielamour la
> poésie l'amour.[31]

30 Roubaud, *Poésie:*, p. 379.

31 Roubaud, *Poésie:*, p. 379. Roubaud accords his description the weight of mathematical terminology, which presents his musings on love and poetry as weighty fact.

[Being two was a sufficient and required condition of poetry. It was a required condition of revolution too. Love poetry[32] was a title by Éluard (Surrealist Éluard), which we can read as a genitive form in old French: love *of* poetry. It would be better to say then: love poetry love. Love of poetry of love.

suddenly I was in love: love poetry love
lovepoetry love lovepoetrylove
poetry love]

The typographical erasure of the boundaries between poetry and love here goes further than an old genitive form: poetry is inspired by love, but as the sequence folds back on itself, it also grows out of a love of poetry, or language itself.[33] The quotation embedded in the text here comes from *Autobiographie, chapitre dix,* where the links between love, poetry and Paul Éluard's writing are explored further through the medium of poetry. In a book subtitled 'poèmes avec des moments de repos en prose' [poems with moments of repose in prose], the extract appears as the 'prose moment' that sets the scene for three Eluardian poems, 'L'AMOUR LA POÉSIE L'AMOUR UN', 'DEUX' and 'TROIS' ['LOVE POETRY LOVE ONE', 'TWO', and 'THREE'].[34] They are Eluardian as far as their content is concerned, made up as they are of words and phrases from the earlier poet's collection *L'Amour la poésie*. However, a look not much further beyond the titles reveals several significant departures from the original material in Roubaud's manipulations of the text.

Roubaud describes *Autobiographie, chapitre dix* as 'l'histoire du vers libre français, en sa période triomphante, classique' [the history of French free verse, in its triumphant, classical period], the autobiographical element

---

He thus playfully mocks his youthful belief in the potential association of love and revolution through poetry.

32 Éluard's title is usually translated into English as *Love, Poetry*. The comma in the English title emphasizes that the title is made up of two separate nouns, rather than the compound 'love poetry', in which 'love' becomes a qualifier of 'poetry'.

33 Roubaud, *Poésie, etcetera*, p. 109.

34 Jacques Roubaud, *Autobiographie, chapitre dix* (Paris: Gallimard, 1977), pp. 22–23. All references to Jacques Roubaud's re-writing of Éluard's *L'Amour la poésie* can be found on these pages. I will only reference the more variable page details from Éluard's original volume in this section.

alluded to in the title being the very words of those poets who have preceded him:

> Les mots des poètes sont le matériau de la biographie d'un poète; ce sont les mots de sa langue et les mots de sa vie, mais les uns et les autres se réfractent à travers la poésie qui l'a précédé, celle qu'il a lue, aimée ou détestée. Ainsi, les poèmes qui m'ont *servi* pour *Autobiographie, chapitre dix* font partie de mon existence en tant que poète.[35]
>
> [The words of other poets are a poet's biographical material: they are the words of his language and the words of his life, but both refracted through the poetry that came before him, the poetry he read, loved, or hated. Thus, the poems that I have *used* to make *Autobiography, Chapter Ten* are part of my existence as a poet.]

The passage recalls the forest of Roubaud's youth, where poetry is absorbed into the memory of the eager reader-poet, just as the *vers* [worms] devour the beech tree leaves that nourish their existence. In this particular volume of his poetry, the process of reading, digesting and subsequently producing material that reflects traces of the traditions that have preceded it are overtly manifest. Roubaud points out his borrowings: 'Je n'ai pas inventé les poèmes d'*Autobiographie*. Je les ai pris dans ma mémoire de poésie, dans les livres que j'ai choisis pour en parler' [I did not invent the poems in *Autobiography*. I took them from my poetry memory, from books that I chose to talk about it].[36] More specifically, these are poems chosen, copied, adapted and at times distorted from '84 livres de poésie par 35 poètes parus entre 1914 et 1932' [84 books of poetry by 35 poets, released between 1914 and 1932].[37]

For Natacha Michel, the effect of Roubaud's collage writing in *Autobiographie, chapitre dix* is a displacement of the voice of the poet. She uses a version of the famous Rimbaudian statement, 'Je est un autre, passé' [I is an other, past], to highlight the presence of past influences in Roubaud's writing here.[38] A close study of Roubaud's adjustments reveals

35 Roubaud, *Description du projet*, pp. 82–83.

36 Roubaud, *Description du projet*, p. 83.

37 Roubaud, *Description du projet*, p. 82.

38 Natacha Michel, 'Roubaud 1978: Les mots de seconde bouche', *Critique*, 35 (1979), 594–609 (p. 596).

another side to the maxim: until the third poem, the personal pronoun 'je' [I] and associated possessive adjectives 'mon' and 'ma' [my], replace the feminine presence in Éluard's writing with that of the male poet himself. For example, Éluard's 'Et le soleil noue ses rayons cherche ton front | Pour te frapper sans cesse' [And the sun knots its rays seeks out your face | To strike you endlessly] becomes for Roubaud 'et le soleil pour | me frapper, invariable, est une serrure' [and the sun to | strike me, invariable, is a lock].[39] The emphasis on the poet himself is also reinforced when the original 'La tête prisonnière dans son corps lié' [The mind prisoner in its linked body] is rewritten by Roubaud as 'mon corps lié' [my body linked].[40] Later in the poems, Éluard's 'dans le fleuve ignorant de ta tête' [in the unknowing river of your mind] is slightly modified to read 'dans le fleuve ignorant de ma | tête' [in the unknowing river of my | mind].[41] This is a distant departure from the Éluard who has been referred to as the poet who offered his readers 'clefs d'or [...] qui ouvrent les chambres de la joie, du désir ou de l'amour' [golden keys [...] that unlock bedrooms of joy, desire or love],[42] for whom 'love is [...] the center and the circumference of his universe'.[43] Éluard is possibly most widely thought of as a love poet and *L'Amour la poésie* is first and foremost an expression of the wonder of love as an inspiration for poetry, full of references to the beauty of the poet-narrator's lover, who is also his poetic muse.[44] Anna Balakian has described the feminine in his poetry as 'the intermediary between the creative sensibility of the poet and the sensations to be conjured from the earth. In her are reflected the beauties of the material world and impressions of the poet'.[45] For Éluard, woman is often 'a force, a haven', associated with images of 'fecundity', she 'inspires

39 Paul Éluard, *Capitale de la douleur* suivi de *L'Amour la poésie* (Paris: Gallimard, 1966), p. 226.
40 Éluard, *L'Amour la poésie*, p. 223.
41 Éluard, *L'Amour la poésie*, p. 149.
42 Jean Ballard, 'Préface', *Cahiers du sud*, 315 (1952), 187–90 (p. 189).
43 Anna Balakian, *Surrealism: The Road to the Absolute* (London: Unwin Books, 1972), pp. 220–21.
44 Robert Nugent, *Paul Éluard* (New York: Twayne Publishers, 1974), p. 50.
45 Balakian, *Surrealism*, p. 220.

[...] him',[46] and it is through love that the poet achieves the most 'precise appreciation' of both 'the self' and 'the outside world';[47] love is a source of creativity for the poet.[48] The lover is the mediating force between the poet and his experience of both himself and the world, facilitating the occasion for poetry. Roubaud's re-shaping of Éluard's lines in *Autobiographie, chapitre dix* thus represents a certain diminishment.

Although Roubaud eventually engages with an addressee, using 'toi' and 'te' [you] several times in the third and final poem in the 'L'AMOUR LA POÉSIE L'AMOUR' trio, the feminine, even love itself, appear at first to be missing from the lines Roubaud has pieced together:

L'AMOUR LA POÉSIE L'AMOUR UN

ma présence n'est pas ici
habillé. moitié du monde
tête prisonnière dans mon corps lié.

dans une solitude d'encre
à proscrire. Sa visi
bilité parfaite me rendait aveugle

voici que le déluge sort
sa tête et le soleil pour
me frapper, invariable, est une serrure.

[LOVE POETRY LOVE ONE

my presence is not here
dressed. half the world
mind prisoner in my body linked.

in a solitude of ink
to ban. Its perfect visi
bility made me blind

46 Charles G. Whiting, 'Eluard's Poems for Gala', *The French Review*, 41 (1968), 505–17 (p. 506).

47 Nugent, *Paul Éluard*, p. 50.

48 Nugent, *Paul Éluard*, p. 64.

> suddenly the deluge comes
> her mind and the sun to
> strike me, invariable, is a lock.]

Images of solitude and confinement abound in the three stanzas, with the intensely physical references to 'tête prisonnière' [mind prisoner] and 'mon corps lié' [my body linked] in the opening verse, notions of prohibition and blindness in the second and finally the closing of the poem on 'serrure' [lock]. That this poetry is somehow representative of Roubaud's young relationship with Michelle may at first seem an incongruous suggestion. However, this constrictive and debilitating imagery becomes more relevant as their affair progresses, or rather deteriorates, following their return to Paris. Space once again plays a role in Roubaud's anecdotal depiction of their situation:

> J'embrassais Michelle successivement [...] en montant ou en descendant ses escaliers, sur tous les bancs des jardins près de l'avenue Gabriel, sous les arbres au bas des Champs-Élysées, sur la place de la Concorde, sur les plates-formes des autobus qui étaient des autobus adéquats aux amoureux, avec plates-formes à l'arrière, par lesquelles on montait dans l'autobus; [...] et l'autobus repartait, et nous nous serrions dans un coin de la plate-forme pour nous embrasser.[49]

> [I kissed Michelle successively [...] going up or down the stairs, on all the garden benches by Avenue Gabriel, under the trees at the bottom of the Champs-Élysées, in Place de la Concorde, on the back deck of those buses that were perfectly suited to lovers, the open, rear decks that we once used to get on and off; [...] and the bus would set off, and we would huddle up close together in a corner of the outer deck to kiss.]

The passage describes displays of affection shared by Roubaud and Michelle, but the proliferation of prepositions of place and verbs of movement point to the fact that there was no single corner for the couple, leaving them unable to consummate their relationship. Perhaps Roubaud represents this lack of intimacy with the missing caress in his poem, which states 'une | seule te fait briller' [one | alone makes you shine] from Éluard's 'D'une seule caresse | Je te fais briller de tout ton éclat' [With one caress alone | I make you shine with all your brilliance].[50] Afraid of

49 Roubaud, *Poésie:*, pp. 379–80.
50 Éluard, *L'Amour la poésie*, p. 163.

Michelle's strict father and with no place of his own, the two resort to secret trysts in locations scattered around the city. It is this lack of their own space that eventually signals the somewhat anticlimactic end of their love: 'Je ne voulais pas attendre. Michelle ne voulait pas ne pas attendre' [I didn't want to wait. Michelle didn't not want to wait].[51]

Despite the emphasis on the male poet in the lines of the poem, the stability of his presence there is called into question from the very beginning, suggesting a sense of ambivalence as the poet speaks through the words of his predecessor. Roubaud describes his own agency in the production of *Autobiographie, chapitre dix* in terms of his selection and subsequent arrangement of the extracts of poetry used: 'et bien sûr dans le choix des moments restitués (comme dans toute autobiographie) comme dans la progression de la présentation, est mon intervention propre, en ce livre' [and of course, my own intervention in this book is in the choice of moments that have been reconstructed (as is the case in any autobiography) and in the order they are presented in].[52] In the same way that a reader might take Roubaud's advice and give weight to the fragments of poetry that feature in this collage, paying particular attention to the way they are presented, or to the order they are presented in, consideration of what is omitted in these lines is critical in the understanding the poet's role in the creation of the text. Like Roubaud, Éluard opens a verse with 'Ma présence n'est pas ici' [My presence is not here], continuing with 'Je suis habillé de moi-même' [I am dressed in myself].[53] A comparison with Roubaud's 'habillé' [dressed], isolated at the beginning of the line by a full stop, is haunted by the missing affirmations of the speaking 'je' [I] in 'Je suis' [I am] and 'moi-même' [myself], deepening the sense of loss of self that has occurred in the transition from one poet to the other.

Proclaiming himself to be 'dans une solitude d'encre' [in a solitude of ink] – though once again the missing personal pronoun and verb 'suis' [am] lead to an effect of dislocation in the speaking voice – directly situates the feeling of solitude in the ink that writes the poem into being. While there

51 Roubaud, *Poésie:*, p. 380.

52 Roubaud, *Description du projet*, p. 83.

53 Éluard, *L'Amour la poésie*, p. 219.

is the sense that Roubaud's writing extends or deepens Éluard's expression, adding new layers of meaning through the manipulation of his words, it is clear that this poem speaks not only of Roubaud's problematic encounter with first love, but also of his experience as poet and the particular feeling of disjunction that occurs in speaking through the poetry of Éluard.

Vers (non) libre

While the adolescent Roubaud falls immediately in love with the novelty of Surrealist poetry and its *vers libre*, the retrospective author looking back on his life's work in *Poésie:* makes no secret of his eventual rejection of the form, represented in particular by the work of Éluard:

> Mon exercice de la poésie jusqu'à ce jour (et Dieu sait que je m'y suis fortement 'exercisé') se caractérise par un manque total de rigueur. J'écris comme cela me vient et ce qui me vient me vient d'ailleurs, d'autres poètes, principalement de surréalistes et postsurréalistes, de Breton, Tzara, Aragon, Éluard; d'Éluard surtout (ce qui est particulièrement débilitant).[54]

> [My practice of poetry until this day (and God knows I put everything into this 'practice') is characterized by a total lack of rigour. I write as it comes to me and what comes to me comes from elsewhere, from other poets, mainly Surrealists and Postsurrealists, from Breton, Tzara, Aragon, Éluard; above all from Éluard (which is particularly debilitating).]

Once associated with the nourishment of the forest *vers* [worms] masticating and digesting beech tree leaves, reading other poets and allowing their influence to flow through the hand composing poetry anew is now anything but productive, described as 'debilitating' even, especially so in the case of Éluard. The choice of Éluard here has much to do with him being the most accessible of these new, adventurous poets: 'C'est que nous lisions Éluard beaucoup. Il représentait la transition moins rude entre la poésie de nos études et celle des temps nouveaux' [It's just that we read Éluard a lot. He represented the gentlest transition between the

54 Roubaud, *Poésie:*, p. 104. Emphasis in the original.

poetry in our studies and that of the newer times].[55] His style of composition will have been the most readily absorbed and regurgitated by the budding young poet.

Roubaud explains his later rejection of Surrealist modes of poetry, rooting his motivation in his concern with form, or lack of it:

> Plus les conditions formelles d'une poésie (et c'est le cas de celle de tous les poètes que je viens de citer) sont molles et floues (plus ceux qui les adoptent se sentent et s'affichent libres par rapport à leurs propres conditions d'exercice), plus la personnalité poétique émerge difficilement. Le sentiment de déjà-vu, déjà-entendu, d'air de famille vague domine leurs productions. [...] je sens qu'impérativement je dois rompre. Je romps.[56]

> The looser and vaguer the formal conditions of poetry are, (the more those who adopt these conditions feel and proclaim themselves to be free in their poetic practices (which is the case for all the poets I have just cited)), the more difficult it is for the personality of the poetry to emerge. The feeling of déjà-vu, the sense that you have already heard this somewhere before, a vague air of familiarity dominates their creations. [...] I feel that it is imperative that I make a break. I am making a break.

He admits he does not find the freedom others proclaim to enjoy in the practice of free verse, instead aligning forms he describes as 'molles et floues' [loose and vague] with lacking poetic originality. In his essay charting the rise and fall of the alexandrine through the history of French verse, *La Vieillesse d'Alexandre*, Roubaud further elaborates on the restrictive elements inherent in so-called free verse. While the form was celebrated for its independence from metric measure and strict rhyme schemes increasingly thought to contort syntax into artificial arrangements for the benefit of sonority, Roubaud points out the dependence of free verse on typography: 'Le vers libre, pour lequel la fin du vers n'est pas définie de *manière interne* par une *mesure rythmique* répétable, a une existence écrite et, puisque destiné à être transmis par l'imprimé, une existence *d'abord typographique*' [Free verse, in which the end of the poetic line is not defined *internally* by a repeatable *rhythmic measure*, has a written existence and, since it is intended to be transmitted in print, a *primarily*

55 Roubaud, *Poésie:*, p. 348.
56 Roubaud, *Poésie:*, p. 104.

typographic existence].[57] Defined by its written or printed presence on the page, the restrictiveness of free verse form's visual existence becomes another dimension to the words of *Autobiographie, chapitre dix*: 'dans une solitude d'encre | à proscrire. Sa visi | bilité parfaite me rendait aveugle' [in a solitude of ink | to ban. Its perfect visi | bility made me blind]. Only a visual reader of this poem, and not a listener to its oral performance, will be conscious of the enjambment ironically breaking up the reference to 'visi | bilité parfaite' [perfect visi | bility], since there is no regularity of rhythm or rhyme indicating line endings and beginnings.

The constrictive qualities of free verse go beyond the necessity of its typography. Roubaud establishes a set of formal characteristics linking *vers libre* to the most classic of French verse forms, the alexandrine. He outlines three negative statements on which free verse is based: unlike the alexandrine, '*Le vers libre standard est non compté*' [*Standard free verse is not counted*], '*Le vers libre commun est non rimé*' [*Common free verse is not rhymed*] and finally, '*Il n'y a pas d'alexandrin dans le vers libre*/L'alexandrin est soumis à un *interdit*' [*There is no alexandrine in free verse*/The alexandrine is subject to a *ban*], citing *Notes sur la poésie* (1936) [*Notes on Poetry*] by Éluard and Breton as evidence of the latter.[58] The result of this negative determination of free verse renders its 'freedom' 'extremely limited' and makes it nothing more than what Roubaud calls an 'anti-alexandrine'.[59] The poet uses a double grammatical negation to explain the consequences of its anti-alexandrine status 'le vers libre commun n'est pas libre de n'être pas cela et la détermination négative qui le caractérise va peser sur son histoire d'un poids considérable' [common free verse isn't free of not being that and the negative determination that characterizes it will weigh considerably on its history], emphasizing its subsistence in the shadow of the traditional verse it so strives to get away from.[60] There are even clear similarities between regular metric verse and free verse in what Roubaud refers to as its 'classic phase'. He outlines two rules respected by both regular and free

57 Jacques Roubaud, *La Vieillesse d'Alexandre* (Paris: Ivrea, 2000), pp. 122–23.

58 Roubaud, *La Vieillesse d'Alexandre*, p. 128.

59 Roubaud, *La Vieillesse d'Alexandre*, p. 129.

60 Roubaud, *La Vieillesse d'Alexandre*, p. 129.

verse: '*(L) La dernière position pleine du vers est plus marquée ou au moins aussi marquée que la précédente*' [*(L) The last full position of the line is more or at least as marked as the previous one*] and '*(F) Si un groupement syntaxique commence à l'intérieur d'un vers, il ne peut s'achever qu'à la fin d'un autre vers*' [*(F) If a syntactical unit begins within a poetic line, it cannot be completed until the end of another line*].[61] Boundaries for metrical and syntactic units are then found to fall in the same place for both verse forms, contributing yet further evidence to the claim that free verse is not, in fact, as free as its name might suggest.

The three 'L'AMOUR LA POÉSIE L'AMOUR' poems in *Autobiographie, chapitre dix* are immediately striking in this respect, for they display a flagrant violation of the rules that make of free verse a form according to Roubaud's own critique. There are no capital letters to head lines or verses, yet a single capital does appear in the middle of a line, which is also in the middle of a verse:

> dans une solitude d'encre
> à proscrire. Sa visi
> bilité parfaite me rendait aveugle
>
> [in a solitude of ink
> to ban. Its perfect visi
> bility made me blind]

Neither the unity of syntactic groupings, nor the fuller final syllable (in relation to that which precedes it), that is, rules *F* and *L*, are respected in Roubaud's rendering. The final line of the second poem reads 'avouer. dans le fleuve ignorant de ma' [confess. in the unknowing river of my], completed only by the first line of the next poem, 'tête je te l'ai dit pour l'arbre' [mind I told you for the tree]. Single words are violently broken up through enjambment over two lines, as in 'visi | bilité' [visi | bility], or even over separate stanzas, 'ne veux pas inventer de béquilles ad || mirables' [I do not want to invent ad | mirable crutches]. Punctuation often appears anywhere but at the end of a line, creating an obvious disparity between

61 Roubaud, *La Vieillesse d'Alexandre*, p. 129.

syntax and what might be thought of as the respiratory unit of a line. For example:

> phore   la perspective ne joue pas pour
>
> moi;   ma mémoire va les cartes,
> bat, d'un concret à un autre
> sans savoir où je devrais la reconnaître.
>
> [phor   perspective plays not for
>
> me;   my memory goes the cards,
> shuffles, from one concrete to another
> not knowing where I should recognize it.]

The sense of fragmentation here is intensified through a comparison with Éluard's original lines, 'Ma mémoire bat les cartes' [My memory shuffles the cards] and later 'Et de félicités | Tu vas d'un concret à un autre' [And with joys | You go from one concrete to another].[62] The former line is made grammatically impossible by Roubaud, who replaces, or 'shuffles', 'bat' [shuffles / (beats)] with intransitive verb 'va' [goes], making the ensuing direct object jarring to the ear. This also leaves the isolated 'bat' offering little communicable meaning, the overall harshness of the syntactic disharmony emulating the words 'd'un concret à un autre' [from one concrete to another]. The replacement of Éluard's addressee 'Tu' [you] with what seems here to be the memory of the poet again locates this disjointed, painful experience within the poet himself.

A similar technique transforms one of Éluard's most renowned images, 'La terre est bleue comme une orange | Jamais une erreur les mots ne mentent pas' [The earth is blue like an orange | Never a mistake words do not lie], into 'la terre est une erreur les mots | j'en rêve que je dors' [the earth is a mistake the words | I dream that I am asleep].[63] A reader of French poetry will almost certainly think of what is absent in Roubaud's line, even more so because its rhythm replicates the eight syllables that compose

62 Éluard, *L'Amour la poésie*, p. 232 and p. 235.
63 Éluard, *L'Amour la poésie*, p. 153.

the original: the rewritten line is haunted by Éluard's composition. The sensuality and vitality of the bold Eluardian image are transformed into 'une erreur' [a mistake]. The words which never lie for Éluard are left free standing, lingering at the end of the line with no follow-up, no purpose. On the surface of it, Roubaud appears to undermine Éluard's imagery, remove his admired lover, his poetic inspiration and leave behind a wreck of broken lines, which are capable only of expressing a sense of futility and suffering on the part of the poet. The sentiment epitomized in the poems' end, 'toutes les raisons disparaissent: souffrir' [all the reasons disappear: suffering], is a desperate negation of the original reference to the loved woman in Éluard's 'Et toutes ses raisons de souffrir disparaissent' [And all her reasons for suffering disappear].[64]

The disparity between the ordered arrangement of the poems into stanzas (there are three poems, each made up of three stanzas of, in turn, three lines each) and the fragmentary lines within these greater structures creates a tension, further exacerbating the impression of imprisonment and constriction. Roubaud adopts a stance reminiscent of Denis Roche in his take on Éluard's poems in *Autobiographie, chapitre dix*, outlined by Roubaud himself as: 'faire comme si le vers libre était libre et tirer, axiomatiquement, toutes les conséquences de la définition' [act as though free verse were free and accept, axiomatically, all the consequences of the definition].[65] If Roubaud's foray into the history of the alexandrine has shown that classic metre continues to be an organizing factor behind freer verse forms associated with the Surrealist movement, the only solution for the further development of the *alexandrine* is: 'rendre *entièrement arbitraire* le découpage en vers par rapport au découpage linguistique' [to make the line breaks *completely arbitrary* in relation to the linguistic units].[66] The above reading has demonstrated that this involves a twofold challenge to the status of common free verse: first, interrogating the harmony between metre and syntax; second, undermining the typographic identity of the verse, highlighting the impossibility of its existence beyond the writing on

64 Éluard, *L'Amour la poésie*, p. 164.

65 Roubaud, *La Vieillesse d'Alexandre*, p. 175.

66 Jacques Roubaud, 'Quatre états de poésie', *Change*, 18 (1974), 85–95 (p. 91).

the page. This next stage in the history of the ageing alexandrine is represented, for Roubaud, by Roche's *Éros énergumène* (1968) [*Eros Possessed*]. Roubaud quotes examples from the latter of lines beginning and ending midway through a word, but the tone of Roche's challenge to metric and syntactic integrity is succinctly demonstrated in Roubaud's selection of the line 'les portes où je dors qui sont deux et fertiles d'' [the doors where I sleep which are two and fertile w].[67] The addition of 'd' to the alexandrine disturbs the reader's count of the twelve-syllable line, but also has a stalling effect: the end of the line is not just missing the final strong syllable stress associated with the alexandrine, it is practically unpronounceable.

Roubaud differs from Roche, however, when he presents his own challenge to the line of free verse from within the space of seemingly ordered stanzas and overarching poem structures, an organizing strategy not used by Roche. The paradox seems to represent what Roubaud refers to as the 'entre-deux' [in-between] of free verse.[68] Speaking of Éluard, among others, he describes the way in which 'tout en fuyant la rime, leurs poèmes étaient de plus en plus envahis de mesures traditionnelles, alexandrins et octosyllabes surtout, flottant comme des ions libres dans une soupe chimiquement encore d'apparence vers-libriste' [while avoiding rhyme, their poems were more and more invaded by traditional metres, mostly alexandrines and octosyllabic lines, floating like free ions in a soup that still vaguely resembled the chemistry of free verse].[69] At the level of form, the avant-gardists' aim of revolutionizing poetic practice through the clean slate of a *tabula rasa* approach proves counterproductive. For any poets that have grown up like Roubaud in the forest of poetry, learning by heart, copying and reciting the traditional poems taught at school in France, giving up on any definition of verse through metrical count or rhyme schemes can only result in the eventual resurgence of the old patterns learned and engrained in memory.[70] This is how it is that classic verse comes back to haunt free verse: the efforts of Surrealist poets to distance themselves from the rhythmic traditions that have come before make of their hopes for innovation a simple negation

67 Roubaud, 'Quatre états de poésie', p. 91.

68 Roubaud, *Poésie:*, p. 353.

69 Roubaud, *Poésie:*, p. 353.

70 Roubaud, *La Vieillesse d'Alexandre*, p. 155.

of past patterns, gradually paving the way for their resurgence in the most contemporary writing.

In his own ironic twist, Roubaud recreates the tension of this 'entre-deux' [in-between], demonstrating the effect of constriction that this mode of composition has on his own poetic practice. By placing his destruction of the axioms sustaining *vers libre* within a greater sense of order in *Autobiographie, chapitre dix*, Roubaud challenges free verse for being neither entirely free, nor versified. The lines of free verse, actually made 'freer' through Roubaud's violation of the customs upholding what he calls classic or standard free verse, are imprisoned in the greater, inescapable framework of conventional versification. The analogy of this type of poetry with 'soup' scattered with 'free ions' captures the sense of the writer's loss of agency when it comes to free verse, conveying it as anything but generative.

A Search for Poetic Autonomy

As Roubaud singles out Éluard as representing a 'particularly debilitating' influence on his own output, he simultaneously builds the beginnings of his theory linking love and poetry on the earlier poet's title, *L'Amour la poésie*. Although his break with Surrealism is expressed in unequivocal terms, the poet's particular relationship with Éluard is one of ambivalence and invites further probing. Roubaud's remoulding of *L'Amour la poésie* is, at least on one level, an effort to unearth the constriction present in Éluard's chosen form, the *vers libre*. The reasons for the poet's suffering, however, must be sought out in his dissatisfaction with his own poetic process and mode of composition. Having pointed out that his creativity in *Autobiographie, chapitre dix* consists in the selection and rearrangement of the words of other poets, Roubaud explains that the collection is as much about re-evaluating his own relationship with free verse: 'j'ai réfléchi et tenu compte de ce qu'était le vers libre pour moi et j'en ai fait une *critique*, en modifiant, dans mes poèmes non inventés, le rapport du vers aux mots, aux phrases qui le composent' [I have thought about and taken account of what free verse meant for me, and I have made a *critique* of it, modifying, in my non-invented poems, the relationship between the poetic line and the words and phrases that compose it].[71] In the words of Natacha Michel, it is a matter of 'prendre pour contenu une autre forme' [taking another form as content].[72] His decision to effect a 'rupture' is not necessarily a personal critique of any single poet writing during '*Le classicisme du vers libre*' [*The classic period of free verse*].[73] Perhaps his decision is not even a complete rejection of the form he seems to criticize so heavily in some of his writing on the period.[74]

Clive Scott signals the 'danger' in attributing the frequent 'parisyllabism' in Éluard's writing to 'traditionalism' or a 'strategy of facilitation'.[75] Instead of a reductive interpretation that concludes 'easier' reading, Scott encourages Éluard's reader to appreciate 'patterns of measures' and 'echoes of measures across line-groups' rather than 'the metricity of the line as line'.[76] Jean-François Puff is another critic who comments on '[le] caractère "facile" qu'on prête à son œuvre' [[the] 'easy' quality that has been attributed to his work], also mentioning Éluard's tendency towards 'limpidité' [ludicity].[77] He believes it is these aspects of Éluard's writing that Roubaud rejects. However, like Scott, Puff recognizes the complex kernel at the heart of Éluard's poetry, explaining that there are no 'distinctions claires' [clear

71 Roubaud, *Description du projet*, p. 83.
72 Michel, 'Roubaud 1978', p. 600.
73 Roubaud, *La Vieillesse d'Alexandre*, p. 117.
74 Although Roubaud seems to frequently stage his rejection of *vers libre* as a choice of poetic form, to argue that he rejects *vers libre* outright would be simplistic. Some of the most personal, poignant poems that feature in his book of sonnets, *Signe d'appartenance* (∈), are in fact written in free verse. In the heart of this collection, which claims to be the poet's first book following his own choice of a new direction of formal 'rigour' (Roubaud discusses the planning and writing stages for *Signe d'appartenance* in detail in *Poésie:*, pp. 447–85), are a number of free verse poems mourning the loss of his brother. See, for example, *Signe d'appartenance* (Paris: Gallimard, 1967), pp. 104–05.
75 Clive Scott, *The Poetics of French Verse: Studies in Reading* (Oxford: Clarendon Press, 1998), p. 267.
76 Scott, *The Poetics of French Verse*, p. 267.
77 Jean-François Puff, *Mémoire de la mémoire: Jacques Roubaud et la lyrique médiévale* (Paris: Éditions Classiques Garnier, 2009), p. 220.

distinctions] in collections *L'Amour la poésie*, *Mourir de ne pas mourir* (1924) [*Dying of Not Dying*] (whose antithetical title is a precursor to the complexity within) or *Capitale de la douleur* (1926) [*Capital of Pain*].[78] Rather these volumes are characterized by 'les contradictions de l'amour vécu' [the contradictions of love lived], which give many of the poems a 'sens obscur, chiffré' [an obscure and coded meaning].[79]

He finds that Roubaud pays homage to the Surrealist poet in *Autobiographie, chapitre dix* through the arrangement of Éluard's words into visual groupings associated with the number nine (three poems, each consisting of three stanzas of three lines), alerting the reader to the mysticism the number nine held for Dante in his great expression of love for Beatrice.[80] Meanwhile Puff draws the reader's attention to the missing element in Éluard's title, the ancient genitive form linking 'l'amour' [love] and 'la poésie' [poetry]: 'le chant' [song], or *entrebescar*, weaving together rhythm and rhyme, that is, 'la dimension métrico-rythmique que recouvre le chant' [the metric-rhythmic dimension of song].[81] Thus, while the themes and images in Éluard's work are often complex and carefully constructed, the implication in Puff's reading is that Éluard's forms do not echo this level of involvement or intricacy.

78 Puff, *Mémoire de la mémoire*, p. 220. Puff's argument centres on the distinction between the *trobar leu* and *trobar clus* styles of the troubadour poets. The *leu* is characterized by 'distinctions claires, péremptoires, tranchées' [definite, conclusive, and clear-cut distinctions] structured by 'ses couples d'antonymes inséparés: joi e dolors, folie et sens' [pairs of inseparable antonyms: joy and suffering, madness and meaning] (Roubaud, *La Fleur inverse: Essai sur l'art formel des troubadours* (Paris: Ramsay, 1986), p. 326). The lexis of the 'closed' or more hermetic *clus* style of poetry is not marked by the clarity of binary pairings, but is interwoven without clear opposition or resolution in an enlacing pattern of rhyme words whose process is known as *entrebescar*.

79 Puff, *Mémoire de la mémoire*, p. 220.

80 Puff, *Mémoire de la mémoire*, pp. 220–21.

81 Jean-François Puff, 'Le modèle des troubadours dans l'œuvre poétique de Jacques Roubaud', *Les Cahiers du Ceracc*, 2 (2003) <http://www.cahiers-ceracc.fr/puff.html> [accessed 5 January 2014] (para. 11 of 14).

Perhaps there is something of Harold Bloom's seminal work, *The Anxiety of Influence*, at play in Roubaud's ambivalent re-writing of Éluard (which also constitutes a reading on the part of the later poet). Bloom links 'poetic history' to 'poetic influence' to the extent that they are 'indistinguishable', and he explains: '[P]oets make that history by misreading one another, so as to clear imaginative space for themselves.'[82] Whether or not Roubaud 'misreads' a certain simplicity into Éluard's poetry – for 'facile' [easy] is a word that seems to recur in discussions about the relationship Roubaud has with the earlier poet – he certainly seems to create the image of a poet from which he distances himself. It is unlikely that Roubaud does not recognize the layers of complexity Puff finds on the semantic level of Éluard's writing, or the echoes of metric play that Scott reads in his forms. However, Roubaud appears to associate his love of Éluard and other Surrealist poets with a concern for the unit of the line, or 'vers' in poetry, which has proved unproductive in his own work of the time. In his reassessment of his relationship with freer verse forms and the writing of his contemporaries, it is possible that Roubaud is, as Bloom describes, clearing his own 'imaginative space'.

Bloom also writes of the poet's reading process as distinct from that of the ordinary reader or critic. This involves the discovery, in the poet, that poetry is 'both external and internal to himself'.[83] Poetic influence is 'the sense – amazing, agonizing, delighting – of *other poets*, as felt in the depths of the [...] solipsist, the potentially strong poet'.[84] The poet's experience is one of ambivalence, at once delighting in the poetry that resonates with his outlook, appreciating the readerly experience and simultaneously feeling the pain of the threat to his own ego. In a passage that closely recalls the experience of Roubaud speaking through the words and broken forms of Éluard's *L'Amour la poésie*, Bloom also refers to a sense of dislocation resulting from this dichotomy within the poet:

82 Harold Bloom, *The Anxiety of Influence: A Theory of Poetry* (New York: Oxford University Press, 1973), p. 5.

83 Bloom, *The Anxiety of Influence*, p. 25.

84 Bloom, *The Anxiety of Influence*, p. 26.

> For the poet is condemned to learn his profoundest yearnings through an awareness of *other selves*. The poem is *within* him, yet he experiences the shame and splendor of *being found by* poems – great poems – *outside* him. To lose freedom in this center is never to forgive, and to learn the dread of threatened autonomy forever.[85]

Roubaud appears to be conveying the difficulty he encounters when trying to create using the forms frequently used in the work of Éluard, at once critiquing these forms and exploring what he feels to be their limits. However, his re-manipulation of Éluard's words may also bear witness to his internal struggle to assert an autonomous identity as poet, as outlined by Bloom in this passage. Roubaud tells his reader that he loves to read poetry, absorbing it so deeply into his memory that he can recite it decades later. However, when following the processes of these same poets, he seems to 'lose freedom in this center'. He is torn between his adolescent ardour with the poets he reads, that early adult identification with the writers who swept him away, and the feeling that he cannot innovate from within the sphere of their influence. Even when composing his defiant *Autobiographie, chapitre dix*, the poet describes becoming entirely absorbed by a re-reading of their words:

> En ce moment je relis les surréalistes pour mon *Autobiographie*, mais je ne les ai pas lus pendant une quinzaine d'années parce que j'étais totalement incapable de les aborder d'une manière qui me permettrait de prendre une distance par rapport à eux […]. J'étais totalement désarmé.[86]

> [I am currently re-reading the Surrealists for my *Autobiography*, but I have not read them for around fifteen years, because I was utterly incapable of approaching them in a way that would allow me to keep some kind of distance from them […]. I was totally disarmed.]

The experience is overwhelming. The impossibility of maintaining a sense of distance on reading these poets he had enjoyed in his youth might be explained through the words of Louis Zukofsky, cited in an article by

85 Bloom, *The Anxiety of Influence*, p. 26.

86 Jacques Roubaud and others, 'Entretien presque imaginaire sur le sentiment des langues', *Change*, 29 (1976), 8–14 (p. 13).

Roubaud on poetic form: 'sometimes a meter's a voice'.[87] For Roubaud, poetic form is constitutive of the poet's voice and identity in poetry, and his acute 'awareness of *other selves*' in his own composition process is manifested in the haunting return of structures and metres that resurge from the poet's unconscious memory during his attempts to write in free verse.

Bloom's focus is the self-reflecting Romantic poet, but in the application of his hypothesis to Roubaud's ambivalent treatment of Éluard, both the approach of the poets to form and the process itself of writing or composing poetry must be foregrounded. The context too is delimited by Roubaud's situation of his battle with Éluard's influence in the particular domain of love poetry. How does Roubaud gain the distance he requires in the fifteen years between feeling 'completely disarmed' by Surrealist writing and once again taking up the poets of his youth for *Autobiographie, chapitre dix*? What composition tools and approaches does Roubaud develop in the time between turning away from Surrealist poetry and beginning his 'autobiographical' pastiche?

Éluard's Muse: Questioning the Specular Relation

A glance at Roubaud's anthology, *Cent vingt-huit poèmes composés en langue française de Guillaume Apollinaire à 1968* [*One Hundred and Twenty-Eight Poems Composed in the French Language from Guillaume Apollinaire until 1968*], sheds further light on Roubaud's reading of Éluard. Subtitled *Anthologie de poésie contemporaine* [*Anthology of Contemporary Poetry*], it groups together poems from the period that features in Roubaud's formal study of the fall of the alexandrine, *La Vieillesse d'Alexandre*, and it is described by the poet as 'Complément' [Complement] to his theoretical text, 'une anthologie de poésie française des cents dernières années "du point de vue formel"' [an anthology of

87 Jacques Roubaud, 'Le silence de la mathématique jusqu'au fond de la langue, poésie', *Po&sie*, 10 (1979), 110–24 (p. 116).

French poetry from the last one hundred years 'composed from a formal point of view'].[88] The collection is a commentary on the poetry explored in his theoretical work and his response in particular to the question of form in the poems concerned. In addition to its complementarity with Roubaud's other studies of the poetry of the time, the author insists on the significance of his selection:

> Il s'agit ici d'un choix, qui indique forcément des *préférences*. L'auteur du choix est un compositeur de poésie, un lecteur de poésie, de cette poésie particulièrement. Il n'était pas né en 1914. Il avait trente-cinq ans en 1968. Les présences et absences sont donc voulues.[89]
>
> [It is about a certain choice, which naturally reveals *preferences*. The author of this choice is a composer of poetry, a reader of poetry, particularly of this poetry. He was not yet born in 1914. He was thirty-five years old in 1968. The inclusions and omissions are therefore willful.]

Roubaud's choice of these poems over other possibilities is made in his capacity as both 'lecteur' [reader] and 'compositeur de poésie' [composer of poetry], reminding the reader of the duality of the reading and writing poet encountered in Bloom's theory, the equivocal nature of the relationship between the material he reads and his creativity, these anthologized pieces and his own poems.

Although Roubaud focuses on the poems' formal traits in his decision-making, the inclusion of Éluard's work is also significant from a thematic point of view. Other than three war poems, published under the chapter heading 'Poésie dans la guerre' [Poetry During the War], the only poems by Paul Éluard in the anthology are 'L'Égalité des sexes' ['The Equality of the Sexes'] and 'L'Amoureuse' ['The Lover'].[90] While these two poems betray some

88 Roubaud, *Description du projet*, p. 137.

89 Jacques Roubaud, *Cent vingt-huit poèmes composés en langue française de Guillaume Apollinaire à 1968: Une anthologie de poésie contemporaine* (Paris: Gallimard, 1995), p. 10.

90 All further references to the two Éluard poems can be found in Roubaud's anthology, pp. 51–52. See also Paul Éluard, *Capitale de la douleur* suivi de *L'Amour la poésie* (Paris: Gallimard, 1966), p. 51 ('L'Égalité des sexes') and p. 56 ('L'Amoureuse').

of the typical formal elements of the period commented upon by Roubaud (the former is a traditional sonnet composed entirely of alexandrines and conventional *rimes croisées* [alternate rhymes] and *rimes embrassées* [enclosed rhymes], and the second poem is written in octosyllabic lines, avoiding rhyme until it culminates in a final rhyming couplet), both pieces also foreground (a) woman, each speaking of her as lover, or more precisely love object. The feminine position in relation to that of the poet is at stake from the outset, taking centre stage in each title.

Nevertheless, as Jean-Jacques Thomas and Steven Winspur point out in regard to 'L'Égalité des sexes', 'there does not appear to be any *equality* of the sexes in the text (contrary to what its title claims)'.[91] Thomas and Winspur identify Éluard's trademark reference to the beauty and illumination in the lover's eyes in the poem, 'la beauté des yeux, beauté des pierres' [the beauty of the eyes, beauty of stones], a frequent motif in his love poetry, tracing their journey from 'un pays arbitraire' [an arbitrary country], through their transformation into tears, 'gouttes d'eau' [drops of water], to the petrification of their 'regard' [gaze] when they become 'pierres nues' [bare stones]. Thomas and Winspur explain that the 'desired person has gradually become objectified into a lifeless image', as the poet addresses his beloved successively as 'ô ma statue' [O my statue], 'ô statue abattue' [O fallen statue] and finally 'ô mon image' [O my image].[92] In fact, it would seem that her presence is in question from the opening of the poem, since it begins with a reference to her disembodied eyes: 'Tes yeux sont revenus d'un pays arbitraire' [Your eyes are returned from an arbitrary land]. Her body never materializes but for its role as 'statue' and 'image', whose existence relies entirely upon the poet's love: 'Mon désir immobile est ton dernier soutien' [My unmoving desire is your last support].

The study by Thomas and Winspur details the typographic and prosodic symmetries in 'L'Égalité des sexes', demonstrating the ways in which they are structured around the central word 'miroir' [mirror], creating a

91 Jean-Jacques Thomas and Steven Winspur, *Poeticized Language: The Foundations of Contemporary French Poetry* (University Park: Pennsylvania State University Press, 1999), p. 162.

92 Thomas and Winspur, *Poeticized Language*, p. 162.

number of mirroring patterns that quite literally emanate from this central point to the outer reaches of the poem.[93] They describe the poem's arrangement as 'a fictional equation established between the desirer and his desired image'.[94] Indeed, the lack of vision accorded to the female, doubled by the deprivation of her own reflected image in 'Le soleil aveuglant te tient lieu de miroir' [The blinding sun is used as your mirror], contributes to the sense that the poet sees in his lover a reflection of himself. He refers to her in possessive terms, '*ma* statue' [*my* statue], '*mon* image' [*my* image] (emphasis my own), where the possessive adjectives also serve to denote his own image or silhouette.

Éluard's artistic conjuring of the lover through the words of poetry and the mirroring effect that ripples outwards from the poem's centre might be read in terms of Luce Irigaray's critical evaluation of masculine subjectivity. In *Speculum de l'autre femme* [*Speculum of the Other Woman*], Irigaray goes back to the origins of psychoanalytic theories of the feminine.[95] The title of Irigaray's chapter dedicated to Freud – 'La Tache aveugle d'un vieux rêve de symétrie' ['The Blind Spot of an Old Dream of Symmetry'] – alludes to the privileging of the visual in the setting of his theory of sexual difference. Beginning with the Freudian notion of female anatomical castration, the gaze is shown to function within a dichotomous structure. Firstly, it involves a paradoxical look at the female body, paradoxical because 'la fillette, la femme, n'aurait *rien* à donner à voir. Elle exposerait, exhiberait, la possibilité d'*un rien à voir*' [the little girl, the woman, supposedly has *nothing* you can see. She exposes, exhibits the possibility of a *nothing to see*].[96] This absence of a sight to behold refers to Freud's well-known account of the discovery, amongst curious children, that the little girl is missing a penis:

93 Thomas and Winspur, *Poeticized Language*, pp. 161–63.

94 Thomas and Winspur, *Poeticized Language*, p. 162.

95 Irigaray also responds to treatments of myth and to philosophical texts, such as Sophocles' *Antigone* and Plato's *Republic*. The wide-ranging essays of the volume each consider an aspect of Western philosophy and culture and its treatment of woman.

96 Irigaray, *Speculum de l'autre femme*, p. 53; *Speculum of the Other Woman*, p. 47.

> La 'castration' pour la femme serait de n'avoir rien à donner à voir, de n'*avoir rien*. De n'avoir rien de pénis, de voir qu'elle (n') a rien. Rien de *même* que l'homme. Donc *rien de sexe* qui se montre dans une *forme* susceptible d'en fonder la réalité.[97]
>
> [Woman's castration is defined as her having nothing you can see, as her *having* nothing. In her having nothing penile, in seeing that she has No Thing. Nothing *like* man. That is to say, *no sex/organ* that can be seen in a *form* capable of founding its reality.]

Female 'castration', therefore, is only relative to the visibility of the male sex organ, whose obvious '*form*' privileges the male as the central term in definitions of gender; that is to say, woman is castrated, lacking, simply because she is visually unlike man. Thus, the first stage in the unveiling of the female predicament posits woman as object of the gaze, in which she 'exposes' and 'exhibits' her visual dissimilarity from the male.

As the Freudian description proceeds, the focus shifts from the image of the female to her reaction, her own gaze. On seeing the male sexual organ for the first time, girls 'at once notice the difference and, it must be admitted, its significance too'.[98] Freud attributes to this realization feelings of 'envy' and being 'wronged' as, somehow, the very appearance of the male genitalia is enough to inform the girl of its value.[99] The notion of envy here presupposes two looks: the first observing the lacking girl and the second emanating from her thereafter, capturing sight of what she misses. Hence, the ease with which the female can be situated as 'other' to a male centre also relies, in part, on her own supposed acceptance of her position, which accompanies her act of looking. In turn, the sole standard of value is attributed to the male sex, reducing the female to a supporting role. Freud's 'tache aveugle' [blind spot] is his inability, in Irigaray's reading, to formulate a positive definition of femininity. Sexual difference is constituted in the feminine not being (like) the male term; it is in this that she is 'other', a reflection of the self-same in which her 'penis-envy' compensates for what is missing.

97 Irigaray, *Speculum de l'autre femme*, p. 54; *Speculum of the Other Woman*, p. 48.

98 Sigmund Freud, *New Introductory Lectures on Psychoanalysis*, ed. by James Strachey, trans. by James Strachey (Harmondsworth: Penguin Books, 1973), pp. 158–59.

99 Freud, *New Introductory Lectures*, p. 159.

The feminist theorist uses the metaphor of the sun to criticize the prioritization of male subjectivity in predominant accounts of psychoanalytic theory beginning with Freud. The male becomes the sun, 'si c'est autour de lui que les choses tournent' [if it is around him that things turn], and woman is aligned with the earth, 'Toujours en voltes, plus ou moins proches du soleil dont elle capte les rayons, les faisant virer selon ses cycles' [Always whirling closer or farther from the sun whose rays she captures and sends curving to and fro in turn with her cycles].[100] Irigaray also refers to the feminine's 'possession par un "sujet", le désir de son appropriation par un "sujet" [...] il (se) projette un quelque chose à absorber, à prendre, à voir, à posséder ... et encore un sol sur lequel se tenir debout, une glace où se mirer' [possession by a 'subject', a subject's desire to appropriate her [...] he projects a something to absorb, to take, to see, to possess ... as well as a patch of ground to stand upon, a mirror to catch his reflection].[101] However, just as the specular image projected in Éluard's poem proves to be flawed, closing the poem as a broken reflection betraying the narrator's own weakness, 'Rompue à ma faiblesse et prise dans mes liens' [Broken by my weakness and caught in my ties], Irigaray explains that the subject who relies on objectification of the other for his own support is necessarily 'multiple, pluriel, parfois di-forme' [multiple, plural, sometimes di-formed].[102] The wordplay bringing out the duality in the deformation of masculine subjectivity designates his projected image as 'Morcellement fantastique, fantasmatique' [A fantastic phantasmatic fragmentation], a '*duplicité*' [*duplicity*] which must inevitably collapse.[103] The feminine figure of 'L'Égalité des sexes' becomes not so much poetic muse as empty 'image' or 'statue'. Éluard appears to question the capacity of the poem, or perhaps poetry in general, to express the structures according to which it functions. The poetic here interacts with social structures, suggesting the failure of specular relations in love and creative partnerships.

The representation of the poet-muse relationship in this poem stands apart from a number of Éluard's other poems centring on love and the

100 Irigaray, *Speculum de l'autre femme*, p. 166; *Speculum of the Other Woman*, p. 134.
101 Irigaray, *Speculum de l'autre femme*, p. 166; *Speculum of the Other Woman*, p. 134.
102 Irigaray, *Speculum de l'autre femme*, p. 168; *Speculum of the Other Woman*, p. 35.
103 Irigaray, *Speculum de l'autre femme*, p. 168; *Speculum of the Other Woman*, p. 35.

feminine lover. The use of metaphor in *L'Amour la poésie* is widely referred to for its transformative and sensually expressive qualities; the line 'La terre est bleue comme une orange' [the earth is blue like an orange] has gained almost iconic status for its voluptuous imagery and radical juxtapositions.[104] There is, in the line, the sense that in love and poetry everything can be turned upside down: the reader is free to take the world in the palm of her hand. The earth is linked to the sweet-tasting orange through roundness of shape, while the incongruous pairing of the small fruit and the immense planet, together with the shocks of colour make the reader pause for breath.

In another example, from *Poésie ininterrompue* [*Uninterrupted Poetry*], the poet-narrator conveys the multiplicity of his lover from the outset, opening with a series of feminine adjectives. The description flows for thirty octosyllabic lines, starting from what might be considered a blank canvas in 'Nue effacée ensommeillée' [Naked erased sleeping].[105] While at first this appears to categorize the feminine space as one of passivity, as the passage develops, the impression on the reader becomes quite altered. In the mass of adjectives, both phonic and lexical patterns are formed. For example, 'Nue' [Naked], 'ensommeillée' [sleeping], 'matinale' [morning], 'Fraîche' [Fresh], 'ébouriffée' [tousled] and 'Ravivée' [Revived] together conjure up images of morning and waking. Meanwhile, the potentially sexual connotations of 'ébouriffée' [tousled] in turn tie it to 'Coquette' [Flirtatious], 'passionnée' [passionate] and 'Étreinte' [Embraced]. The shifting chains of connected adjectives create the sense of an unfurling as the woman awakens and is brought into existence.

At times, the description allotted to the woman is less than favourable. For example, the alliteration in 'Sourde secrète souterraine' [Deaf secret underground] combines definitions suggestive of concealment or barrier, whether the latter are physical or a prevention of understanding. An increasing number of unpropitious traits seep into the portrayal, until it ends with the woman tarnished and broken: 'Surprise dénouée rompue | Noire humiliée éclaboussée' [Surprised lacking broken | Black humiliated

104 Éluard, *L'Amour la poésie*, p. 153.

105 Éluard, *Poésie ininterrompue*, pp. 9–10 for all further references to the poem in this section.

splashed]. Despite this progressive darkening of the tone, moments of brilliance persist, since even towards the end of the piece, the woman in question is 'Ensoleillée illuminée' [Sunny illuminated], 'Fidèle' [Faithful] and 'populaire' [popular]. As a whole, the passage does not simply rely on binary oppositions, but gradually offers additions, contradictions and developments, which both expand upon and annihilate previous definitions, with the result that the reader is, in fact, given no certain perspective in relation to the woman at all. There is the sense that she begins to take shape, visibly moulded into being before the eyes of the reader, but she is outlined by the very same adjectives that proceed to break her down, to the extent that any image captured of her can only ever be fleeting and thus open to renewal as much as destruction.

It has been argued that seemingly more positive portrayals of love similar to these latter two Eluardian examples continue to inscribe the woman as other or object to the male poet-narrator, or subject. Gauthier, for example, suggests that Éluard has presented her as both mother and child, heaven and earth, hope and despair in his writing:

> *Si elle peut être tout, cela signifie clairement qu'elle n'est rien, hors de la cervelle de l'homme.* Elle n'est rien qu'une invention de mâle, encore cette invention fait-elle rien moins que 'réinventer' l'amour, puisqu'elle participe de tous les mythes traditionnels du 'mystère féminin'.[106]

> [*If she can be all, that clearly means that she is nothing, outside the brain of the man.* She is nothing but a male invention, but this invention still does nothing less than 'reinvent' love, since it participates in all the traditional myths of 'feminine mystery'.]

The implication is that, in her multiplicity, she is portrayed as everything the male poet wants her to be, and nothing to herself. Such a perspective would appeal to Lacanian discussions on the structure of the sexual relation. The term 'structure' is chosen here in place of 'interaction(s)' since, according to the psychoanalyst, the male-female relation is always mediated: 'ils sont trois, mais en réalité, ils sont deux plus *a*. Ce deux plus *a*, au point du *a*, se réduit, non pas aux deux autres, mais à un Un plus *a*'

106 Gauthier, *Surréalisme et sexualité*, p. 194. Emphasis in the original.

[there are three of them, but in reality, there are two plus *a*. This two plus *a*, from the standpoint of *a*, can be reduced, not to the two others, but to a One plus *a*].[107] The list of *objets petits autres* includes such disparate things as the gaze, voice and breast. Clearly not all objects as such, they are named so to designate their place as separate from the subject, also referred to as lost objects. The loss is primordial, occurring through the separation of the child from imagined unity with its mother. Occurring prior to the institution of language, this primal castration leaves of itself 'neither images nor words', the *objet a* remaining 'the unobjectified object, the non-represented object, the pre-object'.[108] While the separation is a stage in the establishment of the subject, who very gradually becomes aware of his own 'boundaries', it nonetheless constitutes a castration, a 'severance of the various objects [the subject] previously experienced as part of itself' and so the subject is condemned to remain incomplete, to yearn.[109] Projections of the feminine other as 'everything' are an attempt to fill this void. Yet in psychoanalytic terms, she is also nothing, erased, since 'la réciprocité entre le sujet et l'objet *a* est totale' [the reciprocity between the subject and object *a* is total].[110]

While the critic may see an objectification of the feminine in both *L'Amour la poésie* and *Poésie ininterrompue* [*Uninterrupted Poetry*], the contrast between these poems and 'L'Égalité des sexes' is vast. The use of metaphor and imagery in *L'Amour la poésie* is startlingly new, with the poet's careful arrangement of syntax creating unexpected associations through juxtaposition. In *Poésie ininterrompue*, the poet begins with the blank page: the opening feminine adjectives speak of a woman who is erased, naked, sleeping. Her waking coincides with the stirring of the poem into being, as patterns of adjectives create a space for growth and possibility from out of the silence. In both pieces the poet's imbrication in a love story

107 Lacan, *Encore*, p. 47; *On Feminine Sexuality*, p. 49.

108 Maire Jaanus, 'The *Démontage* of the Drive', in *Reading Seminar XI: Lacan's Four Fundamental Concepts of Psychoanalysis*, ed. by Richard Feldstein, Bruce Fink and Maire Jaanus (New York: SUNY Press, 1995), pp. 119–36 (p. 127).

109 Kaja Silverman, *The Acoustic Mirror: The Female Voice in Psychoanalysis and Cinema* (Indianapolis: Indiana University Press, 1988), p. 7.

110 Lacan, *Encore*, p. 114; *On Feminine Sexuality*, p. 127.

leads to writerly creativity, a space of novelty and discovery that unfolds for the reader as she moves from one word to the next, navigating lexical chains that surprise and make new. In 'L'Égalité des sexes', Éluard appears to deliberately play on female objectification and its constrictive limits for both the narrator and his beloved: the reader faced with the bold, provocative title and the dominant use of mirroring techniques on numerous levels of the poem cannot avoid this interpretation.

The poet's foregrounding of these binary structures pushes the reader to look beyond them. Is Éluard himself staging the inflexibility – the prison – of the sexual relation, also explored by Lacan and Irigaray? Does he attempt to determine its limits within a contemporary understanding of sexuality? The title is certainly suggestive of social comment. Yet it is also about art, the statue and images of the poem not simply props supporting the unconscious. Perhaps Éluard is therefore also playing with the conception of the muse, questioning what it means to unlock inspiration in his lover. This is a possibility that may be explored further through a close reading of 'L'Amoureuse', a poem which, like 'L'Égalité des sexes', appears at first to suggest a binary relation of poet and love object as muse, but which gives way to a multiplicity of semantic layers and a more complex picture of the couple.

Éluard's Muse: Associations, Transformations

Roubaud allots a second place in his anthology to Éluard's 'L'Amoureuse', which bears a number of similarities to 'L'Égalité des sexes'. The feminine lover appears at first to dominate the poem as well as its title:

> Elle est debout sur mes paupières
> Et ses cheveux sont dans les miens,
> Elle a la forme de mes mains,
> Elle a la couleur de mes yeux,
> Elle s'engloutit dans mon ombre
> Comme une pierre sur le ciel.

[She is standing on my eyelids
And her hair is in mine,
She has the form of my hands,
She has the colour of my eyes,
She is engulfed in my shadow
Like a stone on the sky.]

The repetition of the feminine subject pronoun, 'Elle' [She], in the primary position of most lines of the first verse seems to insist on the central and active role of the lover in the poem. Nugent writes of the feminine subject in this poem that 'she is present not only physically, but also becomes one with the lover through their reciprocal awareness of each other's love'.[111] As the poet-narrator enumerates her qualities, she gradually fades into his own image. She stands tall, but no further than on his eyelids; she takes on the shape of his hands, *is* shaped by his hands; she adopts the colour of his eyes, exists in the poem only through the affirmation of his gaze. In assuming his form through the progression of each line of the poem, Éluard's beloved again comes to stand for the poet's mirror image, reflecting his qualities in the shape of her body. Simile at the close of the verse compares her to stone, and the only active verb attributed to her as subject expresses her disappearance into the 'ombre' [shadow] of the poet in 's'engloutit' [is engulfed]. She retreats from visibility into the all-encompassing presence of the poet-narrator, himself so imposing that she fits entirely inside his shadow and is reduced to a supporting role.

If that role is of poetic muse in 'L'Amoureuse', her inspirational qualities are called into question:

Elle a toujours les yeux ouverts
Et ne me laisse pas dormir.
Ses rêves en pleine lumière
Font s'évaporer les soleils,
Me font rire, pleurer et rire,
Parler sans avoir rien à dire.

111 Nugent, *Paul Éluard*, p. 50.

[Her eyes are always open
And she does not let me sleep.
Her daylight dreams
Make the suns vanish,
Make me laugh, cry and laugh,
Speak with nothing to say.]

The culmination of the poem in what Daniel Rivas terms 'a frequent criticism hurled at those who speak for the sake of doing so […] a negativization of uncontrolled speech in everyday discourse', appears at first to devalue the content of the poet's output as inspired by the beloved.[112] Nevertheless, Rivas describes the feminine figure as 'poetic Muse' and interprets the relationship between her and the poet as one of 'identification' after Romantic and post-Romantic French poetry, which would describe the loved woman in terms of the male poet-narrator, 'blurring the differences between the two'.[113] Katharine Conley outlines the role of the muse more specifically in the context of early Surrealist literature and art as representative of the male unconscious: '[S]he is the muse of the automatic writing process who inspires him and prompts his connection to his own inner life.'[114] Breton defines Surrealism itself in terms of this automatic writing process: 'Automatisme psychique pur par lequel on se propose d'exprimer, soit verbalement, soit par écrit, soit de toute autre manière, le fonctionnement reél de la pensée' [Pure mental automatism through which we intend to express ourselves, either verbally, or in writing, or in any other manner, the real functioning of thought].[115] The *Dictionnaire abrégé du Surréalisme* [*The Abridged Dictionnary of Surrealism*], compiled by Breton and Éluard, also refers to the centrality of automatic writing to the literary movement, in 'l'idée génératrice du surréalisme […] le débit torrentiel de l'écriture automatique' [the generative idea of Surrealism […] the torrential flow of automatic writing],

112 Rivas, 'Éluard's "L'Amoureuse"', p. 492.

113 Rivas, 'Éluard's "L'Amoureuse"', p. 491.

114 Katherine Conley, *Automatic Woman: The Representation of Woman in Surrealism* (London: University of Nebraska Press, 1996), p. 1.

115 André Breton, *Manifestes du surréalisme* (Paris: Pauvert, 1972), p. 35.

where the latter part of the definition resonates with the garrulousness at the close of 'L'Amoureuse'.[116] However, reflecting on a photo entitled 'L'Écriture automatique' ['Automatic Writing'], in which a woman is poised ready with a pen to take down the automatic flow of words, Conley points out her 'lack of mental engagement in the process': looking away from both the page and the camera, her body 'inspires' and 'represents' automatic writing.[117] If automatic writing is central to Surrealism, and the artist's muse is the symbol for this process, Conley suggests that she does not participate herself in this artistic production, only creating a pathway for the poet in that direction.

For Rivas, the final line of Éluard's poem, 'a collective wisdom that prizes content at the expense of form', is transformed in the poetic context to express the way the literary text 'speaks', though not in order to 'prove anything', rather to 'state its own conditions of existence as a speaking text'.[118] His reading of this shift is very much in line with the ideas of Chénieux-Gendron, who writes of the significance the notion of 'parler pour parler' [speaking for speaking's sake] held for Éluard. She explains Éluard's work in terms of an impulse seeking out both a transformed and transformative conception of language: 'un nouveau langage, un langage du plaisir, doit être recherché – qui soit délivré de l'obligation de signifier – un langage qui reste ouvert à toutes les virtualités du sens' [a new language, a language of pleasure, must be sought out – one which would be relieved of the obligation to signify – a language that remains open to all the virtualities of meaning].[119] In the light of these readings, the conclusion to 'L'Amoureuse' takes on a quality of ecstasy; it points towards the possibility of a language freed from the constraints of its signifying role, no longer the domain of 'bavards' [chatterboxes] and tedious habit.[120]

116 André Breton and Paul Éluard, *Dictionnaire abrégé du surréalisme* (Paris: José Corti, 1969; repr. 2005), p. 4.

117 Conley, *Automatic Woman*, p. 1.

118 Rivas, 'Éluard's "L'Amoureuse"', pp. 492–93.

119 Jacqueline Chénieux-Gendron, *Le Surréalisme* (Paris: Presses Universitaires de France, 1984), p. 94.

120 Chénieux-Gendron, *Le Surréalisme*, p. 94.

If the reader further probes Rivas's distinction between form and content, or his thought that content is privileged over form in 'L'Amoureuse', the impulse in the poet to both laugh and cry, to speak without any preformed intention, stemming from the dreams of the feminine figure, may also be evocative of definitions of free verse. Perloff, for example, writes that free verse 'tracks the actual movement of thought and feeling, refusing to interfere with its free flow, to inhibit its natural motion; or so, at least, the poem must appear to be doing, no matter how much "craft" has gone into it'.[121] She also mentions the belief that free verse 'tracks the movement of the breath itself', which points to an inherent spontaneity in the form, a closeness to emotions and their fluctuations as reproduced at the close of 'L'Amoureuse'.[122] The emotion of the Surrealist artist too is given prominence by Breton in *Le Surréalisme et la peinture* [*Surrealism and Painting*], charging 'la plume' [pen] or 'le crayon' [pencil] with which he creates his artwork.[123] In the *Manifeste du surréalisme* [*Surrealist Manifesto*], Breton compares the aims of Surrealist creation to Freudian psychoanalysis in terms evocative of these definitions of free verse: 'je résolus d'obtenir de moi [...] un monologue de débit aussi rapide que possible, sur lequel l'esprit critique du sujet ne fasse porter aucun jugement, qui ne s'embarrasse, par suite, d'aucune réticence, et qui soit aussi exactement que possible la *pensée parlée*' [I decided to obtain from myself [...] a monologue of as rapid a flow as possible, on which the critical mind of the subject makes no judgement, which is not obstructed, as a result, by any reticence, and which is as close as possible to *spoken thought*].[124] Definitions of free verse and outlines of the ambitions of Surrealism and its automatic writing processes coincide.[125]

121 Perloff, *Poetry On and Off the Page*, p. 147.

122 Perloff, *Poetry On and Off the Page*, p. 152.

123 André Breton, *Le surréalisme et la peinture* (Paris: Gallimard, 1965), p. 68.

124 Breton, *Manifestes du Surréalisme*, p. 33.

125 There is evidence to show that an element of planning and/or editing went into many of the 'automatic texts' produced by the Surrealists. For example, Jacqueline Chénieux-Gendron points out that the titles and boundaries governing *L'Immaculée Conception* were in fact established in advance. See Jacqueline Chénieux-Gendron, 'Toward a New Definition of Automatism: *L'Immaculée Conception*', *Dada/Surrealism* 17 (1988) 74–90.

Éluard's poem seems to comment on these notions of automatic writing and free verse, placing at the centre of their practice the feminine figure who inspires the poet to write. The muse of 'L'Amoureuse' never sleeps, keeping the poet himself wide-awake throughout her daylight dreams. Moreover, the mirrored reflection of the poet in his feminine love object in 'L'Amoureuse' reveals its cracks when the binary structure is subverted by a mysterious third term in the poem. Rivas spots the phonetic 'pie [qui] erre sur le ciel' [magpie [that] roams in the sky] in the final line of Éluard's first verse going on to explore, among other elements, the metonymic appearance of the magpie in the feminine subject pronoun: 'elle' [she] becomes 'aile' [wing].[126] Éluard's phonic play may also be evoking the letter *l*, which Breton proposes as a solution to the silence that threatens to block the Surrealist writer (Breton himself possibly playing on the *l-elle* relationship) – the letter *l* will be the writer's trigger to continue with his flow.[127] A gendered reading of the text, in line with that of the mirroring in 'L'Égalité des sexes', might see the erasure of the feminine presence from the poem, not only in her assumption of the supporting role, in the shadow of the dominant poet-narrator, but also in her metamorphosis into the image of the magpie, standing thus for the unconscious inspiration and unrestrained form(s) of Surrealist poetry. However, this example of poetic play simultaneously demonstrates the expansive possibilities or 'transformations' existing in a layered interpretation of the poem, placing the woman at the centre of both.[128]

Despite evidence of conflict and violence in the poem, Nugent describes the experience of love in 'L'Amoureuse' as 'a total one', explaining that for Éluard there are 'never two separate experiences', only 'a union of the beloved and the person in love'.[129] Similarly, for Conley, this poem is an example of the Surrealist idealization of reciprocal love, which she sees as 'an effective metaphor for their theoretical goal in automatic writing': that is, a harmony between the poet's unconscious and conscious thoughts.[130]

126 Rivas, 'Éluard's "L'Amoureuse"', p. 493.
127 Breton, *Manifestes du Surréalisme*, pp. 39–40.
128 Rivas, 'Éluard's "L'Amoureuse"', p. 496.
129 Nugent, *Paul Éluard*, p. 50.
130 Conley, *Automatic Woman*, p. 9.

It is a matter of 'liberating' a part hidden deep in the unconscious of the poet, rendering it conscious, the text on the page reflecting the poet's self functioning more as an 'insight' than an 'appropriation'.[131] Even the more encompassing notion of 'insight', however, restricts the potential reach of the text. As Timothy Mathews finds, the power of the poem to transform lies in the potential for association that it poses. He accepts the invitation to connect the impossibility of the lover standing on the eyelids of the poet, and the stone 'lost *on* the sky, "sur le ciel", not in the sky', explaining that each is 'placed on a boundary that cannot be fixed'.[132] For Mathews, the connection captures the simultaneous potential freedom of 'endless, frame-defying association' and also the potential 'alienation of no relation', since 'relation seems to emerge where it cannot and because it cannot'.[133] Rather than seeking out deeper self-understanding or union with the lover, Éluard explores the limits, or potential, of language and image. The poem thus also comments on his poetic process, placing the feminine at the centre of his inquiry.

Despite the potential for transformation to be unlocked in the images and connections that abound in 'L'Amoureuse', both 'L'Égalité des sexes' and 'L'Amoureuse' encourage the reader to assume gendered interpretations from the outset. The form of each poem appears, on the surface, to corroborate such readings, structuring the sexual relation according to the binary mirroring that has been the focus of much work on gender and sexual theory. Irigaray, for example, deconstructs Freudian theory in such a way. She expresses that in both the images and words that constitute a Freudian theory of femininity, it seems the woman hardly features at all. Her sexual organ lacks the visibility which characterizes that of the man, and even her sight is appropriated by male vision, placing her as object of the scene. In the language of the text, she is therefore unrepresented in her own specificity, residing between the words that only describe sexual difference in terms of divergences from the central male term. This leads Irigaray to sum up the

131 Conley, *Automatic Woman*, p. 9.

132 Timothy Mathews, *Alberto Giacometti: The Art of Relation* (London: Tauris, 2014), p. 55.

133 Mathews, *The Art of Relation*, p. 55.

feminine role as that which provides a 'redoublement spéculaire' [specular duplication] of the masculine, fulfilling 'le désir du même, de l'identique à soi, du soi (comme) même, et encore du semblable, de l'alter ego, et pour tout dire de l'auto … et de l'homo … de l'homme' [the desire for the same, for the self-identical, the self (as) same, and again of the similar, the alter ego and, to put it in a nutshell, the desire for the auto … the homo … the male].[134] The progression from notions of similarity to those of specifically masculine association in Irigaray's description confirms the dominance of the one term over the other within the theory of gender, stressing that the theory does not simply posit her as his mirrored equal.

Irigaray further ensures that her use of mirror symbolism is not misinterpreted as a sign of sexual equality by reminding her reader of what is lacking in this 'spécula(risa)tion' [specula(riza)tion]; namely, the penis that the girl does not possess, which she nonetheless compensates for through her envy.[135] However, one must also note the 'speculation' in 'specula(riza)tion' and remember that the female form as a reflection of that of the male is a 'projection' or even a 'project'.[136] Such lexis alludes to the presence of fiction within Freudian theory, identifying its objectifying depiction of woman as one established in order to bolster male subjectivity. In emphasizing the role of form in his choice of these two poems to represent Éluard in an anthology composed, as we have seen, 'du point de vue formel' [from a formal point of view],[137] Roubaud foregrounds the limits of this binary understanding of the sexual relation. Although image and metaphor are sources of extension and transformation in 'L'Amoureuse', form in both of Éluard's poems catalyses the failure of the relation between poet and muse in a way that may be aligned with an Irigarayan reading of a Freudian and to some extent Lacanian theory of femininity.

134 Irigaray, *Speculum de l'autre femme*, p. 63 and p. 26; *Speculum of the Other Woman*, p. 54 and p. 26.

135 Irigaray, *Speculum de l'autre femme*, p. 63; *Speculum of the Other Woman*, p. 54.

136 Irigaray, *Speculum de l'autre femme*, p. 27; *Speculum of the Other Woman*, p. 26.

137 Roubaud, *Description du projet*, p. 137.

Conclusion

In the dialogue between *Autobiographie, chapitre dix* and *Poésie:*, between Paul Éluard and Jacques Roubaud, poetry and love first come together for the poet's younger self. The texts represent a coming of age, in which Roubaud experiences the ardour of first love: his physical desire for Michelle, and unknown territories of poetry. The reader is taken on a journey of discovery, learning how love can be transformative of life and writing, arousing an all-encompassing passion for everyday experience. Like an *amour fou*, the passionate encounter with love of/and poetry transforms Roubaud's existence but is nonetheless fleeting. Roubaud's first love, Michelle, fades into the setting of the poet's youth, existing only as a distant memory to be recounted in his autobiographical prose. Their relation is allowed no space in which to thrive, played out only in moments snatched in various public places. The free verse poems Roubaud attempts to compose at the time are also defined by the poet as momentary: apparently breaking with the ties of tradition on the surface, it is never long before these looser structures are invaded by recognizable metres and phonic patterns memorized from past readings. The poet finds his free verse compositions empty of innovation and stifling to his creativity.

In the poems of *Autobiographie, chapitre dix*, Roubaud challenges Surrealist writers such as Éluard, but the volume is also a reassessment of his own relationship with poetry: 'les pastiches [...] font partie du parcours obligé de l'écrivain, qui doit s'y livrer afin d'être au moins sûr de ce qu'il ne fera plus ensuite' [pastiches [...] are part of the essential development of the writer, who must engage in doing them in order to at least be sure of what he will no longer do going forward].[138] What is presented as a rejection of certain poetic practices and significant figures is also the poet's own reflection on his composition processes. Roubaud writes, for example, of the 'le vers-librisme torride des surréalistes et de leurs émules' [the torrid free verse of the Surrealists and their imitators] on the one hand, adding

138 Jacques Roubaud, *Mathématique:* (Paris: Seuil, 1997), p. 112.

'je m'étais enthousiasmé' [I had been enthusiastic] about it on the other.[139] He describes 'cette gêne' [this embarrassment] and 'cette insatisfaction de plus en plus paralysante' [this increasingly paralysing dissatisfaction] in his attempts to write after the styles of the Surrealists; associating their enterprise with 'qualités intuitives' [intuitive qualities] and 'l'absence de rigueur' [an absence of rigour], he outlines his 'méfiance [...] née d'une incapacité plutôt que d'une réflexion justifiée' [mistrust [...] born of an inability rather than any justified reflection].[140] The implication is that intuitive practices and lack of rigour are accusations levelled at his own processes, swept up, as he often seems to be, in the rapture of the new movement in poetry at the time.

While there is the potential for transformation in Éluard's particular use of image and metaphor, Roubaud foregrounds a sense of frustration at the level of form and its capacity to represent the relation between the poet and his beloved as muse. Although the feminine presence in Éluard's poems is the site of inspiration, she does not herself participate in the poet's creative process from her position in the binary structures where he places her. In a return to the origins of psychoanalytic theories of the feminine, the structures that posited her as muse to the poet, for whom she provided specular identification and insight, also collapse. In those moments in which she appears to be everything to and for the male poet, she fades in a structure where the terms of subject and object are mediated by the *petit a*.

Alain Badiou writes of alternative perspectives on love, proposing that its power to revolutionize lies in 'questions de durée et de processus, et non pas seulement questions de commencement' [issues of duration and process, and not only starting-points]; although 'incertaine' [uncertain], 'mystérieuse' [mysterious] and even 'miraculeuse' [miraculous] at times, the 'rencontre' [encounter] of an *amour fou* exists not at the level of what endures.[141] How might these descriptions be significant for the stage in

139 Roubaud, *Mathématique:*, p. 57.

140 Roubaud, *Mathématique:*, pp. 56–57.

141 Alain Badiou, *Éloge de l'amour* (Paris: Flammarion, 2009), p. 33 and p. 69. Alain Badiou, *In Praise of Love*, trans. by Peter Bush (London: Serpent's Tail, 2012), p. 29 and p. 80.

Roubaud's career as a poet that follows his decision for change? The poet rejects free verse forms epitomized by Éluard's *L'Amour la poésie*, and the automatic writing process, foregrounding the fleeting nature of his first loves, but how does he go on to establish both 'process' and 'duration' in his own poetry forms?

CHAPTER 2

Towards a Definition of Love Poetry, *le vers*

To establish the implications of Roubaud's rejection of free verse forms for his own poetic output, the next stage of my study involves a consideration of the interaction between poetic form and the feminine which is foregrounded in *Trente et un au cube*. Published in 1973, this book is one of the earlier texts listed as belonging to Roubaud's poetry project before the poet's notorious pronouncement of the project's failure and his renunciation of it.[1] As such, the volume serves as a pertinent point of reference from which to consider the various outcomes of Roubaud's 'decision'. How does he respond to the sense of crisis in his creativity and what role does the figure of the feminine beloved play in his formal responses? How far can she be aligned with or distanced from Surrealist visions of love and the muse?

In illuminating the pathways that Roubaud takes in the direction away from the approaches of the Surrealist poets, my readings of the relationship

1 Jean-Jacques Poucel lists the works belonging to the project in his preface to the recent republication of Roubaud's *Description du projet* [*Description of the Project*], p. 8. Roubaud charts the failure of the project in his prose collection *'le grand incendie de londres'* [*'the great fire of London'*]. Over six volumes, he describes the development of what was to be a project involving mathematics and poetry, from its conception following a dream in 1960, to his eventual realization at the time of writing in the 1980s that it would never be completed. In his *Description du projet*, written in 1978, seventeen years after the project's inception, he hints at knowing then its impossibility and utopian proportions (p. 25). In the first volume of the *'grand incendie de londres'* series, first published as *Le Grand incendie de Londres* (Paris: Seuil, 1989) [*The Great Fire of London*], Roubaud announces in the foreword that the project was destined to fail from the outset (p. 8). However, in the same volume, the author also explains the impact of his wife's death on his decision to give up the project (pp. 110–11 and 150–52).

between form and the woman addressed in *Trente et un au cube* also lead towards a definition of love poetry as Roubaud conceives it. It might seem incongruous to speak of defining a genre in which we expect the author to express freely his emotional and sensual experience, maybe to give free rein to his praise of the lover, but that is exactly what the writer of *Trente et un au cube* attempts in and with the volume. Distancing himself from the Surrealist practices of free verse *tabula rasa* and automatic writing, the poet seeks out formal ingenuity and tradition in the creations of the historic troubadours, and he couples this with the solidity and precision of mathematics. Definition, then, in both its meanings.

To understand how Roubaud's engagement with tradition informs the poetry of *Trente et un au cube*, I look to *La Fleur inverse* [The Inverse Flower] (1986), the poet's theoretical work on the formal art of the troubadours, and to his *Description du Projet* (2014) [*Description of the Project*], which gives an insight into his change of composition methods, as well as the Japanese literary models that led him to invent new forms in French poetry. For the sources of the mathematical influence manifested in the title of the poetry volume, I turn to Roubaud's autobiographical prose volume *Mathematique:* (1997) [*Mathematics:*], a book full of anecdotes and personal histories, comparable to *Poésie:*, but whose themes lean away from poetry and towards mathematics.

Trente et un au cube: Moving Away from Specularity

Jacques Roubaud's decision to break away from the dominant methods of poetry composition of his contemporaries evokes the same sense of violence associated with the avant-gardist break with traditional metres, referring to notions of 'rompre' [breaking] and 'rupture' [rupture]. However, the poet is quick to deny any similarity between their revolutionary stance and his own new beginning: 'D'une décision de rupture […]: commencer, c'est rompre; pas pour faire table rase de la poésie du passé (illusion avant-gardiste), mais pour un retour en arrière, jusqu'au nœud de l'erreur, pour prendre un autre chemin' [On the decision for a rupture [...]: to begin is also to make a break; not to make a *tabula rasa* of past poetry (an avant-gardist illusion), but to return to the past, to the crux of the error, to take another route].[2] His 'rupture' does not aim to break free of tradition, rather it turns back towards it, instead distancing his own writing from more recent attempts to deny the patterns of poetry that have come before. Roubaud embarks on an exploration of the sonnet form, citing among other reasons its 'fil formel très ancien, très archaïque; quelque chose capable d'une longue durée poétique' [very ancient, very archaic formal line; something capable of long poetic duration].[3] He seeks a form known for its 'longévité' [longevity] in order to escape the sense of the momentary that had come to characterize contemporary forms of poetry:

> [le sonnet] était capable, comme forme, d'adaptation à des langues, des siècles, des mètres d'une assez grande variabilité; [...] il atteignait donc, par cohésion et métamorphoses, des régions poétiques assez éloignées des conditions poétiques particulières et momentanées, comme celles que j'essayais, précisément, de fuir.[4]
>
> [[the sonnet] was capable, as a form, of adapting to languages, to the passing centuries, to quite a variety of metres; [...] thus, through its cohesion and its metamorphoses, the form was able to reach regions in poetry that were quite distant from the momentary and the particular, the poetic conditions that I was precisely trying to escape.]

This decision for radical change in his methods of composing poetry is famously associated with the compilation of a book of sonnets, *Signe d'appartenance*, so much so that the latter has been hailed as marking Roubaud's birth as poet.[5] Boasting long and short sonnets, prose sonnets and even sonnets of sonnets, this first publication contributing to Roubaud's *Projet* [*Project*] makes no secret of its central concern with form. Nevertheless, I have chosen to trace the implications of Roubaud's 'décision de rupture' for his poetic works in the slightly later volume, *Trente et un au cube*. Preoccupation with form continues to dominate this

2 Roubaud, *Poésie:*, p. 104. Emphasis in the original.
3 Roubaud, *Description du projet*, p. 31.
4 Roubaud, *Description du projet*, pp. 31–32.
5 Claude Roy, *La Conversation des poètes* (Paris: Gallimard, 1993), p. 284.

latter book, still one of the earliest contributions to the then fledgling *Projet*, and it is also a love poem, which makes it most relevant for the particular questions I am asking about Roubaud's formal practice.

Trente et un au cube engages directly with the poet's decision for change: in an echo of the words from his *Description du projet*, Roubaud states in one poem 'je cherche ce qui n'est || pas momentané | dans cette disposition' [I seek that which is || not momentary | in this arrangement].[6] He seeks to escape the momentary through the poetic arrangement itself. The very notion of arrangement, or 'disposition', points to the new dimensions of this poetry. Roubaud's attention is very much given over to the line in *Autobiographie, chapitre dix*, where poetic play challenges definitions of free verse both typographically and phonically. In his '*anthologie de poésie contemporaine*', spaces dedicated to Éluard's poetry are dominated by two-dimensional patterns, with a mirroring effect often occurring within a single line. In stark contrast to these binary patterns, Roubaud's *Trente et un au cube* paraphrases its own 'disposition' as 'chaos mobile' [mobile chaos], thus informing the reader that this poetry is doubly chaotic through its refusal to be stilled. This poem 'qui n'est || pas momentané' [which is || not momentary] is also described in terms of:

liens méticuleux
tissés de son vertical { la blessure blanche au long
segments de soleils violets

[meticulous links
woven in vertical sound { white wound along
segments of violet suns]

The ideas of linking and vertical sound that the poem speaks of are enacted in the typography: the reader's eye follows the vertical movement of the line as its segments shift on the page, then scans the stacked alternatives offered together, enclosed by the bracket on the right. The reader might also visualize the white wound and violet suns that the lines refer to in the overall spacing of the poem as a whole, where the unconventional

6 Roubaud, *Trente et un au cube*, p. 49. All further citations from the volume in the remainder of this section are from this poem.

layout and syllable count result in both small gaps (suns rendered violet through their edges of penned ink lettering) and longer jagged lines of white space. Poetry is no longer centred on the line, counted or without metre, but is thought of in terms of structure with multiple entry-points, or 'architecture'.

The symmetry of the Eluardian poems Roubaud chose to anthologize reproduced the relationship between the poet and his feminine lover, exploring her role of potential support to the writer, his own image and poetic inspiration. Roubaud moves away from Éluard's binary model in favour of a different approach:

> ta | chromatographie sur buvards sonores est | dissolution en aiguilles | cristaux vibratiles gongs || perpétués tu | te déroules reproduite | en quelque sodium | de timbres d'une hauteur | oboesque d'un sifflet ||| pentatonique et | ce qui demeure c'est toujours | fortuit le chemin | d'un sein à un sein de ta | bouche à ta bouche laissé || intact par la lessive d'images conduit | de seuil en seuil de synapses comme inaltérée.
>
> [your | chromatography on blotting papers of sound is | dissolution in needles | vibratile crystals perpetuated || gongs you | unfold reproduced | in some sodium | in tones of a height that is | oboesque of a pentatonic ||| whistle and | what remains is always | unexpected the path | from one breast to a breast from your | mouth to your mouth left || intact by the lye of images driven | from threshold to threshold of synapses as though unaltered.]

The beloved takes on the substance of the poem, represented by an amalgam of colour, sound and chemical substance. In Éluard's 'L'Amoureuse', the merging of lover and poet gave way to an endless deferral, in the form of associations and layers of imagery. Here, she inspires the generation of the poem's form(s). Several techniques are employed to perpetuate an underlying sense of movement in the extract. Vision and the sense of sound overlap, in 'buvards sonores' [blotting papers of sound], 'cristaux vibratiles' [vibratile crystals] and 'sodium | de timbres' [sodium | in tones], suggesting the poem as an entity that may exist written on the page, or be given an aural existence when read aloud. The poem shifts before our eyes: it is the unpredictable spreading of colours in a chromatography experiment on blotting paper, the multiplication of crystals, the crossing of the distance between one breast and another, one mouth and another, ending in the splitting of cells. This doubling of the beloved's body parts, together with the vibrations of colour, seems to present her to the reader through the lens of a prism. She unfolds, grows like the branching lines of the poem: 'tu | te déroules reproduite' [you | unfold reproduced]. She stirs between the senses, escaping both reader and poet in her ungraspable multiplicity.

Origins: Japanese *Tanka* and Troubadour *Canso*

As far as poetic form is concerned, the evocation of crystals will take Roubaud's reader back to the sonnet and its origins in the troubadour *canso*. For the poet, the sonnet is the 'forme mémoire de la canso' [memory form of the canso], the earliest sonnets referred to as '*miroir de la canso*' [*mirror of the canso*]; he explains 'le sonnet n'est pas une canso mais s'approprie une partie de sa définition formelle' [the sonnet is not a canso but appropriates one part of its formal definition].[7] Elsewhere, he clarifies 'le sonnet est initialement une *cobla* de canso troubadouresque qui, par répétition et prolifération, atteint à un statut d'autonomie formelle' [the sonnet is initially a *cobla* of the troubadour canso which, through repetition and proliferation, reaches a status of formal autonomy], that is, it is a single verse of the *canso* that evolves into the later form.[8] In this way, he is able to speak of the sonnet as 'résumant *(cobla)* la forme; cristal de la forme' [summarizing *(cobla)* the form; crystal of the form].[9] More recently, the publication of the title *Quasi-Cristaux* (2013) [*Quasi-Crystals*] shared Roubaud's research of fifty years on the sonnet form. The sonnet is, for Roubaud, a crystal, not only due to its longevity, the gradual sedimentation of its composite qualities over hundreds of years; the poet also

7 Roubaud, *La Fleur inverse*, p. 344.
8 Roubaud, *Description du projet*, p. 108.
9 Roubaud, *Description du projet*, p. 108.

writes of the form's 'capacité de multiplication effervescente' [capacity for effervescent multiplication].[10]

The sonnet's potential for multiplicity is not unlike the success of the 'tanka japonais' [Japanese tanka], which enjoys 'un gigantisme numérique beaucoup plus vertigineux' [numbers of a dizzyingly gigantic scale].[11] It is this Japanese equivalent that forms the basis of the structure of *Trente et un au cube*, with the basic count of 5-7-5-7-7, the syllable count of the Japanese *tanka*, repeated through every level of the text from the metric count of its line unit divided into five fragments, to the number of strophes in each poem, and even in the groupings of the poems within the overall architecture of the book (the latter is made particularly clear by the layout of the credits page according to that pattern at the end of the collection, p. 131). The reference to crystals thus brings together the two traditions in which *Trente et un au cube* is formally inscribed: that of the troubadour *canso* and the Japanese *tanka*.

The proliferation of both sonnets (growing from the *canso*) and *tankas* has at its root a certain amount of collaborative effort among poets. Roubaud's *La Fleur inverse*, presents the troubadour as 'ouvrier' [workman]: more specifically 'forgeron' [blacksmith] or '*fabbro*'.[12] In order to reach 'le diamant' [the diamond], which is both 'la canso et l'amour de l'amant et de la dame' [the canso and the love of the lover and the lady], the poet must work through certain 'équations [...] chimiques' [chemical [...] equations].[13] To prove his love is the greatest, to show his lady is the most worthy of all, his *canso* dedicated to her, singing of her, must be 'unique' and 'Le forgeron lui-même, le troubadour, sort "affiné du feu de la forge d'amour" ' [The blacksmith himself, the troubadour, comes out of 'the forge of love refined by its flames'].[14] The qualities of uniqueness and refinement, known as the *pretz* of the troubadour, or 'l'éclat qui est en ses cansos' [the brilliance that is in his cansos],[15] are achieved through this

10 Roubaud, *Description du projet*, p. 31.
11 Roubaud, *Description du projet*, p. 31.
12 Roubaud, *La Fleur inverse*, p. 200.
13 Roubaud, *La Fleur inverse*, p. 201.
14 Roubaud, *La Fleur inverse*, p. 202.
15 Roubaud, *La Fleur inverse*, p. 254.

constant effort to rise above all other invention: 'Chaque troubadour tente de créer la canso la plus parfaite, celle qui sera plus excellente que toutes les autres cansos. D'où l'axiome: *La canso est la dona du trobar*' [Each troubadour tries to create the most perfect canso, the one that will be the most excellent of all the other cansos. Whence the axiom: *The canso is the lady of the trobar*].[16] When a *canso* is composed, it is measured in the mind of the troubadour against those which already exist, refined and perfected:

> Quand une canso commence dans le jeu et joie de poésie, toutes les cansos lui sont coprésentes. Dans une canso, le trobar tout entier est implicite. [...] Le trobar entier apparaît comme tissé, lié, entrelacé de [...] fils; fils de l'amors et des rimes, formules décasyllabiques dans le registre du «grand chant». Les manières de l'allusion, du passage d'une canso à une autre, représentent un des traits essentiels du jeu formel qu'est le trobar.[17]
>
> [When a canso begins in the play and joy of poetry, all cansos are there with it. In a canso, the entire *trobar* is implicit. [...] The whole *trobar* appears as though woven, linked, intertwined with [...] threads; threads of love and rhymes, decasyllabic formulae in the register of the 'great song'. The techniques of allusion, of movement from one canso to another, represent one of the essential traits of the formal play of the *trobar*.]

There is an enhanced intertextuality among the *cansos*, not only through direct 'allusion', but also in the appropriation and renewal of their technical elements, such as syllabic and rhyme patterns. The striving of the troubadour poets for unique and better forms, their search for the 'diamond' of poetic invention, the *trobar*, constitutes a coherent field of research.

The Japanese counterparts of this European form were chained together in medieval imperial anthologies, creating a 'livre qui est poème de poèmes' [book that is a poem of poems].[18] The poems were intricately linked in such a way that they formed an overall sense of progression, 'par construction de séquences dont les éléments sont des poèmes préalablement

16 Roubaud, *La Fleur inverse*, p. 188.
17 Roubaud, *La Fleur inverse*, p. 286.
18 Roubaud, *Description du projet*, p. 69.

composés et soumis à des principes d'intégration et de progression qui donnent à l'ensemble une architecture propre' [by the construction of sequences whose elements are poems composed beforehand and subjected to principles of integration and progression that give the whole thing its own architecture].[19] The form of the anthology itself thus becomes a poem of poems, a construction rather than a simple gathering of a number of pieces. Like the *canso*, the *tanka* acquires a layer of meaning through association with other texts that together constitute an overarching structure. Maria Muresan explains that a third poem, not included in the anthology but known to a reader from Japanese court society, would provide the link between each poem in the book, extending the notion of collaborative poetic memory from the poets to their readers.[20]

The rapprochement of the *canso* and the *tanka* in *Trente et un au cube* does not serve simply to highlight their technical similarities, however: both Japanese and troubadour verse provide a challenge to what the poet has called 'le momentané' [the momentary]. Roubaud notes the extension of poetic duration through the insertion of the *tanka* into a collective work: 'L'effort du poète collectif, dont l'œuvre est l'anthologie, est de dépasser le temps fragmentaire du *tanka* et le temps erratique du monde physique en les insérant dans un mouvement qui les prolonge' [The collective effort of the poet, whose work is the anthology, is to go beyond the fragmentary time of the *tanka* and the erratic time of the physical world by inserting them in a movement that extends them].[21] When placed in the sequence of the anthology, the circumstances in which the individual poems are composed (for example, the author's name, time and reasons for writing) are erased, making the pieces timeless, 'durables' [durable].[22] Roubaud also outlines the importance for him of a sense of otherness in Japanese literature: 'Le Japon a joué pour moi un

19 Roubaud, *Description du projet*, p. 69.

20 'Maria Muresan, Image-poésie, image-souvenir et *piction*', in *Jacques Roubaud, compositeur de mathématique et de poésie*, ed. by Agnès Disson and Véronique Montémont (Nancy: Absalon, 2010), pp. 333–44 (pp. 334–35).

21 Jacques Roubaud, 'Sur le Shinkokinshū, huitième anthologie impériale japonaise', *Change*, 1 (1968), 73–106 (p. 86).

22 Roubaud, 'Sur le Shinkokinshū', pp. 86–87.

jour le rôle d'un 'ailleurs' poétique, d'une contrée où la poésie fut autre [...], où elle entretint avec la nature (une nature elle-même lointaine, étrange) un rapport privilégié' [For me, Japan once played the role of an 'elsewhere' in poetry, of a country where poetry was other [...], where it had a privileged relationship with nature (a nature that was itself faraway, strange)].[23] Japanese medieval verse opens up another time and place for the poet, far away from what he saw as the stagnancy in his work influenced by contemporary French forms. The curious paradox is that this 'ailleurs' [elsewhere], this environment so 'lointaine' [faraway] and 'étrange' [strange], is really much closer to home than it first seems:

> découvrant la tradition japonaise du 'waka', je me suis senti brusquement en pays familier: c'est un sentiment qui ne trompe guère (ou qui nous trompe de manière convaincante). J'avais su, je savais déjà cette émotion mais je ne savais plus que je savais, je le redécouvrais; et je me souvenais alors du moment où je l'avais su.[24]
>
> [on discovering the Japanese tradition of the 'waka', I suddenly felt like I was in familiar territory; it's a feeling that never lies (or it deceives us in a convincing manner). I had known, I already knew this feeling, but I no longer knew that I knew it, I was rediscovering it; and I remembered then the time when I had known it.]

Feeling at home in the Japanese poetic tradition brings about a pang of nostalgia in the poet, who uses the pluperfect and imperfect tenses to refer, respectively, to an emotion forgotten and rediscovered. His description of this recaptured emotion is reminiscent of the way he speaks of Provençal – 'La langue provençale, que je n'ai pas parlée enfant (qu'aujourd'hui je lis mais je ne parle pas) joue un rôle particulier dans ma mémoire familiale. [...] À la fois proche et absente, elle est pour moi la langue d'origine, la langue perdue de l'âge d'or des langues' [The Provençal language, which I didn't speak as a child (which I read now but do not speak) plays a particular role in my family memory. [...] At once close to me and absent, it is for me a language of origins, the lost language from the golden age of languages].[25] The narrator's grammatical past of the past

23 Roubaud, *Poésie:*, 494.
24 Roubaud, *Poésie:*, 494.
25 Roubaud, *La Fleur inverse*, p. 16.

looks back to the poet's Provençal origins, the 'pays familier' [familiar territory] of his pre-war childhood.[26] Elisabeth Cardonne-Arlyck sees in *Trente et un au cube* an idyllic and nostalgic return to the Carcassonne of the poet's youth, where nature abounds to create a utopic garden.[27] Roubaud's return to the forest of his childhood in *Trente et un au cube* is simultaneously a resituating of himself as poet among all those other writers he had read, absorbed and copied in his adolescence. Roubaud goes back to his childhood origins in Provence, but also to where he believes poetry begins its formal journey: with the troubadours.[28]

Multidimensional Rhythms

The imprint of the troubadour influence manifests itself at moments throughout *Trente et un au cube*, but its prominence at the open and close of the book is undeniable. Just as the troubadour *canso* begins with 'je' [I],[29] brought into existence by the impetus of love which moves the troubadour to speak of his desire,[30] so too this poem of poems takes the lover as its audience:

> JE DÉTIENS MILLION de | syllabes comptées pour toi | pas et tours des roues | hélices selon l'œil mailles | du bruit croisé recroisé || comptées dansées sont | syllabes

26 Roubaud, *La Fleur inverse*, p. 16.

27 Elisabeth Cardonne-Arlyck, *Véracités: Ponge, Jaccottet, Roubaud, Deguy* (Paris: Belin, 2009), pp. 224–26.

28 This overwhelming sense of origin may, for some, represent a deviation from the pursuit of process, and even creativity. However, a key premise in much Roubaldian and Oulipian work is that there is much to be found and 'invented' in old forms. There is a strong sense that futurity can exist in the past, for example, the Oulipians frequently refer to the notion of 'plagiat par anticipation' [anticipatory plagiarism] to describe the invention, or discovery, of a form that has already been discovered.

29 Roubaud, *La Fleur inverse*, p. 141.

30 Roubaud, *La Fleur inverse*, p. 185.

> que je te donne | vibrations s'allongent | couleurs se poussent et battent | suites de mains dyadiques.[31]

> I keep millions of | syllables counted out for you | steps and turns of the wheels | helixes depending on the eye links | of the sound woven in and woven again || counted danced | syllables I give you | vibrations lengthen | colours move over and beat | suites in dyadic hands.

The accumulation of circular shapes and winding actions, like 'tours' [turns], 'roues' [wheels], 'hélices' [helixes] and 'croisé recroisé' [woven in and woven again] recalls the troubadour ethic of *entrebescar*, the interlacing of rhyme words into an intricate pattern that forms the beauty of the *canso*.[32] Moreover, the 'mains dyadiques' [dyadic hands] are suggestive of the work of the artisan, shaping and moulding his words into a form worthy of expressing his love. The axiom '*La canso est la dona du trobar*' [*The canso is the lady of the trobar*] is played out literally in the text when the motif of the artisan's craft recurs: 'mon matériel mes jeux d'orgues || cela qui pénètre | décisivement en toi | cela te façonne | ou t'imprègne de mes traces | résonne de ma métrique' [my material my organ playing || what goes | decisively into you | that shapes you | or fills you with my traces | resonates with my metre].[33] He crafts his verses around the wonder of his *dona* so that their *pretz* may equal her own, and he is motivated by his desire for her, alluded to in the sexual image of the traces he leaves inside her.

At times his efforts come across as an attempt to contain, even constrain her physically within the words of his poem: 'toi énumérante | chantante toi sous mes sibilantes syllabes | accumulées longtemps pour | mieux te réduire pour mieux || t'entraver' [counting you | singing you in my sibilant syllables | collected over time to | reduce you better to || shackle you better].[34] The poem's rhythm strives to capture her essence, to shackle her body in its few lines. If the poet is craftsman, the language of his poetry too becomes malleable material: the alliteration in 'sibilantes syllabes' [sibilant syllables] gives the words another dimension, with phonic

31 Roubaud, *Trente et un au cube*, p. 9.
32 Roubaud, *La Fleur inverse*, p. 321.
33 Roubaud, *Trente et un au cube*, p. 9.
34 Roubaud, *Trente et un au cube*, p. 9.

play echoing the adjective's meaning and somehow making objects of the syllables themselves. Roubaud also writes of 'les nombres | de syllabes que j'entasse || pour toi l'une sur | l'autre' [the numbers | of syllables that I pile up || for you one on top | of the other], where the syllabic units morph into entities that are not only counted, but gathered in piles.[35] This description in poetry is reminiscent of what Roubaud describes elsewhere as '[la] physique du rythme' [the physics of rhythm].[36] The various semantic connotations of the word 'physique' at once evoke the meaning of form, attributing to rhythm a physical shape, and it also suggests material or chemical constitution of an object or substance, if an English reader translates 'physique' as 'physics'. The syllabic rhythm of his verse here takes shape as an object-like entity.

The poet's attention turns to the particular syllable count of *Trente et un au cube*: 'je prends | cet appui sur la parole | ce lent découpage | de l'impair et du premier | de l'impair dans l'impair pour || te parler' [I lean | on words | this slow carving | of odd and primary numbers | of odd numbers within odd to || speak to you].[37] The alternation of odd and primary numbers, and simultaneously of odd numbers within odd numbers, recalls Roubaud's description of the numerical organization of the book. He breaks down 'sa division additive 5+7+5+7+7' [its additive division 5+7+5+7+7] into its various levels, 'cinq subdivisions du livre; [...] cinq "strophes" en chaque poème; [...] cinq "segments" (hémistiches) en chaque "ligne" (vers)' [five subdivisions of the book; [...] five 'strophes' in each poem; [...] five 'segments' (hemistiches) in each 'line' (poetic line)], each bearing the pattern inspired by the syllable count of the *tanka*. He further points out the property of 31 as a prime number, in turn divisible into prime numbers in the above way: 'sa "décomposition" à la japonaise en fait la somme d'un nombre premier de nombres premiers' [its 'deconstruction' in the Japanese style makes it the sum of a prime number of prime numbers].[38] The segmentation of the poem in this extract emulates the multiple layering of the sequence, first outlining its basic division into odd and prime numbers in

35 Roubaud, *Trente et un au cube*, p. 9.
36 Jacques Roubaud, *L'Invention du fils de Leoprepes* (Saulxures: Circé, 1993), p. 74.
37 Roubaud, *Trente et un au cube*, p. 9.
38 Roubaud, *Description du projet*, p. 78.

one fragment – 'ce lent découpage | de l'impair et du premier' [this slow carving | of odd and primary numbers] – then after a pause, indicating what Roubaud calls its 'macroscopie' [macroscopy] in 'de l'impair dans l'impair' [odd numbers within odd].[39]

His carving of the poem into segments is described as 'lent' [slow], perhaps another signalling of the intricacy of his craft. Alternatively, the adjective may reflect the reader's pace, unaccustomed as she will be to the pairing of French syntax with Japanese syllabic rhythms. The author points out the potential obstacle for the reader in the clashing syntactic and metric units: 'Cela peut poser quelque problème de restitution auditive ou, pour l'œil-oreille d'un lecteur, d'adaptation au mètre du poème' [This could pose a problem in an aural rendering of the text or, for the eye-ear of a reader, in adapting to the metre of the poem].[40] However, he is understandably less than sympathetic with the critic who proposes to 'supprimer les frontières de vers et de segments, de «lire en prose»' [get rid of the boundaries between lines and segments, and 'read it as prose'], referencing his 'surdité' [deafness]. Roubaud insists on the significance in *Trente et un au cube* of its rhythm, 'à la fois formellement et dans ce qui est dit dans le poème' [at once formally and in what is said in the poem]: rhythm is key to an understanding of the text's form and content.

Rhythm, then, is there to be considered, contemplated by both the eye and ear of the reader. Yet through his use of the hyphen in 'œil-oreille' [eye-ear], Roubaud appears not to separate the senses of vision and hearing. The first reader of *Trente et un au cube* is the poet's lover, his addressee, whom he invites to receive the poem with all her senses. She mouths the words of the poem with her lips as she follows their sequence with her fingers, 'quand tu les reçois || syllabes remuant | tes lèvres et tes doigts' [when you receive them || syllables moving | your lips and your fingers]; she reads the syllables of the poem aloud and hears it recited to her in a present that ever slips away, 'en la bouche seule | qui les porte (la | tienne) l'oreille seule où | leur point présent se divise || (la tienne la tienne | où elles s'habituent)' [in the sole mouth | that carries them (your | mouth) the sole ear where |

39 Roubaud, *Description du projet*, p. 78.

40 All citations in paragraph are in Roubaud, *Description du projet*, p. 79.

their present point divides || (yours yours | where they reside)]; her hands are blackened with traces of ink from the pages of writing, 'en tes mains (seules | mains à noircir de leur encre)' [in your hands (alone | hands to blacken with their ink)].[41] The reader's 'œil-oreille' [eye-ear] is multiplied for the lover 'en bouche mains yeux oreilles' [in mouth hands eyes ears], rendering it an all-encompassing, sensual experience.[42]

Roubaud theorizes the presence of four dimensions in the poetry reading experience, which he calls 'un quatuor de formes' [a quartet of forms]:

> Il faut distinguer, par exemple, la page superficielle de la forme– poésie écrite de la page interne de la forme-poésie dans la mémoire. La poésie a une forme *écrite* et une forme *eQrite*, qui est l'image visuelle intérieure, mémorielle, de la page de poésie.
>
> De la même manière la forme-poèsie a une composante *orale*, externe et une composante *aurale*, interne. Elle entre par l'œil et par l'oreille, mais surtout, elle entre.
>
> Elle est faite de ces deux couples formels, l'un externe, l'autre interne.[43]
>
> [We must distinguish between, for example, the superficial page of the written poetry-form from the internal page of poetry-form in memory. Poetry has a *written* form and a form which is the visual inner image, in memory, of the page of poetry.
>
> In the same way, the poetry-form has an external *oral* component and an internal *aural* component. It goes in through the eye and through the ear, but above all, it goes in.
>
> It is made up of these two formal couplings, the one external, and the other internal.]

A poem written on the page, read with the eyes, is at the same time perceived aurally in the internal workings of memory. A poem recited and heard is simultaneously seen on 'la page interne' [the internal page] of the inner eye. The poet's words are taken in by his audience, absorbed by his reader, who makes the poetry her own:

> C'est la mémoire qui ira chercher ce qu'il y a dessous, derrière, au-delà de la notation, au-delà de l'exécution. [...] Ce n'est qu'en entrant dans la mémoire intérieure de qui

41 Roubaud, *Trente et un au cube*, p. 9.

42 Roubaud, *Trente et un au cube*, p. 9.

43 Roubaud, *Poésie, etcetera*, pp. 126–27.

> le reçoit et fait sien qu'il accède à un nombre de dimensions respectable, qu'il devient vraiment un poème, et plus une partition.[44]
>
> [It is memory that will go looking for what is underneath, behind, beyond the notation, beyond the execution. [...] It is only on entering the inner memory of the person who receives it and makes it his or her own that it reaches a respectable number of dimensions, that it truly becomes a poem, and no longer a score.]

Poetry then 'enters' the reader, as in *Trente et un au cube* the lover-reader 'receives' its syllables, impregnated with the traces of the poet, penetrated by his material. The description of the same process in sexual terms highlights the particularly personal experience of reading poetry. The poem achieves its full potential of being, its multiple dimensions, through the reader's activation of its words and rhythms, and the insinuating of the poem into memory. The interaction with memory is always a singular process, never the same for any two people.[45] This is why Roubaud insists 'Un poème est toujours fabriqué pour deux: celui qui le compose et celui qui le lit et entend. Et peut-être le retient' [A poem is always made for two: the person who composes it and the person who reads and hears it. And maybe remembers it].[46] The poem exists fully only through both its composer and reader. A poem must also be memorable, or at least 'revisité intérieurement' [revisited inwardly], to be committed to memory and it is partly its rhythm that gives it its hold there.[47]

The 'quatuor' [quartet] in *Trente et un au cube* of 'bouche mains yeux oreilles' [mouth hands eyes ears], does not appear to entirely correspond to Roubaud's theoretical account of the act of reading poetry. Rather the mouth carrying the syllables and the hand blackened by their ink serve to convey the poem as more material, more object-like. They accord it further dimensions of existence, weight and substance. The reader, in fact, learns of the precise physical dimensions of the manuscript when the poet writes in the fourth poem 'j'écris silencieusement sur ma feuille | 21 × 27 | dans la jaune lumière' [I write silently on my page | 21 × 27 | in the yellow light].[48] The measurement stands out in the poem, not only

44 Roubaud, *Poésie, etcetera*, p. 128.

45 Roubaud, *Poésie, etcetera*, pp. 103–04.

46 Roubaud, *Poésie, etcetera*, p. 130.

47 Roubaud, *Poésie, etcetera*, p. 129.

48 Roubaud, *Trente et un au cube*, p. 21.

for its unusual precision in the context of a love poem, but also for its numerical-symbolic notation whose syllabic count is not spelled out in words for the reader. The figures also appear geometrically near the centre of the page of the published edition of *Trente et un au cube,* drawing the eye to itself. In an anecdotal passage in *Poésie:*, Roubaud muses on 'le format 21 × 27' [the 21 × 27 page format], each quarter the perfect space for a sonnet to exist 'seul, compact, serré, événement de poésie singulier' [alone, compact, fitted to the page, a singular event of poetry].[49] He even describes the way that non-sonnets composed on these sheets of paper would acquire 'une caractéristique minimale de la sonnetticité' [a slight characteristic of sonneticity] simply through their arrangement in the same format as the other poems.[50] It is the poet's aside, in the smaller font that indicates a later addition to his daily routine of prose writing, which is most revelatory. Years after the American A4 page format eventually became the norm in France, overtaking the once standard '21 × 27' quite literally with its ostensibly longer rectangle shape (a development Roubaud found 'infiniment disgracieux' [immensely ugly]), it is the original poem arrangement that appears strange to the poet: 'aujourd'hui cependant, sortant les vieux morceaux de papier couverts d'un sonnet de leur refuge de trente ans, ce sont eux que je trouve de forme étrange, trop serrée, comme rabotée' [today however, taking out the old pieces of paper covered in sonnets from their hiding place over the last thirty years, it is they that appear strange to me, too squashed, like their edges have been planed away].[51] It is not that the particular dimensions of any page are more or less suited to sonnet composition, but rather the familiarity of the spatial arrangement to the eye that facilitates the poem's hold in memory, the layout committed to the writer's inner page, 'page interne', of poetry.

The reference to a manuscript's page dimensions is also a feature of 'Still life / Style leaf' by Georges Perec, fellow-Oulipian writer and close friend of Jacques Roubaud. In this enigmatic piece, Perec provides a detailed

49 Roubaud, *Poésie:*, p. 480.
50 Roubaud, *Poésie:*, p. 481.
51 Roubaud, *Poésie:*, p. 480.

account of his writing desk, including the very page of the text's handwritten manuscript, 'de format 21 × 29,7' [in a 21 × 29.7 format].[52] The text loops in on itself at the point where the A4 page features self-reflexively in the description. We learn that it is 'presque entièrement couverte d'une écriture éxagérément serrée, et sur laquelle on peut lire: le bureau sur lequel j'écris est une ancienne table de joaillier' [almost entirely covered in extremely cramped handwriting, and on which can be read: the desk I write at is an old jeweller's table], taking up the same words the essay began with and recounting once again the writer's surroundings.[53] This results in a second description of 'le bureau sur lequel j'écris' [the desk I write on], written on the piece of paper that is (always already) lying on the desk in the original still-life scene. In this contorted *mise en abyme* of sorts, the careful reader will pick up on the tiny alterations that indicate the passing of time, such as the shift of the electronic clock face from 'AM 10:18' to 'PM 12.50'.[54]

Though there is an impossibility about Perec's piece – which he says almost fills the page even before it doubles up on itself and begins all over again – it is relevant for a reading of Roubaud both for its indulgence in spatial play and its evocation of *déjà vu*. The words of the text imply it fits onto a sole A4 sheet of paper. As the writing progresses, the author knows his description is coming to a close towards the bottom of the page, since the entire process has already been carried out. When the reader reaches the halfway point cited above, she knows the essence or shape of the text before it 'begins' (again), having already gone through the account of the desk and what sits upon it. At the very start of the published text, opening with the words 'Le bureau sur lequel j'écris est une ancienne table de joaillier' [The desk I write at is an old jeweller's table], the assumption is that the writer knows what the text contains, what it looks like, as the manuscript is placed on the same desk he embarks on describing; the description already exists on a sheet of paper placed on his desk.[55]

52 Georges Perec, 'Still life / Style leaf', in *L'Infra-ordinaire* (Paris: Seuil, 1989), pp. 107–19 (p. 113 and p. 119).

53 Perec, 'Still Life / Style Leaf', p. 113.

54 Perec, 'Still Life / Style Leaf', p. 112 and 118.

55 Perec, 'Still Life / Style Leaf', p. 107.

In an echo of this sense of the 'already seen', Roubaud tells us that 'toute lecture d'un poème est déjà une relecture' [every reading of a poem is already a re-reading].[56] His explanation lies in the visual form of the poem: 'Mis en présence d'un poème, en tenant compte de ses dimensions et de sa présentation spatiale, on possède déjà immédiatement beaucoup de lui' [In the presence of a poem, just by taking account of its dimensions and its spatial presentation, you already immediately have a lot of it in your possession].[57] An integral part of its committal to memory, the visual appearance of the poem gives away its overall structures and patterns, the shape of what we are about to read or hear. Roubaud details how the play of black lines composing a sonnet positioned on a white page are more easily transposed onto 'une page mentale' [a mental page] through the familiarity of the poem's shape.[58] In fact, he speaks of the page of poetry, whether 'la page existante de | livre ou papier un manuscrit un tapuscrit' [the existing page of | a book or sheet a manuscript a typescript], as 'une mémoire oblique pour éviter le trou de | l'infiniment privé' [an oblique memory to avoid the hole of | the infinitely private].[59] While the poem may exist in a person's memory, that of the poet or reader, its material existence on paper may be thought of as an external support; the poem does not depend solely on its written or printed form, like the typographic line units and enjambments of free verse. However, the singularity of a person's memory, 'l'infiniment privé' [the infinitely private], means that every poem memorized is transformed by and for that person, and also that it faces oblivion, or 'le trou', when that memory fades.

56 Roubaud, *Poésie, etcetera*, p. 130.

57 Roubaud, *Poésie, etcetera*, p. 130.

58 Roubaud, *Poésie:*, p. 42.

59 Jacques Roubaud, *Dors* précédé de *Dire la poésie* (Paris: Gallimard, 1981), pp. 23–24. Spacing reproduced from the original.

Defining Poetry

The 'quartet of forms' or a concern for the multidimensionality of poetry in its construction and reading is central to the composition of *Trente et un au cube* and is one way in which the poet actively moves away from the 'liberté limitée' [limited freedom] of what he called 'le vers libre standard' [standard free verse] that was characteristic of much of Éluard's writing.[60] Roubaud explains that in Éluard's conception of the relation between poetry and love, the missing term is language: 'dans l'équation Poésie = Amour il manque un troisième terme qui s'introduit, c'est la langue' [in the equation Poetry = Love there is a missing third term that comes into it: language].[61] That is not to say that Éluard is not a poet who works very carefully with language in his work, rather Roubaud's conception of 'langue' [language] possesses particular qualities and effects in the context of poetry and its relation to memory:

> La poésie parle, et nous parle. Elle dit; mais en même temps qu'elle dit pour nous, qu'elle suscite en nous, non par la pensée réfléchie mais par la mise en mouvement de notre mémoire, par les choix de langue qui se font à mesure en nous tels que notre mémoire nous les propose en images, en émotions, en d'autres appels et souvenirs de langue, sous l'efficace de sa pénétration, elle transporte en nous quelque chose d'autre: elle parle pour chacun de l'être de sa langue, de la langue à travers laquelle elle parle; elle dit quelque chose de l'histoire de la langue, de sa construction, de son vocabulaire, de sa syntaxe, de ses changements etc. [...] elle emploie la langue à sa manière, unique (et elle est la seule aussi parmi les arts de la langue à le faire de manière essentielle, inséparable d'elle-même). Je nommerai cette manière d'être de la poésie, de son action de mémoire, le nombre et le rythme.[62]
>
> [Poetry speaks, and it speaks to us. It says; but at the same time as saying for us, and stimulating in us (not through pondered thought but through the setting in motion of our memory, through the language choices made in sync with what our memory proposes to us in images, in emotions, in other signals and souvenirs of language), through the effectiveness of its penetration, it transports something else in us: poetry

60 Roubaud, *La Vieillesse d'Alexandre*, p. 123.
61 Roubaud and others, 'Entretien presque imaginaire', p. 10.
62 Roubaud, *L'Invention du fils de Leoprepes*, p. 142.

speaks for each person of the being of their language, of the language they speak through; it says something about the history of language, the way it is constructed, its vocabulary, its syntax, its changes etc. [...] it uses language in its own unique way (and it is the only one of the language-based arts to do it in a way that is essential, inseparable from itself). I will call this manner of being poetry, and its memory action number and rhythm.]

A love of poetry for Roubaud is necessarily a love of language, and it is in poetry that language finds the sedimentation of its very own history. For Roubaud, poetry captures so much of language itself through its insinuation into our personal and collective memories: we recite poetry, learn it by heart and repeat it. Through its particular rhythms and patterns, 'le nombre et le rythme' [number and rhythm], it sticks in our mind, becomes associated with lived moments and interacts with our most personal thoughts and feelings. Language fragments become images, emotions and even morph into other recollections of pieces of language, the links and developments it creates here emphasized through the repeated phrases beginning with 'elle' [it], which flow on each from the one before.

The reader of poetry will have a wealth of rhythms and lines stored in her memory, which are reactivated, renewed through the reading of every new poem. The power of language to multiply associations and interactions lies in memory and the memorability of a poem for Roubaud, as we have seen, is intricately tied in with its rhythm and formal composition.

Roubaud reflects on the relation between poetry and language elsewhere through a definition offered by Gerard Manley Hopkins:

poetry is speech framed for the contemplation of the mind by the way of hearing or speech framed to be heard for its own sake and interest even over and above its interest of meaning (la poésie est parole construite, organisée formée façonnée disposée pour la contemplation de l'esprit selon le chemin (li *sentiers*) de l'ouïe ou parole organisée pour être entendue pour elle-même pour sa valeur et intérêt même au-dessus et au-dela de l'intérêt du sens).[63]

63 Roubaud, 'Le silence de la mathématique', p. 117.

Hopkins goes on to narrow down this idea of '*meaning*' to '*at least the grammatical, historical and logical meaning*'. It is clear from Roubaud's translation of Hopkins's definition that he sees his own work very much through these same words. Hopkins's '*framed*' becomes for Roubaud 'construite, organisée formée façonnée disposée' [constructed, organized formed shaped arranged] an extended translation that encompasses the nature of his writing in *Trente et un au cube*, where his poetry is crafted, arranged, shaped. The definition is also reminiscent of Éluard's ideas on the transformation of language: his motif of 'parler pour parler' ['speaking for speaking's sake'], or as in 'L'Amoureuse', 'parler sans avoir rien à dire' [speaking with nothing to say], also aimed for a use of language over and above accepted everyday meaning, a use freed of the constraints of directed meaning, which is perhaps the '*grammatical, historical and logical meaning*' adopted from Hopkins by Roubaud here.

Roubaud develops his conception of poetry as '*speech framed to be heard for its own sake*' when he describes it as being close to the 'upper limit music' of language:

> … *my poetics*
>
> $\int$ music
> speech
>
> An integral
> lower limit speech
> upper limit music
>
> (une intégrale/limite inférieure la parole/limite supérieure musique/)
> et Zukofsky, en conséquence se désigne ainsi:
> '… the simplest fact of his life, specifically, a writer of music …'[64]

On this occasion, Roubaud borrows the term from Louis Zukofsky, citing and translating the extract it appears in from the American poet's *A-12*. Like Roubaud, Zukofsky places form at the centre of his poetic practice. The two poets also share a love of mathematics, evidenced, perhaps, by the presence of the integral symbol in Roubaud's citation of Zukofsky.

64 Roubaud, 'Le silence de la mathématique', p. 116.

The integral here defines Zukofsky's 'poetics'. It has as its lower limit 'la parole' – speech in its everyday communicative function – and 'musique' as its upper limit – a syntax composed of the rhythm of its words. In mathematics, the limits of the integral are approached, but never reached, which means that Zukofsky's conception of his poetry can never entirely be music or speech. Nevertheless, placing their poetic traditions closer to the upper limit of the integral, Zukofsky and Roubaud classify themselves as 'writer[s] of music'.

The closer the poet is to '[la] limite supérieure' [the upper limit], the further the words of poetry are from their usual semantic designations, performing instead as acoustic instruments. Words no longer exist as representative of what is beyond their letters – the signified – rather they become objects, taking on a sense of materiality that means they are appreciated for their own sake. Éluard's 'parler pour parler' ['speaking for speaking's sake'] appears, on one level, to be relevant in this formula. The Surrealist poet proposed a radicalization of language that would lift it above the plane of the everyday: 'Et le langage déplaisant qui suffit aux bavards, langage aussi mort que les couronnes à nos fronts semblables, réduisons-le, transformons-le en un langage charmant, véritable' [And the disagreeable language used by chatterboxes, a language as dead as the crowns on our heads, let us reduce it, let us transform it into a charming, true language].[65] He hoped for the possibility of a language that would no longer belong to the space of the 'bavards' [chatterboxes] whose use of language as a means to an end had deadened its effects and taken away any pleasure it might bestow.

In his collage piece drawing together fragments of works by various other writers and artists, his contemporaries, Éluard provides the solution for this transformation by way of a citation of Novalis: '*Parler pour parler est la formule de délivrance*' [Speaking for speaking's sake is the formula for release].[66] The fragment that follows, a comment by Fritz Wittels on Freud's talking cure, goes some way towards explaining the way in which

65 Paul Éluard, *Les Animaux et leurs hommes, les hommes et leurs animaux* (Paris: Au sans pareil, 1920), p. 10.

66 Paul Éluard, 'Premières vues anciennes', *Minotaure*, 10 (1937), 49–56 (p. 55).

the notion of 'parler pour parler' ['speaking for speaking's sake'] works towards such 'délivrance' [release]:

> Les analystes [...] laissent parler le malade, sûrs que l'important et le vrai remonteront à la surface même sans qu'ils s'en mêlent. Je présume que c'est par ce chemin que Freud est arrivé à sa découverte fondamentale. Il lui fallait écouter et il a donc écouté. Et à la fin vint la chose cachée, que le flot de paroles était destiné à recouvrir.[67]
>
> [The [...] analysts let the patient speak, confident that that which is important and true will rise to the surface even without their intervention. I presume that this is how Freud came upon his fundamental discovery. He had to listen and so he listened. And in the end came the hidden thing, which the stream of words was supposed to conceal.]

It is in speaking for speaking's sake that that which is 'important' and 'true' resurfaces in language. The difference between the 'flot de paroles' [stream of words] that conceals the 'truth' within it, and the chattering of the 'bavards' that Éluard wishes to leave behind, is that language is freed from constraint in the former, released from its signifying properties that make of it a tool, a means to an end, in Éluard's words, 'mort' [dead]. A third fragment on the same page of Éluard's 'Premières vues anciennes' ['First Ancient Views'], attributed to Gisèle Prassinos, suggests that the route to achieving this potential in language was through the automatic writing practices that had a role in Éluard's poetry and his thought on creativity. In the cited fragment, Prassinos compares the 'trésor' [treasure] uncovered in language through the practice of automatic writing to the supposed innocence perceived in the writing of a young girl of fourteen:

> on y voit apparaître une morale qu'un humour lugubre tient en laisse. Morale de dissociation, de suppression, de négation, de révolte, morale des enfants, des poètes qui se refusent à acquérir et qui resteront des phénomènes tant qu'ils n'auront pas redonné à tous les hommes l'envie de regarder en face ce qui les sépare d'eux-mêmes.[68]
>
> [you see appearing in it the ethics that a gloomy mood keeps restricted on a leash. The ethics of dissociation, abolition, negation, revolt, a moral that belongs to children,

67 Éluard, 'Premières vues anciennes', p. 55.
68 Éluard, 'Premières vues anciennes', p. 55.

to poets who refuse to acquire and who will remain anomalous until they make all men wish to see before them what separates them from themselves.]

The implication is that automatic writing can access something that has been buried under adulthood. The citation suggests that over years of use and familiarity, language is no longer questioned, challenged, or observed as an entity in itself. A further constraint on language is the 'humour lugubre' [gloomy mood] that is not present in the child, perhaps because she has not yet lived sadness, mourning, or those everyday preoccupations that weigh heavily on daily routines. We can infer that Éluard's 'parler pour parler' ['speaking for speaking's sake'] aspires to 'dissociate' from such an everyday, 'negate', even 'abolish' it; his poetics is one of 're-volt' against the mainstream, a search for a prior innocence, a lost self.

In Roubaud's work, it can be said that there is both a response and a resistance to Éluard's poetic practice. Roubaud's 'poetics' – spoken through the words of his fellow poet, Zukofsky – effect a distance, if not a full 'dissociation', from language as 'speech', or 'parole', and this separation from the 'lower limit speech' may be compared, on some level, to Éluard's desire for a language that breaks free of its referent. Yet Roubaud's self-confessed tendency towards 'upper limit music' must be contrasted with Éluard's 'parler pour parler' ['speaking for speaking's sake']. Roubaud's self-alignment with poet Zukofsky in his identification as 'a writer of music' foregrounds the two poets' shared interest in mathematics. Their '*poetics*' is at once defined in the form of an integral and presented by Roubaud in an article whose title places mathematics at the very heart of poetry, its foundation, or base: 'Le silence de la mathématique jusqu'au fond de la langue, poésie' ['The silence of mathematics to the very depth of language, poetry'].[69] To

69 Ann Smock considers the different possible meanings of this title in the context in which it appears in Roubaud's prose volume *Le grand incendie de Londres*. She suggests, for example, that it might refer to the disappearance of mathematical poetry constraints from the prose of Roubaud's volume built around absence, or to the withdrawal of maths, in the face of prose, into the depths of language. These potential readings of the line as it appears much later in Roubaud's oeuvre have somehow transformed the conception I had of it (I had not thought of this sense of retreat), and intensified my feeling that, for Roubaud, mathematics – and

consider the role of mathematics in setting Roubaud's poetry apart from Éluard's conception of 'parler pour parler' ['speaking for speaking's sake'] and the place of 'le nombre' [number] and 'le rythme' [rhythm] in poetry's 'manière d'être [...] son action de mémoire' [way of being [...] its memory action], it will be necessary to look at the role of mathematics more generally in Roubaud's approach to poetry composition, going back to the decision he made to leave behind free verse forms of poetry at the height of the Surrealist movement in his youth, before moving on to the particular presence of mathematics in the construction of *Trente et un au cube*.

A Project of Maths and Poetry

It is impossible to know something of Roubaud and his work and not be aware of the prevalence of mathematics in his writing and life. He regularly introduces himself as: 'Jacques Roubaud, compositeur de mathématique et de poésie' [Jacques Roubaud, composer of mathematics and poetry].[70] The introduction makes reference to Roubaud's professional career as a university professor of mathematics and his life as a poet, which existed alongside his job for many years. The signature merges the disciplines of maths and poetry; Roubaud speaks of composing mathematics like one might do a poem, alluding to the overlap of the two fields in his work. The young Roubaud took up a profession in mathematics with the aim of serving his wish to be a poet. In a list of deductions and arguments compiled to support his decision to make a 'rupture' with his youthful approach to poetry, the very first point is based on mathematics: 'Je vais me servir de la mathématique, disons comme garantie technique et mentor

poetry – have an enigmatic but closely, tightly bound place in language, like the hard, dark kernel hidden at the core of a fleshy fruit. See Ann Smock, *The Play of Light: Jacques Roubaud, Emmanuel Hocquard, and Friends* (New York: SUNY, 2021), pp. 160–61.

70 See, for one of many examples, *Poésie, etcetera*, p. 33, in which Roubaud attaches the signature to a speech he delivered at Osnabrück in 1993.

moral' [I'm going to use mathematics, let's say as a technical guarantee and moral mentor].[71]

Roubaud describes initially embarking on a university career in literature, pinpointing the moment he decided to change paths during a short period in the '*hypokhâgne*', the preparatory class for literary studies at the *École normale supérieure*.[72] He compares the exercise in textual analysis, or 'explication de texte', to the dissection of a frog, in which the object of study (a Nerval sonnet in this particular case) was 'torturé' [tortured] and 'aiguillonné' [prodded].[73] Roubaud reflects that such treatment of poetry would be harmful to his own appreciation of poetry and his composition process. He wanted to be a poet and the only way to do that was to pursue a completely different field for his livelihood. The comparison of the dissected poem to a frog being prodded and maimed points to the importance, for Roubaud, of keeping a poem whole and intact, so to speak. For Roubaud, literary analysis as it was taught at university in his youth took away from the openness to poetry, cutting poems up into sections, smaller parts of themselves. The place of maths in defending the autonomy of poetry was thus, in part, in creating an alternative professional pathway for Roubaud, an escape from teaching, or 'dissecting' poetry.

Roubaud's discovery of the Bourbaki approach to set theory marks a decisive change in his approach to writing poetry.[74] Nicolas Bourbaki – 'ce "mathématicien collectif"' [that 'collective mathematician'] – was the pseudonym for a group of young mathematicians in France in the early 1930s. Roubaud describes the group as the inventors of 'une entreprise générale assez exaltante' [a generally quite thrilling undertaking]: that of reconstructing the edifice of mathematics drawing entirely on the axioms of set theory.[75] While my exploration of Roubaud's writing does not enter into the technical particulars of such a project, certain aspects of the poet's engagement with their work are relevant for a consideration of his

71 Roubaud, *Poésie:*, p. 104. Emphasis in the original.

72 For Roubaud's account of his early change in career path, see *Poésie:*, pp. 298–303.

73 Roubaud, *Poésie:*, p. 302.

74 Roubaud, *Poésie:*, p. 103.

75 Roubaud, *Mathématique:*, p. 47.

approach to poetry composition. Indeed, Bourbaki seems to serve more generally as the 'mentor moral' [moral mentor] Roubaud was seeking in his poetic process.

In his prose volume *Mathématique:*, Roubaud extensively describes his experience of getting to grips with the vast and dense *Traité* [*Treatise*] composed by the Bourbakists.[76] It is his disciplined approach to understanding this mathematical text that he hopes to apply to his poetry writing: 'une chose m'a été certaine dès le début: que le mode de compréhension et de raisonnement dont je m'étais pénétré en des années de bourbakisme, la discipline sévère que je m'étais imposée pour parvenir à le maîtriser, allaient me servir aussi en poésie' [one thing was certain from the beginning: the mode of understanding and reasoning that I had firmly rooted in my mind from the years of Bourbakism, the harsh discipline that I imposed on myself to succeed in mastering it, were also going to be useful to me in poetry].[77] In his reflection on this rigorous study of Bourbakism, Roubaud uses lexis less often associated with poetry. He writes of *penetrating* the topic and its mode of *reasoning*, and of his *harsh discipline* in the pursuit of *mastering* Bourbaki writing. The enterprise itself, both that of the collective pseudonym, Bourbaki, and that of the young Roubaud, undergoing a conversion to their approach to mathematics, is described retrospectively by the poet as making mathematics (la mathématique) 'neuve, porteuse d'une vision et d'une mission' [new, bringing with it a vision and a mission].[78] This understanding of mathematics as a mission to be taken on and completed, a vision to work towards mastering, was, for Roubaud, the perfect way to combat what he called the 'molle' [loose] and 'floue' [vague] poetry of free verse.[79] The poet was seeking something

76 Roubaud states that the 'provocation' of the title *Mathématique:* cannot be justified by the book that follows. His writing in *Mathématique:* is not a monument to the discipline, but continues the series of his prose volumes dedicated to providing an account of the failure of his project of maths and poetry. See *Mathématique:*, pp. 17–20.

77 Roubaud, *Poésie:*, p. 103.

78 Roubaud, *Mathématique:*, p. 68.

79 Roubaud, *Poésie:*, p. 104.

that would insulate his mind from what he was experiencing as a sense of vagueness in literature.[80]

At the time, Roubaud had a very clear idea of what he thought mathematics was, based on the presentation in school education of mathematics as a static, rather than evolving, discipline:

> il y avait <u>cela</u>, (telle construction, tel objet, tel calcul) qui se faisait <u>comme cela</u>, qui s'était toujours fait comme cela [...]. Résoudre un problème mathématique, c'était aller d'un point, l'énoncé, à un autre, la conclusion, préalablement donnés tous les deux, et toujours dans le même sens: il n'y avait à découvrir (et à découvrir vite) que le chemin pour y parvenir.[81]
>
> [there was <u>this</u>, (a certain construction, an object, a calculation) which was done <u>like this</u>, which had always been done like this [...]. Resolving a mathematical problem was a matter of going from one point, the statement of the problem, to another, the conclusion. Both of these points were given beforehand, and always in the same way: you only had to discover (and quickly) the route to get there.]

There was in Roubaud's early conception of mathematics a sense of comfort in its fixity and order. Mathematical questions tackled at school presented a problem that could usually be approached in a limited number of ways. In contrast to the lack of structure Roubaud felt keenly in the forms of Surrealist poetry, maths was about finding a route to a predetermined solution, questions always already answered. Roubaud seems to have found in Bourbakism a sense of familiarity with this conception of mathematics, for he describes the components of their *Traité* [*Treatise*] in similar terms:

> les déductions léchées du Traité, avec la minutie de leur présentation, l'effort constant d'un découpage des chaînes déductives en pas à peu près triviaux [...], la précision pédante et suraffichée des définitions, propositions, lemmes, théorèmes et corollaires, les renvois incessants, chiffrés, typographiquement marqués, aux résultats et notions antérieurement introduits et nécessaires à tel moment d'une démonstration, résultat, comme je l'appris plus tard, de nombreuses rédactions reprises, critiquées collectivement et corrigées d'édition en édition en vue

80 Roubaud, *Mathématique:*, 56.

81 Roubaud, *Mathématique:*, p. 26. Emphasis in the original.

> d'atteindre à des sommets infranchissables de netteté, de clarté et de conviction pédagogiques.[82]
>
> [the polished deductions of the Treatise, with the meticulousness of their presentation, the constant effort to divide deductive chains into practically trivial steps [...], the self-important and frequently referenced precision of the definitions, lemmata, theorems and corollaries, the endless, numbered, typographically marked cross-references to results and notions that had been introduced earlier and were deemed necessary at a certain point in a proof, the result, as I later learned, of several edits collectively redrafted, critiqued and corrected from one version to the next with a view to attaining insurmountable heights of lucidity, clarity, and pedagogical conviction.]

This passage from Roubaud's description of Bourbaki's *Traité* [*Treatise*] is quoted extensively to display the intricacies of its composition. It is an already long extract from an even longer single, unbroken sentence, which has the effect of a building accumulation of mathematical terms, increasing in detail and precision. Almost every noun and adjective is at least doubled or twice qualified in the piece: the 'renvois' [cross-references] are both 'chiffrés' [numbered] and 'typographiquement marqués' [typographically marked], the Bourbakists' 'précision' [precision] is both 'pédante' [self-important] and 'suraffichée' [frequently referenced], all with the aim of reaching the peaks of 'netteté' [lucidity], 'clarté' [clarity] and 'conviction pédagogiques' [pedagogical conviction]. Roubaud's constantly clarified and corrected sentence reflects the thorough nature of the Bourbakist project, the wish to leave no ground uncovered, no aspect of their study uncertain. His own syntax emulates the Bourbakist project of breaking down the deductive chains he speaks of into increasingly smaller chunks, until even the tiniest element of unpredictability is removed so that the steps to follow in a deductive operation become 'triviaux' [trivial]. The building sentence without the reprieve of a full stop to break up the pace of the syntax also emulates the rising to a peak discussed in the semantic content of the extract: the great heights of the Bourbaki aim were unrivalled clarity and conviction. However, what is also encapsulated in Roubaud's sprawling sentence is the impossible

82 Roubaud, *Mathématique:*, p. 55.

level of complication and, eventually, obscurity in the mathematic approach. The Bourbaki quest for 'rigour' and 'perfection' could not be sustained and was doomed to end in failure.[83]

Years later in his account of his mathematic adventure, Roubaud notes 'la distance' [the distance] separating the reality – 'le "réel"' – of mathematics and the Bourbaki approach: 'la présentation idéale d'une axiomatisation, même solidement bâtie comme la leur' [the ideal presentation of an axiomatization, even as solidly built as theirs].[84] He nonetheless basked in the illusion of their intricate formal constructions for a while, enjoying the appeal of this 'espèce nouvelle et irrésistiblement séduisante de calcul' [new and irresistibly appealing type of calculation].[85] The architecture of the Bourbaki method provided certainty and process. Poetry, on the other hand was about composition and invention – 'composer, inventer' – which had nothing to do with the way in which Roubaud conceived of mathematics at the time.[86] As both the narrative and his studies progress, however, the definitions separating mathematics and poetry become less rigid. Roubaud describes maths as a writing process:

> La mathématique n'était pas une concaténation de paroles, n'était pas un univers d'idées. La mathématique s'écrivait, s'inscrivait dans le monde en s'écrivant et s'inscrivant sur le papier, s'y enfonçant, de mine de crayon puis d'encre, en l'assombrissant peu à peu, séquentiellement, dans son ordre, sans ambiguïtés, sans hésitations. Elle se construisait suivant des règles, en échafaudages, en assemblages de signes.[87]
>
> [Mathematics wasn't a concatenation of words, it wasn't a universe of ideas. Mathematics was written, inscribed in the world by being written and inscribed on paper, imprinted there with the lead of a pencil and then in ink, made gradually darker, in sequences, in its order, without ambiguity, without hesitation. It was built following rules, in sections, like scaffolding, in assemblages of signs.]

The description of maths as a progression, constructed 'in sections, like scaffolding', with 'order' and 'assemblages' might be compared to

83 Roubaud, *Mathématique:*, p. 55.
84 Roubaud, *Mathématique:*, p. 47.
85 Roubaud, *Mathématique:*, p. 55.
86 Roubaud, *Mathématique:*, p. 26.
87 Roubaud, *Mathématique:*, p. 77.

metrically composed verse. In this meditation on the written process of mathematics, Roubaud could be describing the inverse of a Surrealist conception of poetry; or poetry written in the manner of *Trente et un au cube*. The numerical pattern underpinning *Trente et un au cube* is a vertical as well as horizontal feature of the poem; it can be counted in syllables across the page as it is followed by the reader's eye, and it visually shapes the number of lines and their organization along the vertical length of the page. The poetic construction thus resembles the scaffoldings and assemblages that Roubaud describes as being a foundational element of mathematics.

The poet's accounts of the two fields of maths and poetry, and his turning to mathematics as a way of coming to terms with the lack of rigour that characterized Roubaud's early writings and the literature of the same time, resonate with the construction of *Trente et un au cube*. In this volume, which closely follows Roubaud's decision to pursue a certain rigour in his poetry, the cubic premise of the book appears to be an attempt to create an ordered, structured space in poetry. The structure of the book resembles Roubaud's early conception of mathematics as a progression to a predetermined solution, rather than 'concatenations of words': patterns of multiplication and syllabic counting define the book's completion from the outset. Bourbakian mathematics appears thus as both 'mentor moral' [moral mentor] and 'garantie technique' [technical guarantee] in the volume, offering Roubaud structure, process and discipline to counter the intuitive practices associated with Surrealism and automatic writing.

The mathematics of Roubaud's autobiographical prose, has a clear presence in *Trente et un au cube*: geometrical shape, counting and multiplication feature as themes and structuring devices in the volume's form. Number is at the heart of the architecture that shapes the book, running through every layer of the text. Yet the lines between mathematics and poetry are increasingly blurred in the descriptions of his early experience of the two disciplines. In Roubaud's accounts of poetic language and its interactions with memory, number is tied in with rhythm; the scale of Zukofsky's 'poetics' adopted by Roubaud, which has 'music' as its upper limit, is expressed in mathematical terms. Rhythm in his poetry is created in the intricate formation of syntactical and syllabic patterns, shaped by the carefully counted silences that determine each poem – and the book as a whole – through the constitution of its stanzas, lines and fragments. The mathematics of the volume's structure is implemented through the sequences that create the constituent parts of the book, from the divisions distinguishing between the thirty-one poems, through to the count of thirty-one syllables that composes each individual line.

Roubaud embraces recognizable poetic structures, such as the *tanka* and the sonnet, giving them an unfamiliarity derived from their translation into the contemporary. In *Trente et un au cube*, the syllabic count of the Japanese *tanka* constantly comes up against the French syntax of the poem. Semantic and rhythmic units frequently clash, creating an overall sense of tension in the piece's sonority. At times, the syllabic units, composed of either five or seven counts, come together to hint at the twelve counts of the French alexandrine. This can only occur as an echo of the line's classic form, since the shift of the hemistich from the sixth count to either the fifth or seventh means it is always an alexandrine at one remove from what the reader might be accustomed to. The result is a rhythm derived, in Roubaud's own words, from 'les retours du même et du différent' [returns of the same and the different].[88] The metrical patterns of *Trente et un au cube* both flirt with and resist a sense of familiarity in memory, thus luring the listener into an engagement with the text and stimulating a sense of curiosity.

The rhythms created in the formal qualities of the poem are at the heart of the distinction between Roubaud's concept of 'poetic language' and Éluard's aspirations for the concept of 'parler pour parler' ['speaking for speaking's sake'] in poetry. For the poet who desired a renewal of language through speaking for speaking's sake, the unexpected images and connections that would arise from unfamiliar juxtapositions in syntax were a signal of the workings of the unconscious and its presence in conscious creativity. If the origins of 'parler pour parler' ['speaking for speaking's sake'] are inextricably linked to the principle of the talking cure, privileging content in speech over form, its ambitions are necessarily tied in with the possibilities of (self-)discovery that exist in the poet's unconscious memory.

In Roubaud's understanding of poetic language, the poem is created as an offering of music to his beloved reader. Carefully constructed and

88 Roubaud, *Trente et un au cube*, p. 41.

constantly refined rhythms entice and draw in his reader; phonic patterns wind their way into memory, triggering recollections of metres heard and recited before. The visual layout of the poem provides another dimension of its 'music': blank spaces frame the text and its components – verses, lines, fragments. The white spaces around the lettering of the text shape it on the page and make it more susceptible to absorption in (and interaction with) memory. The reader is offered the position of the beloved in the text – 'toi' [you] – and her position is vital for the activation of the poem's multiple dimensions on reading.

Conclusion

In *Trente et un au cube*, Roubaud goes back to his poetic origins to explore a conception of poetry as constructed object: the text is the poet's expression of love for his feminine addressee, closely moulded around the qualities of the beloved. She is in the physical body of the text, its words heavy with the *pretz* attributed to her by her troubadour poet. She also adds to the multidimensionality of the poems as addressee, activating its rhythms and associations through a reading of the text – with her *œil-oreille* [*eye-ear*] – and its insinuation in the singularity of her memory. This is a reaction against what Roubaud felt to be the 'debilitating' influence that Surrealism had exerted on his poetic creativity during his youth, as he makes a decision to move away from the automatic writing processes and free verse forms associated with the movement. In *Trente et un au cube*, the poet privileges constructed form and metric definition over a freer *vers libre*; the work of love is a gesture, crafted with his hands.

Through his exploration of form, from the notion of 'aller à la ligne' [starting a new line] embodied by the *vers libre*, to the intricate crafting of multidimensional structures, Roubaud is also considering his own relationship with poetry. His words spoken against Surrealism and his insistence upon a 'rupture' with their practices highlight a concern with his abilities to compose innovatively in free verse. Roubaud chooses Éluard in particular as representative of the oppressive influence of Surrealist poetry on his own composition processes, while incorporating the earlier poet's equation of love and poetry, *lamourlapoésie*, into his own conception of poetic practice. For Roubaud, as for Éluard, the place of the lover in poetry is one that activates a multiplicity of connections, transforming the language on the page. Éluard's use of image challenges the reader's expectations: the juxtapositions created in the syntax of his poems give way to further images, deepening the layers of meaning in the text. However, Roubaud translates this sense of multiplicity through image into a concern with form.

Roubaud speaks of moving on from 'le problème du vers' [the problem of the poetic line] – notably the sense of the momentary he felt had come to characterize contemporary French poetry – to the sonnet as a stage in his poetic growth: 'j'ai combattu mon insatisfaction poétique, mon incapacité à la poésie. [...] Je me suis tourné vers une forme fixe, une "grande forme" ' [I have battled with my dissatisfaction in poetry, my incapacity in poetry. [...] I turned to a fixed form, a 'great form'].[89] Closely linked to the sonnet, the *canso* and *tanka* forms represent both 'process' and 'duration' in a number of ways in *Trente et un au cube*: the constant honing of the form through intertextual comparison; the anthologizing of the poems that makes them part of a sequence, broadening their relevance for the poetic memory of the reader; the careful, thoughtful construction of the text itself. In *Trente et un au cube*, Roubaud reacts not only against a certain poetic form, but the implication it has for the place of memory in poetry. For Roubaud, poetry necessarily engages the conscious memory of the reader and poet, and invokes the traces of poems that have existed before the moment of reading. Moreover, poetry's relation to memory occurs primarily through its form: its visual and aural dimensions, its spatial and rhythmic arrangement, for which the vagueness of 'aller à la ligne' proves insufficient for Roubaud. The feminine addressee is present in all of these elements: she is the poem's first reader, allowing its words to stir and interact with her memory; she is the intricate composition of rhythms, since they sing both of and for her.

Both poets seem to explore the limits of the specularity that has often formed the basis of psychoanalytic interpretations of the place of the female muse to the male poet: Éluard's narrator articulates the failure of

89 Roubaud, *Description du projet*, pp. 30–31.

his lover to provide him with specular support in 'L'Égalité des sexes'. In 'L'Amoureuse', the multiple images and layers of interpretation challenge the binary forms that structure the poem, breaking the mirror reflecting the image of the poet in the face and body of the feminine lover. Roubaud distances his poetry from such binary formal models altogether: his poem is a multidimensional construction that weaves the presence of the feminine into its framework and simultaneously addresses her. At the heart of Éluard's poems and forms foregrounding the beloved is a reflection on the notion of inspiration that triggers automatic writing processes. It is this notion of poetic inspiration that Roubaud rejects, stating 'je n'ai pas besoin d'inspiration en poésie' [I don't need inspiration in poetry], even blaming it for his own writer's block: 'la doctrine de la fureur inspirée, dans sa variante moderne (le surréalisme), fait des ravages, et m'a conduit à l'impasse dont je cherche à me dégager' [the doctrine of the inspired frenzy, in its modern variant (Surrealism), wreaks havoc, and has driven me to the impasse that I'm trying to free myself from].[90] Roubaud's approach to composition manages both the impulses and effects in the creation of poetry: 'la poésie est conçue comme un métier et le poète comme un praticien disposant d'un assortiment de techniques, dont il maîtrise aussi bien les ressorts que les effets' [poetry is conceived as a craft and the poet a practitioner with an assortment of techniques he uses to master poetry's impulses as well as its effects].[91] Roubaud's definition of his own poetry as approaching 'upper limit music' encompasses these principles: mathematics acts as a guarantee against the 'molle' [loose] and 'floue' [vague] qualities of free verse forms, forming rhythms and metres that prioritize the poem's reception.

How far is it possible to truly master the impulses and effects of a poetic text? Roubaud continues to associate his lover with poetry and the act of composition, but if she is woven into the material of the poetry itself, and is also its addressee, what are the implications for her presence on the page and in the sound of the poem?

90 Roubaud, *Poésie:*, p. 107. Emphasis in the original.

91 Henri Scepi, 'Éloge de la contrainte ou ce que peut le poème', *La Licorne*, 40 (1997), 31–46 (p. 35).

CHAPTER 3

The Reader and Roubaud's Love Poem

For Roubaud the composition of poetry is a carefully planned craft, eliminating intangible notions of divine inspiration historically associated with the genre, and recently incarnated in the unconscious experiments and free verse ideals of the Surrealists.[1] In this approach to the poetic process, the presence of the feminine lover is no longer the illuminating glow of inspiration, the light of love and hope that, often inexplicably, stimulates a creative impulse in the poet. In the previous chapter, I began to explore the interaction between the beloved, form and memory in the composition and reading of Roubaud's poetry. In this chapter I formulate what might be thought of as a Roubaldian conception of the poetic muse.

I begin with a reflection on the position of the reader(s) in relation to Roubaud's poetry, focusing on *Trente et un au cube* and a single poem written to introduce a reading of the book at a Paris bookshop in the year it was published. The play of personal pronouns in the piece entangles the reader's position with that of the poet's lover being addressed and reveals something of the route the reader is invited to take through the formal structure of the volume. I then consider the role that form plays in the relation between the poet and the lover he addresses in the poetry volume. At moments in *Trente et un au cube*, she appears to be imprisoned in the poetic structures erected by the poet-narrator: the cube of the volume's title comes to stand as a metaphor not only for the lovers' bedroom, but also for a cubic space in which the poet attempts to detain his love object. I look at this particular aspect of their relation in the book's central poem, where

1 For a consideration of the opposing notions of the poet as prophet and the poet as craftsman, relating to the work of Roubaud and the Surrealists, see Scepi, 'Éloge de la contrainte', pp. 31–43.

the struggle between poet and beloved comes to a climax. Alongside my close readings of this poem, I continue to draw on Lacan's thought on the impossible sexual relation. Lacan attempts a formalization of Freud's ideas of sexual difference through the concepts of set theory, which I compare with attempts to provide an account of the poet-beloved relation through notions of form and structure in *Trente et un au cube*.

In Irigaray's reading of Lacanian theory, she singles out its biological roots in Freud's original text, 'Femininity', to demonstrate the lack of objectivity in Lacan's attempts at formalization. I find, nonetheless, pockets of resistance in her reading of Lacan: spaces of possibility that persist for the position of the feminine in the theory. This foray into Lacanian set theory and Irigaray's pitting of the theory against its Freudian origins lead to a deeper insight into the relation between poet and muse and, in turn, poet and reader in *Trente et un au cube*.

The final part of this chapter builds on my enquiry so far into the impossible sexual relation, seeing in Irigaray's *J'aime à toi* (1992) [*I Love to You*] and *Être deux* (1997) [*To Be Two*] an alternative understanding of the disjunction as a space in which the subjectivity of each term in the couple may exist unimpeded. When aligned with certain moments in *Trente et un au cube* which feature the beloved who sleeps, Irigaray's positive understanding of the disjunction may be used to illuminate the ways that the dividing space between poet and lover, or poet and reader is also a source of meaning and creativity in poetry.

Trente et un au cube: A User's Guide

The opening of *Trente et un au cube* is an invitation to the reader: 'JE DÉTIENS MILLION de | syllabes comptées pour toi' [I keep a million | syllables counted out for you].[2] The words of the poem have been arranged, for her, in rhythms counted in syllables. The chiasmic positioning of pronouns 'je' [I] and 'tu' [you], respectively, at the start of the opening

2 Roubaud, *Trente et un au cube*, p. 9.

fragment and the close of the fragment that follows also invites the reader into a relation with the poet: the counted syllables that make up the book are what bring *you* and *I* together.

In his 'Poème de présentation composé pour une lecture de *Trente et un au cube* à Shakespeare et C°' ['Presentation Poem Composed for a Reading of *Thirty-One Cubed* at Shakespeare and C°'], Roubaud plays on this use of the second-person pronoun 'toi' [you] as his addressee: 'Cela signifiait | ce que chacun voulait vous | l'entendre et moi | l'entendre aussi mais parmi | vous c'est cela voyez vous || cela et pour vous | entendre était cela que je | disais d'elle de | toi mais pour vous elle elle | toi mais qui est ce? c'est toi' [That meant | what each person wanted you || to hear it and me | to hear it too but among | you it is that you see || that and for you | to hear was what I | was saying about her about | you but for you her her | you but who is it? It is you].[3] As the sequences of words in the poem progress, they seem to enact the meaning of his simple opening: 'Cela signifiait | ce que chacun voulait' [That means | what each person wanted]. The poem 'means', or performs meaning, for its addressee. Personal pronouns 'vous' [you (plural)], 'toi' [you] and 'elle' [she] rush around one another in the poem's syntax, colliding and overlapping. The poet attempts to clarify the difference between these pronouns and their role in his poem: 'entendre était cela que je | disais d'elle de | toi mais pour vous' [to hear was what I | was saying about her about | you but for you]. He hints that the person he addresses as 'toi' [you] is in fact 'elle' [her], the love that is the impetus for the poetry. Perhaps then 'vous' [you (plural)] is a polite reference to his reader, who has been accorded the privilege of insight into this expression of passion. No sooner does the poet separate the roles, than he draws them all back together again, as he continues: 'pour vous elle elle | toi mais qui est ce? c'est toi' [for you her her | you but who is it? It is you]. She is at the centre of the address, mediating between 'vous' and 'toi', the reader and the personal address made by the poet. In the end, all these ideas are contained within 'toi' [you] – 'c'est toi' [it is you], which serves at once

3 Jacques Roubaud, 'Poème de présentation composé pour une lecture de *Trente et un au cube* à Shakespeare et C°', in *Almanach de Shakespeare and Company*, 1 (1974), 167–71 (pp. 168–69). All references to the poem are from these two pages, until stated otherwise.

as the most personal of addresses, and the space each reader occupies in *Trente et un au cube*.

The verb 'entendre' [to hear / to understand / to mean] recurs throughout the piece and its doubling in the first line of the poem immediately draws attention to its ambiguity: the poet plays with the difference between his *meaning*, that is his agency as poet, and what his reader *hears* in the lines that he composes. Roubaud keeps the verb in the infinitive, 'vous | l'entendre et moi | l'entendre aussi' [you | to hear it and me | to hear it too], which has the effect of distancing it from any subject. It is as though meaning cannot be shackled exclusively to either poet or reader, denied the commitment of conjugation in line with either pronoun. The poet further probes the ambiguity of the verb 'entendre': 'devais je entendre ce | que j'entendais de toi contre ce | que vous entendiez de toi [...]?' [did I have to mean what | I meant about you against what | you understood about you [...]?]. Must the meaning of 'toi' be the same for both poet and reader? In his defence of poetry, Ben Lerner opens up the possibilities of the poetry genre when he writes that 'to be hailed as a "you" [...] is to be endowed with poetic capacity', since it is also 'to be part of a linguistic community'.[4] Perhaps the work's potential lies in its possibility to expand differently for each reader, precisely in not being restricted to a particular pathway of understanding constructed by the poet.

The full title of Roubaud's 'Poème de présentation' ['Presentation Poem'] gives its intention to present a reading of *Trente et un au cube* at the *Shakespeare and Co.* bookshop in Paris. Reading the published poem decades later, I can only imagine the poet addressing his audience, the singular identities attributed to the pronouns 'je' [I], 'tu' [you] and 'vous' [you (plural)]. The poetry reading event at the bookshop may be considered in the light of Benveniste's 'instances de discours' [instances of discourse].[5] He explains: 'les indicateurs *je* et *tu* ne peuvent exister comme signes virtuels, ils n'existent qu'en tant qu'ils sont actualisés dans l'instance de discours, où ils marquent par chacune de leurs propres instances le procès d'appropriation par le locuteur' [the indicators *I* and *you* cannot exist as virtual signs, they

4 Ben Lerner, *The Hatred of Poetry* (London: Fitzcarraldo Editions, 2016), p. 16.

5 Émile Benveniste, *Problèmes de linguistique générale* (Paris: Gallimard, 1966), p. 251.

only exist when they are being realized in the instance of discourse, where they mark, through each of their own instances, the process of appropriation by the speaker].[6] The play on the ambiguous relationship between 'tu' [you] and 'vous' [you (plural)] remains, but in the instance of the poetry reading there is more a sense that each listener is addressed personally by the poet with 'tu', and that 'vous' refers to the collective audience. The use of 'vous' draws attention to what exists beyond the individual reader, bringing together the group of listeners in their shared experience of the poetry. The reading of verb 'entendre' as *hearing* in the poem gains weight in the instance of this event celebrating the poetry's aural dimension.

The poem is also a response to a particular review by critic Alain Bosquet, which appeared in *Le Monde des livres* [*Le Monde Books*] under the title 'Jacques Roubaud, ou la technique ennemie du poème' ['Jacques Roubaud, or the hostile tactics of the poem'].[7] Jean-Jacques Poucel points out that the 'vous' [you (plural)] of the supplemental poem is therefore also used to address the critic, Bosquet. The context of the live poetry reading imposed by the poem's title and the dimension of listening to the poem that it involves is particularly relevant here; 'voulait vous | l'entendre' may be heard as an invitation to listen closely to the poem's rhythm – *voulez-vous l'entendre* [do you want to hear it[?]]. Poucel explains that this may be a response to Bosquet's claim that the reader of *Trente et un au cube* should disregard the line breaks in the text and instead approach the book as a piece of prose.[8] At an analogous level, Roubaud's poetic response establishes a dialogue with Bosquet which has a third and focal element: the reader.

The critic himself appears to take the side of the reader in his piece: 'Le malheur est que, pour le lecteur de bonne volonté moyenne, Jacques Roubaud se barricade dans ses livres et en interdit l'accès' [The unfortunate thing is that, for the average reader, Jacques Roubaud barricades himself in his books and forbids anyone else from entering].[9] Bosquet

6 Benveniste, *Problèmes de linguistique générale*, p. 255.

7 Poucel, *Jacques Roubaud and the Invention of Memory*, pp. 135–36. For the original review, see Bosquet, 'Jacques Roubaud, ou la technique ennemie du poème', p. 16.

8 Poucel, *Jacques Roubaud and the Invention of Memory*, p. 136.

9 Bosquet, 'Jacques Roubaud, ou la technique ennemie du poème', p. 16.

initially suggests two obstacles to meaning, or understanding, with regard to *Trente et un au cube*:

> Le premier obstacle, pour qui veut lire *Trente et un au cube* est dans l'absence de tout mode d'emploi: le livre-objet ne porte pas de texte au dos, ni sur les revers de la couverture; on chercherait en vain un avant-propos ou une post-face. Le lecteur est obligé de découvrir lui-même son fil d'Ariane. Le deuxième obstacle est physique: chaque texte est imprimé sur une double page repliée sur elle-même; on est donc obligé de la déplier. Pourquoi le format du livre n'est-il pas en largeur pour permettre une lecture normale?[10]
>
> [The first obstacle for the reader of *Thirty-One Cubed* is the absence of a user's guide: the book-object has no text on its back cover, nor inside the cover; there is no foreword or postface. The reader is obliged to find his [or her] own Ariadne's thread. The second obstacle is physical: each text is printed on a double page that is folded over on itself; you are therefore obliged to unfold it. Why is the book's format not of a width that would allow for a normal reading?]

Bosquet's allusion to the myth of Ariadne suggests that the 'ordinary reader' is likely to be disorientated or lost when encountering *Trente et un au cube*, obliged to find her own route through the poem, like the mythological Theseus stumbling blindly through the obscure labyrinth. In the same vein, Bosquet's reference to Roubaud barricading himself in his books, though tongue in cheek, invites a comparison between the poet and the fearsome Minotaur hidden at the centre of the maze. Perhaps Roubaud does ask more of his reader than Ben Lerner when he dismisses 'difficulty' as a reason for avoiding poetry: 'Cette poésie est difficile. Et alors? Est-il indispensable de ne se heurter à aucune difficulté? est-il indispensable de ne faire aucun effort de pénétration, de compréhension?' [This poetry is difficult. And so what? Is it vital that we don't come up against any difficulty? Is it essential not to have to make any effort to get into the text, to understand it?].[11] As Lerner suggests, poetry, or 'poetic capacity' is available to any person willing to respond to a poem's appeal: 'you'. Roubaud asks his reader to invest in his poems and engage with the difficulty she encounters. If disorientation is part of the reading

10 Bosquet, 'Jacques Roubaud, ou la technique ennemie du poème', p. 16.

11 Roubaud, *Poésie, etcetera*, p. 264.

process, the reader must necessarily grapple with the work and find her own path through the text.

In his concern for the reader, Bosquet disagrees. He suggests a need for further clarification – 'un avant-propos ou une post-face' [a foreword or a postface] – an explanatory meta-text addressed to the reader, a user's guide to aid understanding of the poem, from beyond the limits of the poem itself. Roubaud's 'Poème de présentation' ['Presentation Poem'] playfully thwarts this request. The poet's dizzying play on personal pronouns and his ambiguity over the status of meaning and hearing in his repetition of 'entendre' [to hear / to mean / to understand] do anything but guide the reader towards a set interpretation of the volume. Instead, the poem emphasizes the place of the reader in directing the meaning of the text, if only she is willing to engage with the poem and remain open to its possibilities: 'ça signifiait | ce que moi je voulais di | sant cela de toi | que chacun entendait qui | l'entendait s'il voulait s'il || avait les oreilles | ouvertes cela que toi | tu entendais di | rigé vers toi dans le bruit de ces voyelles dislo || quées' [that meant | what I wanted say | ing that about you | that each person heard who | heard if he wanted if he || had his ears | open that which you | you heard dir | ected towards you in the sound of these dislo || cated vowels].[12] The poet's intentions coincide with the reader's understanding as 'ce que moi je voulais' [what I wanted] becomes 'cela que toi | tu entendais' [that which you | you heard]. The 'Poème de présentation' hints at fulfilling the meta-textual function suggested by its title, referring to the sound of its own dislocated vowels. However, it simultaneously undermines Bosquet's hopes for guidance by constantly echoing in its form the themes of disjointedness referred to in its content. For example, the dislocation of its syllables is manifested in the breaking up of the word 'dislo || quées' [dislo || cated] itself over the boundaries of a line. The presentational poem stubbornly reiterates the form that Bosquet so firmly critiques. The theme of meaning-making seems almost to be tossed around in the poem like a ball, alternately passed between poet, 'tu' [you], 'vous' [you (plural)] and 'elle' [she].

12 Roubaud, 'Poème de présentation', pp. 168–69.

Roubaud disorientates his reader throughout the 'Poème de présentation', but perhaps he also provides some form of 'Mode d'emploi' ['User's Guide'] for an approach to *Trente et un au cube* along the way. His stirring of confusion with personal pronouns, intensified by the unfamiliar metre that forces the pronouns to dance around unexpected breaks in syntax, requires a deeper sense of engagement from the reader: I find myself reading and re-reading the lines of the poem in an attempt to follow the intertwined pathways of the multiple addresses. For Stéphane Baquey, a text's form only exists when something in it resists a reading, causing hesitation or slowing down the reader: 'Pour que je perçoive une forme, il faut qu'un aspect d'une œuvre résiste à l'automatisme de ma lecture' [For me to notice a form, some aspect of the work has to resist the automatic nature of my reading].[13] In this sense the poem is a playful attempt on the part of the poet to pull the reader in deeper, to demand the 'effort de pénétration, de compréhension' [effort to get into the text, to understand it] Roubaud suggests have a place in poetry reading.[14]

While the pronouns of address constantly slip into one another, what remains is the prominence of 'toi' [you] as the space shared by lover and reader: 'et c'était tout ce | la que c'était toi partout | ici toi le tout | de toi et c'était cela que cela signifiait' [and it was all that | it was you everywhere | here you all | of you and that was what that meant].[15] For Puff, the alignment of lover and reader in *Trente et un au cube* relates to the poem's difficulty. As I mentioned in my Introduction, Puff explains that both the form and meaning of the book are an expression of Roubaud's theory of rhythm: 'Consubstantielle à la forme du poème, cette théorie en soutient aussi le sens. Cela exige une vraie lecture de la théorie *et* de la poésie, un investissement, intense, dans une complexité que le désir seul peut soutenir, le désir ou l'amour de la poésie' [An integral part of the poem's form, this theory also underpins its meaning. This requires a committed reading of the theory *and* the poetry, an intense investment in a complexity that only desire can maintain, desire or the love of poetry].[16] The level of commitment

13 Stéphane Baquey, 'En quoi un vers peut-il être une forme? (dans la poésie de Denis Roche)', *Formes poétiques Contemporaines*, 2 (2004), 263–74 (p. 263).

14 Roubaud, *Poésie, etcetera*, p. 264.

15 Roubaud, 'Poème de présentation', pp. 170–71.

16 Puff, 'Le déploiement du nouveau chez Roubaud', p. 100.

required of a reader of *Trente et un au cube* means she will necessarily be a lover of poetry; the difficulty of the text, Puff writes, is due to its technical make-up and the fact that its expression is composed formally of its theoretical foundation.

Roubaud goes a step further when he declares that all poetry is, in fact, difficult: 'La difficulté principale de la poésie aujourd'hui est qu'elle est poésie' [The main difficulty of poetry today is that it is poetry].[17] For Roubaud, the difficulty lies in the particular relation of meaning to form in poetry:

> S'il y a sens, c'est sens formel et effet intérieur de sens. Dans toute forme-poésie du présent, d'un type nouveau, il y a difficulté à saisir ce sens, à l'admettre, à le reconnaître parce qu'on est habitué (scolairement et idéologiquement habitué) à chercher autre chose, une des formes habituelles du sens.[18]
>
> [If there is meaning, it is in form and in the inner effects created. In every new type of poetry-form that comes out there is difficulty in grasping the meaning, in accepting it, in recognizing it, because we are used to (academically and ideologically used to) looking for something else, one of the usual forms of meaning.]

A poem's meaning is inseparable from its form, expressible only in that form; it cannot be paraphrased or explained, made simpler. Roubaud makes frequent mention of habits and familiarity in the passage: 'habitué' appears twice in the short extract to describe what readers are used to, 'habituelles' refers to our usual forms of meaning, or understanding, and 'nouveau' here does not signal innovation and the creativity of invention, but that which is strange, unfamiliar, foreign. Poetry is in many cases a departure from our everyday encounters with meaning: it differs from what a conversation might communicate, from what may be read in a newspaper, even from the poetry that readers will have become accustomed to during their schooldays, and therein lies its difficulty.

At the heart of this sense of 'difficulty' is Roubaud's theory of poetry as memory:

17 Roubaud, *Poésie, etcetera*, p. 269.

18 Roubaud, *Poésie, etcetera*, p. 270.

> L'accusation d'incompréhensibilité est associée de manière implicite à l'exigence de compréhension immédiate.
>
> Si la poésie est mémoire, agit sur la mémoire, il n'y a aucune raison que sa pénétration (donc sa compréhension) soit immédiate. Bien au contraire.
>
> [...]
>
> Dans la mémoire naît une compréhension irréfléchie, non traductible, non transmissible, de la poésie.[19]
>
> [The accusation of incomprehensibility is implicitly associated with the demand for immediate understanding.
>
> If poetry is memory, has an effect on memory, there is no reason why its penetration (thus its comprehension) would be immediate. Quite the contrary.
>
> [...]
>
> In memory an unthought-about understanding of poetry takes shape, one that is not transmissible or translatable.]

Poetry is not characterized by the immediate transparency associated with other forms of writing readers engage with regularly. For example, the clear message communicated by journalistic prose, or the suspense-filled syntax of a detective story. Time is the element which differentiates the meaning of poetry from other 'formes habituelles du sens' [usual forms of meaning]. Roubaud's reference to our ideological programming relates to our growing dislike of poetry in a world in which immediacy and convenience are increasingly prioritized – 'on est [...] idéologiquement habitué à chercher autre chose' [we are [...] ideologically used to looking for something else]. To appreciate or understand a poem's meaning, we must eschew our often cursory reading habits in favour of a reading which is slow, repeated, constantly re-thought.

This emphasis on a shift in reading patterns may be an intention of Roubaud's 'Poème de présentation'. The presentational poem's grammatical mobility confuses, slows down, even halts its reader, at times forcing her to go back and retrace her steps. The poem is demanding, requiring the time it takes for the poem and its novel rhythms to become familiar.

19 Roubaud, *Poésie, etcetera*, pp. 270–71.

However, the reader is perpetually alone in her search, for its outcome is an understanding that is 'non traductible, non transmissible' [not translatable, not transmissible]. Roubaud's conception of the comprehension of poetry through memory is not an understanding that comes through explanation or simplification. A poem grows for its reader over time through the resonances it creates and acquires; these are not secrets that can be passed on during a brief transaction.

If Roubaud's 'Poème de présentation' is in fact read as the 'Mode d'emploi' ['User's Guide'] that Bosquet desires, the reader can certainly glean an approach to *Trente et un au cube*. The first step is to embrace the position in the text offered to the reader and respond to the recurring pronoun 'toi' [you] in the 'Poème de présentation'. Through his ludic use of grammar, intermingled with the effects of form in the piece, Roubaud offers the opportunity for closer readings, constructing intricate, intertwining pathways and placing stumbling blocks that slow down the reader and entice her concentration, luring her into a close and active relationship with the text. Roubaud urges the reader to invest time in poetry, here in the individual text, but more generally in regular poetry reading, through which a single poem becomes part of a network of rhythms and poetic intertextuality.

Form: Structuring Reading in Space and Time

The emphasis of Roubaud's intentions regarding formal composition has seemed thus far to be concerned with time, but Bosquet presents his critique of Roubaud's *Trente et un au cube* as a difficult space to be navigated by the ill-equipped reader. Bosquet's double criticism of what he sees as 'la technique ennemie du poème' draws attention to the spatial features and object-like nature of *Trente et un au cube*: on the one hand, the missing user's guide from any cover of the volume, and on the other, the pages that unfold into a landscape format to reveal the extended width of the poems. The pages that fold out to reveal hidden poems are described quite literally as physical obstacles for the reader: 'Le deuxième obstacle est physique' [The second obstacle is physical]. It is an almost comically disproportionate complaint: unfolding the pages for a landscape reading of the book's poems is hardly a laborious task and may even be enjoyed by some for its novelty. It can feel a bit like being let in on a secret, opening out the sheet of a page where an angle remaining in the crease of its fold line creates an enclosure: the cube of the poem that accommodates the reader.

When Bosquet asks: 'Pourquoi le format du livre n'est-il pas en largeur pour permettre une lecture normale?' [Why is the book's format not of a width that would allow for a normal reading?], an immediate reaction might also be to question what constitutes 'une lecture normale' [a normal reading]. The implication is that reading should be physically comfortable and passive. Instead, an experience of reading *Trente et un au cube* is characterized by movement: the reader is active and the book itself is interactive. Each poem is more marked in its beginning and ending, as the reader opens out the page to experience it, and closes it away when it is finished. It makes of each poem a space and of reading a gesture; by unfolding the page, the reader enters into that space and, in a way, activates the poem.

In his 'Poème de présentation', Roubaud posits the book's physical format as the basis of a dialogue between himself and his reader: 'Ainsi cela re | venait de vous à moi de | ces feuilles multiples de | leurs rectangles pliés ou de | quelques oreilles rétine || enfoui cela | revenait jusqu'à moi: toi' [So it came | back from you to me from | these multiple sheets from | their folded rectangles or from | some ears retina || buried it | came back to me: you].[20] Though it is not a matter of a dialogue or conversation in any usual sense of communication, taking place 'en l'absence du | machin communicatoire' [in the absence of the | communicatory thing], the poet points out that the 'cela' [it] of the poem that begins 'Cela signifiait' [It meant] also moves in his direction from the place of the reader.[21] He encourages the reader to be active not only in facing the poem printed on the page, but also in listening to an oral presentation of it: 'vous pouviez ouvrir | les oreilles suivre du | doigt ce que cela | disait de toi l'entendre ou | le réfléchir mais toi? ||

20 Roubaud, 'Poème de présentation', pp. 170–71.

21 Roubaud, 'Poème de présentation', pp. 170–71.

et c'était tout ce | la que c'était toi partout | ici toi le tout | de toi et c'était cela | que cela signifiait' [you could open | your ears follow with | your finger what it | said about you hear it or | think it but you? || and that was all | that it was you everywhere | here you all | of you and that was | what it meant].[22] In Roubaud's 'Poème de présentation', everything comes down to 'toi' [you]: the pronoun of address that is ubiquitous in *Trente et un au cube*, addressing the reader who adds so much to the volume simply by bringing to it her singular experience and understanding, that which can be matched by no other reader. The poet's repetitions of 'toi' [you] are compounded by examples of assonance in 'doigt' [finger] and 'cela' [it / that]. His phonic play draws together the reader's concentration – she follows the words of the poem closely with her finger – and the piece itself – 'cela'. The reference to 'toi' [you] is an opening, a grammatical offering to the reader: an appeal for her to devote herself completely to the act of reading.

The description of the reader actively opening her ears, or following the words of the text with a finger across the page, a combination of hearing, seeing, reflecting and gesture, is similar to the memorable tribute to reading in Michel de Certeau's *L'Invention du quotidien* [*The Practice of Everyday Life*]: 'l'activité liseuse présente [...] tous les traits d'une production silencieuse: dérive à travers la page, métamorphose du texte par l'œil voyageur, [...] enjambements d'espaces écrits, danse éphémère' [the activity of reading has [...] all the characteristics of a silent production: the drift across the page, the metamorphosis of the text effected by the wandering eyes of the reader, [...] leaps over written spaces in an ephemeral dance].[23] Reading takes on the physicality of a dance, the engagement of the body in leaps across the written page. Of the reader, Certeau writes:

> Il insinue les ruses du plaisir et d'une réappropriation dans le texte de l'autre: il y braconne, il y est transporté, il s'y fait pluriel [...]. Ruse, métaphore, combinatoire, cette production est aussi une 'invention' de mémoire. Elle fait des mots les issues d'histoires muettes. Le lisible se change en mémorable.[24]

22 Roubaud, 'Poème de présentation', pp. 170–71.

23 Michel de Certeau, *L'Invention du quotidien: arts de faire* (Paris: Gallimard, 1990), p. XLIX. Michel de Certeau, *The Practice of Everyday Life*, trans. by Steven Rendall (Berkeley: University of California Press, 1984), p. XXI.

24 Certeau, *L'Invention du quotidien*, p. XLIX; *The Practice of Everyday Life*, p. XXI.

> [He insinuates into another person's text the ruses of pleasure and appropriation: he poaches on it, is transported into it, pluralizes himself in it [...]. Ruse, metaphor, arrangement, this production is also an 'invention' of the memory. Words become the outlet or product of silent histories. The readable transforms itself into the memorable.]

The reader brings her life experiences to a text and thus participates in it. Memory creates pockets of recognition: spaces activated by the formation of associations, recollections. Reading appropriates space just as writing does: 'La mince pellicule de l'écrit devient un remuement de strates, un jeu d'espaces. Un monde différent (celui du lecteur) s'introduit dans la place de l'auteur' [The thin film of writing becomes a movement of strata, a play of spaces. A different world (the reader's) slips into the author's place].[25] Certeau draws an analogy between the space of the text and that of an apartment: 'Cette mutation rend le texte habitable à la manière d'un appartement loué. Elle transforme la propriété de l'autre en lieu emprunté, un moment, par un passant. Les locataires opèrent une mutation semblable dans l'appartement qu'ils meublent de leurs gestes et de leurs souvenirs' [This mutation makes the text habitable, like a rented apartment. It transforms another person's property into a space borrowed for a moment by a transcient. Renters make comparable changes in an apartment they furnish with their acts and memories].[26] The act of reading, for Certeau, is about those moments that the reader can make her own, by taking in a text through her particular understanding, shaped by her experiences and memories. His metaphor of the text as habitable, like a rented apartment, encourages an understanding of writing as a space with flexible borders: a malleable shape that expands to allow the reader's recollections, additions and elaborations to build on the text. The text before the reader ignites memories, which are used to cultivate a familiarity with that text, letting her into its space.

The reader of *Trente et un au cube* is coaxed into various literal spaces encompassed by the volume. Roubaud's reflection on the dimensions of the page, for example, coincides with the intimacy of the moment in

25 Certeau, *L'Invention du quotidien*, p. XLIX; *The Practice of Everyday Life*, p. XXI.
26 Certeau, *L'Invention du quotidien*, p. XLIX; *The Practice of Everyday Life*, p. XXI.

which he writes: '(car ma dame | est si profondément en- || dormie) j'écris silencieusement sur ma feuille | 21 × 27 | dans la jaune lumière' [(for my lady | sleeps so | deeply) I write silently on my page | 21 × 27 | in the yellow light].[27] In the same poem, Roubaud signals his specific place in the composition process: 'le papier [...] se remplit || presque entièrement' [the paper [...] is almost || completely filled].[28] This sense of the approaching end is fulfilled in the final poem, where Roubaud observes (in the same central position on the page in which the earlier reference to the dimensions '21 × 27' appears) the shrinking space of the page before him: 'j'ai vu raccourcir devant moi l'espace de blanc étale entre | le front avancé des lettres || dans la transcription | de ce poème et le butoir de sa dernière | feuille tout s'est recouvert | de la terre de la nuit' [I saw shrinking before me the space of white remaining between | the start overripe with letters || in the transcription | of this poem and the end of its last | sheet everything is covered | in earth in night].[29] It is not only his page that gradually fills with the lettering of the poem, but the allocation of sheets set out for the manuscript of the entire book that comes to its 'butoir' [end / stop].

The close of the last poem announces its own overlapping with the book's start in 's'est recouvert' [is covered / overlapped], before leading into two final verses which are largely a repetition of the very first two in the book, starting once again at the beginning with: 'je détiens million | de syllabes comptées pour | toi' [I keep a million | syllables counted out for | you].[30] This circular structure of *Trente et un au cube* thus introduces a sense of *déjà vu* into the text, its end echoing its beginning. It is true, as Thomas and Winspur write, that 'the repetition reinforces the finite nature of the text, as if the book were framed by parentheses'.[31] There is the sense that the book's structure has been conceived in its entirety before the poet begins to set ink to paper. The writer knows where his writing will end, he feels the approach of its final page as though it has already been seen.

27 Roubaud, *Trente et un au cube*, p. 21.
28 Roubaud, *Trente et un au cube*, p. 21.
29 Roubaud, *Trente et un au cube*, p. 129.
30 Roubaud, *Trente et un au cube*, p. 129.
31 Thomas and Winspur, *Poeticized Language*, p. 181.

Each time that the poet signals his place in the construction of the volume, whether he is approaching the bottom of the page, or the last leaf of the book, he creates a shared space for himself and his reader. The reader's eyes reach the end of a poem's page at the same time as the poet's pen; the reader's fingers feel the sparseness of the pages remaining as she reaches the last few poems of the volume. Each reading is a reactivation of the memory of composition. The space of the book is underpinned by the compositional features arising from its numerical foundation, which act as milestones that situate the reader. The *tanka* pattern that permeates every layer of the book creates a sense of familiarity for the reader, who can navigate her way through the poems accordingly: the numbered sections signal the reader's position in relation to the whole volume, and also in relation to the smaller groupings of five and seven poems that make up the overall sequence.

The pattern underpinning the structural foundation of *Trente et un au cube* also extends to the spatio-temporal metaphor on which the volume is constructed. The book's finite structure replicates the totality of a year, signalled in the final poem: 'UNE ANNÉE FINIT [...] une année comparse de la mémoire' [ONE YEAR ENDS [...] one year sidekick of memory].[32] Roubaud's notes on the composition of *Trente et un au cube* also give a year for the period of composition: 'Composé de juillet 1971 à juin 1972' [Composed from July 1971 to June 1972].[33] Whether or not this is accepted as fact, a reader of the volume can trace the shifting seasons through the piece, in a further nod to the Japanese poetry anthologies which would use seasonal motifs to guide the reader from one section to the next and which served as a source of inspiration for this text. The book opens in summer sun and birdsong, 'dans le soleil orange un | oiseau acéré' [in the orange sun a | shrill bird].[34] The reader journeys through the autumn months, 'dans ce | jardin d'automne' [in this | autumn garden], with their fiery shading, 'le feu est cyprès | est saule rouge' [the fire is cypress | is red willow], and gusty showers 'c'était un jardin | que le vent affamé a- || percevait de loin

32 Roubaud, *Trente et un au cube*, p. 129.

33 Roubaud, *Description du projet*, p. 77.

34 Roubaud, *Trente et un au cube*, p. 13.

| le trempant d'eau' [it was a garden | the hungry wind caught || sight of from afar | soaking it in water].[35] She then must survive the winter frost, 'dans cette ville | glaciale' [in this glacial | town] and the melting away of the leaves, 'où des | feuilles tombaient || sur moi dans le noir' [where the | leaves were falling || on me in the dark].[36] Finally, the reader emerges again in summer, among 'belles | nappes de coquelicots' [beautiful | blankets of poppies].[37] On a spatial level, the book is posited as cube: the book's title is reflected visually in the squaring of its unfolding pages, and semantically in the repeated references to the poem itself as 'ce cube' [this cube].[38] This volume alternately figures in the poems as garden, or bedroom, spaces equated in troubadour poetry, where new love and desire are figured as the sweet blossoming of spring.[39]

The book thus lends itself to interaction with memory, offering spaces and temporal markings in which to invest our own recollections and evocations, but also providing markers for the reader to remember elements of the text. After finishing *Trente et un au cube*, features of its structure inevitably stay with the reader: its numbering, its circularity, its rolling seasons. As in Certeau's ' "invention" de mémoire' ['invention' of memory], the act of reading elicits meaning from the stores of individual memory, 'acts and memories' which then 'furnish' or inhabit the space of the text. Perhaps the temporal and spatial structures underpinning *Trente et un au cube* may also be compared to the memory palaces and theatres explored in Frances Yates' influential study, *The Art of Memory*. In the eras she discusses, from the classical period through to the Renaissance, the memory palace or theatre is a mnemonic system in which memory recall is associated with an often imagined locus or location. As Simon Critchley writes in his recent reflection on the art of the memory theatre: 'The time of speech could be mastered by the spatial recollections of *loci*, of *topoi*. One would walk around in one's memory as if in a building or, better, storehouse, inspecting

35 Roubaud, *Trente et un au cube*, p. 37.

36 Roubaud, *Trente et un au cube*, p. 77.

37 Roubaud, *Trente et un au cube*, p. 129.

38 For example, Roubaud, *Trente et un au cube*, p. 69.

39 See Jacques Roubaud, *Les Troubadours: Anthologie bilingue*, p. 6 for Roubaud's comment on this troubadour concept.

the objects therein.'[40] The text is at once a space to be filled with the evocations that are conjured up in a reader's memory, and conversely the text conceived of as a spatially organized system facilitates its assimilation in the reader's mind, becoming an imagined room to be perused at leisure.

The architecture of *Trente et un au cube* encompasses patterns carved in space as well as time; these stimulate associations and also become entangled in the reader's memory. Within these patterns of *Trente et un au cube,* there are points at which references to the material space of the book coincide with the time of its writing, bringing together the reader and poet. It is as though the book's composition is re-enacted on every reading, giving me the sense that I am present in the writing process, given a privileged position in relation to meaning-making in the poems. The book is the space of the cube that envelops the reader and her awareness of time passing: the year that it took to write mirrored in the imagery that gives away the changing seasons.

What though is the relation of form to the poet's lover in *Trente et un au cube* and what more can we learn about the reader's position from this? Close readings of the book's central poem will be my first step towards answering these questions, since it is at the centre of the volume – the volume as the book in the hands of the reader and as the metaphorical cube that the book stands for – that the struggle between the poet and his beloved, between form and love takes place.

The Centre of the Cube: The Beloved

The poet's lover and the numerical sequence that structures the composition of *Trente et un au cube* come together in a climactic encounter in the volume's central poem. The opening incipit posits the female as the structural centre of the cube: 'TE VOICI LE CENTRE: | tu es la seizième lame | de ce cube' [HERE YOU ARE THE CENTRE: | you are the sixteenth edge |

40 Simon Critchley, *Memory Theatre* (London: Fitzcarraldo Editions, 2014), p. 19.

of this cube].[41] Accorded this central position in terms of the geometry of the cube, her presence is structurally pivotal to the book's form. At the centre of the material volume in the reader's hands, poem 16 is the halfway point in the book's thirty-one poems. Visually and formally poem 16 is itself set apart from the rest of the volume, consisting of two large strophes, although the division of the poem into seventeen and fourteen lines, respectively, means that the tanka pattern of 5-7-5 (-) 7-7 still underlies this piece. These strophes are separated by a large white space across the centre of the page. A paradox in the poem's form becomes apparent: while the feminine is addressed in the poem's opening as the sixteenth edge of the book's cubic space, the layout of the page positions her at – or as – its centre, in the space of silence which divides the page.[42]

The poet places his lover in a structural relation to poetic form, citing her position simultaneously as the cube's centremost edge and the space of its centre, but there is also a thematic dimension to the portrayal of space in poem 16. Puff has drawn links between the cubic patterns of *Trente et un au cube* and the bedroom the poet shares with his lover: the etymology of *stanza* intersects the poem both with *chambre* [bedroom] (a material space) and with *strophe* (a prosodic one).[43] The two verses recount a physical, almost violent struggle between the poet and his lover as he attempts to define her position in this poem, to contain her within its boundaries.

A further overlap in the poem's thematic and formal layers occurs in the coincidence of lover and poem in the address, 'tu' [you]. The statement 'tu es la seizième lame | de ce cube' [you are the sixteenth edge | of this cube] addresses the sixteenth poem itself, in addition to the feminine lover who is always somewhere behind that intimate second-person address. Although Roubaud's enthusiasm for the troubadour *canso* has shown that the alignment of poem and lover was in one sense a metaphoric reference to the praise and admiration – the *pretz* – that inspired the expression of love

41 All further references to Roubaud's *Trente et un au cube* in this section are to its central poem, p. 69.

42 The reference to the book's 'cubic space' refers at once to the pseudo-mathematical cubic pattern underlying *Trente et un au cube*, and to the metaphoric space of the cube Roubaud constructs by reference to it.

43 Puff, *Mémoire de la mémoire*, p. 463.

for the lady, in this particular poem, the narrator emphasizes the singular correspondence between his love object and the poem's formal structure.

This central poem of *Trente et un au cube* opens with the poet endeavouring to fix his lover on the page: 'TE VOICI LE CENTRE: | tu es la seizième lame | de ce cube tu | ne bougeras pas pendant | que je te fixe ailes bleues || vertes rouges ma | sauterelle très courtoise | tu ne froisseras | pas cette feuille pendant | que je te cloue' [HERE YOU ARE THE CENTRE: | you are the sixteenth edge | of this cube you | will not move while | I fix you blue green || red wings my | very courteous grasshopper | you will not crumple | this sheet while | I nail you down]. The spaces of the poem, the material book and the lovers' bedroom converge in the unrealizable image of the poet attempting to contain the lover within the page. She is transformed into a grasshopper pinned to the sheet of the poem, calling to mind display cases of captured, lifeless butterflies: she is both courteous and courtly lady, not threatening to disturb the sheet of paper on which the poem is written. Yet from the stillness of her entrapped wings emanates a defiant and dazzling array of colours. Despite the sense of vulnerability in the beloved's metamorphosis into a small insect, and structurally trapped as she is in this cubic space constructed by the poet, there is a sense that her creaturely transformation also allows her to elude his wish to pin her down.

The more the poet persists in his efforts to constrain the winged creature, the more her form continues to be foregrounded: 'tu | seras le centre fixée | comme d'une grande aiguille || entre jaunes bleues | vertes et rouges tes ailes | bien définie par | tes paramètres' [you | will be the centre fixed | as though with a great needle || between yellow blue | green and red your wings | well defined by | your parametres]. In the background, her wings issue an illuminating multitude of bright colours, eluding the poet's grasp through their constant transformation. However, the emphasis on the poet's force has shifted from the earlier line: 'je te fixe' [I fix you] and 'je te cloue' [I nail you down] are replaced by 'tu | seras le centre fixée' [you | will be the centre fixed], removing the poet-subject from the image. Her prison is no longer 'cette feuille' [this sheet], the page of the poem. Instead, her own physical contours are described in terms of limit, or restraint, through use of the word 'paramètres' [parametres], and it is she who incorporates them.

At the same time, her clear definition and outlines make her more accessible to the touch of the poet: 'mes doigts détiennent | l'arc de ton contour | mes doigts silencieusement | révisent la ligne douce || de tes genoux quelque | muscle a bougé pendant la | nuit quelque fumée | s'est engourdie dans tes bras | et je déplace un très peu ||| ton axe nocturne' [my fingers hold | the arc of your outline | my fingers silently | revise the soft line || of your knees some | muscle moved during the | night some smoke | went to sleep in your arms | and I move your nocturnal centre ||| just a touch]. The image is characterized by a stillness so intense that even the slightest movements are notable: the displacement of a muscle overnight, the position of her knees. A sense of intimacy grows in this stillness and the quiet, the feminine's susceptibility to his touch so great that the poet's fingers are able to nudge her body from its own centre. There is sensuality in the physical encounter, but it seems that for the poet-lover to touch her body is simultaneously for him to possess it, to alter it with his fingers.

In some way, this image of the poet re-shaping the feminine form resembles the method of touch Irigaray criticizes for making of the beloved a direct object – 'appropriation, capture, séduction – à moi, vers moi, en moi' [appropriation, capture, seduction – to me, towards me, in me] – so much so that the object becomes alienated from her own being: 'arracher l'autre à son intimité ou intériorité à soi, à sa temporalité [...] le/la faire retomber dans l'immédiateté naturelle d'un toucher simple' [tearing the other from his or her self-intimacy or interiority, from his or her temporality [...] making him/her fall back into the natural immediacy of a simple touch].[44] Like Irigaray's alienating subject, the poet alters feminine being, ever so slightly shifting her place within the night. For both writers, the encroachment of the lover's caress is described in metaphors evoking time: Irigaray refers to touch as stealing the other from their 'temporality', while Roubaud's 'axe nocturne' [nocturnal centre] also evokes the rotation of the earth on its axis, the passing of time, the fading of night into day. The effect is one of displacement; a touch that objectifies the other in seeking pleasure for the self violates the body of the beloved, stealing it away from its centre.

44 Luce Irigaray, *J'aime à toi* (Paris: Grasset, 1992), p. 194.

Perhaps the poet's words are an impossible attempt to still the night and hold the fleeting intimacy and desire forever. He captures the moment in his poem of those nights that too easily slip away into day, but at every re-reading something shifts, the present of the moment cannot be held still. Whether a reference to the elusiveness of time, or the impossible possession of the beloved herself, the object of the poet's touch – 'ton axe nocturne' [your nocturnal centre] – remains at a remove, separated from his fingers by the large blank space dividing the two stanzas that compose this central piece. There is a discrepancy between the poet's possessive touch of his lover in the semantic expression of the poem and the structural layout of the words on the page, which divides him from her and resists the words of the piece.

In *Trente et un au cube*, Roubaud attempts to demarcate the spaces in and of his poem, whose definition overlaps with that of his feminine addressee, but in this climactic centrepiece, she eludes his attempt at categorization. The poet predicts that his lover will rise up and break free of the poem's hold: 'sans doute dans un moment || tu te lèveras | sans effort tu briseras | le temps coagulé | autour de toi dans ces mots [...] annihilant tout effort | de définition sans doute || t'échapperas-tu | très vite de cette feuille | cependant tu restes | en même temps séparée | en même temps retenue' [doubtless any moment now || you will rise up | with no effort you will break | the time coagulated | around you in these words [...] destroying any attempt | at definition doubtless || you will escape | this sheet with haste | yet you stay | at once distanced | at once held back]. The series of verbs in the future tense, 'tu te lèveras' [you will rise up], 'tu briseras' [you will break], and 't'échapperas-tu' [you will escape] drills in a sense of resolve, denoting her inevitable future escape. She will break through the rhythms that surround her, flee the sheet of paper to which she is attached like the winged grasshopper, evading the poet's definition of her. The poet pins her into the sixteenth edge of the cube, but her transformation means she eludes his capture. In the imagery of the poem, the poet expresses control over the centre of her being, but the blank space across the page structurally distances his touch.

Oscillating between imprisonment within the cube and existing as the structure itself, at once captured and elusive in imagery that is both beautiful and troubling, the reader is never sure what to make of her presence. For

Elisabeth Cardonne-Arlyck, the addressee's metamorphosis into a grasshopper and the ensuing struggle is a metaphoric sign of the instability of the love-language-poetry triad that is the foundation of Roubaud's theory of poetry.[45] She explains that the indefinability of the feminine presence means that neither love nor poetry can be pinned down definitively, thus creating a sense of fragility in both the relationship with the beloved and the poetry addressed to her.[46] The central poem of *Trente et un au cube* therefore betrays the discrepancy between the fictional attempt of the poet to secure his love within the words of his poem, and the real impossibility of holding onto her beyond that poem.[47]

Jean-François Puff sees in *Trente et un au cube* the poet's impulse to establish a dialogue: the opening 'je' [I] posits the existence of an addressee, or 'tu' [you].[48] For Puff, the risk faced by the poem is in the failure of this dialogue; if address subjectivizes language, both the poem and poet face oblivion if nobody is there to hear or read its lines.[49] Puff explains this dialogue in terms of 'une postulation en attente de réalisation pleine' [a postulation awaiting full realization],[50] rather than a matter of transparency on the modern model of communication: 'non pas transparence sur le modèle de la communication moderne' [not transparency according to the model of modern communication].[51] He writes: 'dans l'entrelacement du même et du différent, la différence se manifeste fortement comme telle, au risque de rompre le lien, et de renvoyer la voix-guide au soliloque qui toujours la guette' [in the intertwining of the same and the different, difference is manifested strongly as such, at the risk of breaking the link and sending the guiding voice into the soliloquy that forever threatens it].[52] Even if Roubaud's cube is constructed to the most precise of syllabic dimensions,

45 Cardonne-Arlyck, *Véracités*, p. 236.
46 Cardonne-Arlyck, *Véracités*, p. 236.
47 Cardonne-Arlyck, *Véracités*, p. 235.
48 Puff, *Mémoire de la mémoire*, p. 414.
49 Puff, *Mémoire de la mémoire*, p. 415.
50 Puff, *Mémoire de la mémoire*, p. 421.
51 Puff, *Mémoire de la mémoire*, p. 415.
52 Puff, *Mémoire de la mémoire*, p. 421.

the other to whom the poem is addressed ultimately has the freedom not to engage with the poem or the symbolic significance of its form.

Puff also explores Roubaud's references to catastrophe theory in this central poem, comparing the cube evoked to the space of the 'boîte noire' [black box].[53] Puff describes catastrophe theory as the analysis of a sudden change, or leap – *le 'saut'* – in the behaviour of a system, due to continuous changes in one or more of the variables that control it.[54] Operating via a series of inputs and outputs, the 'black box' too records abrupt change, or 'catastrophe'. For Puff, in Roubaud's poem the box becomes a sign of the poet's desire to possess the lover: 'l'espace dans lequel le poète engage tout un effort de détermination, qui vise à la possession par le calcul des paramètres de la substance et du changement de la *dona*' [the space in which the poet makes every effort to reach a definition, one which aims to possess her through the calculation of the parametres of the *dona*'s substance and her change].[55] However, just as Cardonne-Arlyck finds that the poem speaks of its own fiction, Puff too distinguishes the space of the poem from the reality in which the reader is situated:

> Le poème manifeste [...] un exercice singulier de la *mezura*: où la forme prend modèle sur une théorie qui vise à la détermination de ce qui auparavant échappait au calcul. Il s'agit de faire en sorte que la *dona* soit prise dans le poème, abstraite en images et en valeurs rythmiques, et s'offre ainsi à l'organisation d'ensemble qui vise à reconfigurer le temps. La tentative se sait vouée à l'échec: on ne vit pas dans le temps du poème. Pourtant quelque chose y subsiste, quelque chose mis en mémoire.[56]
>
> [The poem demonstrates [...] a singular exercise in *mezura*: where form is modelled on a theory which aims to determine that which previously eluded calculation. It is about making sure that the *dona* is captured in

53 Puff, *Mémoire de la mémoire*, p. 464. Roubaud cites René Thom as one of the influences for poem 16 in his list of 'Remerciements', *Trente et un au cube*, p. 131. Thom was a mathematician well known for his work modelling sudden behavioural changes.

54 For Puff's summary of catastrophe theory, see his *Mémoire de la mémoire*, pp. 463–64. In his outline of the theory, Puff refers to a passage from René Thom's *Paraboles et catastrophes* (Paris: Flammarion, 1983), p. 60.

55 Puff, *Mémoire de la mémoire*, p. 463.

56 Puff, *Mémoire de la mémoire*, p. 464.

> the poem, abstracted in images and rhythmic values, and it lends itself to an overall organization that aims to reconfigure time. The attempt is doomed to failure from the outset: we do not live in the time of the poem. Yet something remains, something held in memory.]

Roubaud's use of form, in particular the rhythm it produces, is likened to the quantifying of that which was previously deemed incalculable. Roubaud applies René Thom's model for measuring abrupt behavioural changes to his expression of love: form appears as an impossible attempt to capture the beloved in time. However, the black box is also a recording instrument, and its rendering of events, no matter how far they stray from continuity, can only be a recording of that event – 'quelque chose mis en mémoire' [something held in memory].

The uncertainty of the addressee's involvement and the distance separating the reader from the fictional space of the poem inform the readings of Cardonne-Arlyck and Puff. Both draw on Roubaud's elaboration of the particular *néant* [nothingness] threatening troubadour love poetry and implicating the reader-beloved to whom the poem is addressed: the *néant* threatens both the poet's verse in its structural life and his love. The reader may not engage with the lines offered by the poet, leaving his poetry redundant and empty of meaning. At the level of the expression of love held in the poetic address, if the beloved turns out not to return the love of the poet, the result may send him into a fatal state of melancholia. An excess of desire or an overwhelming sense of jealousy then threaten to turn his love into madness and, in turn, his verses into collapse.[57]

The troubadour concept of *mezura*, within which Puff inscribes the central poem of *Trente et un au cube*, is the safeguard against this threat. The poet describes its dual powers of resistance in love and troubadour poetry: 'le même mot, *mezura*, désigne à la fois le concept clef de la résistance de l'amour à la force de destruction du "néant" et l'enfermement des mots

57 Roubaud summarizes the link between 'jalousie, effort de possession absolue de la dame' [jealousy, attempt to fully possess the lady] and 'la folie et la mort' [madness and death] represented by 'l'*eros mélancolique*' [the *melancholic eros*] in the introduction to his anthology *Les Troubadours*, p. 18. For a more detailed investigation of Roubaud's interpretation of *eros mélancolique* in troubadour literature see Roubaud's *Fleur inverse*, pp. 86–91 and pp. 94–95.

et des rimes dans les unités proprement indestructibles du vers, de la cobla et de la canso' [the same word, *mezura*, designates both the key concept of love's resistance of the destructive force of the '*néant*' and the enclosure of words and rhymes in the absolutely indestructible units of the poetic line, the *cobla* and the *canso*].[58] It is a stance in love; a defence against its excesses and the obscure forces that lie in wait behind its joy. Roubaud places his *mezura* in the space between two threats to love: 'l'insignifiance' [insignificance], when love is unrequited, and its opposite excess, 'l'insupportable' [the unbearable].

The troubadour *mezura* is also, for Roubaud, a linguistic concept. For the troubadours, Roubaud explains that the *canso* was a necessary way of maintaining unity and intactness of language against what he calls 'la dissolution dans l'étranger ou le dialecte' [dissolution through the use of foreign language or dialect].[59] The poet uses lexis of defence and security when describing the function of *mezura* in verse, writing of 'enfermement' [enclosure], and 'unités proprement indestructibles' [absolutely indestructible units]. Language is tightly secured, respectively, by the metrical units of the line ('vers'), stanza ('cobla'), and poem (the troubadour 'canso'). The layering of form in the respective units of the poem's structure emphasizes the sense that language is protected within multiple interlocking barriers. This description of *mezura* also resonates with the architecture of *Trente et un au cube*, whose *tanka* pattern of 5-7-5-7-7 makes a unit of each line, stanza, poem and the volume as a whole.

Yet at the centremost point of *Trente et un au cube*, rather than the stronghold of *mezura* described in Roubaud's writings, poem 16 reveals its own fragility and uncertainty. Roubaud's central poem reflects on its own future impossibility, its failure: his lover's escape. While trying desperately to hold onto her, the threat of her disappearance keeps her forever at a remove and the resistance of the poet's addressee arises from within the very arrangement that structures the poem. The echoes of ambiguity that ripple out from the centre of the poem's structure to the words at the poem's edges have the effect of creating whispers: for every attempt to define and re-form the beloved, there is a reference to the possibility of her escape,

58 Roubaud, *La Fleur inverse*, p. 287.
59 Roubaud, *La Fleur inverse*, p. 286.

her elusiveness, her invisibility, her enigmatic place in the structure that seeks to define her. *Trente et un au cube* holds a contradiction at its centre which is impossible to resolve. The central place of the feminine in the construction of the poem, and indeed in the volume as a whole, is asserted at repeated instances throughout the two large verses that make up poem 16. She is not simply the image of a love object trapped inside the space of a prison created by her poet, rather she exists as part of the structure itself.

From the outset, the poet aligns her with the edge of the cube: its walls, not its enclosed space. Her central position in the cube is projected into the future in poem 16: 'tu | seras le centre fixée | comme d'une grande aiguille' [you | will be the centre fixed | as though with a great needle]. The poet even insists on her pivotal position in the book's structure against all odds: '(dans cette boîte un | champ de possibles, je dois | t'en séparer pour | que tu sois le centre pur | de ce cube) tu es *centre* || *mobile*' [(in this box a | field of possibilities, I must | divide you from them so | that you may be the pure centre | of this cube) you are its *mobile* || *centre*]. In his final reiteration of her structural centrality, the poet states: 'tu es le centre | de ce cube construit pour | toi' [you are the centre | of this cube built for | you]. In this last reference to her central place in the cube, the poet eliminates any traces of entrapment, regarding the poem's cubic walls as an offering to his love. There is a contradiction in making her the form of the poem, ascribing to its boundaries the curves of her body, and simultaneously attempting to contain her within its cubic dimensions. Her struggle to escape the grasp of the poet takes place at the nexus of the volume in poem 16, but the very possibility of her freedom also lies in her position in its opening words: 'TE VOICI LE CENTRE: | tu es la seizième lame | de ce cube' [HERE YOU ARE THE CENTRE: | you are the sixteenth edge | of this cube]. She cannot remain captured in a structure whose edges coincide with the lines of her own contours.

The Blind Spot in Set Theory: Lacan, Irigaray and Roubaud

Poem 16 brings into play the dynamics between the poet and his beloved: the message of the poem raises the questions of the nature of the poetic muse. The familiar structure of the relation that sees the muse imprisoned within the rhetoric of the male poet is one that we have seen is criticized by Irigaray. She writes of the 'métaphores, survalorisantes ou dénigrantes' [eulogistic or denigratory metaphors], 'tropes' [tropes] and 'chevaleresques oripeaux' [chivalric finery] that the poet uses to portray the feminine in poetry; whether he flatters or chastises the woman that is the object of his writings, his words place her at a remove from herself, 'revêtements' [wrappings], and 'déguisements' [disguise].[60]

Irigaray's criticism is a metaphor for the male psychoanalyst, who writes the feminine into his theory. In *Speculum de l'autre femme*, Irigaray in turn places Freud and Lacan at the heart of their own theories, deconstructing what she understands to be their patriarchal descriptions of the feminine and turning the texts in psychoanalytic theory against their writers. When Irigaray writes of the poet-psychoanalyst that he captures the feminine within 'couches de style ornamental' [layers of ornamental style], a 'sépulture décorative, où elle perd jusqu'à son souffle' [decorative sepulchre, where even her breath is lost], Roubaud's reader might think of the dazzling array of colour pinned into the centre of *Trente et un au cube*.[61] Roubaud's creation of a cube in poetry, his layers of numerical patterning, are presented by the poet himself as an attempt to capture his love therein, an ill-fated wish to possess his beloved and hold her indefinitely in the present moment.

The project of *Speculum de l'autre femme* is encapsulated in the multiple resonances of its title. Through a series of essays presented as readings of texts from Western philosophy, culture and psychoanalysis, Irigaray explores the representation of woman as 'other' to a central male term. She clarifies the possibilities of her title years later, explaining that it might be less ambiguously understood if it were punctuated thus: '*Speculum, De l'autre: femme*' [*Speculum, Of the other: woman*].[62] Her book is an exploration of the 'other', insofar as that 'other' is 'woman'. The title does not, as has often been misconstrued, refer to the second of two women, or the mirror reflection of the author herself, for as Irigaray probes: 'Qui serait

60 Irigaray, *Speculum de l'autre femme*, p. 177; *Speculum of the Other Woman*, pp. 142–43.

61 Irigaray, *Speculum de l'autre femme*, p. 177; *Speculum of the Other Woman*, p. 143.

62 Irigaray, *J'aime à toi*, p. 102.

l'autre femme puisque le générique féminin n'existe pas encore comme représentation ou contenu d'idéalité pour la femme?' [Who would the other woman be if the feminine generic still does not exist as representation or as content of an ideality for woman?].[63] Her writing in *Speculum* deals with the idea that there is no specific conception of 'woman', no 'représentation ou contenu d'idéalité pour la femme' [representation or content of ideality for woman]. Feminine presence in psychoanalysis is instead drawn into the theory simply as the other of the masculine term, what Irigaray calls 'ce redoublement spéculaire' [this specular duplication].[64] Irigaray's title insists that this alterity be positively constructed and that the 'other' be considered for what it specifically represents.[65]

Irigaray's explanation encompasses a consideration of what is possibly the key term in her title, '*Speculum*':

> ce terme est utilisé, à une époque plus ancienne de notre culture, pour désigner l'expression la plus fidèle possible de la réalité. *Speculum mundi*, par exemple, est un titre qui a été fréquent et auquel j'ai pensé. Il signifie miroir du monde non tant comme reflet du monde grâce à un miroir mais plutôt comme pensée de la réalité ou de l'objectivité du monde à travers un discours.[66]
>
> [this term was used, in a more ancient period of our culture, to designate the most faithful possible expression of reality. *Speculum mundi*, for example, was a common title and one I thought about. It means mirror of the world, not so much as a reflection of the world in a mirror, but rather as thought of the reality or the objectivity of the world through a discourse.]

The definition inserts a layer of remove between the various texts that Irigaray responds to and 'la réalité' [the reality] or 'l'objectivité du monde' [the objectivity of the world]. Treating the theories that she deals with as speculative rather than objective is what allows Irigaray first to deconstruct them as discourses, second, to explore the scope within them for the possibility of an alternative, or even opposing view. The speculative

63 Irigaray, *J'aime à toi*, p. 103.
64 Irigaray, *Speculum de l'autre femme*, p. 63; *Speculum of the Other Woman*, p. 54.
65 Irigaray, *J'aime à toi*, pp. 103–04.
66 Irigaray, *J'aime à toi*, pp. 101–02.

root of *Speculum* is therefore offered by Irigaray as the most important meaning of the word for the purpose of her writing in the book. However, its alternative denotation of a gynaecological instrument is perhaps the most recognizable or obvious meaning of the word, particularly in the context of the opening section of *Speculum de l'autre femme*: an extended re-reading of Freud's essay 'Femininity' and his other writings on women. In this particular context, the '*Speculum*' of Irigaray's title is an effort to achieve a vision that takes into account the '*forme*' [form] of femininity.[67] The suggestion is that the problematic 'blind spot' in Freud's theory of castration – the '*rien à voir*' [nothing to see] that characterizes the female sex in relation to the male in his essay – may be eliminated with an approach that considers the specificity of femininity, rather than its difference from (which is ironically also a reflection of) the central masculine term.[68]

In his re-reading of Freud's theory of femininity, Lacan shifts the emphasis away from biologically orientated definitions. Bruce Fink writes of '*formalization without mathematization*' in Lacan's approach to psychoanalytic teaching.[69] The psychoanalyst's provision of symbols – which he refers to as mathemes – plays an important role in summarizing psychoanalytic theory, but Lacan himself explains: 'Le truc analytique ne sera pas mathématique' [The analytic thing will not be mathematical].[70] Fink explains that formalization in the work of Lacan is a move towards 'scientificity', rather than 'measurement'.[71] Fink gives the example of physics to outline the benefits of this approach:

> formalization allowed theorists an independent field of speculation: one could play with the formulas themselves and work out all of their interrelations, without having the slightest idea what the new configurations meant or implied. One could make certain assumptions not because they made any sort of intuitive sense but simply

67 Irigaray, *Speculum de l'autre femme*, p. 54; *Speculum of the Other Woman*, p. 48.

68 Irigaray, *Speculum de l'autre femme*, p. 53; *Speculum of the Other Woman*, p. 47.

69 Bruce Fink, 'Knowledge and Jouissance', in *Reading Seminar XX: Lacan's Major Work on Love, Knowledge, and Feminine Sexuality*, ed. by Suzanne Barnard and Bruce Fink (New York: SUNY, 2002), pp. 21–45 (p. 33).

70 Lacan, *Encore*, p. 105. Lacan, *On Feminine Sexuality*, p. 117.

71 Fink, 'Knowledge and Jouissance', p. 32.

> because they simplified equations; those assumptions could then be tested through experimentation.[72]

Fink's explanation implies that formalization provided a certain level of abstraction, which meant that possibilities in scientific discovery could reach beyond a logic structured by intuition.

Fink concedes that formalization in psychoanalysis is still far from providing an independent basis for theorization in the field, pointing out the prevalence of reading and writing in Lacanian psychoanalysis:

> we see a kind of 'fetishization' of the text, so to speak: [...] an approach to reading Freud's and other texts (e.g., Poe's 'The Purloined Letter') that has spurred great interest in the humanities and in literary criticism in particular and [...] an attention to writing that seeks to have effects on the reader that imply anything but the direct transmission of formulas and mathematically precise equations.[73]

This is clear, for example, in Lacan's presentation of his psychoanalysis as a return to Freud. It is rather, as Elizabeth Grosz puts it, Lacan's work 'produces a certain Freud'; Lacan *re*reads Freud's texts, even re*writes* them on some level.[74] It is necessary to know Freud's texts in some detail before approaching a Lacanian reading, since the French psychoanalyst has a singular approach in his work, offering 'allusions, phrases, and metaphors' instead of direct references or classic footnotes.[75] It is not only Lacan's intriguing approach to the texts he reads that requires a depth of engagement from his reader, but his own multilayering of language that inserts puns, double entendres and ambiguities into his teaching, replicating the process required by analysis itself, 'sifting through layers of meaning, deciphering the text as though it were a long series of slips of the tongue'.[76]

72 Fink, 'Knowledge and Jouissance', pp. 32–33.
73 Fink, 'Knowledge and Jouissance', p. 33.
74 Grosz, *Jacques Lacan*, p. 9. Grosz writes that Lacan produces 'a Freud perhaps more bold and threatening'; one who did not shy away from 'reinvigorating [...] the scandalous quality of psychoanalysis that so thwarted Freud's earliest ambitions for respectability and intellectual acceptance'.
75 Grosz, *Jacques Lacan*, p. 3.
76 Fink, 'Knowledge and Jouissance', p. 33.

Targeting Freudian and Lacanian theories of sexual difference, Irigaray places the writers of psychoanalysis at the centre of their own discourse. She too uses wordplay and lexical ambiguity, but she does so in order to draw out the presence of the Freudian text in Lacanian psychoanalysis, and the speculation in the discourse. Irigaray writes of 'ses plans' [his plans], 'ses contours nets' [his neat outlines], 'sa forme univoquement cadrée' [his univocally framed shape], 'ses calculs de proportions établis une fois pour toutes' [his calculations of proportions established once and for all], 'son unité immuablement réfléchie' [his immovably reflected unit(y)].[77] The references to his 'univocally framed shape' and 'reflected unit(y)' point unmistakeably to the notions of visibility and specularity at play in Freud's observation of sexual difference in the little girl and boy. However, her commentary extends to the Lacanian definition of the feminine, which moves away from biological difference between the sexes to the topological lexis of set theory. Irigaray's choice of vocabulary in this extract aligns the prominence of male sexual form in Freud's theory of castration with the geometric outline of a closed mathematical set. Her reference to his careful outlines, his univocal framing and the precise calculations of proportions might be compared to the 'espace borné, fermé, supposé institué' [limited, closed, supposedly instituted space] posited for masculine sexuality in Lacanian theory.[78] On the contrary, 'la femme se définit d'une position [...] pointée du *pas-tout* à l'endroit de la jouissance phallique' [woman is defined by a position [...] indicated as 'not whole' with respect to phallic jouissance], residing in an open, or non-finite set.[79]

Lacan's distinction between the sexes is not based on biology or genetic make-up. Rather masculinity and femininity are defined as such in his psychoanalysis as relations of the subject to language, or the symbolic order. Fink summarizes the masculine position as 'a whole': 'because there is something that delimits him [...] there is a definable boundary to his set'.[80] The notion of a delimited set, a space enclosed within a defining

77 Irigaray, *Speculum de l'autre femme*, p. 295; *Speculum of the Other Woman*, p. 238.

78 Lacan, *Encore*, p. 14; *On Feminine Sexuality*, p. 9.

79 Lacan, *Encore*, p. 13; *On Feminine Sexuality*, p. 7.

80 Bruce Fink, *The Lacanian Subject: Between Language and Jouissance* (Princeton: Princeton University Press, 1995), p. 109.

boundary, arises from Lacan's use of formulae to distinguish between the categories of masculine and feminine. The masculine position is represented by the constructions: $\exists x\, \overline{\Phi x}$ and $\forall x\ \Phi x$. The latter formula denotes that 'c'est par la fonction phallique que l'homme comme tout prend son inscription' [it is through the phallic function that man as whole aquires his inscription].[81] The phallic function (Φ) as applicable to every subject (x) – or Φx – governs the whole of a man – $\forall x$. Fink paraphrases this formula: 'man is *altogether* determined by symbolic castration [...] every bit of him falls under the sway of the signifier'.[82]

The other formula defining men in a Lacanian perspective – $\exists x\ \overline{\Phi x}$ – offers 'cette fonction [phallique] trouve sa limite dans l'existence d'un x par quoi la fonction Φx est niée [...]. C'est là ce qu'on appelle la fonction du père' [this function is limited due to the existence of an x by which the function Φx is negated [...]. That is what is known as the father function].[83] It can be said that there is some subject – $\exists x$ – for which the phallic function is foreclosed (as represented by the upper bar). This limit that acts as a boundary to the masculine set is provided by the existence – or the 'ex-sistence' of the primal father.[84] The use of wordplay in reference to the position of the primal father indicates his problematic status. While he can be said to 'exist' in the symbolic order, written as he is $\exists x\ \overline{\Phi x}$, he is simultaneously impervious to symbolic castration. The implication is that the primal father knows no limits, for after succumbing to castration, a man can only relate to the *objet a* in another person: 'the lost object which underpins symbolization, cause of and "stand in" for desire'.[85]

Lacan's portrayal of the relation between the masculine and the *objet a* emphasizes the exclusion of the feminine in the formulation. If there is reciprocity, it is between the subject (insofar as the subject is a man) and the *objet a*, which leads Lacan to say of the man that 'tout sa réalisation au rapport sexuel aboutit au fantasme' [the whole realisation of the sexual

81 Lacan, *Encore*, p. 74; *On Feminine Sexuality*, p. 79.

82 Fink, *The Lacanian Subject*, p. 109. Emphasis my own.

83 Lacan, *Encore*, p. 74; *On Feminine Sexuality*, p. 79.

84 Fink, *The Lacanian Subject*, p. 110.

85 Rose, *Sexuality in the Field of Vision*, p. 72.

relationship leads to fantasy].[86] Jacqueline Rose explains the twofold process that makes of woman a 'symptom' for the man: she is 'the place onto which lack is projected' and the site through which that lack is simultaneously 'disavowed'.[87] Defined in this way, she is 'reduced to being nothing other than this fantasmatic place'. Her status as an 'absolute category' and a 'guarantor of fantasy', however, is 'false', since symbolic castration brings about a desire that can never be satisfied; this is why it can be said that 'woman does not exist'.[88]

Lacanian theorization of the feminine is epitomized by the statement 'il n'y a pas *la* femme, la femme n'est *pas toute*' [*woman* does not exist, woman is *not whole*].[89] While not denying the existence of 'real women', this approach places the feminine within a space of instability.[90] Her position is defined purely against that of the masculine, existing as the 'not all' and thus the 'vanishing point' of the system of gender representation.[91] Woman may therefore only ever be 'other' to man, '*his* other' or 'opposite'.[92] The feminine position as negatively defined against the masculine in Lacanian psychoanalysis is reflected in Lacan's formulas of sexuation. The feminine portion of his schema differentiating between men and women is represented by the two formulations: $\overline{\exists x}\ \overline{\Phi x}$ and $\overline{\forall x}\ \Phi x$. The latter formula states that, unlike the masculine position, not all of a woman – as shown by the bar negating $\overline{\forall x}$ – comes under the law of the signifier. Fink confirms that this does not mean that '*some part of every woman* escapes the reign of the phallus', describing the indication as a 'possibility' rather than a 'necessity'.[93] The written formula implies the possibility of another jouissance

86 Lacan, *Encore*, p. 80; *On Feminine Sexuality*, p. 86.

87 Rose, *Sexuality in the Field of Vision*, p. 72.

88 Rose, *Sexuality in the Field of Vision*, p. 72.

89 Lacan, *Encore*, p. 13; *On Feminine Sexuality*, p. 7.

90 Diane Price Herndl, 'Desire', in *Feminisms: An Anthology of Literary Theory and Criticism*, ed. by Robyn R. Warhol and Diane Price Herndl (Houndmills: Macmillan Press, 1997), pp. 485–88 (p. 485).

91 Bronfen, 'Fatal Conjunctions', p. 250.

92 Shoshana Felman, 'Women and Madness: The Critical Phallacy', in *Feminisms: An Anthology of Literary Theory and Criticism*, ed. by Robyn R. Warhol and Diane Price Herndl (Houndmills: Macmillan Press, 1997), pp. 7–20 (p. 9).

93 Fink, *The Lacanian Subject*, p. 112.

to phallic jouissance, one which goes 'right off the scale, right off the map of representation'.[94] The 'radical alterity' to the symbolic order of this possibility in feminine structure is important, for the first formula defining femininity states that there is not even one subject – $\overline{\exists x}$ – (where the subject, x, is a woman) for whom the phallic function is foreclosed – $\overline{\Phi x}$.[95] Woman comes to represent both difference and loss for man in Lacanian theory: 'On the one hand, the woman becomes, or is produced, precisely as what he is not, that is, sexual difference, and on the other, as what he has to renounce, that is, *jouissance*.'[96]

Irigaray builds on precisely this presentation of the feminine 'as what he is not', contrasting the absence of positive definition on the side of the feminine with the bounded space erected by the male theorist for the masculine subject: 'sa forme univoquement cadrée' [his univocally framed shape].[97] She adopts the lexical field of set theory that founds a Lacanian outline of sexuation in her summary of the position of '(la) femme' [(the) woman]:

> La femme ne se peut rapporter à un être, à un sujet, à un tout, simplement désignable. Et pas plus l'ensemble (des) femmes. Une femme + une femme + une femme … n'aura jamais atteint à quelque générique: la femme. (La / une) femme fait signe vers l'indéfinissable, l'inénumérable, l'informulable, l'*informalisable*. Nom commun indéterminable quant à une identité. (La / une) femme n'obéit pas au principe d'identité à soi, ni à un *x* quelconque. Elle s'identifie à tout *x*, sans s'y identifier de manière particulière. Ce qui suppose un excès à toute identification à / de soi. Mais cet excès n'est rien: la vacance de la forme, la faille de la forme, le renvoi à un autre bord où elle se re-touche sans / grâce à rien.[98]
>
> [Woman is not to be related to any simple designatable being, subject, or entity. Nor is the whole group (called) women. One woman + one woman + one woman will never add up to some generic entity: woman. (The / a) woman refers to what cannot be defined, enumerated, formulated, or *formalized*. Woman is a common noun for which no identity can be defined. (The / a) woman does not obey the principle of

94 Fink, *The Lacanian Subject*, p. 113.
95 Fink, *The Lacanian Subject*, p. 113.
96 Rose, *Sexuality in the Field of Vision*, p. 73.
97 Irigaray, *Speculum de l'autre femme*, p. 295; *Speculum of the Other Woman*, p. 238.
98 Irigaray, *Speculum de l'autre femme*, p. 285; *Speculum of the Other Woman*, pp. 229–30.

> self-identity, however the variable *x* for self is defined. She is identified with every *x* variable, not in any specific way. Presupposed is an excess of all identification to / of self. But this excess is no-thing: it is vacancy of form, gap in form, the return to another edge where she retouches herself with the help of – nothing.]

The mathematical lexis of set theory coincides with concepts of definition in language to elaborate on the impossibility of the feminine position in psychoanalytic structures. The impossibility of gathering woman into the space of a finite set – her innumerability – is equated with the lack of a designation that identifies her as 'woman'. For Irigaray, feminine identity is never established, or considered in its own formal specificity. This is why Irigaray can say on the one hand that the feminine 's'identifie à tout *x*' [is identified with every *x* variable], adding paradoxically that this identification takes place in no 'manière particulière' [specific way]. Irigaray is referring in particular to the formula $\overline{\forall x}\ \Phi x$ on the feminine side of Lacan's schema of sexuation. The bar in $\overline{\forall x}$ indicates that 'not all' of woman is governed by the phallic function, leaving the set defining woman as an open category.

Irigaray's repeated references to form and formalization, or more precisely 'vacance de la forme' [vacancy of form], simultaneously encompass the absence of a boundary defining the feminine sex in Lacanian theory and the privileging of biological form, or anatomical difference, in Freud's outline of sexual difference. However, Irigaray's words also refer to the function of the feminine as what Elisabeth Bronfen calls the 'vanishing point' in a Lacanian topology of sexuality; the feminine exists as the measure against which the masculine standard is defined.[99] In Lacanian terms, she stands at once for 'what he is not' and 'what he has to renounce'. Rose takes up the same term used by Bronfen, pointing out: '[T]here is no such system of representation, however elaborated or elevated it may be, in which there is not some point of impossibility, its other face which it endlessly seeks to refuse – what could be called the vanishing-point of its attempt to construct itself as a system.'[100] The feminine is thus placed as an enigmatic, but central

99 Bronfen, 'Fatal Conjunctions', p. 250.

100 Rose, *Sexuality in the Field of Vision*, p. 219.

point in Lacan's system of sexual difference. The system refuses to classify her within a distinct, closed set, but cannot exist without her presence.

Despite her critical approach, Irigaray recognizes in this 'vacance de la forme – the 'rien' that characterizes feminine sexuality – a sense of potential. For Irigaray, the indefinability of woman means that she both exceeds and escapes male concepts:

> Indéfinie, in-finie, *la forme ne s'y achève pas*. Elle n'est pas infinie, mais pas plus *une* unité: lettre, chiffre, nombre d'une série, nom propre, objet unique (d'un) monde sensible [...]. Cette incomplétude de sa forme, de sa morphologie, lui permet à chaque instant de devenir autre chose, ce qui n'est pas dire qu'elle soit jamais univoquement rien. Ne s'accomplissant dans aucune métaphore.[101]
>
> [She is indefinite, in-finite, *form is never complete in her*. She is not infinite but neither is she *a* unit(y), such as letter, number, figure in a series, proper noun, unique object (in a) world of the senses [...]. This incompleteness in her form, her morphology, allows her to continually become something else, though this is not to say that she is ever univocally nothing. No metaphor completes her.]

The centrality of the masculine term as 'all' in definitions of sexual difference means the feminine as 'not-all' is not (de)limited by any 'number' or 'proper noun'. The implication of this is that: 'La / une femme ne peut se recueillir en *un* volume' [The / a woman cannot be collected into *one* volume].[102] The lack of a defining boundary around the feminine set means she exists perpetually as a space onto which the masculine may project his fantasy, it is that which 'lui permet à chaque instant de devenir autre chose' [allows her to continually become something else]. Irigaray finds that the feminine in Lacan's definition is dependent on masculinity, whether it is that of the masculine set against which woman is defined simply as what he is not, or more generally because definitions of the feminine are written from what Irigaray perceives to be the deeply entrenched patriarchal viewpoint of male theorists. However, there is a glint of possibility in Irigaray's words. In the capacity of the feminine to continually become something else, she is elusive. While her image is continually substituted for the projections of masculine desire, it seems

101 Irigaray, *Speculum de l'autre femme*, p. 284; *Speculum of the Other Woman*, p. 229.

102 Irigaray, *Speculum de l'autre femme*, p. 297; *Speculum of the Other Woman*, p. 240.

that her indefinability opens up a field of potential: no metaphor completes her. Her position is characterized, through the words of Irigaray, by movement, positing her structure as the site of change and possibility.

Irigaray recycles the lexis of set theory used to delineate the terms of sexual difference at this level in Lacan's theory both in order to highlight its flaws and to seek out the spaces for feminine resistance within that very theory. Without attempting to assimilate the poetic text to Irigaray's theory, there is a sense of potential in Irigaray's deconstruction of Lacanian sexuation that may be used to unlock Roubaud's cube. Like the feminine subject in Freudian and Lacanian theory, Roubaud's feminine love is written into the story. In each case, her 'form' is set out by the pen of the male theorist, or mathematician-poet. The feminine position in psychoanalysis is defined in relation to the masculine, whether it is in relation to the visibility of the male sex, or the neat finitude of the masculine in set theory. Roubaud attempts to detain his love inside his cube of poetry, carefully calculating the outlines of his structure from the multiplication of syllables. In Irigaray's reading of Lacan, and Roubaud's portrayal of his lover in poetry, there is the sense that the feminine position cannot be pinned down, in words or figures.[103] The spaces of set theory and the volume of the cube fail to encapsulate the feminine presence, and in both texts an attempt at formalization produces the portrayal of her elusiveness. She exists in their carefully constructed structures as a 'point of impossibility'.

What becomes of Freud's castration scene without the presence of the little girl, whose anatomy and gaze affirm the dominance of the male sex? Without that which does not belong to the set – the existence of the

103 The language of rigid precision that Irigaray uses to outline the Lacanian approach to sexuation – his clean lines, his unequivocally framed form(s), his carefully calculated proportions established without room for adjustment (see *Speculum de l'autre femme*, p. 295) – and the broad context of Roubaud's mathematically orientated form in poetry in which I have quoted it bring to mind the feminist writings and performances of Juliana Spahr and Stephanie Young, and their conception of foulipo. They consider the place of the 'messy [...] and gendered body' in constraint-based writing and ask why these restrictive techniques seem to appeal more to men than they do to women writers. See *The noulipian Analects*, ed. by Matias Viegener and Christine Wertheim (Los Angeles: Les Figues Press, 2007), pp. 1–4, 5–13 and 99–101. For my citation in this footnote, see the editors' note on p. 1.

'not-all' – what binds the 'whole' in a Lacanian definition of masculinity? Without his addressee, Roubaud's cube would have no intention. There is no explicit dialogue between Roubaud and the position of the feminine in psychoanalysis, but my alignment of the central poem in *Trente et un au cube* with Irigaray's reading of Lacanian sexuation illuminates correlative elements in the two structures. The feminine presence is at once that which is locked into a structure erected by the male writer, and also that which simultaneously supports and eludes that structure.

'comme un corps diaphane …'

The ambiguous relationship between a poem's form and the lover it addresses is explored in depth in Roubaud's essay-length meditation on poetry, 'Le silence de la mathématique jusqu'au fond de la langue, poésie'. In the article, Roubaud explores the relationship between poetry, love and language, and considers the place and nature of mathematics in this triad. His approach in the piece is to develop an argument through the construction of a list largely composed of intertextual references and quotations from other poets' writings, accompanied by his own commentary, translations and poetic extracts. Each point builds on the last and the reader is left to infer the relationship between each and, indeed, the overall argument.

The enigma of form and its relation to the beloved is considered through the words of Cavalcanti's poetic treatise on love: 'Dona me prega' ['A Lady Entreats Me']. Cavalcanti's poem appears frequently as an intertextual reference in Roubaud's work, both in his poetry and his prose. In this particular essay by Roubaud, Cavalcanti's verse is followed by Roubaud's own translation from the Italian into French. The extract from Cavalcanti's poem is also accompanied by some words from the troubadour poet Arnaut Daniel (also translated into modern French by Roubaud) and an extract from '"Mantis", an Interpretation' by Louis Zukofsky.[104] The three names

104 Arnaut Daniel's full poem, 'Doutz brais e critz' ('Doux bruits et cris'), along with a modern French translation, is included in Roubaud's anthology of troubadour poetry *Les Troubadours*, pp. 232–35.

are poets that appear periodically in Roubaud's œuvre and they form a small network of poets linked through their intertextual borrowings. Cavalcanti's 'Dona me prega' ['A Lady Entreats me'] is influenced by lines from Daniel's earlier poem.[105] Zukofsky too draws on Cavalcanti's sonnet in his *A-9*. The poets are also drawn together more precisely by poetic form, each of them writing in either the sestina or sonnet tradition. Roubaud has described the sestina as the culmination of the *canso*, bearing the traces of intricacies and developments in the form over time and he also links the sonnet to the *canso*, explaining that the newer form evolved from one verse – or *cobla* – of the troubadour song.[106] Roubaud shares the poets' interest not only in the relation of poetic form and love, but more particularly the relation of the *canso* and sonnet forms to memory.

The extracts from the three poets in Roubaud's essay show the impact of their intertextuality 'par transmission d'ondes' [through wave transmission]: Roubaud's use of the list form particularly draws out the similarities that ripple through the extracts.[107] The selections from poems ranging from the troubadour tradition to contemporary American poet, Zukofsky, bring together the woman's body, form, light and the diaphanous:

> *in quella parte*   *dove sta memora*
> *prende suo stato*   *si formato come*
> *diaffan da lome*   *d'una scuritate*
>
> en cet endroit où se tient la lumière, l'amour (la poésie) 'formé' comme un corps diaphane l'est de lumière, lui, d'obscurité car, je le répète, la langue […] est *ce qui donne lumière et qui illuminé resplendit* (diaphane)
> ainsi la dame
> que.l seu bel cors baizan rizen descobra. e qe.l remir contra.l lum de la lampa
> (son corps, *contre* la lumière de la lampe. *formato come / diaffan da lome*)

105 Roubaud highlights the connection, saying of the two lines quoted from Arnaut Daniel's poem: 'ils préfigurent les développements de Guido Cavalcanti dans sa *canzone doctrinale* sur la nature de l'amour' [they prefigure Guido Cavalcanti's developments in his *doctrinal canzone* on the nature of love]. See Roubaud's anthology *Les Troubadours*, p. 235.

106 Roubaud, *Description du projet*, p. 108.

107 Roubaud, 'Le silence de la mathématique', p. 115.

poésie:
.... the simultaneous / the diaphanous / historical / in one head. [108]

[*in quella parte* *dove sta memora*
prende suo stato *si formato come*
diaffan da lome *d'una scuritate*
en cet endroit où se tient la lumière, l'amour (la poésie) 'formé' comme un corps diaphane l'est de lumière, lui, d'obscurité
car, je le répète, la langue [...] est *ce qui donne lumière et qui illuminé resplendit* (diaphane)
ainsi la dame
[in that place of light, love (poetry) 'formed' like a diaphanous body is so formed by light, the body itself, of darkness
for, I repeat, language [...] is *that which gives light and which, iluuminated, shines brightly* (diaphanous)
and the lady too]
que.l seu bel cors baizan rizen descobra. e qe.l remir contra.l lum de la lampa
(son corps, *contre* la lumière de la lampe. [(her body, *against* the light of the lamp)] *formato come / diaffan da lome*)
poésie: [poetry]
.... the simultaneous / the diaphanous / historical / in one head.]

In the last of the lines cited, a reinterpretation of Cavalcanti attributed to Zukofsky, 'the simultaneous' captures the duality of Roubaud's use of form in *Trente et un au cube*: it is suggestive of the cube that at once contains the lover and whose parameters coincide with her own silhouette. The image which draws the multiple poetic extracts and translations together here, however, is that of the diaphanous body, resplendent against the light of the lamp against a background of darkness. In Cavalcanti's lines, echoes of internal rhyme and alliteration bring together the place of love in the intellect, '*quella parte*'; the state or essence and the formation of love, '*suo stato*' and '*si formato*'; and finally, the darkness, or obscurity of which the body of love (or poetry, as Roubaud adds in brackets in his translation, just beneath the Italian text) is composed, '*scuritate*'. While

108 Roubaud, 'Le silence de la mathématique', p. 115. Typographic layout and line indentation reproduced from the original. Bracketed English translations of Roubaud's own French translations are included below, integrated into a second citation of the original text.

the thematic focus of Cavalcanti's piece is love and its effects, Roubaud's exegetic translation highlights the reflection on poetry itself, which is equally present in the poem. The phonic patterns here draw out terms which contribute to the sense of materiality or the shape of the object described, 'l'amour (la poésie)' [love (poetry)]; the emphasis is on its place, its formation, its body.[109] To break into this object would be impossible, for it is a space characterized by its black obscurity.

The notion of poetry as impenetrable object is reminiscent of Roubaud's description of *mezura* as creating secure layers in a *canso* through its interlocking rhythm and rhyme patterns. The image also echoes Roubaud's aphorism: 'La poésie dit ce qu'elle dit en le disant' [Poetry says what it says in saying it].[110] The suggestion is that poetry should remain, in some sense, 'obscure', but this 'obscurity' is not so much a matter of intellectual difficulty or impenetrability; rather the poet is insisting on a comprehension which does not rely on explanation, paraphrase or simplification of a poem's content at the expense of its form. Instead, form is privileged as that which allows a poem to express meaning, and the choice of verb 'dire' [to say] also evokes poetry's phonic dimension. In Roubaud's reading of Cavalcanti's poem, the object that takes its place in the mind of the reader is the poem just as it is: intact, shaped and formed by its sounds and rhythms. The visual layout of a poem is developed in relation to its phonic patterning, forming dimensions that interact with one another.

In Cavalcanti's verse, the poem is apprehended *where memory resides*: 'dove sta memora'. The use of the verb in 'prende suo stato' and the past participle 'si formato' imply that the poem, in fact, only acquires its final shape through being remembered, or memorized. Roubaud has expressed the view that a poem is never the same for two different readers, only taking on its full potential when it is absorbed into an individual's

109 In Chapter 1, we saw that Roubaud adopts Éluard's title *L'Amour la poésie* as a tribute to the troubadour genitive in which juxtaposition of the nouns designates 'l'amour *de la* poésie'. The placing of 'la poésie' in parentheses in this case suggests that love and poetry are interchangeable concepts, at least in Roubaud's reading of 'Dona me prega' ['My Lady Entreats Me'].

110 Roubaud, *Poésie, etcetera*, p. 77. Emphasis in the original.

memory and allowed to interact there with the past, with personal reminiscences and with fragments of other poems.[111] Roubaud conveys this effect in his translation of Cavalcanti's 'memora' as 'lumière' [light]. The freer translation creates a dual movement of light: a reader's memory is a space that illuminates any poem she appreciates, and in turn, the words of poetry are a diaphanous material that shines brightly upon its immersion in the stores of the reader's personal and poetic memories, there triggering new associations and connections. A similar treatment of diaphanous light occurs in Roubaud's *Exchanges on Light*, a slim volume that features the voices of philosophers, scientists and poets exchanging on the nature and meaning of light. In the words of one speaker, 'all form is a form of light that manifests in the object that it informs'.[112] The same speaker later explains: '[T]he begetting light and the splendor begotten weave together and illuminate one another.'[113]

Ann Smock draws a connection between the image of the diaphanous woman and 'photography's "not-of-this-world" character [...], its kinship with dream and fantasy, and memory': 'Sometimes, when Roubaud mentions a long-desired lady appearing naked and all luminous in a dark room, *chambre noire*, it is hard to tell if this happens in a bedroom at night or a darkroom (a stanza – of a poem – is a "chambre" too).'[114] I cannot help but wonder at the resonances in Smock's comparison of the image to a photograph, that object which serves as a memory in and of itself, often replacing the original memory of an occasion we may have held in our minds, and becoming the source of later projections of our imagination back into the past. Through its documentation in the form of a photograph, a memory shifts and contorts, just as the poem expands to accommodate what it brushes against in memory.

Imagined as diaphanous material, the poem is an invitation to the reader: a point of self-reflexivity and interactivity. Roubaud emulates the movement of this network of light in the form, or arrangement of his

111 Roubaud, *Poésie, etcetera*, pp. 101–08.

112 Jacques Roubaud, *Exchanges on Light*, trans. by Eleni Sikelianos (Iowa City: La Presse/Fence Books, 2009), p. 10.

113 Roubaud, *Exchanges on Light*, p. 13.

114 Ann Smock, *The Play of Light*, p. 139.

argument in 'Le silence de la mathématique'. Fragments of poetry from different times and languages are juxtaposed, bringing out the intertextual links and imagery which connect them. His choice of form enacts the way in which 'the diaphanous / historical' resides 'in one head', one line stimulating the recollection of another, like the successive collision of waves.

In the same way that the language of poetry is illuminated by the light bestowed on it in memory – *illuminé resplendit* [illuminated, shines brightly] – the body of the beloved lady glows against the lamplight. The diaphanous quality attributed to her body by the observer-poet is evocative of the lexis of Irigaray's criticism in regard to Lacanian theory on the not-all of the feminine: 'Cette incomplétude de sa forme, de sa morphologie, lui permet à chaque instant de devenir autre chose, ce qui n'est pas dire qu'elle soit jamais univoquement rien. Ne s'accomplissant dans aucune métaphore' [This incompleteness in her form, her morphology, allows her continually to become something else, though this is not to say that she is ever univocally nothing. No metaphor completes her].[115] Just as Irigaray writes of the feminine who perpetually becomes 'something else', or 'something other' to herself through the incompleteness of her definition in psychoanalysis, the diaphanous silhouette of the poet's lover appears to have no substance unique to her, her form instead activated by the lamplight and reflecting the vision of her beholder. In Irigaray's later writings, the diaphanous is that which protects and envelops male sexuality, making of the feminine a lifeless statue: 'Et si, pour surmonter la douleur de ta première nuit, tu veux que je devienne cristalline, diaphane, milieu te permettant de transparaître délivré de l'obscur de ta naissance et de ta conception, tu me prives de ma retouche. Du lieu où j'ai lieu' [And if, to overcome the pain of your first night, you want me to become crystalline, diaphanous, a transparent place that saves you from the darkness of your birth and conception, you deprive me of retouching myself. Of the place where I take place].[116] If feminine presence in Lacan's theory confirms the 'all' of male sexuality through her exclusion from the set, we might compare her diaphanous material in Roubaud's writing to the very lines that Lacan uses to delineate the

115 Irigaray, *Speculum de l'autre femme*, p. 284; *Speculum of the Other Woman*, p. 229.
116 Luce Irigaray, *Passions élémentaires* (Paris: Minuit, 1982), p. 28.

masculine, those 'neat' lines that Irigaray mocks. If her exclusion from the set confirms the set's completeness, its wholeness, we might seek her out in the form itself that secures its space. Like that which is diaphanous, she reflects what the writer requires her to be: what Irigaray called 'son unité immuablement réfléchie' [his immovably reflected unit(y)].[117]

In my reading the feminine comes to be associated with form in a similar way in Roubaud's *Trente et un au cube* and the classification of sexuation that Lacan establishes through set theory. She is the central axis on which *Trente et un au cube* is built, the lines which form the edges of his poetic cube. Whether in Roubaud's poem or Lacan's use of set theory, the diaphanous quality associated with the feminine means her presence is determined by the masculine term in the relation. She exists in both theory and poem as a reflection of *his* vision. In Irigarayan interpretations of Lacanian theory, the feminine lacks her own specificity, serving as the 'vanishing point' of gender representation. However, there is a paradox in the effects of form: the implications of this mean that within the forms constructed by both Roubaud and Lacan, her 'diaphanous' status means she perpetually evades classification. Despite her position of incompleteness in set theory terms, her place in the structure remains essential for the existence of the central male term:

> De repérage, en fin de comptes, plus ultime que le sujet, qui ne se soutient que par un effet en retour de quelque objectivité, de quelque objectif. S'il n'est plus de 'terre' à (re)fouler, à travailler, à (se) représenter, mais aussi encore et toujours à désirer (s)'approprier, matière opaque qui ne se saurait pas, quel socle subsiste-t-il pour l'ex-sistence du 'sujet'?[118]
>
> [As a benchmark that is ultimately more crucial than the subject, for he can sustain himself only by bouncing back off some objectiveness, some objective. If there is no more 'earth' to press down / repress, to work, to represent, but also and always to desire (for one's own), no opaque matter which in theory does not know herself, then what pedestal remains for the ex-sistence of the 'subject'?]

117 Irigaray, *Speculum de l'autre femme*, p. 295; *Speculum of the Other Woman*, p. 238.

118 Irigaray, *Speculum de l'autre femme*, p. 165; *Speculum of the Other Woman*, p. 133.

Irigaray emphasizes the objectification of the feminine, not only in 'objectif' [objective] and 'objectivité' [objectiveness], but also in her references to the feminine as 'repérage' [benchmark], 'socle' [pedestal], 'terre' [earth] and 'matière' [matter] that the masculine subject bounces off. The multiple layers of meaning that characterize Irigaray's word choices come together in her use of 'représenter' [represent], since it refers to the illusory place of the feminine as guarantor of a fantasy that cannot be, both for the subject and the male theorist who projects that subject. Irigaray's *Speculum* reveals that the position of the feminine in Lacanian theory is part of a discourse that needs to be reconsidered, and is not in fact 'objective' at all. Nevertheless, the presence of the feminine in Lacanian theory is the necessary platform for the existence of the masculine subject in the system. Irigaray's use of the term 'ex-sistence' points to the ambiguous status of the primal father, the boundary that limits the masculine set and the unenclosed position of the feminine in relation to that jouissance which escapes the reign of the phallus, going 'right off the scale'.[119] Irigaray thus alludes to the place of the feminine as instrumental in the confirmation of masculine subjectivity through her place as support to this exceptional status. The feminine is then aligned with the boundary itself that confirms the set of man in Irigaray's re-writing of Lacan; without the impossibility of 'woman', the finitude of man's status cannot be.

Just as the feminine presence is necessary to prevent the collapse of Lacan's structure of sexual difference, so too Roubaud's poem cannot exist in its fullest being without its addressee. She may not be 'all', but she is nonetheless a guarantor of the structure into which she has been written. Roubaud's feminine also escapes classification. She is at once the reflection of the poet's vision, his creation, and she is also the material of the poem illuminated by each eye that runs over it, created in the unpredictability of the reader as other, who gives the text life and simultaneously threatens its failure. Her diaphanous nature represents the potential that exists in any single reading of the text; the possibilities offered to the reader who is invited to 'activate' the poem. As in Irigaray's deconstruction of Lacanian

119 Fink, *The Lacanian Subject*, p. 113.

theory, feminine otherness is at once a threat to the masculine term and the site of possibility. Equally, when the poet invites readerly engagement, there can be no guarantee of what experiences of his work will ensue.

Roubaud's feminine beloved can thus be read through the model of Lacanian set theory and in Irigaray's reading of it. As in Irigaray's analogy of the psychoanalyst as male poet, Roubaud writes the feminine into his poem. She is there aligned with the poem's form: a diaphanous substance. As such, her presence necessarily reflects the poet's vision of her, just as the structure of the feminine in Lacan's system of sexuation is defined against the complete set delineating masculinity. As diaphanous substance, the form of the poem is also reflective of the presence of the reader. The reader contributes to the creation of meaning in a poem through its interaction with the spaces of memory. In this conception of poetic form, the poet allows the institution of meaning in the text to escape him. Similarly, the feminine is that which eludes definition and its Lacanian theorist: as the 'not-all' of Lacan's system of representation, she exceeds, surrounds, escapes and dwarfs male concepts. The poet attempts to capture her in words and figures, but she resides within the boundaries he constructs, and precisely because of that she eludes his cubic prison, indistinguishable from the very structures he creates.

The Disjunction: From the Impossible Relation to *'j'aime à toi'*

Reminded repeatedly throughout poem 16 that the feminine addressee is the centre itself of the cube, or volume of poetry – 'tu es le centre | de ce cube construit pour | toi' [you are the centre | of this cube built for | you] – the reader is left contemplating the blank space that occupies the middle of the page. This interval at the halfway point in the poem is made more noticeable by the fact it is the largest to intervene in any poem of *Trente et un au cube*: other poems are composed of five strophes, with a double line space between each, while this central piece is made up of only two verses, separated by a gap of approximately five line spaces.

Contrary to Irigaray's critical analogy of the psychoanalyst as poet who silences the muse, Roubaud's use of the blank space has been the source of feminine resistance against the poet's pen. The poet's fingers are prevented from adjusting, or recreating the axis on which she turns, the core of her being, when the poet's statement at the end of the first strophe, 'je déplace un très peu' [I move just a touch], is separated from 'ton axe nocturne' [your nocturnal centre] at the beginning of the next section by the break in the page; the separation at this particular point in the syntax suggests that the feminine presence eludes the poet, he does not reach his object.

Roubaud offers a mathematical definition of the dividing space that separates the lovers in *Trente et un au cube* in the form of a mathematical, or more precisely, topological citation: 'dans un espace accessible, tout point est fermé, ou (ce qui revient au même) si deux points sont distincts, il existe un voisinage de chacun d'eux qui ne contient pas l'autre' [in an accessible space, each point is closed, or (which amounts to the same thing) if two points are distinct, there is a neighbourhood of each of them that does not contain the other].[120] The statement is attributed to Nicolas Bourbaki, the collective pseudonym for the group of mathematicians whose ambition to reformulate mathematics had been so present in the beginnings of Roubaud's path as a composer of maths and poetry, and it appears isolated on the page preceding the twelfth poem in the book. The quote is not acknowledged in detail, referenced only in the list of 'Remerciements' [Acknowledgements] at the close of the volume, where 'Nicolas Bourbaki' is typed in alongside the twelfth bullet point down the page. It is one of the few direct citations in the volume whose origin and precise mathematical meaning are unlikely to be instantly recognizable by most poetry readers; many of the other quotes and intertextual references that abound in *Trente et un au cube* are fragments of poetry that will be familiar to the regular French poetry reader, or even someone who has grown up learning well-known poems as a school pupil in France.

Roubaud does not offer any clues as to the signification of the Bourbaki citation in *Trente et un au cube*. It is quoted elsewhere in Roubaud's œuvre, appearing a number of years later in prose volume *Mathématique:*, where

120 Roubaud, *Trente et un au cube*, p. 52.

Roubaud tells his reader that it is: 'l'axiome de Fréchet' [Fréchet's axiom], or more precisely 'L'axiome dit (par Bourbaki) de Fréchet' [The axiom attributed (by Bourbaki) to Fréchet].[121] In *Mathématique:*, Roubaud recollects the earliest period of his studies in mathematics, particularly his embarking on Bourbaki's *Topologie générale* [*General Topology*], the third in a series of vast and complicated volumes. Roubaud does not explain the meaning of the axiom in precise mathematical terms, only mentioning in passing that it applied, in the field of mathematical topology, to 'une séparation plus faible, celle des espaces accessibles' [a weaker separation, that of accessible spaces].[122] Nevertheless, his narrative does implicitly suggest a way in which the reader of *Trente et un au cube* may approach the axiom. Roubaud reassuringly describes the intense difficulty that even he encountered on his first attempts to read Bourbaki's *Topologie générale* [*General Topology*]:

> J'ai lu et relu d'innombrables fois ces définitions, toute cette première page et les pages suivantes, sans rien comprendre [...]. Mais je n'ai pris que peu à peu conscience du fait que la difficulté essentielle venait non d'une extrême impénétrabilité du sujet [...] ni d'une incapacité congénitale de ma part à le comprendre (heureusement), mais de ce que je ne savais pas lire.[123]
>
> [I read and reread those definitions countless times, all that first page and the following pages, without understanding a thing [...]. But I only gradually realized that the essential difficulty came not from the extreme impenetrability of the subject [...], nor from a congenital inability on my part to understand it (fortunately), but from the fact that I did not know how to read it.]

Roubaud's own struggle to understand the Bourbakian Treatise justifies the hesitation of the reader to seek out the mathematical origins of his mysterious quote on accessible space. Roubaud's battle, as he reminisces, is a question of reading approach. He describes switching from a mode of reading suited to prose, which involved speeding through the narrative driven by its suspense, to one which he applied to poetry: reading slowly, until much of the text was learnt entirely by heart.[124] Only then was he

121 Roubaud, *Mathématique:*, p. 167.
122 Roubaud, *Mathématique:*, p. 167. Emphasis in original.
123 Roubaud, *Mathématique:*, pp. 159–60.
124 Roubaud, *Mathématique:*, p. 160.

able to read the text in a manner particularly befitting mathematics: 'C'est avec une extrême méfiance que j'en vins à me hasarder à redire ces enchaînements raisonnables autrement, à les résumer, à les paraphraser, à en venir à l'idée que la mathématique est paraphrasable' [Very warily I attempted to go through these chains of reasonings again, to summarize them, to paraphrase them, to come to the idea that mathematics can be paraphrased].[125] In this, Roubaud found the insurmountable difference separating maths and poetry: while mathematics can, indeed must, involve paraphrasis, poetry cannot be paraphrased, or explained.

In *Trente et un au cube*, a book subtitled 'poésie' [poetry], the same lines of Fréchet's axiom are read as poetry rather than mathematical theory. Taken out of their mathematical context, the lines acquire new possibilities of meaning. Roubaud himself seems to encourage this sense of freedom in their interpretation, when he muses on what the words evoke for him:

> Le charme de cet axiome venait du fait qu'il se pouvait, dans un tel espace que, pour certains de ses couples de points, chacun des voisinages de l'un des points de tels couples rencontre nécessairement l'un des voisinages de l'autre et qu'ils se trouvent ainsi enchevêtrés l'un à l'autre par la topologie de leur espace, leur monde. C'est, je crois, ce qui se passe dans la mémoire, dans la difficile séparation des souvenirs.[126]
>
> [The charm of this axiom came from the fact that it was possible, in such a space, that for some of its pairs of points, each of the neighbourhoods of one of the points in these pairs necessarily encounters one of the neighbourhoods of the other, and they find themselves tangled up together through the topology of their space, their world. This is, I believe, what happens in memory, in the difficulty separating different recollections.]

Set against the backdrop of reminiscences of his early encounters with the world of mathematics, the axiom is transformed into a metaphor for the author's memory processes. Through his transposition of the topological definition into the domain of memory, Roubaud manifests its semantic flexibility in his writing. The lines describe a structural relationship or interaction that may be applied to concepts and objects outside of

125 Roubaud, *Mathématique:*, p. 161.

126 Roubaud, *Mathématique:*, p. 167.

mathematics. Furthermore, his acknowledgement of the axiom's 'charm' somehow adds a personal perception, or sentimental value to the words, subtracting from their mathematical quality. This understanding permits a reading of the citation in *Trente et un au cube* that departs from its mathematical source, moving towards a lexical analysis of the shapes and structures it refers to: perhaps it could be interpreted as a 'formalization' of the poet-lover relation in *Trente et un au cube*.

There are some resonances between the Bourbaki quote included in Roubaud's volume of love poetry and Lacan's outlining of the structure of the disjunctive sexual relation. Read as a description of love in structural terms, the Bourbaki quote insists on a distance between the couple: there is a part of oneself, a section of one's surrounding space, or 'voisinage', which remains inaccessible to the lover. The poet refers to two distinct points, each surrounded by an area that cannot be penetrated by the other. The mathematical phenomenon can be represented visually by the convergence of two circles, neighbourhoods of the points at their centres. Much like a Venn diagram, one circle, or neighbourhood, slightly overlaps the other, leaving its remaining space – the majority – out of reach.[127] This structural understanding of the distinction of the two points, isolated from one another by the boundaries of the neighbourhoods within which they reside, resembles the problematic relationship of the '*deux*' in Lacan's work: the psychoanalyst refers to 'l'impossible d'établir la relation d'eux' [the impossibility of establishing the relationship between 'them-two'].[128] Lacan reformulates the notion more specifically as an impasse in the sexual relation: 'l'impossibilité d'établir [...] l'Un de la relation *rapport sexuel*' [the impossibility of establishing [...] the One of the relation 'sexual relationship'].[129]

Lacan evokes Aristophanes' myth of love in his account of the impossible sexual relation. In Plato's *Symposium,* the character explains that we are sundered beings, left to seek out our other half once physically separated from us by Zeus. Love, then, is the attempt 'to combine two in one'

127 For an illustration of the axiom, see Thierry Vialar, *Handbook of Mathematics* (Paris: Books on Demand, 2015), p. 206.

128 Lacan, *Encore,* p. 12; *On Feminine Sexuality,* p. 6.

129 Lacan, *Encore,* p. 13; *On Feminine Sexuality,* p. 7.

and 'heal the human sore'.[130] To a certain extent, Lacan appears to echo this when he states 'L'amour [...] n'est que le désir d'être Un' [Love [...] is but the desire to be One], and he also refers directly to Aristophanes' account in his theory of the subject.[131] However, he does not endorse the ancient Greek representation of love, calling it 'pathétique' [moving] but 'leurrante' [deceptive].[132] He substitutes it with the evidence of analytic experience, which reveals that the search of the subject is not for his 'complément sexuel' [sexual complement], but for 'la part à jamais perdue de lui-même' [the part of himself lost forever].[133] For Lacan, the 'représentants' [representatives] or 'figures' [figures] of this lost part of ourselves are the *objets a*, those reminders of primordial wholeness.[134] While love may constitute our wish for oneness, it does not grant that wish. Instead, it is 'ce qui nous conduit à l'impossible d'établir la relation d'eux' [[that] which leads us to the impossibility of establishing the relationship between 'them-two'].[135] The use of 'd'eux' here specifies the love relationship as that which necessarily involves two, alluded to in the homophony that designates *deux*. Thus, rather than fulfilling our search for that missing part of ourselves, making the subject whole, the unity of 'Un' [One] is always supplanted by the disparity of 'd'eux/deux' [of the others/of them-two], and the only relationship characterized by oneness is that narcissistic 'mirage' of specularity.[136]

Lacan's reference to 'la relation *rapport sexuel*' [the relation 'sexual relationship'] refers at once to the defining structures that differentiate the sexes, summarized in the formulae of sexuation, and to the (im)possibility of a sexual relationship between those defined as masculine and feminine in psychoanalysis. Badiou transposes the implications of the formulae defining sexual difference into everyday terms, explaining that pleasure is the source of a separation between lovers:

130 Plato, *Lysis Symposium Gorgias*, trans. by W. R. M. Lamb (London: Harvard University Press, 1925), p. 141.

131 Lacan, *Encore*, p. 12; *On Feminine Sexuality*, p. 6.

132 Lacan, *Les Quatre Concepts*, p. 187.

133 Lacan, *Les Quatre Concepts*, p. 187.

134 Lacan, *Les Quatre Concepts*, p. 180.

135 Lacan, *Encore*, p. 12; *On Feminine Sexuality*, p. 6.

136 Lacan, *Encore*, p. 46; *On Feminine Sexuality*, p. 47.

> Jacques Lacan nous rappelle que dans la sexualité, en réalité, chacun est en grande partie dans sa propre affaire [...]. Il y a la médiation du corps de l'autre, bien entendu, mais en fin de compte, la jouissance sera toujours votre jouissance. Le sexuel ne conjoint pas, il sépare. Que vous soyez nu(e), collé(e) à l'autre, est une image, une représentation imaginaire. Le réel, c'est que la jouissance vous emporte loin, très loin de l'autre.[137]
>
> [Jacques Lacan reminds us, that in sex, each individual is to a large extent on their own [...]. Naturally, the other's body has to be mediated, but at the end of the day, the pleasure will be always your pleasure. Sex separates, doesn't unite. The fact that you are naked and pressing against the other is an image, an imaginary representation. What is real is that pleasure takes you a long way away, very far from the other.]

Badiou's reading of Lacan emphasizes the physical distance between the lovers: pleasure divides, pursued and enjoyed by the individual through the mediation of the other's body. For Badiou, perceived notions of intimacy and proximity in the sexual encounter are illusory. In an experience that is summed up as 'pressing against the other', bodily contact is just a means to individual pleasure.

While the homophony in the 'd'eux' of Lacan's 'relation d'eux' points to the discrepancy of the 'two' in the sexual relation, in Lacan's formulation it is the 'Others' – 'eux' – who come between the two lovers. Fink describes the 'Other' in Lacan's work as having many 'faces' or 'avatars', whose nuances shift from one period of the psychoanalyst's thought to the next.[138] Fink also writes of the 'Other' as 'language', 'demand' and 'desire'.[139] These three 'faces' of the Lacanian Other find themselves inextricably linked and as such, *they* form the barrier – 'eux' – which denies the possibility of the sexual relation.

Lacan makes the poignant observation that 'Ce qui parle n'a à faire qu'avec la solitude' [That which speaks deals only with solitude], suggesting that the subject in speech is destined to isolation and loneliness.[140] Soler takes up the notion, pinpointing an 'impossibility' in speech, 'you speak with your lover, and the person who listens to you understands your words

137 Badiou, *Éloge de l'amour*, pp. 12–13; *In Praise of Love*, p. 18.
138 Fink, *The Lacanian Subject*, p. 13.
139 Fink, *The Lacanian Subject*, p. 13.
140 Lacan, *Encore*, p. 109; *On Feminine Sexuality*, p. 120.

and sentences, and you can repeat them. You can even explain them. When you speak, you can develop meaning […]. You can communicate that meaning and you can explain meaning, but the constant question for the listener is, what is he getting at? What is he after?'[141] Soler's repeated use of the conjunction 'and', in addition to the insistent rhetorical anaphora in which 'you can' frequently recurs, both have the effect of delaying the critical questions. In a sense, it is as though the twists and turns in her explanation replicate what has been called the 'sliding', 'metonymy' or 'desire' in language.[142] It is that which cannot be grasped, that lack, that absence of the referent which recalls the profound loss implicated in 'that first moment of symbolisation'.[143] The void instils itself between speaker and other, or speaker and lover, for what the subject says is far removed, in both syntax and meaning, from what the listener hears. Thus, the 'impossibility' in speech is simply the 'impossibility to say what you want'; once our demands are put into words, something is lost and our interlocutor can never respond to us with what we truly demand.[144]

The disjunction between poet and beloved is most prominent in the book's central poem, where the division between them is effected in the silent interval that separates the poem's two stanzas. More than a structural division between the two terms of the couple, however, the space of silence on the page of the poem is aligned with the beloved herself. Even if the alignment is one that prevents the controlling touch of the poet, the reader may feel a sense of ambivalence towards her position in the quiet heart of the poem. Silence is explicitly used as a tool of restraint against the feminine in parts of *Trente et un au cube*. At times in the volume, the poet's voice dominates, even muzzles her: 'que || ma voix te joigne | ma voix te place sur le plan de la page que […] ma voix te | muselle' [in the hope || my voice reaches you | my voice places you within the framework of the page

141 Colette Soler, 'The Subject and the Other (I)', in *Reading Seminar XI: Lacan's Four Fundamental Concepts of Psychoanalysis*, ed. by Richard Feldstein, Bruce Fink and Maire Jaanus (New York: SUNY Press, 1995), pp. 39–44 (p. 50).

142 Soler, 'The Subject and the Other (I)', p. 50.

143 Rose, *Sexuality in the Field of Vision*, p. 55.

144 Soler, 'The Subject and the Other (I)', p. 50.

[…] my voice muzzles you].[145] She is silenced in the poet's representation of her across the pages of his poem: 'ma voix te plie. te silence' [my voice folds you. silences you].[146] In the reference to folding, the reader might think of the foldout pages of the book in her hands, another reminder of the metaphoric relation between the poet's lover and the material of the poem. Roubaud's terms evoking the repression and manipulation of his love in these examples seem to resonate with the terms dividing poet and muse, psychoanalyst and feminine object in the early writings of Irigaray, where the theorist finds in the poet-muse relationship a stifling of the feminine.

There are silences in *Trente et un au cube* which are associated with the woman sleeping:

> ainsi vont les suites | de silences jusqu'au point | de la nuit où tu t'endors, || séparent (j'explore | le filtre des voisinages | du point de ton som | meil j'adhère au germe proche | de ton inconscience | tourne || au-dessus de ton | engourdissement) approchent | d'avant (dans le chaud | de tes paroles s'engour | dissant le chaud de tes jambes || se repliant se | fermant dans les draps) les suites | de silences convergent vers le point unique | de ton sommeil l'approchent le || plus infiniment | possible d'avant et d'après (accompagnant | ta respiration, graduées | par tes poumons plongeant de ||| plus en plus profond | dans ton sommeil).[147]
>
> [so go the sequences | of silences up to the point | of the night where you sleep, || they separate (I explore | the filter of neighbourhoods | from the point of your | sleep I join the seed near | to your unconsciousness | turn || above your | drowsiness) they approach | from before (in the heat | of your words drift | ing off the heat of your legs || folding | closing in the sheets) the sequences | of silences converge at the single point | of your sleep they approach it as || infinitely as possible | from before and from after (accompanying | your breathing, graduated | by your lungs plunging ||| deeper and deeper | into your sleep).]

In the first line of this extract, the blank spaces separating the segments become 'les suites | de silences' [sequences | of silences] that the poem speaks of: both 'suites' [sequences] and 'point' [point] are followed by a space and preposition 'de' [of], punctuating the noun phrases with short silences. The poet continues in the language of topology encountered

145 Roubaud, *Trente et un au cube*, p. 117.
146 Roubaud, *Trente et un au cube*, p. 117.
147 Roubaud, *Trente et un au cube*, p. 81.

earlier in the Bourbaki citation, writing of 'le filtre des voisinages' [filter of neighbourhoods] that he explores, following the sequence of silences until he reaches the central 'point unique | de ton sommeil' [single point | of your sleep]. Recalling the distinct points in topology between which 'il existe un voisinage de chacun d'eux qui ne contient pas l'autre' [there is a neighbourhood of each of them that does not contain the other], here the woman's sleep can only be approached up to a certain limit. In sleep, she necessarily leaves the poet alone. The topological limit is also representative of the poet's sexual frustration, for he notes the legs of his lover 'se repliant se | fermant dans les draps' [folding | closing in the sheets]. The silences are aligned with her breathing, becoming gradually heavier as the extract progresses. When the poet nears the sleeping woman at the centre, the passage ends in a sequence of alliterative play on the letter 'p' in 'par tes poumons plongeant de ||| plus en plus profond' [by your lungs plunging ||| deeper and deeper]; in this the reader hears the deepening of her breathing as it occurs in the words of the poem.

The poet too listens to her breathing as she sleeps: 'et dans ta nuit | depuis le point de ta nuit ||| je ne suis rien (j'écoute ta respiration | engourdie je longe | le chaud de tes jambes serrées longues) je cherche encore || un coin dans ton sommeil que déjà le jour me | sépare biffant | les étoiles' [and in your night | from the point of your night ||| I am nothing (I listen to your slow | breathing I follow | the heat of your long closed legs) I still search || for a corner in your sleep but daylight already distances | me erasing | the stars].[148] The reader is taken further into the night as the first two segments culminate in a repetition of 'nuit' [night]. The poet himself then falls silent, 'je ne suis rien' [I am nothing], only listening intently to his lover's breathing, following the heat emanating from her legs that exclude him.

The encounter between the poet and the woman who sleeps in Roubaud's poem might be compared to an inquiry by Irigaray into the productive function of silence and separation in a relationship between two individuals:

> Ce silence est un espace-temps qui t'est offert, sans rite ni vérité préétablie, a priori. Il est constitution d'une ouverture à toi, à l'autre qui n'est et ne sera jamais mien. Ce

148 Roubaud, *Trente et un au cube*, p. 81.

> silence est possible grâce au fait que ni *je* ni *toi* ne sont tout, que nous sommes l'un et l'autre limités, marqués par le négatif, différents sans hiérarchie. Ce silence est le premier geste du *j'aime à toi*. Sans lui, le 'à' est impossible tel que je l'entends. Ce silence est condition d'un possible respect de moi et de l'autre dans leur limites.[149]

> [This silence is a space-time which is offered to you, without ritual or preestablished truth, *a priori*. It constitutes an overture to you, to the other who is not and never will be mine. This silence is possible due to the fact that neither *I* nor *you* are everything, that we are both limited, marked by the negative, different but without hierarchy. This silence is the first gesture of *I love to you*. Without it, the 'to' is impossible in the way that I understand it. This silence is the condition of a possible respect for myself and for the other in our respective limits.]

The definition of silence as a space-time echoes the limited proximity of Roubaud's topological points, each defined by an area of space that remains inaccessible to any other point. Irigaray writes of the limits of each term in the relationship not as constraint, but as a space in which the individuality of *I* or *you* may thrive without the encroachment of the other upon their being. The philosopher posits silence as the first stage in the process of '*j'aime à toi*' [*I love to you*], a way of loving that is based on an irreducible distance between the lovers, in which the preposition 'à', or 'to', is a mediating space between two people: 'Le "à" est le lieu de non-réduction de la personne à l'objet. Je t'aime, je te désire, je te prends, je te séduis, je t'ordonne, je t'instruis, etc. risquent toujours d'anéantir l'altérité de l'autre, de le/la transformer en mon bien, mon objet, de le/la réduire au/en mien' [The 'to' is the space of non-reduction of the person to the object. I love you, I desire you, I take you, I seduce you, I order you, I instruct you, etc. always risk shattering the alterity of the other, transforming him/her into my property, my object, reducing him/her to/into mine].[150] The beloved is no longer object. According to the feminist philosopher, true lovers are 'Eloignés par [leur] différence, mais présents l'un à l'autre' [Distanced by [their] difference, but present to one another].[151] To clarify, the presence involves trust, love and respect for the other, but

149 Irigaray, *J'aime à toi*, p. 182.
150 Irigaray, *J'aime à toi*, p. 172.
151 Luce Irigaray, *Être Deux* (Paris: Grasset, 1997), p. 27.

the distance means allowing the alterity of the other to survive.[152] This involves being faithful to myself, avoiding the temptation to become (like) the other, but also requires the acceptance that the other can never be completely revealed to me, appropriated by me, remaining, in part, a 'mystery'.[153] The aim is to protect the subjectivity of each term in the relationship, avoiding the collapse of intimacy into sameness.

Although Irigaray's ideas build constructively on the Lacanian disjunction, finding in the separating spaces constituting the (impossible) relation a positivity that allows for individual subjectivity, to accept that there will remain an element of 'mystery' in a lover may be a difficult reality to grapple with. We have seen that sleep and silence at times represent the suppression and manipulation of the beloved in *Trente et un au cube*, signalling the dominant position of the poet who writes his love object into the text. There are also allusions in these moments to a sense of anxiety felt by the poet. Sleep is a separating space that isolates him, and he is left yearning in his lover's absence: '(ton sommeil | dans la chaleur de | tes jambes fermées) qui m'exclut sans espoir' [(your sleep | in the heat of | your closed legs) which excludes me without hope].[154] Jean-François Puff too points out that the woman's sleep is often a source of anxiety for the poet, who is excluded from her embrace.[155]

Roubaud does not attempt in *Trente et un au cube* to portray an impossible ideal, the mythical unity of the love relation that sees two become one. Instead, he alternates between feelings of insecurity in separation and those silences that allow the presence of his lover to grow, her breathing emanating through the words of the poem in sleep. The poet himself is overwhelmed with a silence so absolute that he becomes engrossed in the rhythm of her breathing: 'les || suites de silences | m'enveloppent me recouvrent' [the || sequences of silences | envelop me cover me].[156] As Irigaray states, the space between is a 'geste' [gesture], an act of giving, or offering oneself: 'T'écouter

152 Irigaray, *Être Deux*, p. 16 and p. 94.

153 Irigaray, *Être Deux*, pp. 22–23.

154 Roubaud, *Trente et un au cube*, p. 81.

155 Puff, *Mémoire de la mémoire*, p. 459.

156 Roubaud, *Trente et un au cube*, p. 81.

demande donc que je me rende disponible' [Listening to you thus requires that I make myself available].[157]

Spaces of Silence in the Composition of *Trente et un au cube*

To remain silent and listen, to relinquish possession and allow the 'mystery' of another person is an act of giving, because it involves an exposure to risk: what if she leaves? What if I am left alone? When the poet reveals this fear in poem 16 of *Trente et un au cube*, the alterity of his lover is expressed in terms that see her flee the page on which he inscribes the rhythms of his poem, while he simultaneously addresses her as his (first) reader. What do the silent spaces in the volume therefore mean for the poet and his relation with (the beloved as) his reader?

The poet's gesture is described as the weaving of pockets of protective silences around his lover: 'déjà le jour | a vieilli les silences que | je cousais autour | de toi (séquences brodées | de silences ordonnant || ta surface endormie disposant caches chemins repères sur | ton corps en sommeil) je repars de rien, séparé' [already daylight | has aged the silences that | I stitched around | you (embroidered sequences | of silences ordering || your sleeping surface laying out hiding places pathways landmarks on | your body in sleep) I start over again, separated].[158] Roubaud's reference to stitching, or sewing, is a reminder of his troubadour intentions, part of his *entrebescar* process intricately constructing patterns of rhyme words into systems that are able to activate the memory of the person who reads, hears, or recites the poem. He entwines silences into the poem, the blanks between segments that create the jagged rhythm of *Trente et un au cube*. The spaces here are linked to the body of his lover, but rather than erasing her presence or silencing her, they create secret pockets of resistance, routes of possibility and monuments to her being: 'caches chemins repères' [hiding places pathways landmarks]. The use of the word 'repères' [landmarks]

157 Irigaray, *J'aime à toi*, pp. 183–84.
158 Roubaud, *Trente et un au cube*, p. 81.

in particular is suggestive of Roubaud's theory of poetry as memory, in which the role of silence in rhythm is to create memorable patterns and divisions in language.

The poet reverses the process of writing in black ink on a white page, when he states: 'J'ARRANGE LE BLANC | dans le noir je prends pied dans | ta substance' [I ARRANGE WHITE | in black I get a foothold in | your substance].[159] The composition of the poem consists in blank spaces being built into the black architecture of writing rather than the flowing of black ink along the page. The silences associated with the feminine lover, her respiration and the web of rhythm the poet weaves around her take on a substantial quality that distances them from notions of emptiness or void. The blank spaces in *Trente et un au cube* are a tangible and enduring material entity: 'les pierres || blanches de l'espace' [the white || stones of space].[160] If the reader follows these stepping stones to the centre of the labyrinth, she finds the feminine lover is the breathing heart of the poem:

> musique de toi transmise | entre blanc et noir | par les fusées elliptiques | et les carreaux d'étendue || patchwork buissonant | où progressent les silences | car tu es le lieu | de leur migration tu fixes | les silences dans ton pouls [...] musique de toi | détournée du blanc dans | le noir (l'étendue | cantatrice de ta peau | identiquement traverse || le vide nocturne).[161]
>
> [music transmitted from you | between white and black | through the elliptic rockets | and the vast patchwork of || squares branching | where the silences spread | for you are the place | of their migration you fix | the silences in your pulse [...] music of you | diverted from white into | black (sprawling | cantatrice of your skin | identically crosses || the nocturnal void)]

The contrast of the black-inked words against the white spaces of the page becomes the squares of a patchwork quilt, the singing skin of the woman spread across the void of night. This 'musique' [music] is at once the poem that sings of her in black and white, and the silences that emanate from

159 Roubaud, *Trente et un au cube*, p. 49.
160 Roubaud, *Trente et un au cube*, p. 69.
161 Roubaud, *Trente et un au cube*, p. 49.

her own body, her breathing: 'ton pouls' [your pulse]. She is the diversion of white spaces in black writing, 'détournée du blanc dans | le noir', and these are constitutive of the text, acquiring an importance greater than that of the writing.

In *Trente et un au cube*, the poet writes that the blank spaces in his text retain the presence of his addressee: 'pour | t'entraîner je dispose au | blanc de mes discours | les mêmes bornes fenêtres | étoiles composées' [to | lead you I arrange in the | white spaces of my speech | the same boundaries windows | composed stars].[162] The spaces are bordered or framed; windows in the text that take on the beauty of stars. A similar transition takes place in Roubaud's meditation on spoken poetry, *Dire la poésie* [*Saying Poetry*], in which he compares the windows in the room to sheets of paper:

> les ouvertures dans le mur
> pas vraiment des fenêtres de grandes feuilles de papier
> semi transparent translucide.[163]
>
> [the openings in the wall
> not really windows large sheets of paper
> half transparent translucent.]

These openings in the walls undergo a transformation of light and sound:

> la lumière
> brouillant les arbres à travers les feuilles de papier
> translucide au silence créant cette marge violette et
> verte et mélangée de bruit à ma voix disant ces
> poèmes.[164]
>
> [light
> blurring the trees through the sheets of translucent
> paper in the silence forming this margin of violet and
> green mixed up with noise beside my voice saying these
> poems.]

162 Roubaud, *Trente et un au cube*, p. 9.
163 Roubaud, *Dors*, p. 10.
164 Roubaud, *Dors*, p. 16.

The silent, almost transparent sheets of paper come alive with the noise of green and purple hues. Some of their colour comes from the interaction of light with the trees beyond the windows: the poet's distraction during the poetry reading is built into the poem, memories of the moments of composition absorbed into the spaces dividing its units of words. The distraction of colours and sounds becomes a margin to Roubaud's voice, incorporated into his written text. Yet there is a sense that these margins, the 'feuilles de papier' [sheets of paper], or windows, represent spaces that exceed the poet. However planned and crafted these sections of his poetry might be in reality, they appear to the reader as moments in which the poet's mind wanders.

The 'feuilles de papier' that are Roubaud's windows are like the diaphanous body of the poem in the reader's memory, the woman's resplendence in the lamplight of Cavalcanti's 'Dona me prega': like the lady glows more brightly under the gaze of her lover, so too a poem is illuminated by its interaction with a person's memory. For Roubaud, it is a poem's rhythm that coincides and clashes with the patterns memorized throughout a lifetime of poetry reading and recitation. It is then the blank spaces in a poem – 'marge […] à ma voix' [margin […] beside my voice] – that shape it for its reader. These spaces become imbued with the memories of the reader – senses of familiarity and contrast conjured up by a poem's metre – and so, like diaphanous windows they let the reader into the poem, allowing her contribution to its existence through reading.

In *Trente et un au cube,* the tree leaves outside brush against the bedroom window of the lovers, leading the reader into the intimate space within:

> le || feuillage pressant | la fenêtre voulant dire | entrer octobre un | matin ton ventre sous mes | mains toi séjournant dans la || compagnie du so | leil bougeant de mes mains som | brement et lumi | neusement […] à | la fois grimpant dans mes mains || qui t'ouvrent te referment comme des feuillages | si toi dans mes mains | et de la main du soleil | t'ouvrant t'élevant bougeant.[165]

165 Roubaud, *Trente et un au cube*, p. 85.

> [the || leaves brushing against | the window saying | come in October one | morning your middle under my | hands you lying in the || company of the | sun stirring from my hands dark | ly and lu | cidly [...] at | the same time climbing in my hands || which open you close you again like leaves | if you in my hands | and from the hand of the sun | opening you raising you stirring.]

In the extract, the feminine figure is the page of the poem, which the poet folds and opens in his hands. She stirs, 'grimpant' [climbing] and 'bougeant' [stirring], until she seems somehow to overflow his grasp, unfurling like the tree under the light of the sun, 't'ouvrant t'élevant' [opening you raising you]. The sun shining into the room hints at the possibility of escape offered by the window in the text; it is at once a space through which the poet symbolically invites the reader into his text and a reminder that the poem opens out onto the unknown in doing so.

Towards the end of the volume, the poem itself is referred to again in terms evoking its movement:

> – permutations circulaires de groupes | traçants courant elles-mêmes ||
> sur un fond fixe de | gouttes de crayons ou d'encres | – glissements de sons | en presque durées égales | en presque constantes é- || lévations et chutes | et moments de retour [...] ce po- || ème entre dans ta | vue. qu'il y bouge, qu'il force | ton angoisse. ce | la suffira. je ne de | mande pas d'autre utili || té. qu'il soit cela | seulement. qu'il t'y enferme. | ensuite vienne le | sens que tu lui donneras | le demain de ta lecture || ton parcours parmi | ses milliers de syllabes le | paraphe de ton œil au travers de ses lignes | (de ton doigt sur ses arêtes).[166]

> [– circular permutations of groups | plotting flowing themselves || against a fixed background of | drops of pencil or ink | – shifting of sounds | at a nearly regular pace | with nearly constant ri || ses and falls | and moments of return [...] this po || em comes into your | sight. may it stir there, may it force your worry. that | will be enough. I ask for | no other utili || ty. may it be that | only. may it enclose you. | then comes the | meaning you will give it | the tomorrow of your reading || your route among | its thousands of syllables the | signature of your eye across its lines | (of your finger over its bones).]

The extract shifts before the reader's eyes, shot through with the same sense of flux that characterizes much of *Trente et un au cube*. Circular

166 Roubaud, *Trente et un au cube*, p. 121.

permutations and sliding sounds effect rises, falls and returns, tracing their itinerary in droplets of pencil and ink. The poem's reference to itself is heard in these sounds played out 'en presque durées égales' [at a nearly regular pace] and the 'permutations circulaires de groupes' [circular permutations of groups], evoking the multiplication of *tanka* patterns that run through the book's various levels. The poet expresses his intention for the poem to move before the gaze of his lover, to enclose her, also his reader, within it. However, it is during her subsequent readings of the poem, 'le demain de ta lecture' [the tomorrow of your reading], that she will bestow (her) meaning onto the poem. In the 'paraphe de ton œil' [the signature of her eye], her eye writes the text as she reads; her finger imposes the signature of her presence along its lines, fleshing out its bones with the fulfilment of its potential that her reading brings. The poem is an offering to the lover-reader, an invitation for her in turn to bestow meaning upon the text: 'le | sens que tu lui donneras | le demain de ta lecture' [the | meaning you will give it | the tomorrow of your reading]. It is a meaning as individual as each signature – 'paraphe' – and perhaps it is possible to say that the poem changes in some way on each reading and in relation to each of its readers.

Spaces of silence in the poetic structure of *Trente et un au cube* are like windows: providing a view beyond that of the poet and allowing the reader in. Just as feminine subjectivity is given space to breathe in Irigaray's re-writing of the love relation, so too the reader is encouraged to fill the spaces of potential in Roubaud's poetry. The conclusions of my readings of *Trente et un au cube* cannot, however, exclude those spaces that stifle and threaten the feminine presence in the volume. There is a vacillation in Roubaud's text between different understandings of the disjunction in the relation. Although it represents a source of anxiety, yearning and a wish to possess the other, the space between lovers may at other moments be interpreted as a positive one that allows for the coexistence of both terms in the relation. Through the spaces that constitute the rhythms of the poems, there is an opening up of the text to the creation of meaning within it, independent of the written lines of the poet. Perhaps it can be said that meaning in *Trente et un au cube* is the result of a collaborative effort between the poet and his reader, just as the poet-lover accepts that a space-between, with the anxiety and mystery that sustains, is the way in which his beloved's existence may have space to breathe.

Conclusion

In *Trente et un au cube* the numerical underpinning of form carves out spaces in the text, markers of place and time, which mobilize an interaction with memory. At times its unexpected patterns slow down or halt the reader, forcing a re-reading and a closer engagement with the lines of the poem.

The otherness of the reader can be considered in the light of Lacan's theorization of the feminine, and particularly in the way in which Irigaray deconstructs the system. She reads Freud in Lacan's schema of sexuation, comparing the geometrical spaces envisaged in set theory to the visual prominence of male anatomy in the earlier psychoanalyst's theory of castration. While Lacan moves away from biological concepts in Freud, Irigaray finds in both a patriarchal writing of woman into the story. The psychoanalyst is likened to the male poet, who gains support in his creativity from the muse: she is an empty figure, a blank canvas onto which the writer projects his fantasy. However, Irigaray draws out the possibility for resistance in Lacan's theory: the feminine not only eludes the masculine term, but as that which cannot be contained, her potential exceeds him. The very system that constructs the feminine in the negative image of masculinity, the 'not-all' that confirms that which is 'whole', necessarily fails without her presence. When Roubaud aligns poetic form with the diaphanous body of the loved woman, it is, on the one hand, because the poem's form reflects the careful construction of the poet. Yet as diaphanous material, a poem's form also reflects the presence of the reader whose commitment to reading is essential for the fulfilment of meaning in the text. In the same way that Lacan's feminine eludes classification through the theorist's definition of her as 'what he is not', so too the fullest potential of the poet's work escapes him.

Feminine otherness to Roubaud's male poet – the dazzling of her wings, her creaturely transformation – distances her from him. Through the many references to the addressee's position at, or as, the central axis of the poem, she also comes to be aligned with the unusually large space of silence that separates the two verses of the sixteenth poem: the true centre of the book and the space that divides the poet's touch from feminine form. I have read this distance separating the lovers in *Trente et un au cube* through the structure of the sexual disjunction, or the impossibility of the sexual relation in Lacanian psychoanalysis. The sexual relation in Lacan's work is a layered concept: it is at once the relation between the masculine and feminine terms in the psychoanalyst's formulae of sexuation and the coming together of the two in sexual terms. Just as Lacan's conception of the sexual relation may be understood on multiple levels – which are nonetheless interrelated – so too does the disjunction function in different ways between the poet and his beloved. The distance gives rise to anxiety – the knowledge that the beloved cannot be possessed and the loss on the part of the poet who relinquishes some of his control, allowing for the interactions between the text and the singular investment of each reader in the poem. The separation between the lovers is also a space in which each individual subject is allowed the space to be, comparable to the space-between that characterizes the Irigarayan love relation both in *Être Deux* and *J'aime à toi* – titles which exemplify the respected subjectivity of both terms that constitute the relation. I offer no resolution of these contrasting interpretations of the disjunction, since Roubaud includes examples of them all in his treatise on love. There is violence and manipulation in his treatment of the feminine – a reminder that she exists in *Trente et un au cube* as the poet represents her on the page. He also distributes spaces throughout the text in which her presence grows, acknowledging her breathing as the beating heart of the poem.

The reader does not require a 'mode d'emploi' [user's guide] to tackle the jagged rhythms and unfamiliar forms of *Trente et un au cube*; the volume is itself a treatise on poetry as much as it is one on love. Through an engagement with its form, the reader learns the value of commitment to poetry and with time, the navigation of the book's unknown spaces becomes a familiar route that can be mapped out and explored in memory.

By opening out the folded page enclosing each poem and taking up the position of Roubaud's addressee, the reader accepts the poet's offering, millions of syllables counted out between poet and reader. The relationship that follows does not constitute a dialogue in the conventional sense; there is no two-way conversation made up of statements or questions and replies, but it is founded on an interaction. Without the reader, the book's cubic structure collapses. In this way, *Trente et un au cube* is Roubaud's user's guide to poetry.

CHAPTER 4

Form, Love and Loss

Roubaud's later writings reach beyond their boundaries towards the poet's life experiences even more so than his early poetry volumes. The poet has written of his work as existing in the interstice between two periods of mourning in his life: 'pris entre deux "bords" de mort' [held between two 'edges' of death].[1] The impetus for Roubaud's first major poetry collection, *Signe d'appartenance*, came when the poet was mourning the loss of his brother. He writes of *beginning to speak*, 'selon ma manière de dire qui est la poésie' [in my manner of speaking which is poetry], binding together the existence of poetry and the need for self-expression.[2] Yet life alters the creative path of the poet; the unexpected overwhelms and just as it once was the trigger for the beginning of poetry, it also has the power to silence it.[3] Following the unexpected death of his wife, Roubaud comes up against the second of his ' "bords" de mort' ['edges' of death]. He tells his reader: 'j'étais comme silencieux' [I was as though silenced].[4]

The works of Roubaud's œuvre written after 1983 inevitably bear the weight of the loss of Alix Cléo, and they are shaped by it. My study began with Roubaud's construction of an approach to love in poetry. While *Trente et un au cube* reflects Roubaud's attempt to formalize love through

1 Jacques Roubaud, *Quelque chose noir* (Paris: Gallimard, 1986), p. 132.

2 Roubaud, *Quelque chose noir*, p. 131.

3 In a radio interview, Roubaud explains that he had planned the trajectory of his poetry publications from the outset, aiming for nine works that would culminate in the recently published *Octogone* [*Octagon*] in 2014. *Quelque chose noir* [*Some Thing Black*] cannot have been part of that plan, since it was written in response to the unexpected passing of Alix Cléo. See Roubaud's radio interview 'Page 124 – Oubli', *Le Carnet d'or*, France Culture, 19 April 2014.

4 Roubaud, *Quelque chose noir*, p. 132.

the language of poetry and mathematical structure, in later volumes *Du noir tombe* (1985) [*Darkness Falls*] and *Quelque chose noir* (1986) [*Some Thing Black*] there is what might be described as an undoing of form, and what Roubaud has called his 'aphasie' [aphasia] in poetry.[5] The collection titles themselves signal formlessness and a lack of measure, or definition; their indeterminate references to the colour black and 'some thing' a far cry from the numerical precision and cubic shaping evoked by the title of *Trente et un au cube*.

What has thus far been a theoretical account of the relation between the poet-narrator and his muse will become a close reading of the particular creative partnership between Jacques Roubaud and his late wife, Alix Cléo, within the parameters of Jacques Roubaud's writing. The disjunction that I found to be part of the lovers' collaboration in *Trente et un au cube* becomes concretized, as the texts I will be reading were all produced after the death of Alix Cléo, and in response to it. They include *Du noir tombe*, *Quelque chose noir* and *Octogone* [*Octagon*]. Although some parts of these texts will be characterized by moments lived by the poet, this study does not slip into the realms of life writing and autobiographical analysis. I continue to focus on the links between love and poetic form, through close readings of Roubaud's writings. Roubaud's later works draw on and expand the conceptions of love and poetic form that constitute *Trente et un au cube*, and my readings reflect this development.

I began this book with the particular intertwining of form and love that characterized Roubaud's outlook on poetry composition as he embarked on life as a poet. Now I reconsider the place of form in Roubaud's poetry through readings of *Du noir tombe* and *Quelque chose noir*, written in the wake of Alix Cléo's passing. What becomes of poetic form when love is lost, and silence threatens to engulf language completely? Without the poet's first reader and when fading memories of her are all that the poet has left, what is the role of form in poetry, and what is the position of the reader in relation to the text?

In the last part of my study, I focus on the nature of the creative collaboration that goes on between Alix Cléo and Jacques Roubaud as the

5 Roubaud, *Quelque chose noir*, p. 131.

poet mourns his loss. Alix Cléo was a photographer, writer and translator, who shared creative projects with her husband and frequently worked with him.[6] Having suffered with asthma since her childhood, a pulmonary embolism took her life suddenly in January 1983. Is it possible to speak of collaboration even after the poet's beloved has passed away? Does the creative partnership necessarily end with her death, or is it somehow appropriated by the person left behind? I consider the role of one of Alix Cléo's photographs – *Quinze minutes la nuit au rythme de la respiration* [*Fifteen minutes at night to the rhythm of breathing*] – in Jacques Roubaud's writing.[7] Although my particular focus is Roubaud's poetry, I look at the place of the photograph in a passage from the author's prose volume *Le Grand incendie de Londres* [*The Great Fire of London*]. Not only does the passage in question bear traits of Roubaud's adoption of the troubadour poetry aesthetic, *entrebescar*, but it also anticipates – and retrospectively interacts with – a poem that appeared in Roubaud's recent collection published by Gallimard, *Octogone*. In *Trente et un au cube*, the beloved's breathing was the beating heart of the poems' rhythm. How does Alix Cléo's breathing shape Roubaud's writing through her photograph after she is gone?

When Darkness Falls: Love, Mourning and the Unravelling of Form

Quelque chose noir is often the point of departure for commentators working on Roubaud's poetry of love and mourning. The volume contains some of the first poems written after Alix Cléo died: its final poem,

6 See, for example, their joint translation of Gertrude Stein's *Lifting Belly*, published in *Action poétique*, 82–83 (1980), 90–97.

7 This particular photo taken by Alix Cléo is reprinted in Hélène Giannecchini, *Une image peut-être vraie: Alix Cléo Roubaud* (Paris: Seuil, 2014), p. 115. See also the catalogue to the posthumous exhibition of Alix Cléo's work at the *Bibliothèque nationale de France*, *Alix Cléo: Photographies*, ed. by Anne Biroleau-Lemagny, Hélène Giannecchini and Dominique Versavel (Paris: BNF, 2014), pp. 154–55.

'Rien' ['Nothing'], is dated 1983, the year of her death, and the title of its first poem gives its composition date as May 1985, 'Méditation du 12/5/85' ['Meditation from 12/5/85'].[8] The discrepancy in the dates is accounted for in the book's opening:

> Je me trouvai devant ce silence inarticulé un peu
> comme le bois certains en de semblables moments
> ont pensé déchiffrer l'esprit dans quelque rémanence
> cela fut pour eux une consolation ou du redoublement
> de l'horreur pas moi.[9]
>
> [I found myself before this silence inarticulate a bit
> like wood some in such moments
> thought about deciphering the spirit in some remanence
> it was a consolation for them or an intensification
> of the horror not me.]

A world apart from the opening lines of *Trente et un au cube*, in which the addressee, the poet's lover, was the impetus for the production of the words on the page – 'JE DÉTIENS MILLION de | syllabes comptées pour toi' [I KEEP A MILLION | syllables counted out for you] – the poet in *Quelque chose noir* faces emptiness.[10] The silence referred to is not one that structures the poetry, a tangible component of the poem's form. Instead, it engulfs the poet, leaving him inarticulate, motionless, stuck in his grief. There is no 'toi' [you], only the impersonal 'certains' [some] from whom the speaker distances himself; it is a reference that doubles his isolation. The opening to the volume begins – 'Je' [I] – and ends – 'moi' [me] – with the poet alone. The *passé simple* [simple past] tense takes the reader back to a past distanced from the present, however, and the beginning of *Quelque chose noir* marks the end of this silence he describes. The book is thus testimony to a hiatus in Roubaud's life as a poet.

8 Roubaud, *Quelque chose noir*, pp. 11–12 and pp. 145–48.
9 Roubaud, *Quelque chose noir*, p. 11.
10 Roubaud, *Trente et un au cube*, p. 9.

This interruption in poetry writing is expressed visually in the poem title '1983: janvier.   1985: juin' ['1983: January.   1985: June'].[11] The large gap between the dates represents the void in Roubaud's poetry production and the full stop after 'janvier' [January] marks a definitive ending in the poet's life, the point after which nothing will ever be the same. There is no full stop after 'juin' [June], however, suggesting that the pathway towards poetry remains open onwards from the point of *Quelque chose noir*. In the first line of '1983: janvier.   1985: juin' ['1983: January.   1985: June'], Roubaud explains: 'Le registre rythmique de la parole me fait horreur' [The rhythmic register of language horrifies me].[12] He cannot bring himself even to read poetry: 'Je ne parviens pas à ouvrir un seul livre contenant de la poésie' [I can't bring myself to open a single book of poetry], preferring instead 'de la prose inoffensive' [inoffensive prose].[13] With love wrenched from the formula that defined Roubaud's existence as a poet, poetry as he knows it becomes impossible. The intertwining of love and language – 'lamourlapoésielamour' [lovepoetrylove] – that was the principal concern of *Trente et un au cube*, is now inconceivable. In 'Aphasie' ['Aphasia'] Roubaud presents the particular stages of the undoing of his poetic theory:

> Jakobson dit que l'aphasie mange la langue à l'envers de son acquisition. Les articulations les plus récentes partent les premières.
>
> Une bouche qui se défait commence par les lèvres.
>
> J'ai pensé la même chose du vers. les règles du vers disparaissent une à une dans sa destruction, selon un ordre, aussi, aphasique. Comme si les poètes défaisaient leur bâtiment étage par étage. Sans le faire exploser d'un coup.
>
> Devant ta mort je suis resté silencieux.
>
> Je n'ai pas pu parler pendant presque trente mois.
>
> Je ne pouvais plus parler selon ma manière de dire qui est la poésie.[14]
>
> [Jakobson says that aphasia eats away at language in the reverse order of its acquisition. The most recent articulations are the first to go.

11 Roubaud, *Quelque chose noir*, p. 33.
12 Roubaud, *Quelque chose noir*, p. 33.
13 Roubaud, *Quelque chose noir*, p. 33.
14 Roubaud, *Quelque chose noir*, p. 131. Punctuation reproduced from the original.

> A mouth's undoing begins on its lips.
>
> I have thought the same thing about verse. the rules of verse disappear one by one as it is destroyed, in an order that is also aphasic. As though the poets were taking down their building floor by floor. Not blowing it up in one go.
>
> Faced with your death I remained silent.
>
> I could not speak for almost thirty months.
>
> I could no longer speak in my manner of speaking which is poetry.]

The mouth is the site of the fusion of poetry and love in *Trente et un au cube*, bringing together the language of poetry and the kiss. In 'Aphasie', the 'chant' [song] constructed in *Trente et un au cube* is unravelled from the very lips on which it began. The passage in the later volume alludes to the principles behind the construction of *Trente et un au cube* in its reference to the notion of order and rules forming a 'bâtiment' in poetry. The cubic construction that held the poet's lover in its centre is now undone floor by floor, demolished before the eyes of the reader who follows the prosaic lines on the page. Nevertheless, insofar as *Quelque chose noir* is the point at which Roubaud's silence is broken, its poems dated from May 1985 marking 'presque trente mois' [almost thirty months] after the death of Alix Cléo, it necessarily presents itself as a volume of poetry.

The form of the poems in *Quelque chose noir* has drawn much critical attention, often centred on the question of genre. Christelle Reggiani writes of the volume that 'la poésie précaire paraît constamment à la limite de *verser* dans la prose' [the precarious poetry seems constantly on the verge of lapsing into prose].[15] Elisabeth Cardonne-Arlyck finds in *Quelque chose noir* a 'poétique ablative' [ablative poetics] and a 'raréfaction [...] des moyens' [rarefaction [...] of methods]; she contrasts its poems to those of *Trente et un au cube*, pointing to a 'poétique austère de la phrase, qui [...] n'use quasiment jamais du divorce de la mesure et de la syntaxe' [austere poetics of the sentence, which [...] hardly ever sees a divergence between metre

15 Christelle Reggiani, 'Portrait de l'artiste en poète: paradoxes de l'auteur roubaldien', in *Jacques Roubaud, compositeur de mathématique et de poésie*, ed. by Agnès Disson and Véronique Montémont (Nancy: Éditions Absalon, 2010), pp. 135–46 (p. 143). Emphasis in the original.

and syntax].[16] While the clashing boundaries of syntactical and metrical measure are the source of texture in *Trente et un au cube*, *Quelque chose noir* is described in terms of its sparse idiom: 'Peu d'enjambements mais des phrases qui se prolongent au-delà de la ligne, comme des versets ou des paragraphes de prose, ou s'arrêtent avant, comme des vers. [...] Des poèmes, donc, de privation' [There are few enjambments, but there are sentences that go on beyond the end of the line, like verses or paragraphs of prose, or they stop short, like lines of poetry. [...] They are therefore poems of deprivation].[17]

The concern in both analyses is with the line of poetry or '*vers*'. Reggiani's wordplay in her reference to a poetry constantly about to '*verser* dans la prose' [lapse into prose] highlights the '*vers*' as the point at which the distinction between poetry and prose is blurred. Cardonne-Arlyck points out the missing play between the syllabic and syntactic lines that was a prominent feature of *Trente et un au cube*. In *Quelque chose noir*, there are lines, sometimes paragraphs, of prose. Poems characterized by shorter lines bear little trace of tangible syllabic patterning, placed at a remove from the line of lyric poetry by the simile in Cardonne-Arlyck's evaluation: '*comme* des vers' [*like* lines of poetry]. In Jean-François Puff's words, *Quelque chose noir* is a 'négation stricte de la poésie' [strict negation of poetry], haunted at every step by what is missing from it:

> on se souvient du modèle de l'*entrebescar* rythmique – l'entrelacement des langues dans le baiser – et des conceptions des troubadours, qui lient indissolublement amour et poésie. De cela il saurait plus être question. Pas plus d'ailleurs que l'un des effets du rythme comme jeu de langage, qui est la reconfiguration du temps.[18]
>
> [we think back to the model of the rhythmic *entrebescar* – the intertwining of the tongues in the kiss – and the troubadour concepts that inextricably link love and poetry. It can no longer be a question of that. And it is no longer possible to see the reconfiguration of time in the effects produced by rhythm as language play.]

16 Cardonne-Arlyck, *Véracités*, p. 247.
17 Cardonne-Arlyck, *Véracités*, p. 247.
18 Puff, *Mémoire de la mémoire*, p. 377.

The aesthetic of *entrebescar* present in so much of Roubaud's poetry is now but a memory, the entanglement of rhythms, rhymes and lexical fields unravelling in the wake of Roubaud's bereavement. What Puff had seen as an attempt to reconfigure time through the contours of rhythm in *Trente et un au cube* is impossible in a life full of the before and after of death.

Comparisons with Roubaud's earlier works of poetry are inevitable, as the lines between Roubaud's poetic theory, composition processes and the poetry itself are rarely clear-cut. It is therefore understandable that many readings of *Quelque chose noir* allude to that which came before, present now only as a shadow, or an echo of a possibility. Ben Lerner writes of the experience of loss expressed in poetry, identifying the phenomenon that seems to bring together commentators on Roubaud's poems of mourning: '[T]he felt unavailability of traditional lyric categories; the instruction to read [the] writing as poetry – and especially as lyric poetry – catalyzes an experience of their loss, like a sensation in a phantom limb.'[19] Roubaud's volume, published as part of Gallimard's poetry collection, is subtitled as '*Poésie*' [*Poetry*]. Nevertheless, the reader cannot help but feel that the dynamics have changed and that the poetry alluded to, both on the cover of the volume and within, is somehow a distant memory. What *was* 'catalyzes' what is now unavailable in poetic form.

Before entering into my reading of the relationship between form and love lost in *Quelque chose noir*, I want to pause to consider the nature of the poetic silence that defined Roubaud's existence for thirty months after Alix Cléo's death. Although silence, in many forms, is central to *Quelque chose noir*, and despite the ambiguity in the genre of the poems, I will be working from the premise that the book does nevertheless mark the end of a definitive silence in poetic output, and a new beginning in poetry composition. With these assumptions in mind, I turn back to *Du noir tombe*.

The slim volume is made up of nineteen poems by Jacques Roubaud, accompanied by artwork – 'dessins' [drawings] – by Jean-Gaudaire Thor. The first poems of *Quelque chose noir* are dated May 1985, but the publication date of *Du noir tombe* is also 1985, and a note at the end of the latter

19 Ben Lerner, *The Hatred of Poetry* (London: Fitzcarraldo Editions, 2016), pp. 90–91.

book indicates a composition period of slightly earlier that same year: '*Du Noir Tombe*, de JR est une suite de 19 variations écrites spécialement pour ce projet, en mars–avril' [*Darkness Falls* by JR is a series of nineteen variations written specially for this project in March–April].[20] If *Quelque chose noir* marks the breaking of the poet's silence, the 'suite de 19 variations' [series of nineteen variations] of *Du noir tombe* just falls within that period of silence, and is somehow characterized by it.[21]

As with *Quelque chose noir*, there are allusions in the work to Roubaud's previous poetic concerns. The book's nineteen poems are divided into six groups of three, leaving one solitary poem at the end. Each of the three poems in a group contains almost exactly the same words, in the same order, the first line of each appearing thus:

1. nuit
2. nuit
3. nuit
4. un silence
5. un silence
6. un silence
7. la nuit
8. la nuit
9. la nuit
10. le noir
11. le noir
12. le noir
13. un silence
14. un silence
15. un silence
16. une couleur
17. une couleur
18. une couleur
19. fenêtre

20 Jacques Roubaud, with Jean-Gaudaire Thor, *Du noir tombe* (n.p.: Colorature, 1985). Not paginated.

21 It is worth mentioning that there are not many copies of the small collection easily available. On discovering a copy in The Kandinsky Library in Paris, and noting the dates of composition and publication, I considered the possibility that its scarcity might in some way be linked to its creation during the months of silence I have

1. night
2. night
3. night
4. a silence
5. a silence
6. a silence
7. the night
8. the night
9. the night
10. darkness
11. darkness
12. darkness
13. a silence
14. a silence
15. a silence
16. a colour
17. a colour
18. a colour
19. window

The view as a list of the first words of each poem shows the sestina pattern underlying the overall structure of the series; invented by troubadour Arnaut Daniel, the sestina comprises six stanzas and an envoi. Roubaud situates 'le secret de la sextine' [the secret of the sestina] in the complex permutation of rhyme words – 'mots-rimes' – that creates echoes throughout the form.[22] The poet describes the pattern as 'une imbrication' [interlocking] of 'assonances-consonances sur les mots-rimes' [assonances-consonances in the rhyme words], an intertwining which also draws out 'une dissonance dans les assonances' [a dissonance in the assonances].[23] The 'rhyme words' do not necessarily rhyme, creating both assonant and consonant sounds.[24] The phonic effect produced is not random; rather the shifting pattern is generated by the mathematically

referred to above. See Chris Andrews on 'paranoid interpretation' and the tendency of the reader to 'go "too far"' in *How to Do Things with Forms: The Oulipo and Its Inventions* (Montreal: McGill-Queen's University Press, 2022), pp. 178–83.

22 Roubaud, *La Fleur inverse*, p. 296.

23 Roubaud, *La Fleur inverse*, p. 295.

24 Roubaud, *La Fleur inverse*, p. 294.

structured movement of the same set of words appearing in each of the poem's six stanzas.

Roubaud uses the figure of the snail to represent the 'imbrication' of the 'mots-rimes' in a sestina. The rhyme words are listed vertically according to their order within the first stanza and a spiral is drawn working inwards from the sixth position at the bottom of the list, through the first at the top, and ending at the third position in the centre. The trajectory of the spiral from this sixth position inwards gives the order of the rhyme words for the next stanza and the same steps can be followed for each new sequence until the series of six stanzas is complete. The order produced in the sequences can be represented thus, where each number represents a rhyme word and each letter a new stanza:

a. 1 2 3 4 5 6
b. 6 1 5 2 4 3
c. 3 6 4 1 2 5
d. 5 3 2 6 1 4
e. 4 5 1 3 6 2
f. 2 4 6 5 3 1

Following this permutation, the pattern of rhyme words is different in each of the six stanzas, ensuring a constantly original and stimulating formal structure.

The particular permutation of rhyme words in the sestina is what leads Roubaud to write of its 'séduction poétique musicale et formelle' [musical, poetic and formal seduction].[25] The troubadour *canso* was linked with this notion of seduction: an appeal to the beloved lady, its structural ingenuity was tied up in desire. For Roubaud, the shape of the '*escargot*' [snail] used to calculate the sequences of rhyme words in the sestina is a symbol of the interconnectedness of the poem's formal and amorous ambitions: 'elle lie la permutation au poème plus fermement, l'*escargot* étant un animal pour qui chair et ongle sont particulièrement proches' [it ties the permutation more tightly to the poem, the *snail* being a creature in which flesh and shell are bound particularly closely together].[26] In addition to the entangling of

25 Roubaud, *Description du projet*, p. 107.
26 Roubaud, *La Fleur inverse*, p. 296.

flesh and skeleton, content and form, the image is suggestive of the secure structure of the rhyme words, which holds together the poem 'fermement' [tightly]: the sestina's arrangement is an example of the *entrebescar* technique that Roubaud placed at the heart of his love poetry in *Trente et un au cube*.

This aside into the intricacies of the sestina form indicates the ways in which it is not similar to the list of the poems that make up *Du noir tombe*. While the overarching architecture of six sections and an envoi in the book does invite a comparison with the form, the distinctive intertwining of the sestina's six stanzas through the engineered movement of assonant and consonant words is not present in the collection. Instead, the wording of each of the three poems belonging to a group is almost identical and each threefold repetition of a poem is followed by three repetitions of the next. There are no organized patterns or sequences interconnecting the six groups, apart from the aleatory recurrence of references to night – 'nuit' [night], 'la nuit' [the night], or 'le noir' [darkness] – and silence which dominate the short collection. Roubaud appears to hint at the sestina form from within the arrangement of *Du noir tombe*, but delving beyond the surface reveals that the differences are greater than the similarities. The comparison itself between the sestina and *Du noir tombe* highlights the starker nature of these poems which are imbued with the sombre tones of the poet's grief, and we are reminded of Puff's analysis: mourning his love has meant the impossibility of *entrebescar*.

Further comparisons between *Du noir tombe* and Roubaud's other poetic concerns and works are invited in the note that closes the book. Referring to the nineteen 'variations', Roubaud insists that they are particularly unlike those that make up a previous work: 'Elles sont toutes différentes de celles constituant le livre *Dors*, publié chez Gallimard en 1981' [They are completely different from the ones that make up the book *Sleep*, published by Gallimard in 1981].[27] The statement naturally arouses the curiosity of the reader, particularly one who is accustomed to the intertextualities and multiple connections that both form a network within Roubaud's oeuvre and spill out beyond it. Why – or how – are the 'variations' of *Du noir tombe*

27 Roubaud, *Du noir tombe*, not paginated.

so completely different from those that make up the poet's earlier book? What might a comparison with *Dors* add to a reading of *Du noir tombe*?

The first difference in the poet's approach in the two books is shown in their respective titles. The poetic voice of *Dors* addresses its listener in the second-person singular form; the title is the mark of a volume that is explicitly oral. In a piece of introductory writing to *Dors* entitled 'Indication' ['Instruction'], Roubaud defines the book as 'un programme de lecture' [a programme of reading] whose poems 'ont été conçus pour être dits, pour être transportés réellement par la voix' [have been conceived to be spoken, to be transported by the voice].[28] Not only are the poems to be read aloud, but when the reader reaches the end, the poet advises that the entire sequence is to be read again 'dans l'ordre inverse' [in reverse order].[29] Roubaud goes on to say that the written page is not to be understood as 'une notation, une partition de la voix' [a notation, a score for the voice], and the silences in the vocalization of the poems are not to be equated with the blanks on the page. Instead, the two modes of reading are described as 'presque autonomes' [almost autonomous]:

> l'une et l'autre lecture construisent, imaginaire, un *double*, qui est cette poésie, absente de chaque poème, s'il est entendu ou lu, mais plutôt se situe derrière chacun, un peu derrière chacun, à l'écart oblique et qui derrière chacun vous regarde.[30]
>
> [the one and the other reading form an imaginary *double*, which is this poetry, absent from each poem, whether it is heard or read, but rather is situated behind each one, a little behind each one, separate oblique and which from behind each one watches you.]

There is an echo in these instructions of Roubaud's theory of memory in poetry reading. The poet encourages the reader to become well acquainted with the poems, first approaching them in the sequence in which they are printed on the page, then in reverse order. Another double is that of the voice and the visual page. The twofold notion of a reading

28 Roubaud, *Dors*, p. 33.

29 Roubaud, *Dors*, p. 33.

30 Roubaud, *Dors*, p. 33. Spacing reproduced from the original here and in later citations from the volume.

that watches on from behind the reader reiterates the significance of the multidimensionality – the interconnection of the phonic and spatial features – of a poem, and its interaction with memory. Meanwhile, the qualifiers 'à l'écart   oblique' [separate   oblique] and the reference to the '*double*' suggest that a reading can be separate enough from the reader to be able to watch on over the process, almost like a presence lingering uncannily in the background. This silent observer might stand for the element of otherness in reading, the unknown that the poet invites into his text when he asks for the reader's participation in it.[31]

The multiple layers of reading that characterize *Dors* collapse in *Du noir tombe*. Its title signals the onset of a darker time, and rather than sleep, night now brings with it death. There is no second-person address to connect with the reader of the poems, only the 'Je' [I] of the poet's voice and the loneliness of night:

la nuit
je m'éveille
et je vois
dans la nuit
je vois
la nuit et
rien.[32]

[night
I wake
and I see

31 In his translation of Roubaud's text, *Sleep preceded by Saying Poetry*, Matthew B. Smith reproduces this sense of the uncanny, doubled reading. He reads aloud his English translation simultaneously to a recording of his reading of the poetry in French. When he stumbled over words and confused sounds in his live reading, he incorporated some of these 'happy accidents' into his final translation. See his 'Note on the Translation' in *Sleep preceded by Saying Poetry* (Providence: La Presse, 2019).

32 *Du noir tombe*, poem no. 7. As the volume is not paginated, I will refer to the poems by number according to the sequence in which they appear in the book. I also replicate the original spacing of the poems as it appears in *Du noir tombe*.

in the night
I see
the night and
nothing.]

The consecutive repetitions, which occur within individual poems as well as across groups, do not necessarily tease the reader's memory in the way we have seen elsewhere in the poet's oeuvre. This more subdued approach can be contrasted with Roubaud's own description of the poems in *Dors*:

> les poèmes se répondent dans leur succession, de séquence à séquence, en des figures d'intrication, où interviennent non seulement le lexique mais les longueurs des vers, les intervalles qui les séparent dans la page, multiples impairs et rythmés d'une même unité, les glissements de temps et de nombre, les couleurs.[33]

> [the poems respond to one another in their succession, from one sequence to the next, through devices of interrelation involving not only the lexis used, but also the length of the lines, the intervals that separate them on the page, the uneven and rhythmic multiples of a unit, the shifts in time and number, the colours.]

The 'succession' of poems in *Dors* hints at the numerical structuring of *Trente et un au cube*; the collection is divided into three sections, each with thirty-one poems. Those thirty-one poems are in turn divided into smaller groups of poems counted according to the *tanka* pattern: 5-7-5-7-7. This Japanese influence on the structure of *Dors* is made evident through lists – almost like contents lists – that precede each of the five subsections in a sequence and indicate the key words, or titles, from which the poems grow. For example, opening section one is the list:

1. dormir
2. nuit
3. un silence
4. fenêtre
5. la nuit.[34]

33 Roubaud, *Dors*, p. 34.
34 Roubaud, *Dors*, p. 43.

1. sleep
2. night
3. a silence
4. window
5. the night.

While the longer second section is given thus:

1. dors
2. nuit
3. lumières
4. un silence
5.
6.
7. la nuit.[35]

1. sleep
2. night
3. lights
4. a silence
5.
6.
7. the night.

Often the titles outlining each sequence of 5-7-5-7-7 are the same across the three streams of thirty-one poems, but slight modifications from one to the next mean that none of the three sections are identical. Despite the structural nod to *Trente et un au cube*, the poems themselves of *Dors* are characterized more by a sense of variation and modification open to chance and circumstance than by the intricate intertwining of the *entrebescar* aesthetic. As Roubaud states in his 'Indication', the poems respond or react to one another, they are made up of slips – 'glissements' – that are often no more than interruptions which 'interviennent' [occur].

In the text that precedes *Dors*, entitled *Dire la poésie* [*Saying Poetry*], the poet accounts for the sense of shifting that characterizes the work:

35 Roubaud, *Dors*, p. 46.

> Je veux dire que pendant les six ou sept années où
> ces poèmes ont existé avant d'être posés en ce livre
> à chaque lecture à chaque copie manuscrite
> de leur ensemble quelque chose changeait je
> leur faisais subir des variations minimales l'ensemble
> de ces poèmes était accumulation de variations
> minimales.[36]
>
> [I mean that during the six or seven years that
> these poems existed before being placed in this book
> on every reading in every handwritten copy
> of the collection something changed I
> subjected them to minimal variations the gathering
> of these poems was the accumulation of minimal
> variations.]

The published work comprises a set of poems that has evolved over several years; it incorporates tiny changes that have occurred in the sequences in their alternating states of being performed and written down. Roubaud's use of the imperfect tense to describe the alterations emphasizes their movement over time: multiple and cumulative. In another passage in *Dire la poésie* the poet describes how the sound of a dripping tap infiltrated the sequences:

> une goutte
> ponctuation à ma voix toujours la même se
> préparait à tomber du robinet qui ne fermait pas je
> l'attendais elle absorbait mon attention retirant
> de ma voix basse lisant les poèmes toute intention
> toute persuasion toute certitude afin encore que la
> voix continue d'elle-même au-delà de ce qui était
> déjà écrit peut-être pour le répéter pour le bouger
> d'un mot déplacer d'un intervalle d'une ligne
> pour aller un peu plus loin avant que la goutte d'eau
> à nouveau tombe.[37]

36 Roubaud, *Dors*, p. 18.
37 Roubaud, *Dors*, pp. 17–18.

[a drop
punctuating my voice always the same was
preparing to fall from the tap that would not turn off I
was waiting it absorbed my attention removing
from my low voice reading the poems all intention
all persuasion all certitude so that the
voice continues of its own accord beyond what was
already written maybe to repeat it to shift it
by a word move an interval a line
to go a little further before the drop of water
falls again.]

The sequences bear the traces of the circumstances in which they were composed, read and reread, assimilating the rhythms punctuating the poet's thoughts at the time. The dripping tap featured in this explanatory extract does figure in *Dors*, appearing simply as 'une goutte' [a drop] across six of the poems.[38] The water droplet draws the reader's attention to the quiet of night and the poet's distraction:

une goutte

une goutte

va

tomber.

tu attends

qu'elle

tombe.

quelque chose

à

attendre.[39]

[*a drop*

a drop

38 The poems entitled 'une goutte' do not appear in consecutive order; they feature in the sixteenth and twenty-seventh positions of each of the three sequences of thirty-one poems that make up *Dors*.

39 Roubaud, *Dors*, p. 52.

will
fall.

You wait
for it
to fall.

Something
to
wait for.]

As the sequence builds, there is a sense of accumulation and time passing, regulated by the intervals anticipating the droplets falling, and the moments in which they fall:

une goutte

une goutte
tombe.

tu
l'entends.

rien d'autre
ne change.[40]

[*a drop*

a drop
falls.

you
hear it.

nothing else
changes.]

40 Roubaud, *Dors*, p. 59.

It is not only the waiting and the dripping water that mark the progression of time, but also the lexical and typographical shifts. The next poem under the title of '*une goutte*' repeats the structure of the first in the series cited above, but the verb 'attendre' [to wait] (and 'attends' [wait]) is replaced by 'croire' [to believe] (and 'crois' [believe]).[41]

The fourth poem is very close to the second in its vocabulary and themes:

> *une goutte*
>
> une goutte
> tombe
>
> tu peux l'en
> tendre
>
> rien d'autre n'a
> rrive.[42]
>
> [*a drop*
>
> a drop
> falls
>
> you can he
> ar it
>
> nothing else ha
> ppens.]

Lexical modifications see the move from 'change' [changes] to 'arrive' [happens] at the end of the poem, and the addition of the modal verb 'peux' [can] in the centre of the poem alters the syntax ever so slightly. The effect of these varying repetitions in poems scattered among others that do not mention the 'goutte' at all, is the creation of echoes that resonate through the different sequences.

One of the final in the series of six poems built around the dripping faucet speaks of the role of memory in poetry:

41 Roubaud, *Dors*, p. 75.
42 Roubaud, *Dors*, p. 81.

une goutte

une goutte
tom
bait.

revenait
en
arrière.

quelque chose
en
mémoire.[43]

[*a drop*

a drop
was fall
ing.

was
going
back.

something
in
memory.]

No longer waited for, the falling drop becomes a memory embedded in the preceding sequences that make up the text. The poem's reference to the drop as memory also recalls the point in the 'Indication' where the poet describes the dripping tap regulating the rhythms of his poetry composition. This network of resonances is one of many that ripple through the collection, offering instances of familiarity and intimacy between poet and reader. It is an example of the 'figures d'intrication' [devices of interrelation] and the 'glissements de temps et de nombre' [shifts in time and number] with which Roubaud defines *Dors*.

The mood of the poems in *Du noir tombe* is sparse and sombre in comparison to those of *Dors*, with the themes of darkness, night and silence

43 Roubaud, *Dors*, p. 97.

prevailing. Any references to sound are overshadowed by a sense of its struggle or failure to penetrate the darkness. Sounds are described as 'split' ('le bruit | se scinde') or 'drying up' ('les bruits | sèchent'), suffocated in the poems by repetitions of 'nuit' [night], 'noir' [darkness] and 'silence' [silence]. Instead of the 'figures d'intrication', the 'glissements de temps et de nombre' and 'les couleurs' characteristic of the sequences in flux that comprise *Dors*, movement in *Du noir tombe* takes another form. The shifts that occur from one poem to the next within each group of three are visual, involving typographical differences and slight changes in punctuation: the same words are arranged differently over lines; the full stop changes position, at times vertically distanced from the end of the poem, appearing somewhere below it; and the spacing of the lettering varies, sometimes appearing dense and a little squashed, other times spaced out.

In poem 15, the inadequacy of the written format of the poem is foregrounded:

unsilence

un

silence.

fu

yant

dan

slan

uits
ansp

oint

.

[asilence

a

silence.

flee

ing

in

the

pointl
essn

ight

.]

The suddenly condensed font is visually obvious when compared to the preceding poems, but it is a feature which is impossible to reproduce when reading aloud. Similarly, the enjambments of unpronounced letters – 'slan / uits' and 'ansp / oint' – cannot be transposed through voice to a listener, which means that the poem is, aurally, exactly the same as the preceding poem, in which none of the words are split over lines and the spacing of the lettering is presented in a way that does not attract attention.

The variations occurring from one poem to the next are such that they would not be transmissible in an oral rendering of the page; they are silent. Perhaps this is one way in which the poems can exist within Roubaud's period of silence: there is a stifling of rhythm in the pure repetitions that characterize an aural representation of *Du noir tombe*. The 'variations' are notably visual in form and can be contrasted in this way to the 'programme de lecture' [programme of reading] of which *Dors* is a part. According to Roubaud's theory of poetry, this means a diminishment of multidimensionality and thus a broken link between the poems and memory. The two-dimensionality of the visual arrangements that constitute *Du noir tombe* are a response to the loss of his first reader: 'La poésie, parce que j'avais pris l'habitude de la dire à haute voix, de lire en public, et pour elle, avec qui je vivais, s'est arrêtée pour moi' [Poetry, because I had got into the habit of reading it aloud, reading in public, and for her, whom I lived with, stopped for me].[44] No longer able to read aloud for Alix Cléo, the purpose of poetry, particularly its 'upper limit music', for Roubaud is called into question. From January 1983, Roubaud describes preferring the 'neutralité' [neutrality] of prose: 'besoin ni des yeux d'un lecteur ni des oreilles d'un

44 Roubaud, *Le Grand incendie de Londres*, p. 55.

auditoire' [no need for a reader's eyes or an audience's ears].[45] For the full possibilities of poetry to be activated, Roubaud asks his reader to approach it with eyes and ears, yet the reader of *Du noir tombe* is cut off from any profound engagement with the poem's sound and the variations in form that usually establish rhythm in a text here remain silent.

The 'intrications' [interrelations] of colour that Roubaud explains are characteristic of *Dors* are also notably absent in *Du noir tombe*. Although the blackness of night is the most frequent shade to recur, colours such as blue, white, black, yellow, red and grey are interspersed throughout the sequences that make up *Dors*.[46] The only colour to be mentioned in the poems of *Du noir tombe* – and it is mentioned again and again – is black. The single variation on this comes towards the end of the book in the sixteenth, seventeenth and eighteenth poems, in which the expected 'noir' [black] is replaced by a generic reference to colour: 'une couleur tombe' [a colour falls]. The 'dessins' [drawings] by Jean-Gaudaire Thor also bring blocks, lines and splashes of black paint to the pages of Roubaud's arrangements. These are only interspersed with interjections of pale grey, until the nineteenth and final poem welcomes a rough-hewn triangular patch of yellow, topped with a flourish. Alongside the yellow, across the centre of the double-page spread of the final poem, is an imposing black rectangle, with two white spaces looking out from it, like eyes. A dash of black paint downwards across the page from the bottom of the rectangle, appearing almost like a tail, gives the shape an animalistic appearance. Elements of the drawing find their echoes in the words of Roubaud's arrangement:

> fenêtre
>
> je m'éveille
>
> et je vois
>
> au milieu
> de la chambre

45 Roubaud, *Le Grand incendie de Londres*, p. 55.

46 See Roubaud, *Dors*, p. 43, p. 44, p. 46, p. 51, and p. 55 for the first mention of each of the colours listed, respectively.

le bruit

de la fenêtre

qui avance.[47]

[window

I wake

and I see

in the middle
of the room

the sound

of the window

that moves forward.]

The rectangle that looks back at the reader is suggestive of the window and the sense of sight that is part of the textual arrangement, and I cannot help but see in the yellow form to its right a manifestation of light. Yet the image presents a paradox, as it is not light that the poet sees flowing in through the window, but 'le bruit | de la fenêtre | qui avance' [the sound | of the window | that moves forward].

The senses of sound and vision also overlap in poem 16:

une couleur
tombe.

je l'entends.

[a colour
falls

I hear it.]

The vision of noise approaching through the window and the sound of colour falling compound the notion of a poetry and rhythm that are expressed visually, or typographically, on the page in *Du noir tombe*. Or does

47 Roubaud, *Du noir tombe*, poem no. 19.

this development in which colour is heard and sounds morph into things seen point beyond the fallen darkness of *Du noir tombe* towards the possibility of the poet breaking his silence? The ending of the collection with the sense of progression, or beginning, in the final word 'avance' [moves forward], in conjunction with the singular appearance of the window and the brightening patch of yellow paint in Gaudaire-Thor's paintings, seem to offer such a possibility. This final poem suggests the light at the end of the tunnel of silence.

Addressing the Beloved: Reading Obliquely in *Quelque chose noir*

Thinking of form in *Du noir tombe* in the light of certain aspects of earlier collection, *Dors*, brings into focus several key differences between those texts, and between Roubaud's works written before and after the death of Alix Cléo. From *Dors* to *Du noir tombe*, the multiplicity of colours is subdued, the lexical variations are exchanged for unvaried aural repetition and the poet's preoccupation with voice turns into a concern with the visual. The poems that compose *Du noir tombe* are characterized by silence: it is a *sestina* whose *chant* is missing, and the poet draws attention to this loss through his rapprochement of the two works. The poems of the later work may be described as two-dimensional in relation to those of *Dors*; they are missing the phonic dimension that makes of rhythm an enticement of memory in the reading process.

Situated somewhere between Roubaud's silence and his formal return to poetry, *Du noir tombe* may be thought of as a window into *Quelque chose noir*.[48] The title of *Du noir tombe* appears in the later volume's sixth poem, on line 5:

48 I choose the adjective 'formal' to refer to the breaking of the poet's silence with *Quelque chose noir* for two reasons: it is the collection that Roubaud himself names as his first since Alix Cléo's death and it bears some of the formal traits that are characteristic of his poetry before Alix Cléo's death.

Où es-tu?

Où es tu :

qui ?

Sous la lampe, entourée de noir, je te dispose:

En deux dimensions

Du noir tombe

Sous les angles. comme une poussière:

Image sans épaisseur voix sans épaisseur

La terre

qui te frotte

Le monde

dont plus rien ne te sépare

Sous la lampe. dans la nuit. entouré de noir. contre la porte.[49]

[*Where are you?*

Where are you:

who?

Under the lamp, wrapped in darkness, I set you down:

In two dimensions

Darkness falls

In every corner. like dust:

Image without depth voice without depth

The earth

that rubs against you

The world

you are no longer separated from

Under the lamp. in the night. wrapped in darkness. against the door.]

The second-person addressee was absent from *Du noir tombe*, but in *Quelque chose noir* she is aligned with the two-dimensionality that characterizes poetry since she went away. The poet begins his poem asking where he might look for his love in a world defined by her absence – 'Où es tu:' [Where are

49 Roubaud, *Quelque chose noir*, p. 19.

you:] – but his use of the colon alters the nature of the question, now hesitating over the identity of Alix Cléo in death – 'qui?' [who?].

The rest of the poem is an attempt to answer this question: 'En deux dimensions' [In two dimensions]. On the one hand, the poet mentions her image without depth, and her voice without substance. These flat representations of the poet's lost love correspond to mentions throughout *Quelque chose noir* of the reminders left behind by Alix Cléo of her life. He writes, for example, of being 'Entouré d'images de toi, choisies par ton regard. choisies et par ta pensée éclairées' [Surrounded by images of you, chosen by your eye. chosen and illuminated by your thought].[50] The poet is surrounded by Alix Cléo's presence in the form of her work, which still fills the apartment they shared when she was alive. The photographer was the subject of many of her own works, so it is her own photographic image that is multiplied throughout the poet's living space. However, the poet is ambivalent about these presences of his late wife:

> Chaque image de toi – je parle de celles qui sont dans mes mains, devant mes yeux, sur les papiers – chaque image touche la trace d'une reconnaissance, l'illumine,
>
> Mais elle est pourtant révolue, elles sont révolues, chacune et toutes, ne constituent en leurs configurations aucune vie, aucun sens, aucune leçon, aucun but.[51]
>
> [Every image of you – I mean those that are in my hands, before my eyes, on paper – every image of you touches the trace of a recognition, illuminates it,
>
> But it is nevertheless past, they are past, each and every one, they do not constitute in their configurations any life, any meaning, any lesson, any aim.]

While Alix Cléo's photographs evoke memories of her presence, each offering a sense of her, a familiar trace that resonates with the observing poet, the form he recognizes in them is irrevocably past. It is this ambiguity that Roland Barthes captured in his mantra: '*Ça-a-été*' [*That-has-been*].[52] The essence of a photograph lay, for Barthes, in what he called the photographic

50 Roubaud, *Quelque chose noir*, p. 78. Punctuation reproduced from the original.

51 Roubaud, *Quelque chose noir*, p. 112.

52 Roland Barthes, *La Chambre claire: note sur la photographie* (Paris: Gallimard, 1980). See pp. 119–22 for Barthes's meditation on the *Ça-a-été* of the photograph.

referent: 'la chose *nécessairement* réelle qui a été placée devant l'objectif, faute de quoi il n'y aurait pas de photographie' [the *necessarily* real thing that was placed in front of the lens, without which there would be no photograph].[53] While in painting, reality may be feigned and referents need not be rooted in any real existence, the photograph bears witness to what has been: 'dans la Photographie, je ne puis jamais nier que *la chose a été là*' [in Photography, I can never deny that *the thing has been there*].[54] An uncanniness results: 'Il y a double position conjointe: de réalité et de passé' [There is a double and linked position: of reality and the past].[55] Representative of what has been, the real of the photo is also necessarily past. It is this distance that is compounded in Roubaud's poem by his use of the adjective 'révolue' [past]: belonging to the moment in which the image was captured, the photographic referent is not simply changed by time in relation to the poet's present but is itself no longer.

Roubaud experiences the images of Alix Cléo as objects. Prepositions signalling the positions of the photos – '*dans* mes mains, *devant* mes yeux, *sur* les papiers' [*in* my hands, *before* my eyes, *on* paper] – place them tangibly within the poet's reach.[56] The list of prepositional phrases also suggests an accumulation, an abundance of photographs. Yet these two-dimensional objects are without substance: 'elles [...] ne constituent aucune vie, aucun sens, aucune leçon, aucun but' [they [...] do not constitute any life, any meaning, any lesson, any aim]. The presence they create points more to death than life; signifiers without their referent, they are empty signs. As such, they can hold no future for the poet, who sees in them what he has lost.

Recordings of Alix Cléo's voice have the same effect on the poet:

> Ta voix se déplaçant en bruissant dans le magnétophone, j'entends les efforts de ton souffle, dans la nuit, devant le magnétophone à ton lit.
>
> Je l'entends après des centaines de nuits inchangée et pourtant il n'y a rien en elle d'un présent, rien que la magie mécanique ait pu, par la mimésis en limailles, translater d'aucun de tes moments, pleins, séparés, difficiles de souffle, révolus, pour être là en ton nom, comme un recours.

53 Barthes, *La Chambre claire*, p. 120.

54 Barthes, *La Chambre claire*, p. 120.

55 Barthes, *La Chambre claire*, p. 120.

56 Emphasis my own.

Et c'est pourquoi peut-être, tu es en elles, vue, et voix, le plus irrémédiablement, morte.[57]

[Your voice moves crackling in the tape recorder, I hear the efforts of your breath, at night, before the recorder by your bed.

I hear it unchanged after hundreds of nights and yet there is nothing in it of the present, nothing that mechanical magic has been able to translate into iron filings from any of your full, distinct, difficult moments of breathing, past, to be there in your name, like a reprieve.

And maybe that is why you are most irrevocably dead there, in them, image, and voice.]

Prepositions situate the reality of the moment in which Alix Cléo made the voice recording: '*dans* la nuit, *devant* le magnétophone *à* ton lit' [*in* the night, *before* the recorder, *by* your bed].[58] The recording bears the qualities of her voice, the difficult breathing of someone who suffered with asthma. Yet the sound is tinny and mechanic, removed from its original moment. Again, the reminder of Alix Cléo's presence is precisely what recalls her absence, and the description connecting the souvenir object with the poet's present reality is constructed with negatives: 'rien de' [nothing of], 'rien que' [nothing that]. These flat portrayals of Alix Cléo's image and voice are empty reminders of what once was.

In the lines following the references to her image and voice 'sans épaisseur' [without depth], Roubaud outlines the real of her current existence:

La terre
        qui te frotte
Le monde
        dont plus rien ne te sépare.[59]
[The earth
        which rubs against you
The world
        you are no longer separated from.]

57 Roubaud, *Quelque chose noir*, p. 112.
58 Emphasis my own.
59 Roubaud, *Quelque chose noir*, p. 19.

While the photos and voice recordings remind the poet of the temporal distance separating him from the Alix Cléo of these souvenirs, the references to the present of her body assert its proximity to the earth where she now lies. The vertical play on the spacing of the line follows the thoughts of the poet to her body buried underground. The contrast in 'Où es-tu?' ['Where are you?'] is stark, the physicality of the objects indefinitely retaining images of Alix Cléo irreconcilable with the thought of her decaying corpse.

The question 'Où es tu: qui?' [Where are you: who?] acts as a premise for the poem, which goes on to assert the impossibility of fixing Alix Cléo's identity in death: the question is intensified rather than answered. Photographs, recordings, her closeness to the earth that envelops her skin all signify her physical distance from the poet. A reply to the question of the title takes place across a re-writing of one line from the poem: 'Sous la lampe, entourée de noir, je te dispose: | En deux dimensions' [Under the lamp, wrapped in darkness, I set you down: | In two dimensions]. Qualified by a feminine adjective, this opening line refers to the poet's addressee, and the poet arranging the material of her presence on the page.[60] At the close of the poem, it is the poet who sits under the light of the lamp, surrounded in darkness: 'Sous la lampe. dans la nuit. entouré de noir. contre la porte' [Under the lamp. in the night. wrapped in darkness. against the door]. Full stops replace the commas of the first line, and the spatial and temporal position of the poet in his bedroom under nightfall is clearly demarcated with the additions 'dans la nuit' [in the night] and 'contre la porte' [against the door]; his position in the room is more sharply defined than that of Alix Cléo. They are distanced, they can exist only separately, but Alix Cléo is here aligned with Roubaud, as he writes something of her existence into the poem.

60 In her translation of *Quelque chose noir*, Rosmarie Waldrop writes 'I spread you out' for 'je te dispose'. Waldrop's translation here emphasizes the lack of definition that characterizes the existence of Alix Cléo in Roubaud's writing, her multiplicity in death. See Jacques Roubaud, *Some Thing Black*, trans. by Rosmarie Waldrop (Elmwood Park: Dalkey Archive Press, 1990), p. 17.

In the absence of the poem's first addressee, the position of the reader too comes into question. In *Trente et un au cube* the pronoun 'tu' [you] was at the centre of the overlapping positions of lover and reader, making the poem an offering of love and a gesture to the reader. What are the implications of the reader of *Quelque chose noir* taking up the position of the poet's lost love?

In 'Dialogue', Roubaud posits the notion of the poem as dialogue:

> Je n'ai jamais pensé à un poème comme étant un monologue
> parti quelque part de l'arrière de ma bouche ou de ma main
>
> Un poème se place toujours dans les conditions d'un
> dialogue virtuel
>
> L'hypothèse d'une rencontre l'hypothèse d'une
> réponse l'hypothèse de quelqu'un
>
> Même dans la page : la réponse supposée par la ligne,
> les déplacements, les formats
>
> Quelque chose va sortir du silence, de la ponctuation,
> du blanc remonter jusqu'à moi.[61]
>
> [I have never thought of a poem as being a monologue
> issued somewhere from the back of my mouth or from my hand
>
> A poem is always placed in the conditions of a
> virtual dialogue
>
> The hypothesis of an encounter the hypothesis of a
> reply the hypothesis of someone
>
> Even on the page: the reply assumed by the line,
> the spacing, the format
>
> Something will come out of the silence, the punctuation,
> the blank space will come back to me.]

61 Roubaud, *Quelque chose noir*, p. 124.

The existence of the poem relies on its hypothetical addressee. It would even be possible to speak of an interlocutor, since Roubaud places dialogue, encounter and reply – 'dialogue', 'rencontre' [encounter], 'réponse' [reply] – at the centre of the poetry reading (and writing) process. The poem alludes to the multidimensionality that is such a prominent part of Roubaud's poetry theory: the poem as both oral and written entity, issued from the poet's 'bouche' [mouth] or 'main' [hand]. The form of the poem, the line, the spacing and the typography were all part of its connection with memory in *Trente et un au cube*; and although the poetic *vers* becomes 'ligne' [line], in 'Dialogue' the poet writes of form again as eliciting a response from the reader.

In the second half of the poem, Roubaud equates the reader's participation in the text with authorship:

> Quelqu'un de vivant, de nommé: un poème d'amour
>
> Même quand l'omission, l'indirection, l'adresse pronominale
> rendent possible cette translation: qu'un lecteur soit devant la page,
> devant la voix du poème comme au moment de sa naissance
>
> Ou de sa réception: lecteur lecteur   ou   lecteur auteur
>
> Ce poème t'est adressé et ne rencontrera rien.[62]
>
> [Someone living, named: a love poem
>
> Even when omission, indirection, pronominal address make this translation possible: a reader before the page, before the voice of the poem just as when it takes shape
>
> Or when it is received: reader reader   or   reader author
>
> This poem is addressed to you and will encounter nothing.]

62 Roubaud, *Quelque chose noir*, pp. 124–25.

The closing line sums up the uncertainty that the poet is faced with: addressed to the poet's deceased wife, the poem will encounter only nothing. A love poem, for Roubaud, exists for and because of the beloved: 'Quelqu'un de vivant, de nommé' [Someone living, named]. Yet the reader's position as contributor to the poem – 'lecteur auteur' [reader author] – remains even in the absence of the primary addressee. The poet refers to 'omission' and 'indirection', which he says are both a form of transfer – 'translation' – made possible through the umbrella of the pronominal address, 'tu' [you]. While lexical and phonic play centred on the coincidence of the reader's and lover's position in Roubaud's 'Poème de présentation', 'Dialogue' proposes that the reader has an oblique relationship to *Quelque chose noir*. If the reader approaches the poetry through 'omission', 'indirection' and 'translation', there is the sense that she is at one remove from the poem, rather than invited into its most intimate space – the *stanza*, or *chambre* [bedroom] that constituted the premise of *Trente et un au cube*. In Roubaud's treatise on love and poetry, the numerical sequence of the tanka generated the markers in space and time connecting the positions of the reader and the poet's beloved, and this network activated in the reading process was the source of possibility for expanding meaning in the text. What is the nature of the reader's relationship with form in *Quelque chose noir*?

Form in *Quelque chose noir*

The formal elements of *Quelque chose noir* are less tightly wound into its structure. The title itself indicates uncertainty, vagueness, its indefinable 'some thing' a world apart from the precision and finitude that characterized *Trente et un au cube*. Jean-François Puff pinpoints the unplanned nature of the volume: 'ce livre, *Quelque chose noir*, apparaît au lieu d'autre chose' [this book, *Some Thing Black*, appears in place of something else], the thing for which it is 'substitut' [substitute] being the 'Projet' that had occupied Roubaud's plans since his decision to write poetry within a consciously formal schema.[63] The book's existence therefore signals loss on two levels: that of Roubaud's love, and that of the dual project in mathematics and poetry he had planned for many years, a great architecture built of interlocking, interrelated component parts. *Quelque chose noir* could not have figured in Roubaud's plans for a poetry project, and the period of silence to which it attests can only emphasize that fact. The book bears the weight of Roubaud's grief and, as Jean-Jacques Poucel concludes, it is 'the absence of a loved one' which is 'the work's generating principle'.[64]

The first poem of *Quelque chose noir* to be written, 'Rien' ['Nothing'], is dated 1983, but it is the last to appear in the order of the book and it is separated from the rest of the collection by a page giving its title and date of composition. The format of this final poem distinguishes it from the others in the volume; it is aligned to the right-hand side of the page, a position which Benoît Conort refers to, using Roubaud's own terms, as being up against the edge or boundary of death: 'il bute sur la marge comme sur "un bord" de mort' [it comes up against the edge as though against 'an edge' of death].[65] The layout of the poem has a particular effect: set apart from the rest of the book both by the blank space that dominates the left-hand side of the two pages on which it is printed, as well as by its title page, there is a sense that the poem attempts to escape the volume. This is compounded by the tapering off of the poem on its second page to its final reference to nothingness:

tant d'absence

que tes yeux
s'approchent

de rien.[66]

63 Jean-François Puff, 'L'Écriture photographique de *Quelque chose noir*', *Formes Poétiques Contemporaines*, 2 (2004), 313–24 (p. 314).
64 Poucel, *Jacques Roubaud and the Invention of Memory*, p. 198.
65 Benoît Conort, 'Tramer le deuil (Table de lecture de *Quelque chose noir*)', *La Licorne*, 40 (1997), 47–58 (p. 56).
66 Roubaud, *Quelque chose noir*, p. 128.

[so much absence

that your eyes
approach

nothing.]

Figuring in the top right-hand corner of the page and surrounded by the vast whiteness of the space that remains, the poem's end disappears into the nothingness that it evokes. The poem has an ambiguous status; it is both the 'chronological' beginning of *Quelque chose noir*, written shortly after Alix Cléo died, and it marks the volume's physical end; it speaks of the loss of Roubaud's love, and it represents the conception of *Quelque chose noir*. It is, as Poucel writes, Alix Cléo's absence that provides the impetus for this poetry volume and as the point where her loss intersects with the beginning again of Roubaud's poetry composition, 'Rien' brings a sort of circularity to *Quelque chose noir*.

The term – 'bute[r]' [come up against] – used by Conort to describe the arrangement of 'Rien' takes the reader back to the last pages of *Trente et un au cube*, whose 'butoir' [end / stop] the poet referred to as the end of his composition process came into sight.[67] Roubaud's earlier work too had a circular quality: its time span covered a single year with its evolving seasons, its overlapping verses brought together its ending and beginning, guiding the reader towards a re-reading of the book. The possibility of perpetual repetition and transformation was in line with the poet's theory of poetry as memory: multiple readings of the poetic work drew out new associations and embedded parts of the poetic text more deeply in the mind of the reader. The circularity of *Quelque chose noir* works differently. The reader is brought back, on each reading, to the death of the poet's wife. The return to 1983 that closes a reading of the volume points to an impasse: the poet of *Quelque chose noir* is enclosed in his grief. There is no resolution, or consolation; there is no cathartic end to this elegy. In fact, the poet himself explicitly rejects some of the sentiments traditionally

67 Roubaud, *Trente et un au cube*, p. 129.

associated with elegiac genres in the book's opening poem.[68] The return, on the volume's final page, to the poet's earliest moments of grief also signals that the work of composing has not been the 'recompense' that is sometimes afforded the author of the elegy, or as Jahan Ramazani summarizes in his study of the genre, 'the *implicit* work of mourning carried out by the poet himself'.[69]

The positioning of this last poem along the right-hand page edge, however, seems to direct the reader outwards and away from the text, rather than back to its first page. There is not the obvious push from the poet for a re-reading that there was in *Trente et un au cube* and the temporal scale of *Quelque chose noir* is not modelled on any cycle, or coherent period, in the manner of the earlier volume. While the structure of *Trente et un au cube* was finite and precise in its guidance of the reader towards the end of the book, 'Rien' is separated from the patterning that runs through *Quelque chose noir*. For there is, in the later volume, a 'cubic' sequence underpinning the different layers of the text: there are nine sections, or chapters, in the book, each comprising nine poems, and every poem is made up of nine lines. The lines differ in shape and form; rarely constructed with any distinguishable metric count, they vary from being short, spaced out and quite sparse to approaching the length of a short paragraph of prose. The cubic measure of nine stops short of the level of the poetic line. The last poem in *Quelque chose noir*, 'Rien', appears alone, in or as its own section, following the ninth line of the ninth poem of the ninth section. It is something of a number ten in a book of nines, and so challenges the numerical sequence that otherwise structures the volume.

Even where the number nine appears, on the surface, to uphold the volume, there is an undoing at its very root. Three does not, for Roubaud, represent a holy trinity, but is rather the multiplicity that death induces:

> Tes photographies reproduites   les phrases reproduites de ton
> Journal   avec sa ponctuation particulière: un.

68 Roubaud, *Quelque chose noir*, p. 11.

69 Jahan Ramazani, *Poetry of Mourning: The Modern Elegy from Hardy to Heaney* (Chicago: University of Chicago Press, 1994), p. 3. Emphasis my own.

Tes lambeaux de cadavre se défaisant se délitant à l'anéantissement sobrement et rigidement fleurir d'aucune façon imaginable sinon par la désuétude la résurrection de certains mots les bibliques n'appartenant pas à ma tradition: deux.

Le rectangle de la pièce tapissée de papiers bruns japonais et son agencement d'objets le tien à peu près intact depuis presque trente mois où je reçois la lumière plein les mains: trois.

Ce sont trois fois toi trois des irréductiblement séparés déplacés réels de toi perdus en une diaspora qu'unit seule ce pronom: toi.[70]

[Your reproduced photographs the reproduced lines of your Journal with its particular punctuation: one.

The bits of your corpse coming undone falling apart at its destruction soberly and rigidly flourishing in no way imaginable or else through obsolescence the resurrection of certain words biblical ones not belonging to my tradition: two.

The rectangle of the room decorated with brown Japanese paper and its arrangement of objects yours almost untouched for thirty months where I receive plenty of light: three.

These are three times you three of the irreducibly divided shifted reals of you lost in a diaspora united only by this pronoun: you.]

For the poet, there is no question of an afterlife, and there are no words to console him with the possibility of Alix Cléo's resurrection. The figure three does not symbolize the hope of a holy alliance, but the cold fact that Alix Cléo's identity is multiple in death. The plural nouns that abound in this extract from 'Je vais me détourner' ['I am going to turn away'] add to the sense of fragmentation. Individual words and syntactical clauses float formlessly on the page in the irregular spacing that shapes the poem, despite being reined in by the count of three and the pattern of colons that equates these numbers with a mode of address directed to Alix Cléo: 'toi' [you]. The dominance of nouns and present participles over active verbs

70 Roubaud, *Quelque chose noir*, p. 61.

compounds the feeling of stasis that has ruled the poet's existence for the thirty months since his wife's death.

She is in the writings and photos that she left behind, her presence in these works particularly poignant as her body was more often than not the subject of her photographic creations, and her journal held some of her most intimate thoughts. Together they constitute what Roubaud has referred to as 'un multiple autoportrait' [a multiple self-portrait], and Alix Cléo's principal activities.[71] Already fragmented in this first of three points listed by the poet, Alix Cléo's body is the subject of the second. Echoes of alliteration and assonance draw together terms denoting decomposition, undoing and destruction: 'se défaisant' [coming undone], 'se délitant' [falling apart], 'anéantissement' [destruction] and 'désuétude' [obsolescence]. While the other two of Alix Cléo's identities are presented as having a particular form – her distinctive use of punctuation that shapes her journal entries, the rectangular room whose layout has remained untouched for thirty months – her body, 'lambeaux de cadavre' [bits of [her] corpse], is described only in terms connoting formlessness.

In 'Je vais me détourner', number and references to shape only intensify the absence of metrical shaping in the poem. The count of 'un' [one], 'deux' [two], 'trois' [three] that appears to offer a semblance of order and a set of limit points actually forms the gateway to further multiplication: 'trois fois   toi   trois des irréductiblement séparés   déplacés réels de toi' [three times   you   three of the irreducibly   divided shifted reals of you]. The square root of nine stands for the unravelling of the poem, the dissolution of the poet's love, rather than a solid structural foundation. The three repetitions of 'toi' [you] in the final 'stanza' of this extract are echoes of their homophone, 'trois' [three], and the effect of the whole is to lose the poet's addressee in a chorus of phonic repetitions. The reader too enters

71 Alix Cléo Roubaud, *Journal (1979–1983)*, ed. and intro. by Jacques Roubaud, 2nd edn (Paris: Seuil, 2009), p. 13. Emphasis in the original. Jacques Roubaud edited Alix Cléo's journal posthumously, publishing everything that she had written in it during their years together 'à l'exception de quelques passages d'ordre strictement privé' [except a few strictly private passages] (p. 8). Jacques Roubaud is not listed as editor on the book's cover. See pp. 7–15 of the *Journal* for his introduction.

into an uneasy relationship with this text; while an abundance of addresses in 'tu' and 'toi' [you] have previously functioned to draw the reader into a closer engagement with the poetry, here they successively exclude her and place her in an unstable position in relation to the poem. Unlike the 'Poème de présentation', the play on the second-person singular pronoun in this poem does not tempt the reader to follow the thread in search of a definitive attachment to 'tu' and 'toi' [you]; it is no longer a matter of determining the respective positions of the reader and the beloved in the text, since her position is already multiple.

The strings of nine that run through the form of *Quelque chose noir* are not held together tightly. Cardonne-Arlyck writes of a 'variation constante [...] de la densité respective des lignes noires et des blancs' [constant variation [...] of the respective density of the black and white lines] creating 'espacements mobiles' [mobile spacing] and, in turn, 'un rythme qui n'est pas celui sonore de la parole, mais silencieux de l'espace graphique' [a rhythm which is not the heard rhythm of speech, but silent, and a characteristic of graphic space].[72] She also finds that the varying degrees of aphasia manifested in each of the poems itself contributes to their poetic value: 'La comparaison de l'évolution de la poésie au progrès de l'aphasie invite d'ailleurs à lire les poèmes comme manifestant divers degrés de l'affection, les plus proches de la prose étant les plus atteints' [Comparing of the evolution of the poetry to the progression of the poet's aphasia invites us to read the poems as revealing different degrees of affliction, the ones closest to prose being the most affected].[73] Poetry as a way of writing and feeling in *Quelque chose noir* is thus located in the comparison between poems, their differences and variations.

Comparison is also at the heart of Jean-François Puff's evaluation of genre and form in *Quelque chose noir*. Puff asserts that 'l'entrelacement des mots dans le poème, par le vers, par la rime' [the intertwining of the words in the poem, through the poetic line, through the rhyme] which characterized Roubaud's subscription to the troubadour aesthetic in *Trente et un*

72 Cardonne-Arlyck, *Véracités*, p. 247.
73 Cardonne-Arlyck, *Véracités*, pp. 247–48.

au cube is replaced in *Quelque chose noir* 'par "la ligne, les déplacements, les formats", par "blancs", "ponctuation", "silence" ' [by 'the line, the shifts, the formats', by 'blank spaces', 'punctuation', 'silence'].[74] Puff cites Roubaud's 'Dialogue' to qualify his analysis of rhythm in *Quelque chose noir*, describing the shift from rhyme and metric shaping to blank space, punctuation and typographical features that occurs from *Trente et un au cube* to the later book of love poetry. While Puff concedes that there are rhythmic elements in *Quelque chose noir*, he defines these as 'non non rythme' [non non rhythm] and 'surface', which replace the concepts of 'rythme' [rhythm] and 'volume' that were central to *Trente et un au cube*.[75] Puff interprets the notion of two-dimensionality in *Quelque chose noir* as the manifestation of a failure. Alix Cléo is described as prisoner of the two-dimensional surface: whether it is a question of the poems in which she is memorialized by her husband, or her own photographic works which feature her image.[76] As Roubaud himself writes repeatedly in *Quelque chose noir*, these are only flat representations from which the person that Alix Cléo once was becomes increasingly unrecognizable.

Form is loosely structured by number in *Quelque chose noir*: patterns carve out spaces in the text, and the numbers nine and three recur throughout the poems like a leitmotif. However, if the beloved is still to be sought out within the form of this love poem, it is because multiplication in *Quelque chose noir* is a reflection of death. As Elisabeth Bronfen writes: '[D]eath is a decomposition of forms, the breaking of aesthetic unity.'[77] The undoing of the beloved's body – 'se défaisant se délitant' [coming undone falling apart] – is also the dissolution of form in this book of poems dedicated to her. The practice of formal poetry and its ambition are continually threatened at their edges, whether it is the final tenth poem, 'Rien', that defies the book's pattern, or the fraying root of three that leads to the shift in the relationship between the poet and his love, the poem and its reader.

74 Puff, *Mémoire de la mémoire*, p. 416.

75 Puff, *Mémoire de la mémoire*, p. 504.

76 Puff, 'L'Écriture photographique', p. 322.

77 Elisabeth Bronfen, *Over Her Dead Body: Death, Femininity and the Aesthetic* (Manchester: Manchester University Press, 1992), p. 60.

Time and the Reader in *Quelque chose noir*

Moments of self-reference in *Trente et un au cube* created an overlap between the manuscript in the process of being composed and the printed book in the reader's hands. The year it took Roubaud to write *Trente et un au cube* coincided with the time span of the book's themes, mapping out a route that guided the reader through the text. By contrast, the reader's pathway through *Quelque chose noir* is not marked out by signs familiar to the reader. References to time figure in relation to Alix Cléo's life and her death: the thirty months of silence broken by the composition of the volume, the dates of the first poems written in 1985 after that interlude, the earliest dated poem 'Rien' from 1983, and the 'jour de juin' [day in June] that was the couple's wedding day.[78]

One poem in particular traces the events occurring in the year before Alix Cléo died:

Roman, III

> Cette année-là, les nouvelles ne furent pas bonnes. L'un mourut avant le printemps, d'un cancer du poumon. Son dernier livre resta inachevé. Il y travailla jusqu'au dernier moment.
>
> Juste après, au printemps, un autre toussa. C'était un cancer encore, du poumon encore. Il lui rendit visite après l'opération. Il y avait un parc où attendre, parmi du soleil. En regardant la radio, on voyait très bien l'absence, nouvelle, d'un poumon : par comparaison, un manque d'ombre sur le cliché. Seul un arc noir, vers le haut.
>
> À la fin d'août, l'homme dont nous parlons se rendit à La Bourboule chercher sa femme, pour rentrer avec elle à Paris. Il changea trois fois de train, sur de petites lignes. Il l'attendit à la sortie de l'établissement de bains et ils marchèrent en remontant la Dordogne, jusqu'en dehors de la ville, où ils s'embrassèrent. Il était onze heures du matin et trop tôt pour aller dans la chambre, à l'hôtel. Son dos s'était doré, elle respirait mieux.

78 See Roubaud, *Quelque chose noir*, p. 47 for 'Un jour de juin'. The poem is based on an epithalamium written by Georges Perec as a gift to the couple on their wedding day. The original epithalamium can be found in Georges Perec, *Beaux présents belles absentes* (Paris: Seuil, 1994), pp. 61–65.

En décembre, en somme, tout était encore possible. Le premier janvier de l'année suivante (l'année dont nous parlons), elle colla leurs deux noms sur la porte, avec la date en dessous, suivie d'un point d'exclamation:

19..![79]

[*Novel III*

That year, the news was not good. One died before the spring, from lung cancer. His last book remained unfinished. He worked on it up until the end.

Just after, in spring, another coughed. It was cancer again, of the lung again. He paid him a visit after the operation. There was a park to wait in, in some sun. Looking at the X-ray, we could see very clearly the absence – recent – of a lung: by comparison, there was no shadow on the negative. Only a black curve, near the top.

At the end of August, the man we are talking about went to La Bourboule to pick up his wife, to return with her to Paris. He changed trains three times, on the smaller lines. He waited for her at the entrance to the spa and they walked along the Dordogne, until they reached the outskirts of the town, where they kissed. It was eleven o'clock in the morning and too early to go to the hotel room. Her back was golden, she was breathing better.

In December, in short, everything was still possible. On the first of January the following year (the year we are speaking about), she stuck their two names on the door, with the date underneath, followed by an exclamation mark:

19..!]

The first half of the poem has been cited here at length to highlight its framing within 'that year'. The poet traces events from before and during spring, through the end of August, to December, and then finally to January of the following year. Time references head each section of the poem, and they lead sentences within paragraphs. The piece and the events it recounts are structured chronologically, and the timescale of the poem might be compared to the temporal foundation on which *Trente et un au cube* was built. In this poem, as in the earlier volume, there are references to the times of year and the signs of the changing seasons: the sun shining

79 Roubaud, *Quelque chose noir*, pp. 55–56.

over the park, Alix Cléo's tanned skin, the actions marking a new beginning on 1 January.

The title 'Roman, III' ['Novel III'] anticipates the narrative tone of the piece: the sentences build up into paragraphs of prose and the use of the *passé simple* [simple past] prepares the reader for a story. Yet there is the sense that the narrator does all he can to keep the reader at a distance. The title alludes to form, but gives no indication of subject, or theme. The main characters are given as 'Il' [He] and 'elle' [she], 'L'un' [One] and 'un autre' [another], designations that become confused if the reader does not follow carefully their respective threads, for example, when they appear together in the third sentence of the second paragraph: 'Il lui rendit visite après l'opération' [He paid him a visit after the operation]. The reiteration later in the poem – 'l'homme dont nous parlons' [the man we are speaking about] – does not clarify much, 'l'homme' [the man] never having been identified in the piece. Logic tells the reader that a new character – 'Il' [He] – has entered the story, visiting the second person to be touched by lung cancer – 'lui' [him] – but the use of the definite subject pronoun is disorientating, suggesting that the subject in question is already known. Perhaps the reader is to assume that the protagonist here is '[l']homme abandonné, à cause d'une mort' [[the] man left abandoned because a death] who has a role in the previous poem, 'Roman, II' ['Novel II'].[80] In both cases, Jacques Roubaud is the main character. Nevertheless, the reader of 'Roman, III' ['Novel III'] comes in at a point after which the tale has begun. The anonymity of the two men – Georges Perec, who died of lung cancer in 1982, and Claude Roy, who was diagnosed with the same disease in that same year, having a lung removed because of it – who are close friends of our protagonist, excludes the reader from their circle of intimacy. This is the poet's story; these are his memories.

The same strategy of omission is used in reference to the year, the new year with which the story ends: 'l'année dont nous parlons' [the year we are speaking about]. The year we are speaking about is not given: '19..!'. In the end, the new year hoped for does not materialize in the poem's story and time remains stuck at Alix Cléo's death:

80 Roubaud, *Quelque chose noir*, p. 53.

> Vue d'après, cette année-là lui semble presque paradisiaque : les dernières photographies, comme allégées de l'angoisse [...].
>
> Il peut interpréter cela comme une prescience, des adieux. Les images ne s'en trouvent pas alourdies.
>
> Il se souvient de bonheurs légers, clairs, précaires. Les heures bavardes dans la cuisine, Christmas shopping in Manchester.
>
> Les nuages tournant dans les carreaux de miroir disposés, collés contre le mur à gauche des oreillers. Les nuages, ainsi, entrant dans le golfe de toits à gauche de l'église les regardaient, ensemble, l'après-midi. Puis ils s'embrassaient.
>
> Mais, c'est vrai, cette année-là les nouvelles ne furent pas bonnes.[81]
>
> [Looking back, that year seems almost like heaven to him: the last photographs, as though relieved of anxiety [...].
>
> He interprets it as foresight, goodbyes. The images are not weighed down by it.
>
> He remembers light, precarious joys. Hours chatting in the kitchen, Christmas shopping in Manchester.
>
> The clouds shifting in the squares of mirror arranged, stuck to the wall to the left of the pillows. Thus the clouds entering the bay of roofs to the left of the church watched them, together, in the afternoon. Then they kissed.
>
> But it is true, that year the news was not good.]

Moments of happiness are remembered with greater intensity in the light of what was to follow. Lightness is a theme that pervades this second part of the poem, whether it is Alix Cléo's last photos that are 'allégées de l'angoisse' [relieved of anxiety], 'pas alourdies' [not weighed down], or the poet's memories of times that were 'légers, clairs' [light], but the memories are also 'précaires' [precarious], teetering on the edge of tragedy. The lighter moments in the descriptions of the poem's second half can be contrasted with the very fixed narrative of the poem's opening four paragraphs. There are no longer time references to introduce each section, the poem instead following the meandering of Roubaud's thoughts and his recollections of that year. The use of the *passé simple* [simple past] that dominates the earlier part of the narrative is swapped for the imperfect

81 Roubaud, *Quelque chose noir*, p. 56.

and present tenses of a primary character who looks back on his past. At least until the final line of the piece, which brings these lighter thoughts back down to earth with a sinking feeling.

Time in *Quelque chose noir* is not a space the reader has in common with the poet; the dates that figure in the volume are personal to him, and the grief is not shared. The narrative structure and pronominal vagueness of 'Roman, III' have a distancing effect and there are frequent reminders in the poem that this is the telling of somebody else's story. The presence of the clouds in the poem, however, represents a different possibility for the reader and her engagement with memory in or through the text. The way the clouds are reflected in the mirrors in the couple's room foregrounds the distinction between the inside and outside spaces of the poem: the interior of the apartment and the outside sky, the ordinary every day and the intimate life of husband and wife – hours spent chatting at the kitchen table – and the reader's place as onlooker. The clouds' reflection in the squared mirrors of the poem seems somehow to beckon the reader closer. Perhaps it is their outside presence in the room that parallels the position of the reader, or maybe it is that the clouds are the subject of the verb: 'les regardaient' [watched them]. The reader too watches on from outside, at one remove through the mirrored reflection; it takes some delving beyond the space of the text for the reader to place the key characters in the tale, and the numbers in the gaps where the date should be.

The poems in *Quelque chose noir* are not interlinked in the manner of *Trente et un au cube*, where the principles structuring the medieval Japanese anthologies meant consecutive poems were connected through themes and key pivot-words. There is no such discernible pattern in the poem titles of *Quelque chose noir*. Florence Marsal points out the repetitions that occur both in these titles and the references to Alix Cléo's photographs that surround the poet, describing the effect in *Quelque chose noir* as one which 'imprisons the reader and the poet in a time that repeats itself identically, with no possible escape'.[82] Where there are series – 'Méditation du 12/5/85',

82 Florence Marsal, 'Mourning and the Call to Possible Worlds in Jacques Roubaud's Poetry', *Sites: Journal of Twentieth-Century/Contemporary French Studies*, 6 (2002), 357–69 (p. 361).

'Méditation du 21/7/85', 'Méditation du 8/5/85' ['Meditation from [...]'] and 'Nonvie', 'Nonvie, I', 'II' and 'III' ['Nonlife [...]'], for example – the individual titles involved may be interspersed between other poems, across more than one section, or appear consecutively. In this there is something of writer Alex Ronan's description of grief as an experience that 'moves in waves rather than in a straight linear progression'.[83] Despite the overarching architecture based on the number nine, there is little in the way of visible ordering between one poem and the next, and perhaps this is reflective of the disorderly nature of mourning for the lover left behind. Culture writer, Julia Cooper, explains: '[L]inearity is a concept we have grafted onto time, probably so that it feels less immense to us. [...] And we likewise insist that grief follow a linear progression. The compulsion to slot grief into divisible stages along a narrow path is to ward off an overwhelming feeling of total engulfment.'[84] Roubaud captures this paradox in *Quelque chose noir*, where the most precise markers of time – those which outline the narrative of the poet's life with Alix Cléo – give way to those that betray the non-linearity of grief. The narrator who attempts a chronological re-telling ends up aimlessly watching the clouds pass above the world that carries on outside his window, without him and without his love.

The reader is not invited to engage with the temporal and spatial markings of *Quelque chose noir* in the same way as in *Trente et un au cube*. In the latter volume, time and space unfolded to encompass the reader, bringing her into a familiar relation with the text, an intimate link that promoted the stimulation of memory. In *Quelque chose noir*, references to time and space disorientate, refusing the formation of patterns or distinguishable sequences that might more readily elicit the investment of the reader's memory. Instead, memory is singularly that of the poet and of his fading souvenirs of Alix Cléo's life. The poet's second-person singular address is thrown into doubt and the reader self-consciously takes up the position of observer, her relationship with the text existing at a remove.

83 Quoted in Julia Cooper, *The Last Word: Reviving the Dying Art of Eulogy* (Toronto: Coach House Books, 2017), p. 44.

84 Cooper, *The Last Word*, p. 52.

Spatial Metaphors and the Impossibility of Memory

Calling each poem in *Quelque chose noir* a square or 'carré', Jean-François Puff sees in the cubic nine-by-nine-by-nine of the entire volume a projection of the apartment that Jacques Roubaud now inhabits alone.[85] It is a space described as 'réduit' [reduced] in relation to that of *Trente et un au cube*, which Puff demonstrated was a privileged space-time for the beloved constructed in rhythm, and the reduction is evidence of the failure of a joint project in photography and poetry that the poet had hoped to pursue with his spouse: 'la chute du projet comme lieu de mémoire extériorisé dans une œuvre conjointe de photographie et de poésie' [the failure of the project as an exterior memory-space in a joint œuvre of photography and poetry].[86] I am intrigued by Puff's reference to an exteriorized memory-space and the possibilities this project might have encompassed. Before imagining these, I will consider the implications of his premise that *Quelque chose noir* is the textual manifestation of a failure. In the reduced relation between poetry's form and thematic spaces it represents in the volume, what is lost? If the poems' form in *Quelque chose noir* is indicative of a failure, what are the implications of this for the memory spaces they were tied in with in Roubaud's previous love poetry? What is the nature of the reduced connection that Roubaud weaves between poetry, space and memory in *Quelque chose noir*?

When the poet evokes the space around him, it is invariably that of his apartment. In 'Dès que je me lève' ['When I get up'], the continuity of the poet's morning routine in his apartment space is heavy with stasis and aimlessness:

> Dès que je me lève (quatre heures et demie, cinq heures), je prends mon bol sur la table de la cuisine. Je l'ai posé là la veille, pour ne pas trop bouger dans la cuisine, pour minimiser le bruit de mes déplacements.

85 Puff, 'L'Écriture photographique', p. 323.
86 Puff, 'L'Écriture photographique', p. 323.

> Je continue de le faire, jour après jour, moins par habitude, que par refus de la mort d'une habitude. Être silencieux n'a plus la moindre importance.[87]
>
> [When I get up (four thirty, five o'clock), I take my bowl from the kitchen table. I put it there the night before, so as not to move too much around the kitchen, to minimize the noise of my movements.
>
> I continue to do this, day after day, less through habit than through the refusal of the death of a habit. Being quiet no longer matters in the slightest.]

The actions the poet carries out upon waking are defined by passiveness. The double negative in 'refus de la mort d'une habitude' [refusal of the death of a habit] demonstrates the poet's reluctance to change, rather than a reason or impulse for his decisions. He goes on in the poem to describe the coffee he makes: 'Je verse un fond de café en poudre, de la marque ZAMA filtre, que j'achète en grands verres de 200 grammes au supermarché FRANPRIX, en face du métro Saint-Paul' [I pour a drop of instant coffee, of the ZAMA filter brand, which I buy in big 200 gram jars at FRANPRIX supermarket, opposite the Saint-Paul metro station].[88] The repetition and monotony in the poet's routine – the presence of drab brand names, measurements of coffee that nobody cares about and directions for the local supermarket – echo through the details he offers and their prosaic grammatical arrangement. In some sense these characteristics of the writing match up with the terms Ramazani has used to define the modern elegy: 'In becoming anti-elegiac, the modern elegy more radically violates previous generic norms than did earlier phases of elegy: it becomes anti-consolatory and anti-encomiastic, anti-Romantic and anti-Victorian, anti-conventional and sometimes even anti-literary.'[89] Even more than being anti-literary and anti-elegiac, however, Roubaud's writing here is situated at the negative pole of the lyric, at the farthest reach away from 'upper limit music'.

Poetic form is called explicitly into question when Roubaud cites a line from Rimbaud's 'Les Amis' ['Friends'] in the poem: 'Je pense: "Et l'affreuse

87 Roubaud, *Quelque chose noir*, p. 27.
88 Roubaud, *Quelque chose noir*, p. 27.
89 Ramazani, *Poetry of Mourning*, p. 2.

crème/Près des bois flottants/" ' [I think: 'And the horrible scum/Near the floating wood'].[90] The poet reappropriates the line in a description of the coffee he has made, its 'archipels de poudre brune [...] îles noires bordées d'une boue crémeuse qui sombrent lentement, horribles' [archipelagos of brown powder [...] black islands lined with a creamy mud, which darken slowly, dreadful].[91] Through the quote, the prose poem points beyond itself to the lyric form, which is evoked in the forward slashes marking out the line breaks in the original poem. Only appearing as a citation of itself in prose, the lyricism of lyric poetry is doubly challenged by the translation of Rimbaud's richly symbolic description of a landscape to the purpose of depicting the sight of a badly stirred coffee. The Rimbaud citation also has a connection with *Trente et un au cube*. There the same extract laid out in verse form acts as an epigraph to Poem 15. This earlier poem is also centred on the poet's morning: 'ainsi dans la pause | qui précède les jours aux | premiers roulements | de pigeons amoureux quand | je m'éveille contre ta || chaleur repliée' [thus in the pause | that precedes the days at the | first cooings | of the pigeons in love when | I wake against your || folded heat].[92] The cooing pigeons and the warm proximity of his lover can be contrasted, however, with the emptiness and silence that fill the mornings of 'Dès que je me lève': 'je m'assieds sur la chaise de cuisine, [...] face au fauteuil, laid et vide' [I sit on the kitchen chair, [...] opposite the armchair, which is ugly and empty].[93] The spaces of Roubaud's apartment are described in terms of Alix Cléo's absence.

If poetic form is diminished in *Quelque chose noir*, it is because the real spaces it represents are lacking. The apartment is a place that Alix Cléo used to dwell in: 'Je m'éloigne peu souvent de cet endroit comme si l'enfermement dans un espace minime te restituait de la réalité, puisque tu y vivais avec moi' [I rarely leave this place as if being closed up in a small space would make you real again, since you lived there with me].[94] The

90 Roubaud, *Quelque chose noir*, p. 28.
91 Roubaud, *Quelque chose noir*, p. 28.
92 Roubaud, *Trente et un au cube*, p. 65.
93 Roubaud, *Quelque chose noir*, pp. 27–28.
94 Roubaud, *Quelque chose noir*, p. 36.

hypothetical structure denotes the impossibility of restoring Alix Cléo's presence but does not stop the poet from closing himself off from the world in the home he shared with his wife. There are echoes of the cubic prison of *Trente et un au cube* in the rest of the poem whose beginning is cited here. Its title – 'Dans l'espace minime' ['In the small space'] – designates the hermetic space of the apartment, but also the failure of that space to hold on to the woman he loves:

> Cela qui m'occupe, entièrement, et me détourne du dehors, de m'éloigner, de quitter les chambres, les mouvements de soleil, c'est l'espace, l'espace seul, tel que tu l'avais empli d'images, de tes images, de tes étoffes, de ton odeur, de ta sombre chaleur, de ton corps.
>
> Disparaissant, tu n'as pas été mise ailleurs, tu t'es diluée dans ce minime espace, tu t'es enfuie dans ce minime espace, il t'a absorbée.[95]
>
> [What occupies me, completely, and distracts me from the outside, from getting away, from leaving the rooms, the movements of the sun, is the space, the space alone, just as you had filled it with images, with your images, with your stuff, with your scent, with your dark heat, with your body.
>
> Gone, you were not placed elsewhere, you were diluted in this small space, you fled into this small space, it absorbed you.]

The poet is losing her still. Space is no longer a tool used by the poet to navigate memory processes, instead revealing his failure to retain the traces of Alix Cléo's presence. In the extract space overwhelms the poet, always the subject of verbs which divide him from the outside world, and the use of reflexive verbs – 'tu t'es diluée' [you were diluted], 'tu t'es enfuie' [you fled] – suggests that the beloved has eluded the poet's grasp. There is a tension between the sense that she has actively escaped into 'ce minime espace' [this small space] and the closing notion that it has absorbed her. The effect of the poet's play on subject and object verbs leaves him standing alone. The space of the poem cannot draw in the lover, and the link between memory and space is one that speaks of impossibility.

95 Roubaud, *Quelque chose noir*, pp. 36–37.

There are efforts in this poem and the one that follows to stop up the area that absorbs Alix Cléo's memory. Roubaud describes staying indoors, dominated by the apartment that surrounds him. However, the shifting light of the sun coming through the windows is a reminder of the world beyond: 'À sa descente, comme à sa montée, le soleil pénètre, s'il y a du soleil, et suit son chemin reconnaissable, sur les murs, les planchers, les chaises, courbant, couchant les portes' [When it sets, just as when it rises, the sun penetrates, if there is sun, and follows its familiar path, on the walls, the floors, the chairs, curving, bending the doors].[96] The sun penetrates the apartment space, altering its lines, and the poet is passive before its movement: 'Je laisse le soleil s'approcher, me recouvrir, s'éteindre' [I let the sun come near, cover me, fade away].[97] In 'Fins' ['Endings'], the poet describes closing up the apartment at daybreak: 'la nuit avertie de sa fin, je me lèverai, je fermerai les portes, les lampes, le lit' [the night warned of its ending, I will get up, I will shut off the doors, the lamps, the bed'].[98] Despite these attempts to enclose the space, the sun's movement reveals the gaps in the structure: 'la flaque de soleil couché devant la porte, [...] déjà se remue, se retire' [the puddle of sun that lies in front of the door, [...] already moves, retreats].[99]

The leaking space of the apartment where the traces of Alix Cléo's memory are diluted is comparable to the broken rhythms that infuse the poetry of *Quelque chose noir*. The prosaic lines lack the embrace that characterized *Trente et un au cube*. The title of poem 'Fins' encapsulates succinctly the metaphor of poetic form for space. The plural noun refers at once to the ending of night as daylight spills into the room and to the position of the poem at the close of the book's second section. It also anticipates the poem's finishing: 'Maintenant, vient une fin, je renonce' [Now, an ending comes, I give in].[100] However, throughout 'Fins', the poet questions the nature of another ending. He asks: 'quelque chose s'achève mais

96 Roubaud, *Quelque chose noir*, p. 36.
97 Roubaud, *Quelque chose noir*, p. 37.
98 Roubaud, *Quelque chose noir*, p. 38.
99 Roubaud, *Quelque chose noir*, p. 38.
100 Roubaud, *Quelque chose noir*, p. 39.

comment savoir quoi?' [something is ending, but how to know what?] and later wonders 'Quelque chose qui est à sa fin, toute proche [...] je ne parviendrai pas à savoir quoi' [Something which is at an end, so near [...] I will not figure out what].[101] The French noun 'fin' can denote an aim, or purpose, but the questioning, and the vague references to the 'some thing' of the book's title, as well as the sense of resignation in the poet as he closes the poem rule out that ambition. The poem distances this collection from the conscious gesture that built *Trente et un au cube*, a volume conceived of in its entirety from the outset of its composition. Rather the reader encounters loose endings and the withdrawal of the poet faced with the impossibility of defining the space that surrounds him and the poems that he writes across the page.

If each poem is to be considered a square and the volume a projection of the poet's living-prison space, there remains the question of the number nine as a structuring element in *Quelque chose noir*, even as a cubic patterning that has a reduced grip on the words of poetry compared to the sequence that generated *Trente et un au cube*. In *Autobiographie, chapitre dix*, the number nine was seen to pay homage to the love poetry of Paul Éluard, through an allusion to Dante's love for Beatrice. Dante is said to have met Beatrice for the first time when he was nine and their second meeting took place nine years later; the number nine also became a symbol in the poet's dreams and visions, or the times at which they occurred.[102] The number is also a mark of death in Dante's writing. There are nine circles in Dante's *Inferno*, and Virgil and Dante enter the most significant part of hell, the City of Dis, in the ninth canto.

In 'Méditation des sens' ['Meditation of the Senses'], the poet's memory of Alix Cléo through the various senses is experienced as a descent into hell:

> On y descend par une spirale, une damnation.
>
> De la vue, à la voix.   de la voix, au souffle, parfum, odeurs.

101 Roubaud, *Quelque chose noir*, p. 38.

102 See Andrew Frisardi's introduction to his translation of Dante Alighieri's *Vita Nova* (Evanston: Northwestern University Press, 1994), in particular his exploration of the significance of the number nine in the work, pp. liii–lvi.

De l'odeur au goût: mordre, enfoncer, salives.

Fond du puits, intérieur ultime est le toucher.

Le toucher absolu du corps. la jouissance et la décomposition.

Le toucher des mains, de la chair, la coexistence en un même lieu mental, en un même corps des corps, le dire dans la bouche, le goût, le souffle, l'entrelacement qui respire pénètre.

Pour la méditation des cinq sens, là était la recollection de mortalité

Si la distance évanouissante des deux corps, brûlant de leur infiniment présente brûlure: paradis veillant sur son envers.

Toutes stations que maintenant je descends en enfer, par le souvenir.[103]

[It is a spiral descent, a damnation.

From sight, to voice.   from voice, to breath, perfume, scents.

From scent to taste: biting, sinking in teeth, saliva.

Bottom of the well, the last interior is touch.

The absolute touch of the body. pleasure and decomposition.

The touch of the hands, of the flesh, coexisting in the same mental space, in one body of bodies, the saying in the mouth, taste, breath, the intertwining that breathes, penetrates.

For the meditation of the five senses, there was the recollection of mortality

If the fading distance of the two bodies, burning from their infinitely present burning: paradise watching over its opposite.

All stations that I pass on my descent to hell, through memory.]

The intensity of memory stifles the poet. To remember the bodily presence of the beloved is to yearn, but the thought of her physicality brings with it the reminder of her mortality. Space in this poem does not represent the dilution of memory, but the intensification of its depth. The movement downwards is marked by 'stations' of remembering and the successive linking of the senses in the poem's opening with prepositions

103 Roubaud, *Quelque chose noir*, pp. 82–83.

'de' [from] and 'à' [to]. The downward spiral and the well are symbols of the poet's suffering, his desire not only thwarted, but an eternal reminder of the decay and decomposition of the mortal body.

In this poem the narrator confronts the memory of Alix Cléo that is not contained in the two-dimensional photos that fill the apartment, or the tinny voice recordings she left behind. Smell, taste and touch are senses that cannot be traced in the physical objects that Alix Cléo owned or created: 'Les autres traces, venues des autres sens ne sont qu'en moi. Quand je trébuche dessus, j'étouffe' [The other traces, issued from the other senses are only in me. When I stumble on them, I feel stifled].[104] The poet describes the effect of these sensorial memories on him as physical obstacles that he stumbles against, so overwhelming that they cut short his breath and suffocate him. Yet there is a paradox in the poet's expression of his suffering: the traces of Alix Cléo that stem from the senses of smell, taste and touch are memories that are singular to the poet. Her physicality exists now only through and in Roubaud:

> Et c'est pourquoi aussi la vie qui te reste, s'il te reste, est imprimée en moi, suaire, entremêlée en moi, refusant de se défaire.
>
> Et de céder comme ta chair à la complaisante décomposition non imaginable, et de s'immobiliser comme l'image et la parole dans les parenthèses documentaires. Cette vie qui est cela:
>
> Ton odeur, ton goût, le toucher de toi.[105]
>
> [And that is also why the life you have left, if you have any, is imprinted in me, a shroud, entangled in me, refusing to be undone.
>
> And to yield like your flesh to indulgent unimaginable decomposition, and to stop still like the image and speech in documentary parentheses. That life which is this:
>
> Your scent, your taste, your touch.]

He suggests that Alix Cléo's existence, whatever form that may take beyond the 'parenthèses documentaires' [documentary parentheses] of the photos and recordings that capture her for a fleeting moment, is

104 Roubaud, *Quelque chose noir*, p. 34.
105 Roubaud, *Quelque chose noir*, p. 113.

henceforth inextricably intertwined with his own. The poet considers conjuring up some form of presence for his feminine addressee: 'je pourrais te donner forme, parler, te refaire, un dos, un ventre, une nudité humide noire, je ne m'y abandonne pas' [I could give you form, speak, remake you, a back, a middle, a black moist nakedness, I do not allow myself to do it].[106] The words glance back at the poet-narrator of *Trente et un au cube*, who centred feminine form on the axis of his poetry cube, but the proposal in *Quelque chose noir* ends in the poet's resignation. He allows no comfort or illusion to assuage his longing, even temporarily, and renounces the possibility of reconstructing Alix Cléo in the imaginative work of poetry memory. Alix Cléo's memory is confined to documentary recordings and sensory evocations yearned for in the body of the poet, but the nine infernal rings of Dante's poem are a symbol of Jacques Roubaud's prison rather than her own.

Beyond the Text: Alix Cléo's Last Photo

I have described the relationship between reader and poem, or memory and poetic form as 'oblique' in *Quelque chose noir*, but the poet does offer ways into the apartment space he inhabits and into the story he shares with Alix Cléo, notably so in two poems, both entitled 'Cette photographie, ta dernière' ['This photograph, your last']. The poems appear, respectively, at the opening and the close of the book's sixth section and they each describe the poet's view of a photograph taken by Alix Cléo. The photo hangs on the apartment wall in the position in which Alix Cléo had placed it, between the very two windows that are pictured in it: 'Posée, au cœur, de ce qu'elle montre' [Placed at the heart of what it shows].[107] The poems present a spatial and literal *mise en abyme*, as well as a textual one.

106 Roubaud, *Quelque chose noir*, p. 37.

107 Roubaud, *Quelque chose noir*, p. 91. Spacing reproduced from the original in all citations of poems from the collection to follow in this chapter.

A number of repetitions resonate through the poems, mirroring the picture within a picture that they depict. Their openings describe the room in the evening light. The first begins:

> Cette photographie, ta dernière, je l'ai laissée sur le mur, où tu l'avais mise, entre les deux fenêtres,
>
> Et le soir, recevant la lumière, je m'assieds, sur cette chaise, toujours la même, la regarder, où tu l'as posée, entre les deux fenêtres,
>
> Et ce que l'on voit, là, recevant la lumière, qui décline, dans le golfe de toits, à gauche de l'église,   ce qu'on voit,   les soirs, assis sur cette chaise, est, précisément,
>
> Ce que montre l'image laissée sur le mur, sur le papier brun sombre du mur, entre les deux fenêtres.[108]
>
> [This photograph, your last, I left it on the wall, where you had put it, between the two windows,
>
> And in the evening, getting the light, I sit, on this chair, always the same, to look at it, where you placed it, between the two windows,
>
> And what I see, there, getting the light, which fades, in the bay of roofs, to the left of the church,   what I see,   in the evenings, sitting on this chair, is, precisely,
>
> What the image left on the wall shows, on the dark brown paper of the wall, between the two windows.]

The second of the poems opens:

> Cette photographie, ta dernière, je l'ai laissée sur le mur, entre les deux fenêtres, au-dessus,
>
> De la télévision désaffectée, et le soir, dans le golfe de toits à gauche de l'église, quand la lumière,
>
> Se concentre, qui en même temps, s'écoule, en deux estuaires obliques, et inchangeables, dans l'image,
>
> Je m'assieds, sur cette chaise, d'où l'on voit, à la fois, l'image intérieure la photographie, et autour d'elle, ce qu'elle montre,

108 Roubaud, *Quelque chose noir*, p. 91.

Qui seulement, le soir, coïncide, par la direction de la lumière, avec elle.[109]

[This photograph, your last, I left it on the wall, between the two windows, above,

The disused television, and in the evening, in the bay of roofs to the left of the church, when the light,

Is concentrated, which at the same time, flows, in two oblique and steadfast streams, in the image,

I sit, on this chair, from where I see, at the same time, the image inside the photograph, and around it, what it shows,

Which only coincides with it, in the evening, through the direction of the light.]

The time setting is the same in each extract, reflecting the light conditions that went into the composition of the photograph itself. The position of the photo between the windows remains unchanged, even since Alix Cléo placed it there months before the writing of these poems. Roubaud too sits in the same chair – 'sur cette chaise' [on this chair] – taking up his familiar position before the picture and the windows looking out of the apartment. The phrase evoking the poet's point of view and the source of light through the window, 'dans le golfe de toits, à gauche de l'église' [in the bay of roofs, to the left of the church], is repeated not only in each poem, but throughout the volume, arising as a leitmotif that the reader comes to memorize.

The repetitions that occur between the homonymous poems are interspersed with differences. These extracts alone show the more condensed nature of the second of the two poems. There is also a shift in tone, when the poet refers to the 'télévision désaffectée' [disused television] under the picture in the second poem; the disused TV set replaces Alix Cléo in the description of where the photo is placed and infuses the two poems with a distinct sense of before and after. It cannot really be said that Alix Cléo is present in either text, since both stage her disappearance from the room as a contrast to her presence in the photograph. However, the personal pronouns that address Alix Cléo are more visible in the first of the poems. Referring to what he sees in the image, the poet writes:

109 Roubaud, *Quelque chose noir*, p. 103.

parcequ'en ce cœur, le cœur de ce qu'elle montre, que je vois, il y a aussi, encore l'image elle même, contenue en lui, et la lumière, entre, depuis toujours, depuis le golfe de toits à gauche de l'église, mais surtout il y a, ce qui maintenant manque

Toi. parceque tes yeux dans l'image, qui me regardent, en ce point, cette chaise, où je me place, pour te voir, tes yeux,

Voient déjà, le moment, où tu serais absente, le prévoient, et c'est pourquoi, je n'ai pas pu bouger de ce lieu-là.[110]

[because in this heart, the heart of what it shows, what I see, there is also, still the picture itself, contained in it, and the light, comes in, as ever, from the bay in the roofs to the left of the church, but above all there is, what is now missing

You. because your eyes in the picture, which watch me, in this spot, this chair, where I place myself, to see you, your eyes,

Already see, the moment, when you would be absent, foresee it, and that is why, I have not been able to move from this spot here.]

In the play of pronouns staging the difference between photograph and reality, presence and absence, the isolation through punctuation of 'Toi' [You] in the penultimate section gives greater impact to the image of Alix Cléo. The pronoun is followed by the only full stop that appears in the body of either poem. The poet writes of a time before, when his wife could foresee the moment she would no longer be there, and this sense of a change to come is compounded by the use of the conditional tense: 'le moment, où tu serais absente' [the moment, when you would be absent]. The close of the second poem can be contrasted with this:

tu regardes,

Vers le point où je m'assieds, te voir, invisible maintenant, dans la lumière,

Du soir, qui pèse, sur le golfe de toits entre les deux fenêtres, et moi,

110 Roubaud, *Quelque chose noir*, pp. 91–92. Spelling and typography reproduced from the original.

Absent de ton regard, qui dans l'image, fixe, la pensée de cette image, dédiée à cela, les soirs de maintenant, sans toi, au point,

Vacillant du doute de tout.[111]

[you look,

Towards the spot where I am sitting, looking at you, invisible now, in the light,

In the evening, which weighs heavy, on the bay of roofs between the two windows, and me,

Absent from your gaze, which in the picture, fixes the thought of the picture, dedicated to this, the evenings of now, without you, in the spot,

Which falters with the doubt of everything.

The conditional tense is replaced by the factual present and the pronouns standing in for Alix Cléo fade from prominence. The sparser lines of the second poem also reflect an emptiness; the void that marks Roubaud's existence since Alix Cléo's death is more prevalent.

In these readings what becomes clear is that the play of similarities and differences holds the reader's attention. The matching titles and opening words of the poems, the identical positions, oppositions and the network of gazes that are part of the layout of the room pose a challenge for the reader, arousing a desire to find out what remains and what shifts in the detailed patterns of the two texts and their portrayals of the living space. They act as a palindrome that opens and closes section six of *Quelque chose noir* and speaks of a before and after. In these instances, the two poems also emulate the form of the photograph in question: *51 rue des Francs-Bourgeois*.[112] In the photo, Alix Cléo and Jacques Roubaud both face the camera, Alix Cléo seated at the table on the left, and Roubaud reclining on the sofa, reading a newspaper, along the right-hand side. Their opposition is repeated by two windows between them that look out onto the street, and over the gulf in the rooftops to the left of a church. The poems

111 Roubaud, *Quelque chose noir*, pp. 103–04.

112 The photograph is the last image to appear in Alix Cléo's *Journal*, p. 221. The photographs printed in the *Journal* appear chronologically in the text, sometimes to accompany events or moments recorded in the book's writing, sometimes not.

reflect the doubling that is present in the image itself and they are also like photographs in their combined form: in their repetitions of the same and the barely perceptible shifts in detail, the poems are like two photographs of Roubaud's view.

For Michel Monte, the poems express a 'vacillement' [faltering]: the refusal to fix 'un sens clair et unique' [a clear and single meaning], which is in tension with 'l'attitude obsessionnelle du scripteur' [obsessive attitude of the writer], and thus 'le signe de la douleur' [a sign of pain].[113] In the movement from the first to the second of the poems, the tone becomes visibly starker and more pained. However, the poems are also a tribute to Alix Cléo, reflecting through the medium of poetry the form that was her craft and passion. They have a particular effect on the reader: the poems pull the reader into the sameness and difference of their detail and into the room that Roubaud inhabits. We study the texts like someone looking into the depths of a photograph to make out more clearly the forms that are not immediately visible. The textual *mise en abyme* functions as a formal analogy with its visual counterpart: when faced with a picture within a picture, the viewer cannot help but look more closely at the smallest image, identifying the features that make it a version of itself. However, while the repeated reference to the 'point' [spot] where Roubaud sits compounds the effect of the *mise en abyme*, situating the onlooker in the inside space of the apartment, the poet's view through the windows sends the reader beyond. Because of its repetition, the phrase – 'le golfe de toits à gauche de l'église' [the bay of roofs to the left of the church] – is a memorable one in *Quelque chose noir*; resurging like a refrain in the mind of the reader. The line directs our attention outside the apartment and across the boundaries of the text, visually and spatially, but also (inter)textually when the view arises in the collection's final poem, 'Rien':

ce morceau de ciel
désormais
t'est dévolu

113 Michèle Monte, '*Quelque chose noir*: de la critique de l'élégie à la réinvention du rythme', *Babel*, 12 (2005) <http://babel.revues.org/1093> [accessed 15 December 2013] (para. 49 of 58).

où la face aveugle
de l'église
s'incurve.[114]

[this piece of sky
from now on
is yours to keep

where the blind side
of the church
curves.]

The reference to the 'morceau de ciel' [piece of sky] comes up in Roubaud's sonnet anthology *Quasi-Cristaux* [*Quasi-Crystals*], in an entry that gives part of a letter written by Baudelaire discussing the qualities of the sonnet form:

> *parce que la forme est contraignante, l'idée jaillit plus intense.* [...] *Avez-vous observé qu'un morceau de ciel aperçu par un soupirail, ou entre deux cheminées, deux roches, ou par une arcade, etc. donnent une idée plus profonde de l'infini que le grand panorama vu du haut d'une montagne?* [...] (L'image du 'morceau de ciel' fait penser à Oscar Wilde).[115]

> [*because the form is restrictive, the idea emerges more intensely.* [...] *Have you noticed that a piece of sky glimpsed through a cellar window, or between two chimneys, two rocks, or through an arcade, etc. gives a more profound sense of infinity than the vast panorama seen from the top of a mountain?* [...] (The image of the 'piece of sky' reminds me of Oscar Wilde).]

114 Roubaud, *Quelque chose noir*, p. 147.

115 Roubaud, *Quasi-Cristaux: Un choix de sonnets en langue française de Lazare Carnot (1820) à Emmanuel Hocquard (1998)* (Paris: Martine Aboucaya et Yvon Lambert, 2013). Emphasis from the original; the italic font represents the extract from Baudelaire's letter. The volume is not paginated, rather the poems are arranged in chronological lists; this extract can be found following the first poem listed under 1874.

The sonnet's timelessness and its universal appeal, for Baudelaire, stems in part from its inbuilt constraint and the density that its form imposes on its content, and the image of the 'piece of sky' evoking infinity more effectively than the panoramic vista is used to illustrate this thought. Roubaud's bracketed aside on Oscar Wilde is most revealing, however. The reference he makes is to 'that little tent of blue', the view from the cell window in Wilde's *The Ballad of Reading Gaol*, written while the author was imprisoned. In this context, the 'morceau de ciel' represents an unattainable glimmer of freedom and hope for the writer who is trapped in his grief.

Alix Cléo is identified with this view from the windows, the gulf formed by the rooftops to the left of the church: 'le golfe de toits' [the gulf formed by the gap in the roofs] is also 'le golfe de toi' [the gulf of you], and the 'morceau de ciel' [piece of sky] is dedicated to her in Roubaud's poetry. In *Quelque chose noir*, the elegiac nature of the writing and the emphasis in the text on the void left behind in the wake of Alix Cléo's passing make it tempting to interpret 'le golfe de toits à gauche de l'église' [the bay in roofs to the left of the church] as an expression of the beloved's irrevocable absence. The gulf is bottomless in *Quelque chose noir*, representing the dissipation of Alix Cléo's memory, or it is engulfing, the suffocating intensity of grief. Ann Smock too identifies a network of connections where the line recurs in other writing by Roubaud. She traces the origin of the clouds entering the bay of roofs back to *La Boucle* [*The Loop*], the branch of Roubaud's prose narrative which revolves around some of the earliest memories from his childhood. There the clouds come to stand for 'a monster from his childhood', specifically the 'Monstre de Strasbourg' who had featured in frightening tales he told his siblings after nightfall. Eventually Roubaud realizes that the clouds rolling through the inlet of sky are associated with 'the ghost of a monstrous event from the past, […] an imminent, brutal disappearance'.[116]

Yet there are spaces in *Quelque chose noir* set out for Alix Cléo. Citations from her *Journal*, its particular use of punctuation, and references to her photographic work abound in the volume. In his 'Postface' written for

116 Smock, *The Play of Light*, p. 95.

Hélène Giannecchini's book on Alix Cléo's photography, *Une image peut-être vraie* [*A picture that may be true*], Roubaud writes of *Quelque chose noir* as a form of posthumous collaboration with the prose of the *Journal*. He describes the *Journal* as being 'comme œuvre de prose [...] et généralement mis en rapport avec le livre de poésie que j'ai publié en 1986, *Quelque chose noir* qui, de manière très apparente, répond et dialogue avec lui' [like a work of prose [...] and generally linked with the book of poetry that I published in 1986, *Some Thing Black*, which visibly responds to and dialogues with it].[117] How far it is possible to speak of collaboration in the given situation is difficult, however. If Alix Cléo's *Journal* is to be described as a work of prose, intended to be read as a published volume, Jacques Roubaud's position as its editor cannot be ignored. The question of Alix Cléo's independence from her husband and the possibility that she may be accepted as a writer in her own right arises in Giannecchini's study. Writing of Jacques Roubaud's decision to publish only the parts of the journal that were recorded during the years he and Alix Cléo spent together as a couple, Giannecchini discusses the limits of Alix Cléo's position as the poet's wife:

> Rien n'existe alors, avant 1979, le début de leur amour? La vie d'Alix est associée à celle de Jacques Roubaud au point que les événements antérieurs sont abolis; tout est réduit à leur histoire. En voulant permettre à son travail d'être vu, Jacques Roubaud s'y est lié. Si bien qu'Alix n'est souvent que la femme morte du grand écrivain, son état civil occultant alors sa production. Au mieux, elle est la muse pour laquelle il a érigé un tombeau dans son recueil de poèmes *Quelque chose noir*. Ce n'est pas ce qu'il voulait, il aurait aimé parfois être, lui, le mari de la grande photographe, réduit à sa simple fonction conjugale.[118]
>
> [So nothing exists before 1979, the beginning of their love? Alix's life is linked with Jacques Roubaud's to the point that previous events are abolished; everything is reduced to their story. In wanting her work to be seen, Jacques Roubaud became linked to it. So much so that Alix is often just the dead wife of a great writer, her civil status thus eclipsing her production. At best, she is the muse for whom he erected a tomb in his collection of poems *Some Thing Black*. That is not what he wanted, sometimes he would have liked to be the husband of the great photographer, reduced to his simple conjugal role.]

117 Giannecchini, *Une image peut-être vraie*, pp. 188–89. For Roubaud's 'Postface', see pp. 185–95.

118 Giannecchini, *Une image peut-être vraie*, p. 74.

Jacques Roubaud had wanted to bring Alix Cléo's work the success and acclaim she did not have the chance to enjoy while she was alive. Giannecchini also suggests that Roubaud would have preferred to live in Alix Cléo's shadow, in matters of art and creativity, rather than the opposite. Readers of *Quelque chose noir* and the *Journal* will know that the poet's fame fuelled some of Alix Cléo's anxiety as a writer. In her *Journal*, she writes of the struggle to become a writer: 'J'ai voulu,à tort,être écrivain.Épouser un poète était le moyen de ne pas l'être' [I wanted,wrongly,to be a writer.Marrying a poet was the way not to be one].[119] Writing becomes an impossibility directly correlated with the status of her husband: 'impossibilité d'écrire,mariée à un poète' [impossibility of writing,married to a poet].[120] Roubaud later responds to Alix Cléo's expression of anxiety in his poetry volume: 'Impossible d'écrire, marié(e) à une morte' [Impossible to write, married to a dead woman].[121] The poet attributes the words to a feminine subject through his bracketed addition of the 'e' to the adjective form. Perhaps in the words of his poem Roubaud does realize his wish to reduce his role to that of Alix Cléo's spouse.

The visible grammatical adjustment is one way that the poet sends the reader elsewhere in search of the source of his wordplay: Alix Cléo's writing. Roubaud similarly directs the reader of *Quelque chose noir* to Alix Cléo's photography. While her photographs are not published in the French edition of *Quelque chose noir*, selected images figure in the English translation of the volume and in the second edition of Alix Cléo's *Journal*.[122] Poucel describes the absence of photographs in *Quelque chose noir* as a gesture that 'concretizes the experience of loss by divorcing the text from its occasion'.[123] He goes on to write that the decision not to publish the photographs as part of the poetry volume is part of a 'poetics of absence and restraint found elsewhere in the poems'.[124] The omission of the photographs from a volume that speaks of them repeatedly epitomizes the experience of loss that is the

119 Alix Cléo, *Journal*, p. 193. Typography reproduced from the original.
120 Alix Cléo, *Journal*, p. 143. Typography reproduced from the original.
121 Roubaud, *Quelque chose noir*, p. 63.
122 Images from Alix Cléo's series *Si quelque chose noir* are included at the end of *Some Thing Black*.
123 Poucel, *Jacques Roubaud and the Invention of Memory*, p. 178.
124 Poucel, *Jacques Roubaud and the Invention of Memory*, p. 178.

poems' subject, but the tension created by the references to images the reader cannot see will push many to seek out the sources that Roubaud is alluding to. 'Cette photographie, ta dernière' ['This photograph, your last'] is identifiable as the photo entitled *51 rue des Francs Bourgeois*, the last of the images to appear in the *Journal*, printed just above Alix Cléo's last diary entry.[125] Roubaud's poem title – *this photograph, your last* – leaves space for the reader to explore, to search for possible answers to the writer's clues by following his trail of intertextual links. As a reader faced with the title, 'Cette photo' ['This photo'], I want to know *which* photo. I want also to compare the image to the dimensions of the room and the network of gazes described in Roubaud's poems. I am curious to see what has been given in words. The duo of poems relies on the visual, not just describing the detail of the images and the real memories they trigger, but also emulating the medium of photography through their comparative form. They arouse interest in their subject, which is also the subject of the photographs, and like the *mise en abyme*, encourage a deeper fascination with their detail.

As Giannecchini shows, Roubaud has a desire to have Alix Cléo's work seen. The view through the apartment window and his emphasis on writing and images that are not in the reader's hands make of *Quelque chose noir* a point within a network. After bringing the reader into the intimacy of the home he shared with Alix Cléo, he leads her away from the volume, to the *Journal* and photographs of his late wife. Memory in *Quelque chose noir* is, in this way, tied up with the role of the reader, and there are, in the volume, spaces of mobility and collaboration. The poet's references lead to an external memory space of sorts, one that the reader activates by following the threads of intertextuality. Perhaps Roubaud has created something of what Puff described as 'lieu de mémoire extériorisé dans une œuvre conjointe de photographie et de poésie' [exterior memory-space in a joint œuvre of photography and poetry]. The poet directs his reader to Alix Cléo's *Journal* and photography collection, and without these diversions a reading of *Quelque chose noir* feels somehow incomplete. The memory of the reader is solicited in order to perpetuate the appreciation of the art Alix Cléo composed.

125 Alix Cléo, *Journal*, p. 221.

Despite his wish not to dominate the posthumous reception of Alix Cléo's work, it is true that the poet's existence remains associated with it, as Giannecchini writes: 'En voulant permettre à son travail d'être vu, Jacques Roubaud s'y est lié' [In wanting her work to be seen, Jacques Roubaud has become linked to it]. His popularity as a writer and the textual 'tombeau' [tomb] he has created in Alix Cléo's memory have contributed to the interest in Alix Cléo's work that she had wished for. Does this reduce the role of Alix Cléo to that of 'femme morte du grand écrivain' [dead wife of the great writer] or muse? The question raised by Giannecchini returns me to the theoretical writings of Luce Irigaray and her questioning of the position of woman as other – or muse – in psychoanalytic structures she found to be ingrained with patriarchal tropes. Perhaps it is impossible not to view Roubaud's uses of Alix Cléo's writings and photographs as examples of appropriation. However, some readers have interpreted both the direct and adjusted citations from her *Journal* in *Quelque chose noir* as a form of dialogue. For example, Marie Fabre focuses on the dialogue that begins in the *Journal*: 'les adresses à l'être aimé, seul interlocuteur direct du journal' [the instances of address directed to the beloved, the only direct interlocutor of the journal].[126] Roubaud's role in editing and publishing the diary is considered to be a fulfilment of this dialogue begun in the original writing of the text.

Véronique Montémont writes of Roubaud's use of citation as 'un acte d'amour ultime' [a last act of love], 'la seule manière de rester en contact avec la disparue, de se glisser dans ses mots, dans son regard, de continuer à être *avec elle*' [the only way to stay in contact with the deceased, to slip into her words, into her gaze, to continue being *with her*].[127] His absorption of Alix Cléo's language in *Quelque chose noir* is thus a way of maintaining some form of contact with her after she is gone, through the voice of her writing. Moreover, Montémont emphasizes Roubaud's own silence following his

126 Marie Fabre, 'Hommage à Alix Cléo Roubaud', *Terres de femmes*, 155 (2017) <http://terresdefemmes.blogs.com/mon_weblog/2010/01/hommage-à-alix-cléo-roubaud.html> (para. 3 of 10).

127 Véronique Montémont, '"Je t'aime jusque là" (Jacques Roubaud éditeur du *Journal* d'Alix)', in *L'Écrivain éditeur*, ed. by François Bessire, 2 vols (Geneva: Droz, 2002), II, pp. 207–19 (p. 211).

wife's death.[128] The critic attributes Roubaud's renewed possibility for expression to his wife, 'par le truchement de la voix de la jeune morte' [through the voice of the dead young woman].[129] It is Alix Cléo's voice that speaks through the published *Journal*, for Roubaud remains silent as editor: 'ne fournit aucune note, aucune explication, aucun commentaire de texte, prouve que sa démarche est pure de tout égoïsme et entièrement tournée vers la mise en lumière de l'autre' [adds no note, no explanation, no textual commentary, proves that his approach is not tainted by egotism and is entirely dedicated to bringing the other to light].[130]

Montémont and Giannecchini agree that Roubaud's intentions to increase awareness of Alix Cléo's work are noble, though there is a question in the work of the latter critic regarding the impact of the poet on perceptions of Alix Cléo and her work. Giannecchini contributes to the discussion as author of the first full-length study on the work of Alix Cléo: one of very few works to consider the period of the photographer's life before she met Roubaud. While some readers have recognized a movement towards dialogue in the poetry volume, and while it is clear in the book that Roubaud intends the reader to go beyond his poetry to the photography and prose of Alix Cléo, the role the poet has in citing and editing his wife's writings gives them a context that lies within his own *œuvre*.

In what light are we to view the spaces carved out for Alix Cléo in *Quelque chose noir*? Roubaud uses them to direct his reader through a window out of the text, creating connections beyond the volume for the reader to pursue. The poet's aims are to broaden collective memory of his late wife's creative projects through formation of an external memory structure highlighting her photographs and journal writings, but the question of the positioning of the beloved in the poet's text arises. Is Alix Cléo muse, overshadowed by the work of Roubaud? Or is the poet able to step aside, as Montémont suggests, to foreground the work of his late wife?

128 Montémont, '"Je t'aime jusque là"', p. 208.
129 Montémont, '"Je t'aime jusque là"', p. 211.
130 Montémont, '"Je t'aime jusque là"', p. 209.

Breathing, Form, Collaboration

While the breath of the lover captured as the rhythmic beat of the poem in *Trente et un au cube* represented the space created for the reader's involvement with the text, in *Quelque chose noir*, rhythm and the breathing of Alix Cléo take a very different shape. Alix Cléo's respiratory difficulties are well documented in her *Journal* and in Roubaud's writings, and the spacing of the words that compose some of the poems in *Quelque chose noir* has been linked with the breathlessness of the poet's asthmatic wife. Geneviève Guétemme sees the traces of Alix Cléo's jagged breathing in the punctuation used by Roubaud in his poetry: 'Jacques Roubaud reprend notamment, dans *Quelque chose noir*, la ponctuation, sans espace entre certains mots et pleine de blancs, du *Journal*. Cette ponctuation qui accélère et distend les phrases, présente une image de l'asthme d'Alix, de son manque de souffle et ses appels d'air' [In *Some Thing Black* Jacques Roubaud notably takes up the punctuation of the *Journal*, the lack of spacing between certain words and, elsewhere, the many blank spaces. This punctuation that speeds up and stretches out the sentences presents an image of Alix's asthma, of her lack of breath and her gasping for air][131] Beyond this homage to Alix Cléo and its monument to her suffering, Guétemme finds that the spaces in common in the two works represent not only Roubaud's own grief, but also his continuation of Alix Cléo's work:

> Dans les textes de Jacques Roubaud, les points intempestifs, les retours à la ligne et les espacements d'interlignes visualisent son souffle à lui: coupé par la mort d'Alix. Ils montrent aussi qu'il s'est approprié le travail d'Alix sur le vide et la coupure et qu'il le continue.[132]

131 Geneviève Guétemme, 'Le *Journal* d'Alix Cléo Roubaud: étude d'un paratexte photographique, poétique et amoureux', *Essays in French Literature and Culture*, 49 (2012), 59–78 (p. 68).

132 Guétemme, 'Le *Journal* d'Alix Cléo Roubaud', p. 68.

> [In Jacques Roubaud's texts, the untimely full stops, the line breaks and spaces between lines visualize his own breath: cut short by Alix's death. They also show that he took over Alix's work on emptiness and rupture, and that he continues it.]

Guétemme's description brings together the poet and his beloved, and suggests a common aim in their writing.

Alix Cléo's respiration is also referred to as rhythm in *Quelque chose noir*, but rather than figuring in an emphasis on music and sound in poetry, her breathing is the subject of a poem entitled 'Art de la vue' ['Art of Seeing']:

> La netteté, la décision extrême de l'intention visuelle
>
> Sans aucun doute cette absence d'hésitation est liée à l'ubiquité photographique, qui fragmente chaque mouvement en une séquence de gels
>
> Mais du froid de l'immobilité acquise dans le sel la chaleur du corps solarisé s'évapore comme la sueur brumeuse au dessus des chevaux dans l'hiver new-yorkais de Stieglitz
>
> D'un côté le littéral, l'absolutisme maniériste, les rayons lumineux conduits, forcés comme, à l'écrire
>
> De l'autre, sur fond minimal géométrique (donné) le geste de tenir l'appareil sur la poitrine (contre le cœur, les seins) la pose nocturne interminable, aux seules étoiles, 'quinze minutes la nuit au rythme de la respiration'
>
> Image avalée par le souffle.[133]
>
> [The sharpness, the extreme decisiveness of the visual intention
>
> Without a doubt this absence of hesitation is linked to photographic ubiquity, which breaks up each movement into a sequence of stills
>
> But from the cold of the stillness gained in the salt the heat of the solarized body evaporates like the fog of sweat above the horses in Steiglitz's New York winter
>
> On one hand the literal, the manneristic absolutism, the rays of light driven forward, forced as in writing
>
> On the other, against a minimal geometric background (given) the act of holding the camera on her chest (close to her heart, her breasts) the endless nocturnal pose, for the stars alone, 'fifteen minutes at night to the rhythm of breathing'

133 Roubaud, *Quelque chose noir*, p. 99.

Image swallowed by breathing.]

The visual is at the forefront as Roubaud describes Alix Cléo's *Quinze minutes la nuit au rythme de la respiration*. The photo is a memory of the moment it was taken: in the black of night, Alix Cléo lies naked on the ground before a row of cypress trees in Roubaud's childhood home of Saint-Félix. With the camera resting on her chest, the long exposure of the photo over fifteen minutes produces an image marked by Alix's jagged breathing, an image which bears little resemblance to its visual referent.[134] In his poem Roubaud captures the contrast between the decisiveness behind the composition of the image and the hazy result, and he evokes Stieglitz's *Terminal* to highlight a series of oppositions in Alix Cléo's photo. *The Terminal* juxtaposes definition and blurry edges, immobility and movement, cold and heat; in the foreground, hot steam rises from horses in the cold winter snow, while a set of powerful verticals in the building and colonnades behind them make up the background of the photo. In Alix Cléo's photo the movement of her breathing, the heat of her tanned body in Roubaud's memory and the exposure of the photo taken over fifteen minutes may be contrasted with the immobility of the resulting image and its inflexible freezing of time within a sequence. The differences distinguish the 'littéral' [literal], the lines of darkness and light that make up the image, from the memory of the night on which it was composed, and Alix Cléo's 'geste' [act] of holding the camera against her chest.

The dichotomy between what the viewer sees and the memory it represents characterizes Roubaud's response to the photograph elsewhere in his writing. At first glance the photograph looks something like an X-ray; jagged lines separate what appear to be black hills along the lower half of the image from a white sky across the top. Grey smudges blur the lines between black and white and also the lower sections of the black slopes. Roubaud describes the photograph as he sees it positioned on his writing desk five years after it was taken:

134 Giannecchini, *Une image peut-être vraie*, p. 119.

> montagnes très abruptes, plusieurs plans de montagnes s'enfonçant vers un arrière de l'image, relief imaginé par le devenir gris des noirs; montagnes regardées du plancher d'une vallée sombre, sombre de la muraille de noirs qui se dresse verticalement devant elle; vallée sombre et sans détails, à peine touchée, minimalement, de quelques photons tombés du ciel sans couleur; montagnes s'enfonçant dans d'autres montagnes, grises, éclairées de très loin.[135]
>
> [very steep mountains, several heights of mountains sinking into the rear of the image, a depth imagined in the fading of blacks into greys; mountains observed from the floor of a dark valley, dark with the great wall of black that towers vertically in front of it; dark valley, without details, hardly touched, only minimally, by a few photons fallen from the colourless sky; mountains sinking into other mountains, grey ones, lit up from very far away.]

The source of this extract is not without significance. The passage describing the photo appears for the first time in Roubaud's *Grand incendie de Londres*, written in 1985, but is taken up again in 2014, in the poet's 'Postface' to Hélène Giannecchini's *Une image peut-être vraie*. The reappearance of the extract in the first book-length dedication to the work of Alix Cléo places Jacques Roubaud in the position of critic, or reader, albeit one close or privileged enough to provide a 'Postface'. Despite its context, respectively, in a self-declared volume of prose and a critical study of Alix Cléo's photography, Roubaud's reading of Alix Cléo's photo has some of the qualities of a poem. Repetitions abound in the passage, so that one phrase describing the 'montagnes' [mountains] successively sinks into another, much like the slopes themselves of the image. Words create shifting shapes: 'image' [image] ripples into 'imaginé' [imagined], the 'sombre' of 'vallée sombre' [dark valley] is repeated after the quick breath of a comma, and greys and blacks merge into one another in the darkness. Alliterations and assonances drive the writing on: 'p', 'v' and 'to' sounds recur in 'plusieurs plans', 'verticalement devant elle; vallée sombre' and 'photons tombés'; 'verticalement' echoes in 'minimalement' and 's'enfonçant'. The effect, compounded by the repeated use of semi-colons and the lack of full stops, is one of breathlessness, perhaps in homage

135 Roubaud, *Le Grand incendie de Londres*, pp. 396–97. See also Roubaud's 'Postface' in Giannecchini's *Une image peut-être vraie*, p. 191.

to the photographer and her subject. The repetitions and modulations create a sense of speed and unstoppable flow.

As the writing on the photo moves on, the perceived image of the mountains morphs into one of smoke, and then flames:

> Ce seraient montagnes sauf que les airs, au-dessus, sont envahis aussi de noir: du noir cette fois comme une fumée; les montagnes ne sont pas solides, profondes, mais de fumée épaisse, noires de fumée dont on ne voit pas les flammes, ou plutôt dont les flammes sont noires elles-mêmes, sont la fumée même; un feu noir; un feu-fumée d'une seule noire couleur; un feu sombre qui renvoie la lumière qui l'exhibe, qui le dessine, qui le pénètre de gris en arrière et le dissipe en fumées.
>
> Ce ne sont pas des montagnes, ce sont des flammes inclinées vers la gauche, des flammes obscures qui ne poussent pas toutes droites vers le ciel, mais s'inclinent sous la lumière visible à droite, la lumière lointaine qui les enveloppe de sa clarté, les définit comme flammes; les flammes s'inclinent sous la lumière, et sous le vent invisible aussi, venu du coin lumineux, à droite, où le golfe de lumière est le plus profond; le vent et la lumière viennent de là, comme la photographie le révèle.[136]
>
> [They would be mountains if it were not for the space above them also invaded by black: black like smoke this time; the mountains are not solid, deep, but made up of thick smoke, black with a smoke whose flames are not visible, or rather whose flames are themselves black, are the smoke itself; a black fire; a fire-smoke made up of one black colour; a dark fire that expels the light that exposes it, gives it shape, infuses it from behind with grey and disperses it into wisps of smoke.
>
> They are not mountains, they are flames leaning towards the left, dark flames that do not push straight up towards the sky, but which bend under the light that can be seen on the right, the faraway light which envelops them, defines them as flames; the flames bend under the light, and under the invisible wind too, which comes from the corner of light, on the right, where the stream of light is deepest; the wind and the light come from there, as the photograph shows.]

The description accumulates in the building of subordinate clauses that connect either through repetition of the nouns or adjectives that close the previous clause, or through prepositional phrases and relative clauses that create a branching out in the passage. The interweaving of nouns such as

136 Roubaud, *Le Grand incendie de Londres*, p. 397. Also in Giannecchini, *Une image peut-être vraie*, p. 191.

'fumée' [smoke], 'flammes' [flames] and 'lumière' [light] is evocative of the *entrebescar* technique that has been so important in Roubaud's writing, hinting again at the presence of poetry in this written account of Alix Cléo's photo. The *entrebescar*-like woven strands in this text also establish a particular relationship with the photograph in question. The sense that the elements of syntax in the text blend and merge through repetition and adjustment emulates the forms that make up the photograph: the spaces of colour – white, grey, black – separated by blurred lines and the peaks that seem at times to run into one another. Roubaud thus incorporates the rhythm of Alix Cléo's irregular breathing into his writing, through his account of the photograph that he takes as his subject, in the spaces that join the visual and the textual is the jagged breathing of Alix Cléo.

The pace of Roubaud's reading of Alix Cléo's photo is punctuated by the paragraph changes, signalling on each occasion corrections to the poet's and in turn the reader's understanding of the nature of the photo. The peaks in the photograph are not, in fact, mountains. They are first manifestations of thick smoke, and then they are flames bending in the wind. The true subject of the photograph is revealed in instalments it seems. Further on in the passage, Roubaud writes: 'La photographie n'est pas de flammes, même noires, pas de montagnes avalées par l'obscurité de nuit, mais de cyprès; les cyprès dans la nuit bougies noires bougées de vent, flames-fumées' [The photograph is not of flames, even black ones, not of mountains swallowed by the darkness of night, but of cypress trees; cypress trees in the night black candles flickering in the wind, smoke-flames].[137] Following the image through the eyes of the poet, the reader first imagines the trees bending in the wind, but the indication of the photograph's subject shifts again when the poet remembers that on the night the photograph was taken, the air was still:

> Mais les cyprès, alors, ne bougeaient pas: au moment dont je me souviens, le moment que j'écris, octobre, il y a du cers tiède qui s'enveloppe autour de mes jambes, qui vient battre obstinément la colline en haut de la restanque, et les cyprès s'inclinent, non vers

137 Roubaud, *Le Grand incendie de Londres*, pp. 397–98. Also in Giannecchini, *Une image peut-être vraie*, p. 192.

la gauche dans un souffle venu de l'autre direction mais vers l'avant; ils s'inclinent de la tête comme ils le font toujours, comme des flammes, comme des bougies nocturnes dans une chambre fenêtre ouverte, comme des montagnes chargées de nuit quand on les contemple fixement. En octobre de cette année antérieure, dans le cers tiède de deux heures du matin, je me souviens, comme je me souviens maintenant, de la photographie intitulée *Quinze minutes la nuit au rythme de la respiration* (les deux souvenirs se superposent, deviennent indistincts; je me souviens maintenant, devant l'image, et je me souviens m'être souvenu), du moment d'août, nocturne aussi; à ce moment les cyprès ne bougeaient pas. Et, Alix se levant, regardant l'allée des cyprès, l'air était chaud, immobile, en repos dans la nuit, il n'y avait pas de vent.[138]

[But the cypress trees were not moving then: at the time I remember, the same time of year I am writing in now, October, there is the mild Cers wind that wraps itself round my legs, which stubbornly lashes the hill that rises above the dry stone wall, and the cypress trees bend, not towards the left in a breeze coming from the other direction but forward; they bend their heads like they always do, like flames, like candles at night in a bedroom with the windows open, like mountains heavy with night when you look at them intently. In October of that earlier year, in the mild Cers of two o'clock in the morning, I remembered, as I remember now, the photograph entitled *Fifteen minutes at night to the rhythm of breathing* (the two memories overlap, become indistinct; I remember now, looking at the image, and I remember remembering), that moment in August, also at night; the cypress trees were not moving then. And, Alix standing up, looking at the alley of cypress trees, the air was hot, still, peaceful in the darkness, there was no wind.]

There are three memories intertwined with the image shown in the photo: the occasion when the photo was taken by Alix Cléo, on a hot August night in 1980, the moment in October 1985 when Roubaud writes, and the October of the year before. Just as the original memory and the memory of that memory become confused in the mind of the poet, so too it becomes unclear for Roubaud's reader whether the metaphors that made of the photographic forms mountains, smoke and flames are inspired in the poet by the view of the cypress trees he encounters in October 1984, or whether the photo itself made him think of the trees 'comme des flammes, comme des bougies [...], comme des montagnes chargées de nuit' [like flames, like candles [...], like mountains heavy

138 Roubaud, *Le Grand incendie de Londres*, p. 399. Also in Giannecchini, *Une image peut-être vraie*, pp. 193–94.

with night]. The similes used to describe the trees leaning in the October wind resonate with the objects and shapes the poet attributed to the forms in Alix Cléo's photograph. The memories overlap and the poet's future vision of the photograph is included in the intertwining of past times remembered.

An echo of Roubaud's description of *Quinze minutes* sounds in the poet's recent collection published by Gallimard: *Octogone* (2014). The volume's opening poem, 'Entrecimamen', is a return to Roubaud's childhood home and troubadour heritage.[139] In the prose poem, Roubaud pays tribute to his origins in the form of a wind that swirls through the peaks and lows of southern French terrain:

> Dans les branches les plus hautes de grands arbres, des pins, des sapins, cèdres, mélèzes, sous le vent fort mais régulier, qui n'est pas le vent de tempête qui choque, entrechoque, embarrasse, punit, arrache, déracine, mais le beau grand vent constant, pressant, pressé des provinces méditerranéennes, le 'cers' du Minervois, des Corbières.[140]
>
> [In the highest branches of the tall trees, pines, firs, cedars, larches, in the strong but regular wind, which is not the wind of the storm that shocks, shakes, troubles, punishes, rips, unroots, but the great fair wind that is constant, driving, driven from the Mediterranean provinces, the Cers of the Minervois, of the Corbières.]

Layers of assonance, alliteration and lexical repetitions produce rhythm. Successive clauses pick up phonic and lexical elements of what has come before, which pushes the poem ahead in a way that reflects the force of the incessant wind, and also evokes the form of Roubaud's meditation years earlier on Alix Cléo's *Quinze minutes*. Near the end of the poem, there are further parallels between the two pieces of writing, when the poet becomes breathless in the face of the driving wind:

> sur la colline, […] le visage heurté, giflé de draps d'air, la bouche emplie d'un bâillon d'air froissé, presque m'étouffant, m'asphyxiant, presque étranglé, garrotté, suffocant, l'oscillation de flamme de bougie des cyprès aux plumeaux vert-noir, leurs affrontements, leurs confrontations aux gestes-paraphes des pins, et des amandiers

139 The troubadour term 'entrecimamen' signifies 'entrelacement' and is a reference to the 'entrebescar' technique in noun form.

140 Jacques Roubaud, *Octogone* (Paris: Gallimard, 2014), p. 9.

> en dessous, jusqu'à ce qu'enfin, et toujours, en chacun des lieux envahis par le vent en vienne à s'établir, s'imposer, créant comme une oasis de tranquillité au cœur d'un tourbillon, un '*entrecimamen*'.[141]
>
> [on the hill, [...] my face struck, lashed by sheets of wind, my mouth stopped with a gag of crumpled air, almost stifling me, asphyxiating me, almost strangled, muzzled, suffocating, the flickering of the candle flame of the cypresses with their green-black tufts, their clashes, their confrontations with the movements-flourishes of the pines, and of the almond trees below, until finally, and still, in each of the places invaded by the wind, an *entrecimamen* comes to be established, imposed, creating something of an oasis of calm in the heart of the whirlwind.]

Silenced, suffocated by the gusts of air, the poet sees a row of cypress trees dancing in the wind, their movement like the candle flame he saw in Alix Cléo's photograph. Deep in this dedication to the troubadour craft are the echoes of a memory rooted in *Quinze minutes*. The 'entrecimamen' that is the subject of the poem is the intertwining of lexical items and phonic assonances, but also of reading and memory: his poem bears traces of his reading of Alix Cléo's photograph from decades before. The poet invests the spaces of the photo with his recollections and thoughts of when it was taken, and the times he had returned to the setting. In turn, he allows its lines and shapes to stimulate his memory and to infuse his compositions, to create new directions. Roubaud's memory interacts with the form of the photograph in the ways that he set out for poetry.

Roubaud's writing in the given extracts reflects the characteristics that are singular to the image: the blurred lines, the running into one another of its various elements. It is also possible to see in Roubaud's lexical repetitions and limited variation on nouns and adjectives the few colours that make up the image: shades of black, white and grey. Beyond this emulation of the visual in his writing, the shapes that Roubaud sees as he observes the photograph positioned on his desk may be aligned with his conception of poetic language. Formulated in vocabulary used by Zukofsky, poetic language is described as being nearer to 'upper limit music' than 'lower limit speech'; the referent fades from the fore as rhythm and sound are privileged in Roubaud's definition of poetry. Words in Roubaud's poetic language at

141 Roubaud, *Octogone*, pp. 10–11.

times acquire an object-like materiality, becoming self-referential in the foregrounding of their phonic qualities. In the poet's reading of *Quinze minutes*, the shapes of the photo are mountains, smoke and flames blown by the wind. For the reader following the poet's account, particularly in the absence of the image itself, the lines and forms in the photograph successively become the objects that Roubaud describes them as: mountains, flames, smoke, windblown trees. The lines and colours that make up the image take on a material existence, constantly shifting and performing independently of their referent, like the words of poetry whose music and rhythm are heard before and above semantic meaning. Rhythm is at the heart of the image. As the beloved's breathing punctuated the lines of *Trente et un au cube*, providing the spaces that are vital for the reader's interaction with the poetry, so too Alix Cléo's respiration forms the photograph. Rhythm draws in and encompasses the reader, eliciting her involvement with the work.

In this alignment of the photograph with poetic form, Roubaud is in that position of reader. He is Alix Cléo's reader and he engages with her photograph in the same ways that he elicits a response from the reader of his poetry. As editor of Alix Cléo's *Journal* and writer of *Quelque chose noir*, the poet embraces the work of Alix Cléo; her words and photographs acquire new resonances and increased readership, but from within the context of Roubaud's own œuvre. In the extract from his prose volume *Le Grand incendie de Londres*, and more importantly as part of his 'Postface' in Hélène Giannecchini's study of Alix Cléo's photography, this text is a reading that places the poet in a different position in relation to his wife from that of poet to lover, muse, or addressee. He is her reader; he becomes immersed in the piece's form, allowing a network of associations and connections to grow from his vision of the photo, fulfilling his continuing notion by which the reader is required to be part of the meaning generated in a poem.

Grief and *Biipsisme*: Different Forms of Silence

Reflected in Roubaud's texts published after Alix Cléo's passing is a sense of conflict between the poet's silence in grief and the need to speak.

Against the backdrop of many months during which the poet feels an impossibility to express his experience in poetry, in *Quelque chose noir*, the poet writes: 'On ne peut pas me dire: "il faut le taire" ' [They cannot tell me: 'you must be quiet'].[142] This struggle is recognized by Sandra Gilbert as a reaction to an untimely death: '[A]nyone who has suffered the shock of a death that is unexpected or experienced as wrongful has had to engage with what is impossible to tell yet somehow essential to speak, if only stammeringly.'[143] Gilbert's summary captures, on the one hand, a feeling of shock, or disbelief in mourning. There is often associated with bereavement an inability to articulate the loss that is felt – it is the unthinkable, the unspeakable – but Gilbert additionally suggests that the survivor feels they have been wronged. Perhaps it is this feeling of injustice that is the source of the impulse to speak: a will to explain, justify and in that way understand the unfathomable.

Elisabeth Bronfen points out what is frequently referred to as an impossibility in language when it comes to death:

> Placed beyond the register of images that the living body can know, 'Death' can only be read as a trope, as a signifier with an incessantly receding, ungraspable signified, invariably always pointing back self-reflexively to other signifiers. Death remains outside clear categories. It is nowhere, because it is only a gap, a cut, a transition between the living body and the corpse, a before (the painful fear, the serene joy of the dying person) and an after (the mourning of the survivor), an ungraspable point lacking any empiric object.[144]

Death is beyond the line of what can be experienced by the survivor, which perhaps goes some of the way towards accounting for the silence that grief instils in that person. Bronfen's description resonates with aspects of *Quelque chose noir*: the sense of a before and after that defines the experience of the mourner, the identification of death as a 'gap' or 'cut', the 'ungraspable point'. Roubaud's references to his everyday life

142 Roubaud, *Quelque chose noir*, p. 22.

143 Sandra M. Gilbert, *Death's Door: Modern Dying and the Ways We Grieve* (London: Norton and Company, 2006), p. 99.

144 Bronfen, *Over Her Dead Body*, p. 54.

following the death of Alix Cléo point to a life divided into the before and after of his wife's loss, a before and after to poetry and the ability to write it. As poet he also grapples with finding a way not only to address Alix Cléo but identify her.

The vacillation between silence and the impulse to speak experienced by the mourner is articulated rather differently by Jacques Derrida in his dedication to his late friend, Roland Barthes:

> Deux infidélités, un choix impossible: d'un côté ne rien dire qui revienne à soi seul, à sa propre voix, se taire ou au moins se faire accompagner ou précéder, en contrepoint, par la voix de l'ami. Dès lors par ferveur amicale ou reconnaissante, par approbation aussi, se contenter de citer, d'accompagner ce qui revient à l'autre, plus ou moins directement, lui laisser la parole, s'effacer devant elle, la suivre, et devant lui. Mais ce trop de fidélité finirait par ne rien dire, et ne rien échanger. Il retourne à la mort. Il y renvoie, il renvoie la mort à la mort.[145]
>
> [Two infidelities, an impossible choice: on the one hand, not to say anything that comes back to oneself, to one's own voice, to remain silent, or at the very least to let oneself be accompanied or preceded in counterpoint by the friend's voice. Thus, out of zealous devotion or gratitude, out of approbation as well, to be content with just quoting, with just accompanying that which more or less directly comes back or returns to the other, to let him speak, to efface oneself in front of and to follow his speech, and to do so right in front of him. But this excess of fidelity would end up saying and exchanging nothing. It returns to death. It points to death, sending death back to death.]

Derrida opposes silence to speaking in honour of the friend who has passed away, nonetheless describing both as 'infidelities'. In speaking on behalf of a friend who is no longer living, there is the risk of imposing only one's own presence. The poignancy of Derrida's dilemma is derived from the situation of both figures in the sphere of philosophy and critical thought: to speak *for* the deceased equates to an erasure of sorts, an

145 Jacques Derrida, 'Les morts de Roland Barthes', *Poétique*, 47 (1981), 269–92 (pp. 276–77). English translation in Jacques Derrida, *The Work of Mourning*, ed. by Pascale-Anne Brault and Michael Naas (Chicago: University of Chigaco Press, 2001), p. 45.

overshadowing. Derrida proposes 'quoting' the friend as an alternative, describing this particular form of silence as 'accompanying' that which comes back to the other, 'letting' him speak, and 'effacing oneself' before his speech. However, his conclusion that citation in this case amounts to 'saying and exchanging nothing' tells us that there is no act of giving in silence, no dedication, no homage.

There are many differences between the context of Derrida's eulogy and the relationship between Jacques and Alix Cléo Roubaud as it is figured in the written and photographic publications of the couple. The context of friendship is exchanged for one of marriage, and while Roland Barthes enjoyed great success in the literary domain, Alix Cléo's writings betray her sense of anguish as an aspiring writer. Nonetheless, the impasse expressed in this extract from Derrida's writing is also perceptible in the different forms of silence that characterize Roubaud's writing following Alix Cléo's death. Perhaps the differences between the two partnerships themselves raise important questions: between the notably unequal literary statuses of Alix Cléo and Jacques Roubaud, does it always come back to the voice of the poet? Can we speak of 'infidelity', after Derrida, in the opposition of the poet's silence, or his use of citation, to a 'saying and exchanging'?

Somewhere between (citation as) silence and speaking that risks coming back 'to one's own voice' is Roubaud's *biipsisme* [*biipsism*]. The term encapsulates the writer's theory of love tied in with a conception of poetry that follows a line back into the troubadour tradition. For the two linked in love, *biipsisme* means unity without erasing difference: 'Chacun, une y est l'autre de l'un, une. L'inséparabilité y est absolue, mais sans indistinction: parce que l'amour est de ce monde et du corps' [In biipsism, each person is the other of the one. Inseparability is absolute, but not without indistinction: because love is of this world and of the body].[146] There are similarities to Irigaray's conception of love as protecting the distance that maintains difference in the two subjects that enter into a relation, but Roubaud's idea places more emphasis on the ideal, utopian aspects of the fusion: 'Dans ce monde, s'il avait pu être pensé, la pensée de l'autre, toujours, aurait été la pensée de

146 Jacques Roubaud, 'L'Amour, la poésie: Hypothèses', in *De l'amour*, ed. by École de la Cause freudienne (Paris: Flammarion, 1999), pp. 81–104 (p. 103).

l'"autre de deux"' [In the world of biipsism, if it could have been imagined, the thought of the other would always have been the thought of the 'other of two'].[147] Opposed to the notion of solipsism, Roubaud's definition relies on the extension of thought beyond the self. The poet's reference to the other world of *biipsisme* and his use of the past conditional in the description signal its impossibility, more so since in the latter citation the poet speaks from the world of one left behind: 'Le monde d'un seul, mais qui aurait été deux' [The world of one who is alone, but who would have been two].[148]

The fullest definition of *biipsisme* comes into being in poetry. Roubaud writes of a poem composed in two voices, the '*voix-guide*' [*guide-voice*] and '*voix-écho*' [*echo-voice*]. Rather than dominating the sequence, in a twist created by a constraint elaborated by the poet, the '*guide-voice*' finds itself submitting to the same constraint as the '*echo-voice*':

> La deuxième voix écoute et pèse et rumine et se remémore ce que dit la voix première, qui parle pour elle et qui ne parle qu'afin d'assurer que ce qu'elle aura dit ne rendra pas la seconde voix muette mais au contraire à la sienne parfaitement accordée. Aucune des deux voix, en fait, ne commande l'autre; elles se soumettent toutes les deux à la règle, qui est la *Règle d'Amour*.[149]
>
> [The second voice listens to and weighs up and thinks about and recalls what the first voice says, which speaks for the second and which only speaks to make sure that what it says will not render the second voice silent but, to the contrary, will keep it in perfect harmony with its own. Neither of the two voices, in fact, controls the other; they are both subjected to the rule, which is the *Rule of Love*.]

The constraint involves a series of repetitions of 'nos jours' [our days] and 'nos nuits' [our nights]. Every time the guiding voice says either 'nos jours' or 'nos nuits', the reply from the echoing voice must be 'nos jours'. When the guiding voice doubles his or her utterance – 'nos jours, nos jours', or 'nos nuits, nos nuits' – the reply from the echoing voice is 'nos nuits'.[150]

147 Roubaud, *Le Grand incendie de Londres*, p. 210.
148 Roubaud, *Le Grand incendie de Londres*, p. 209.
149 Roubaud, 'L'Amour, la poésie', pp. 84–85.
150 For a detailed description of the constraint that structures the poem and its effects, see Roubaud, 'L'Amour, la poésie', pp. 81–86.

The constraint limiting the '*voix-guide*' is that he or she must make sure the '*voix-écho*' never falls silent, for the echoing voice must repeat exactly what the guiding voice says, even if there is a delay and the echo becomes interspersed with further utterances from the guide. For example:

nos jours	
	nos jours
nos nuits, nos nuits	
	nos nuits
nos jours, nos jours	
	nos nuits
[our days	
	our days
our nights, our nights	
	our nights
our days, our days	
	our nights]

The echoing voice must be given the opportunity to say both of the 'nos nuits' that make up the guiding voice's second utterance, before then taking up the echoes of 'nos jours nos jours', the third pronouncement from the guiding voice:

nos nuits	
	nos jours
nos jours	
	nos jours
nos nuits, nos nuits	
	nos nuits
[our nights	
	our days
our days	
	our days
our nights, our nights	
	our nights]

In this way, the guiding voice is subjected just as much as the echoing voice to the constraint structuring the poem. Roubaud sets out his explanation as a dialogue, in which his interlocutor asks just what the reader might be thinking:

> – La seconde voix n'est-elle pas le souvenir de la première ? la première l'anticipation, l'imagination de la seconde ?
> – En effet, en amour, deux voix se revoient et se prévoient l'une l'autre.[151]
>
> ['Is the second voice not the memory of the first ? And the first voice the anticipation, the imagination of the second ?'
> 'Indeed, in love, two voices both hear and anticipate each other.']

If the '*voix-guide*' does not stay in tune with the sequence of echoes, he or she will either silence the second voice, or the poem will end in a cacophonous repetition of endless 'nos jours', or 'nos nuits'.

The poet gives an extended example of the two voices at work, ending in a numerical palindrome: 'Cela fait 53 paroles pour la voix-guide, 35 pour la voix-écho' [That makes 53 utterances for the guide-voice and 35 for the echo-voice].[152] The mathematical play gives rise to a close of the discussion on love and a definition of love poetry:

> La première voix du poème, la voix-guide, avance en assurant la préservation exacte de son passé. Il me semble dans ces conditions que ton poème n'est pas un poème de l'amour mais seulement du souvenir de l'amour. Et même pas du souvenir réel de l'amour réel, mais du souvenir imaginé d'un amour rêvé.
>
> – Sans doute. Mais tout amour ne vit que de préparer la pérennité de son souvenir.[153]
>
> ['The first voice of the poem, the guide-voice, moves forward ensuring the exact preservation of its past. Given these conditions, it seems to me that your poem is not about love but about the memory of love. And not even about the real memory of a real love, but about the imagined memory of a dreamed love.'
>
> 'No doubt. But every love lives only to prepare the permanence of its memory.']

151 Roubaud, 'L'Amour, la poésie', p. 85.
152 Roubaud, 'L'Amour, la poésie', p. 86.
153 Roubaud, 'L'Amour, la poésie', p. 86.

In a movement echoing the palindrome that brings together the fifty-three words spoken by the guiding voice, and the thirty-five uttered by the echo, the poem as a whole enacts the expression of love and its memory.

Jean-François Puff draws the notion of the '*voix-guide*' and the '*voix-écho*' into his analysis of *Quelque chose noir*, seeing in Roubaud's adoption of fragments from Alix Cléo's *Journal* 'la tentative de renversement de la voix-guide en voix-écho' [the attempt to transform the guide-voice into an echo-voice] and the hope of restoring what he describes as 'un impossible dialogue, par l'entrelacement de voix à jamais séparées' [an impossible dialogue, through the intertwinement of voices separated forever].[154] Véronique Montémont too writes of an experience of '*biipsisme*' between the poet's *Quelque chose noir* and Alix Cléo's *Journal*, though pointing out the irrevocable distance across time that it highlights: 'Ce qui est absolument tragique, c'est que l'échange se fait à contretemps' [What is absolutely tragic, is that the exchange takes place across the impossible distance of time].[155] The disjunction effected by time is situated beyond the grave by Elisabeth Cardonne-Arlyck: 'une sorte de dialogue d'outre-tombe' [a sort of dialogue from beyond the grave].[156] The notion of dialogue, particularly in line with Roubaud's elaboration of the interconnected '*voix-guide*' and '*voix-écho*' for which careful listening and response are key, breaks the dichotomy between speaking and silence in Derrida's dedication to Barthes. However, in the descriptions given in these readings of Roubaud's texts, each of the three writers simultaneously classifies the dialogue that occurs between Roubaud's *Quelque chose noir* and Alix Cléo's *Journal* as somehow impossible. Although the voices of the two volumes address one another, perhaps Roubaud's interweaving of Alix Cléo's journal entries and his responses to them in poetry can only ever be citation at most.

The harmonious sequence of the guiding and echoing voices relies on the presence of the respective silences that allow the other's utterance to

154 Puff, *Mémoire de la mémoire*, p. 442.

155 Véronique Montémont, *Jacques Roubaud: L'amour du nombre* (Lille: Presses Universitaires du Septentrion, 2004), p. 248.

156 Elisabeth Cardonne-Arlyck, 'Poésie, forme de vie', *L'Esprit Créateur*, 32:2 (1992), 89–101 (p. 101).

take place. Each voice anticipates and bounces off the other, the act of listening as vital in the sequence as that of speaking – 'deux voix se revoient et se prévoient l'une l'autre' [two voices hear and anticipate each other]. When Roubaud reads Alix Cléo's photo *Quinze minutes* and when its forms are experienced as the rhythm of 'upper limit music', I see the same play of guiding and echoing voices that makes up his philosophy of *biipsisme* in poetry.

Through the poetic constraint linking the *guide-voice* and the *echo-voice*, Roubaud says that in love poetry there is an effort to preserve love past – 'la voix-guide […] avance en assurant la préservation exacte de son passé' [the guide-voice […] moves forward ensuring the exact preservation of its past]. As the echoes of his reading ripple out from the prose text of *Le Grand incendie de Londres* and from his 'Postface' in Giannecchini's *Une image peut-être vraie* to recent poetry collection *Octogone*, we look back to the poet's memory of those moments spent with Alix Cléo, moments manifested in the rhythm of her breathing that shapes the irregular lines in *Quinze minutes*. The interaction of the guiding and echoing voices in Roubaud's *biipsisme* seeks to ensure the permanence of love's memory in the future, 'la pérennité de son souvenir' [the permanence of its memory]. The writing that resonates with the rhythm of Alix Cléo's breath is also the extension of love's memory into the future. The image at the centre of Roubaud's readings is renewed, stimulating fresh associations and connections on every re-reading. It is not in silence or the act of quoting, but in reading her that the poet finds the space for Alix Cléo's voice to guide.

Conclusion

Comparisons of Roubaud's earlier and later works – those published after the death of Alix Cléo – reflect the poet's changing relationship with poetic form and his experience of loss. At times, this has meant searching for aspects of his writing that are no longer present and some of my readings are inevitably concerned with negation. The multidimensionality of Roubaud's poetic structures – the way the poem's written shape interacts with and evokes the phonic, and vice versa – is replaced in *Du noir tombe* by a poetry that functions visually, in silence. Without the beloved that Roubaud had placed at the centre of poetic form, that form is somehow diminished, no longer structured from the level of the syllable. This loss of multidimensionality is foregrounded in *Du noir tombe* through a direct comparison with *Dors*, signalled by the poet himself. His statement that *Du noir tombe* is not like *Dors* is also an invitation to the reader to consider the changes that occur from the first to the second volume and thus to reflect on the definition of poetry in the absence of the woman he loves.

Du noir tombe is linked through its title to *Quelque chose noir*. In the latter volume, poetic form and the rhythm that entails in Roubaud's work continue to be defined as diminished, particularly in comparison with *Trente et un au cube*. The place of form as a marker in the text for the interactions of memory fails; memories are those of the poet and the reader is somehow excluded from many of the spaces that make up the volume. Poetic spaces seem, in Roubaud's grief, not to stimulate memory, but rather to dilute what the poet knows of Alix Cléo, or to engulf his senses in infernal yearning. But the reader takes a different position in relation to *Quelque chose noir*. It is precisely in directing the reader away from the text that Roubaud creates a network for the engagement of the reader's memory. In encouraging his reader to seek out Alix Cléo's photographs, to search for references that he both borrows and adapts from her personal journal, the poet not only widens collective memory of the photographer's creations, but also elicits deeper responses from the reader to those parts of his writing that speak through Alix Cléo's words and images. In this way, Roubaud dedicates an external memory space to Alix Cléo, but remains necessarily a central figure within the network he constructs. The place of the beloved in contributing to meaning in his poetry is therefore uncertain.

Alix Cléo is present in Roubaud's writing as the centre of his poetic form through the rhythm of her breathing. Her uneasy respiration infuses Roubaud's description of *Quinze minutes*, filtering through to recent publication *Octogone*. Through his writing on Alix Cléo's photo in prose volume *Le Grand incendie de Londres* and the passage's renewed context in a volume dedicated to the work of his late wife, Roubaud moves from the role of poet to that of reader. He engages with the form of *Quinze minutes* as a reader of his poetry would: he invests the spaces of the photo with his memories and allows the forms in the image to elicit associations and discoveries in his mind as he observes it. Layers of reading and memory become intertwined until it becomes unclear where precisely the divisions between them lie, and the structure of the relationship between poet and reader is recreated, this time between photographer and poet.

Conclusions

Windows on Form

Throughout this study, Jacques Roubaud has been connected to his reader, or to the activity itself of reading, through a series of windows that appear in his texts. The young poet looks out of his bedroom window into the forest beyond. He listens to the chomping beech tree worms – *vers* – that come to represent the absorption and production of poetry, a reading and writing process so engrained in him that it is likened to the nourishment of the tiny creatures. The young poet's window opens out onto poetic influence: the forest situated in Roubaud's childhood region reminds the adult poet of his troubadour roots and is also a land of escape where he would spend his days discovering and reading contemporary poetry. When Roubaud turns away from the free verse forms and the *tabula rasa* approach of the Surrealist movement, it is not in order to shake off the traditions in poetic form that have come before him, but to actively engage with them, to adopt them into his own practice and to renew them.

Roubaud's commitment to an exploration of the richness of established poetic forms is manifested in *Trente et un au cube* through a return to the medieval Japanese *tanka*. The poet's intertwining of a metre inspired by this form with French syntax gives rise to a singular rhythm in the volume that flirts, but never quite matches up, with the classic alexandrine in its counts of five and seven syllables. Structure in *Trente et un au cube* is visual and aural, leaving behind the dependence on typography that characterized standard free verse for the poet: the shape of the poetry on the page doubles the beat of its rhythm, and listening to a poem conjures up an image of its text and the spacing of its fragments. It is through the interaction of these dimensions in reading, the echoes between the visual and phonic shaping of the poem, that the poem enters into a relation with memory. There, fragments of the poem interact with the stores of poetic traces and trigger associations and connections. The reader's memory of poetry is in turn a model for the understanding of poetry as memory: the intertextuality that informs the rhythms, structure and the literary fabric of the book produces a hybrid poetry that is at once strange and familiar, difficult and embracing.

In *Trente et un au cube*, the window into the lovers' bedroom is an invitation to the reader to come closer, to immerse herself in the poems. The dimensions of the poetry collection and entry points into its architecture are multiplied through the use of numerical patterning, which facilitates the creation of pathways for the reader who navigates its pages. Markings in space and time – the year over which it unfolds, the bedroom, the spring garden, the edges of the cube – insinuate their way into memory, providing points of familiarity in the book and inviting the reader to invest in its spaces. Form thus structures the reading process and offers the reader the spaces in which to build her own meaning within the parameters of the book.

While windows draw the reader into the spaces of *Trente et un au cube*, those encountered in Roubaud's works written after Alix Cléo's death tend to look out beyond their texts. At the close of *Du noir tombe*, a window lets a glimpse of light and a hope of sound into the poem collection, for its 'variations' exist only silently, on the page. These arrangements do not signal a return to the practice of 'aller à la ligne' that Roubaud describes in Surrealist free verse, rather their forms speak through what is missing: the 'upper limit music' that characterizes Roubaud's self-inscription in the troubadour tradition. The shift in form represents loss and an impossibility in poetic expression tied to the poet's bereavement. Falling within a period of silence in Roubaud's poetry output – an 'aphasia', in the words of the poet – *Du noir tombe* is also a window into *Quelque chose noir*, the collection of poems that breaks that silence imposed by grief.

In *Quelque chose noir* the textual dimensions are symbolic of the poet's apartment space and the flat representations of his deceased wife that fill it. Unlike the poetry cube that was an attempt to detain the poet's lover in space and time, *Quelque chose noir* betrays Alix Cléo's irrevocable absence, its pared-down form a sign of the poet's own confinement: in the routines that structured his life before his wife died and which now fulfil no purpose but to remind him of her loss, and in the empty home they used to share. The poet's view of the inlet of sky produced in the gap between the roofs opposite his apartment develops into a leitmotif in the volume. Identified with the poet's late wife, the view from the window signals the failure of poetic form to hold onto the memory of his beloved and directs the reader away from *Quelque chose noir* towards a network of texts and photographs by Alix Cléo. Through the multiple intertextualities in the volume, the poet constructs an external memory space of sorts, building the collective memory of Alix Cléo's *œuvre*. This movement from a personal to a collective engagement with memory is for the poet a way of continuing Alix Cléo's creative project in her absence. In the development of my readings along the chronological trajectory of Jacques Roubaud's poetry composition, form has become less fixed around definitions of the poetic line and the prosodic elements of metre and structure that are the foundation of his early works of love poetry. In every instance, form catalyses a particular interaction with the memory of the poetry reader and creates an invitation to take an interactive role in relation to the texts.

(Re)presenting the Beloved 'in Theory': Chapters 1, 2 and 3

Intrinsic to Roubaud's journey in poetic form is his engagement with the feminine addressee in his love poetry. I began my enquiry referring to the poetic 'muse'. A traditional conception of the muse figures in models criticizing the structures of the sexual relation in Freudian and Lacanian psychoanalysis, representing what Irigaray perceives to be the objectification of the feminine for the advantage of the masculine in male-dominated theories. In the same way that Irigaray uses the structure of the poet-muse relation to illuminate her psychoanalytically inspired vision of the sexual relation, I have used Freudian, Lacanian and Irigarayan readings of the feminine and masculine positions as a lens through which to read Roubaud's poetic address.

I found some of the elements in Irigaray's criticism increasingly active in my readings of poems by Paul Éluard. The Surrealist poet foregrounds a mirroring between the poet-narrator and muse that might be compared to the reflection of the self-same that Irigaray criticizes in Freud's essay on feminine castration. I also explored the connection between free verse forms and the automatic writing processes that were prominent in the Surrealist movement, with the muse acting as a source of inspiration to the poet's creativity. At first glance, she appears to be central to both of the poems by Éluard that Roubaud selected to represent his engagement with Surrealism: her femininity dominates Éluard's titles, 'L'Amoureuse' and 'L'Égalité des sexes', and she is foregrounded in the texts. However, a closer reading of the poems sees her fade into the reflected image of the poet, leaving her with no substance unique to her. It is a shift that takes place in the poems' form; the poetic line that stages the dynamics of the relation between poet and beloved comes up against a limit in the binary opposition of the two terms, anticipating Irigaray's critique of the analogy of masculine subjectivity with the mirror image.

An exclusive focus on the formal structure of these two of Éluard's love poems would overlook the associations and transformations that occur on the syntactical plane and its interaction with the lexical. Existing in multiple layers of semantic possibility, Éluard's muse inspires a renewal of language through its removal from the domain of the everyday: the exceptional state produced in love is conceived as an initial step towards new discoveries hidden in the deepest recesses of the poet's unconscious. Éluard's ambitions for a 'parler pour parler' ['speaking for speaking's sake'] in poetry link automatic writing processes explicitly to the principles of the Freudian talking cure, privileging unexpected juxtaposition over form and conventional structural arrangement.

While Roubaud's conception of poetic language appears to echo Éluard's wish to distance language from the ties of the referent, his 'upper limit music' incorporates the numerical and mathematical patterning evident in the traditions of poetic form to produce a poetry that is built on that very premise, revealing a multiplicity of spatial and temporal dimensions that interact with reading and shape it. The feminine love in *Trente et un au cube* does not bring divine inspiration to the writing process, instead she is located in the forms conceived and crafted by the poet; like crystals that form over hundreds of years, she and the poem together unfurl through a myriad of associations and connections that extend over time, creating an inextricable link between form and memory. Her alignment with the form itself of poetry leads me to develop my foray into psychoanalytic representations of the sexual relation: just as the Lacanian feminine is accounted for in structures conceived by the male theorist, the feminine lover in *Trente et un au cube* is written into the story by the poet. Just as the feminine in Lacanian theory exists as the 'vanishing point' of the system of sexuation, as Irigaray emphasizes, so too Roubaud's addressee is identified within the very outlines that attempt to contain her.

The comparison between the position of Roubaud's lover in *Trente et un au cube* and the Lacanian feminine illuminates the structures of reading into which readers themselves are invited. Although the spatial metaphor of the volume witnesses an attempt to detain the beloved within its walls, it is in her alignment with the form itself of the book that she is given the possibility of resisting the poet's hold. As the feminine other who eludes the poet, she produces the expanded possibilities offered in a reading of the text – spaces to be activated by the interaction with the reader's memory. The disjunction in the relation of poet to lover continues to represent a creative space in *Trente et un au cube*, both for the feminine position and the poet's, when read through Irigaray's notion of 'j'aime á toi' [I love to you]. The acceptance that an element of mystery will always remain between lovers allows the subjectivity of both terms in the relation to survive. The poet's silence, a further leitmotif, is read as an offering to his other, an invitation to enter the spaces of the poetic text through the rhythm of her own breathing.

My comparison of *Trente et un au cube* with texts that show something of Roubaud's engagement with Éluard's poetry explores the development in the poet's approach to the formal representations of love in poetry. The distancing of his poetic practice from certain structures and writing processes associated with Surrealist literature is simultaneously a formulation of love in poetry. While at times, Roubaud's poetic representations of love are rooted in his lived experiences – for example, his encounter with first love, Michelle, is inseparable from his reminiscences of his first loves in poetry – *Trente et un au cube* sets out a theoretical account of what it means for the poet to address his beloved in poetry.

In the Introduction to this book, and following Irigaray's poet-theorist analogy, I asked whether the love poet necessarily silences his beloved when he writes her into his lyric and addresses her as his other. I have found moments in which the wish to possess her overwhelms the poet-narrator, moments of violent struggle, yearning and anxiety. Through comparative readings of Roubaud's presentation of love in *Trente et un au cube* and varying but interconnected models of the masculine-feminine relation in psychoanalytic terms, however, I have also been able to show that there are spaces in Roubaud's poetry offered to his lover and, in turn, his reader. When the feminine enters his text through its silences and blank spaces, rather than meaning an erasure of her presence, she exists as the heart of the text's form: the source of its singular rhythm, the impetus for its creation.

When Silence Is Grief: Chapter 4

My readings of *Trente et un au cube* in proximity with the theories of Freud, Lacan and Irigaray have been a springboard for my exploration of texts written by the poet in the wake of Alix Cléo's death. An understanding of Roubaud's approach to love and form in poetry composition enabled me to uncover the differences and developments in his later writings: differences that reveal loss not just of love but of the possibility to articulate it through poetic form. These shifts are particularly evident in *Du noir tombe*. The ideas that I developed in relation to the shared position of addressee and reader in *Trente et un au cube* enabled me to explore the changed position of the reader in *Quelque chose noir*.

The understanding of poetic form as an engagement of memory is at the heart of findings in Chapter 4. *Quelque chose noir* ceaselessly plays out its inability to hold onto the memory of the beloved, its spaces alternately diminishing what remains of Alix Cléo and suffocating the poet who yearns for her. This is not an elegy in which the poet works through his own grief and Jacques Roubaud does not recreate Alix Cléo as substitute. The poet directs us outwards, away from his own writing, and the reader's singular engagement with poetic form is activated in the intertextual network created through *Quelque chose noir*: an external memory space for the work of Alix Cléo. Finally, my consideration of Alix Cléo's photo, *Quinze minutes*, in terms of Roubaud's conception of poetic language – one that encompasses a link between form and memory through the prioritization of rhythm over the referent, or 'upper limit music' as Roubaud refers to it – has led me to place Roubaud himself as Alix Cléo's reader. In this final move, Roubaud makes the gesture of Irigaray's 'j'aime à toi' [I love to you]. Much like the poet-narrator in *Trente et un au cube* who listens intently to his lover's breathing as she sleeps, and the guide-voice that prepares a space for the echo-voice in *biipsisme*, Roubaud reads Alix Cléo's photograph, allowing the rhythm of her breath in turn to penetrate his writing.

Reader-Addressee

That I set out to explore my reasons for being drawn to a particular text by a certain writer is more than a platitude or pleasing cliché. I have experienced the ways in which Roubaud invites the reader into a deep engagement with his texts through the questions posed by form, the shaping of the poems on the page and for the ear of his addressee, the intricacy of his crafted rhythms and the spatio-temporal metaphors on which his poetry is built – the volume of the cube, the lovers' bedroom, the apartment he shared with Alix Cléo, her last photo. My findings have illuminated my personal relationship with Roubaud's love poetry, my close readings of his poetic and theoretical texts forming the basis of my enquiry into those aspects of the poems that have pulled me in.

I admit to being intrigued by the poet's address: the pronouns 'tu' and 'toi' are omnipresent in his poems and those pronouns offer me, his reader, the privileged position of his beloved, to whom he speaks through the poetry. Roubaud offers his poem as a gift in *Trente et un au cube*; to reach his addressee is the purpose and ambition of his rhythmic formation, which is composed and intricately crafted in words and number: 'JE DÉTIENS MILLION de | syllabes comptées pour toi' [I KEEP A MILLION |

syllables counted out for you].[1] In this opening to *Trente et un au cube*, it feels as though this poem has been written for me.

Poetic address, particularly that of the male poet who writes to his lover, has often been the context of an objectification, the feminine other serving as a pretext for the poet's (self-)reflection and creativity. When I embarked on this work, Irigaray's consideration of the structures of address in traditional lyric poetry as a central element in her critique of psychoanalytical approaches to the feminine resonated with my early experiences of Roubaud's poems. In *Trente et un au cube*, a struggle at the heart of the volume betrays the poet's will to control and manipulate the woman he addresses. In *Quelque chose noir* the use of direct and adjusted citation that is interpreted as dialogue with Alix Cléo by some critics is simultaneously a resituating of her writing in the context of the poet's work. These problematic moments sometimes betray the yearnings and anxieties of the poet-narrator, and his difficulty in allowing the 'mystery', as Irigaray puts it, of his partner to exist. At other times, they are the manifestation of grief and the impossible wish to hear the other speak.

In a reversal of Irigaray's account of psychoanalytic theory in terms that evoke the male poet, I turned to the Lacanian positioning of the masculine and feminine to shed light on the depictions of love in Roubaud's poetry. By bringing Lacan into proximity with Roubaud in this way, I have found that the desire to hold the other closer, to possess her, to impose on her a certain form gives rise in Roubaud's poetry to her elusiveness and resistance. This equates to an inclusive, immersive experience for the reader of love poetry: the otherness of the feminine represents the power of the reader to contribute to meaning-making in the text. I see in the poet's attempts to define her the knowledge that she both eludes and exceeds him. Just as Irigaray proposes an acceptance of the disjunction between two lovers and a fostering of the space between them, Roubaud's poetry incorporates within its lines a gesture that opens out his text to the other. The subject who listens intently to the breathing of his lover offers a space for her own subjectivity; the poet who is now reader of his beloved lets her into the collaborative space of his composition.

1 Roubaud, *Trente et un au cube*, p. 9.

Bibliography

Agamben, Giorgio, *Stanzas: Word and Phantasm in Western Culture*, trans. by Ronald L. Martinez (London: University of Minnesota Press, 1993).
Alighieri, Dante, *Vita Nova*, trans. and intro. by Andrew Frisardi (Evanston: Northwestern University Press, 2012).
Andrews, Chris, *How To Do Things with Forms: The OuLiPo and Its Inventions* (Montreal: McGill-Queen's University Press, 2022).
Badiou, Alain, *Éloge de l'amour* (Paris: Flammarion, 2009).
—— 'La scène du deux', in *De l'amour*, ed. by École de la Cause freudienne (Paris: Flammarion, 1999), pp. 177–90.
Baetens, Jan, *Romans à contraintes* (Amsterdam: Rodopi, 2005).
Balakian, Anna, *Surrealism: The Road to the Absolute* (London: Unwin Books, 1972).
Ballard, Jean, 'Préface', *Cahiers du sud*, 315 (1952), 187–90.
Baquey, Stéphane, 'En quoi un vers peut-il être une forme? (dans la poésie de Denis Roche)', *Formes poétiques Contemporaines*, 2 (2004), 263–74.
Barthes, Roland, *La Chambre claire* (Paris: Gallimard, 1980).
—— *Le Discours amoureux: Séminaire à l'École pratique des hautes études 1974–1976 suivi de Fragments d'un discours amoureux: inédits*, ed. by Claude Coste (Paris: Seuil, 2007).
—— *Fragments d'un discours amoureux* (Paris: Seuil, 1977).
Bec, Pierre, 'Jacques Roubaud et les troubadours', *La Licorne*, 40 (1997), 9–20.
Bénabou, Marcel, and others, *Un art simple et tout d'exécution: Cinq leçons de/sur l'Oulipo* (Saulxures: Circé, 2001).
Bens, Jacques, 'Queneau Oulipien', in *Atlas de littérature potentielle*, ed. by Oulipo (Paris: Gallimard, 1981), pp. 22–33.
Benveniste, Émile, *Problèmes de linguistique générale* (Paris: Gallimard, 1966).
Berger, John, *About Looking* (London: Bloomsbury, 2009).
—— *Understanding a Photograph*, ed. and intro. by Geoff Dyer (London: Penguin Classics, 2013).
—— *Ways of Seeing*. (London: BBC and Penguin Books, 1972).
Biroleau-Lemagny, Anne, Hélène Giannecchini and Dominique Versavel, eds, *Alix Cléo Roubaud: Photographies* (Paris: Bibliothèque nationale de France, 2014).
Blanchot, Maurice, *L'Espace littéraire* (Paris: Gallimard, 1955).
Bloom, Harold, *The Anxiety of Influence: A Theory of Poetry* (Oxford: Oxford University Press, 1973).

Bloomfield, Camille, and Claire Lesage, eds, *Oulipo* (Paris: Bibliothèque nationale de France and Gallimard, 2014).

Bosquet, Alain, 'Jacques Roubaud, ou la technique ennemie du poème', *Le Monde des livres*, 22 February 1974, p. 16.

Bouretz, Claudine, 'Séquence', *Fragmentaires*, 2 (1984), 26–37.

Breton, André, *Arcane 17* (Paris: Pauvert, 1971).

—— *Manifestes du surréalisme* (Paris: Pauvert, 1972).

—— *Le Surréalisme et la peinture* (Paris: Gallimard, 1965).

Breton, André and Paul Éluard, *Dictionnaire abrégé du surréalisme* (Paris: José Corti, 1969; repr. 2005).

—— *Notes sur la poésie* (Paris: G.L.M., 1936).

Bronfen, Elisabeth, 'Fatal Conjunctions: Gendering Representations of Death', in *Lacan, Politics, Aesthetics*, ed. by Willy Apollon and Richard Feldstein (New York: SUNY Press, 1996), pp. 237–60.

—— *Over Her Dead Body: Death, Femininity and the Aesthetic* (Manchester: Manchester University Press, 1992).

Burke, Carolyn, 'Irigaray through the Looking Glass', *Feminist Studies*, 7:2 (1981), 288–306.

Cardonne-Arlyck, Elisabeth, 'Invoquer l'autre', *Écritures contemporaines: La revue des lettres modernes*, 4 (2001), 73–87.

—— 'Poésie, forme de vie (Jacques Roubaud)', *L'Esprit Créateur*, 32:2 (1992), 89–101.

—— 'Roubaud mélancolique', in *Jacques Roubaud, compositeur de mathématique et de poésie*, ed. by Agnès Disson and Véronique Montémont (Nancy: Absalon, 2010), pp. 307–17.

—— *Véracités: Ponge, Jaccottet, Roubaud, Deguy* (Paris: Belin, 2009).

Carmody, Francis J., 'Eluard's Rupture with Surrealism', *PMLA*, 76:4 (1961), 436–46.

Caws, Mary Ann, *André Breton* (London: Twayne, 1996).

Certeau, Michel de, *L'Invention du quotidien: arts de faire* (Paris: Gallimard, 1990).

Chénieux-Gendron, Jacqueline, *Le Surréalisme* (Paris: Presses Universitaires de France, 1984).

—— 'Toward a New Definition of Automatism: *L'Immaculée Conception*', *Dada/Surrealism*, 17 (1988), 74–90.

Cixous, Hélène, *Le Rire de la Méduse* (Paris: Galilée, 2010).

Cixous, Hélène and Catherine Clément, *La Jeune Née* (Paris: Union générale d'éditions, 1975).

Conant-Ouaked, Chloé, 'L'écriture plasticienne de Jacques Roubaud: une performance littéraire', in *Jacques Roubaud, compositeur de mathématique et de poésie*, ed. by Agnès Disson and Véronique Montémont (Nancy: Absalon, 2010), pp. 345–58.

Conley, Katharine, *Automatic Woman: The Representation of Woman in Surrealism* (London: University of Nebraska Press, 1996).

Conort, Benoît, 'Tramer le deuil (Table de lecture de *Quelque chose noir*)', *La Licorne*, 40 (1997), 47–58.

Consenstein, Peter, *Literary Memory, Consciousness, and the Group Oulipo* (Amsterdam: Rodopi, 2002).

—— 'Remarques celées, remarques clairvoyantes', in *Jacques Roubaud, compositeur de mathématique et de poésie*, ed. by Agnès Disson and Véronique Montémont (Nancy: Absalon, 2010), pp. 125–33.

Cooper, Julia, *The Last Word: Reviving the Dying Art of Eulogy* (Canada: Coach House Books, 2017).

Copjec, Joan, *Imagine There's No Woman* (London: Massachusetts Institute of Technology Press, 2002).

Critchley, Simon, *Memory Theatre* (London: Fitzcarraldo Editions, 2014).

De Ferrari, Guillermina, 'Representing Absence: The Power of Metafiction in Jacques Roubaud's *Le Grand Incendie de Londres*', *Symposium*, 49:4 (1996), 262–73.

Delattre, Andre, 'Personal Notes on Paul Éluard', *Yale French Studies*, 2 (1948), 103–05.

Delay, Florence, and Jacques Roubaud, 'La pluralité des proses de J. Roubaud', *Quai Voltaire*, 10 (1994), 17–27.

Derrida, Jacques, 'Les morts de Roland Barthes', *Poétique*, 47 (1981), 269–92.

—— *The Work of Mourning*, ed. by Pascale-Anne Brault and Michael Naas (Chicago: University of Chicago Press, 2001).

Disson, Agnès, 'Roubaud japonais: feuilles de styles, feuilles de route', in *Jacques Roubaud, compositeur de mathématique et de poésie*, ed. by Agnès Disson and Véronique Montémont (Nancy: Absalon, 2010), pp. 249–60.

Dolar, Mladen, 'At First Sight', in *Gaze and Voice as Love Objects*, ed. by Renata Salecl and Slavoj Žižek (London: Duke University Press, 1996), pp. 129–53.

Duncan, Dennis, *The Oulipo and Modern Thought* (Oxford: Oxford University Press, 2019).

Éluard, Paul, *Les Animaux et leurs hommes, les hommes et leurs animaux* (Paris: Au sans pareil, 1920).

—— *Capitale de la douleur* suivi de *L'Amour la poésie* (Paris: Gallimard, 1966).

—— *Poésie ininterrompue* (Paris: Gallimard, 1946; repr. 1953).

—— 'Premières vues anciennes', *Minotaure*, 10 (1937), 49–56.

Fabre, Marie, 'Hommage à Alix Cléo Roubaud', *Terres de femmes*, 155 (2017) <http://terresdefemmes.blogs.com/mon_weblog/2010/01/hommage-à-alix-cléo-roubaud.html>.

Felman, Shoshana, 'Women and Madness: The Critical Phallacy', in *Feminisms: An Anthology of Literary Theory and Criticism*, ed. by Robyn R. Warhol and Diane Price Herndl (Houndmills: Macmillan Press, 1997), pp. 7–20.

Fink, Bruce, 'Knowledge and Jouissance', in *Reading Seminar XX: Lacan's Major Work on Love, Knowledge, and Feminine Sexuality*, ed. by Suzanne Barnard and Bruce Fink (New York: SUNY Press, 2002), pp. 21–45.

—— *The Lacanian Subject: Between Language and Jouissance* (Princeton: Princeton University Press, 1995).

Fowlie, Wallace, *Age of Surrealism* (London: Dennis Dobson, 1953).

Freud, Sigmund, *Beyond the Pleasure Principle*, ed. by Todd Dufresne, trans. by Gregory C. Richter (Toronto: Broadview Editions, 2011).

—— *New Introductory Lectures on Psychoanalysis*, ed. and trans. by James Strachey (Harmondsworth: Penguin Books, 1973).

Fuss, Diana, *Dying Modern: A Meditation on Elegy* (London: Duke University Press, 2013).

Gallop, Jane, '*Quand nos lèvres s'écrivent:* Irigaray's Body Politic', *Romanic Review*, 74:1 (1983), 77–83.

—— *Reading Lacan* (New York: Cornell University Press, 1987).

Gauthier, Xavière, *Surréalisme et sexualité* (Paris: Gallimard, 1971).

Giannecchini, Hélène, 'Alix Cléo Roubaud', *Area*, 19–20 (2009), 97–112.

—— 'Alix Cléo Roubaud, absolument photographe', *Chroniques de la Bibliothèque nationale de France*, 61 (2012), 22–23.

—— 'Alix Cléo Roubaud: dualité de la lumière', *Les Cahiers du refuge*, 188 (2010), 5–8.

—— 'Un futur antérieur sans cesse déchiré', *Les Écrits*, 132 (2011), 37–42.

—— *Une image peut-être vraie: Alix Cléo Roubaud* (Paris: Seuil, 2014).

Gilbert, Sandra M., *Death's Door: Modern Dying and the Ways We Grieve* (London: Norton, 2007).

Grosz, Elizabeth, *Jacques Lacan: A Feminist Introduction* (London: Routledge, 1990).

Guétemme, Geneviève, 'Alix Cléo et Jacques Roubaud: l'amour, la mort', *Nouvelle revue d'esthétique*, 10 (2012), 11–25.

—— 'Alix Cléo Roubaud: celle qui se voyait "autre"', in *Autoportrait et altérité*, ed. by Sandrine Lascaux and Yves Ouallet (Mont-Saint-Aignan: Presses universitaires de Rouen et du Havre), pp. 77–89.

—— '*Éros mélancolique* de Jacques Roubaud et Anne F. Garréta: écriture, photographie et disparition', *Nottingham French Studies*, 51.3 (2012), 342–53.

—— 'Le *Journal* d'Alix Cléo Roubaud: étude d'un paratexte photographique, poétique et amoureux', *Essays in French Literature and Culture*, 49 (2012), 59–78.

—— 'Transgression photographique: Alix Cléo Roubaud ou comment photographier la mort', *Irish Journal of French Studies*, 12 (2012), 27–42.

Hanrahan, Mairéad, 'Literature and Mathematics: The Difference', *Journal of Romance Studies*, 7:3 (2007), 7–25.

Hardy, G. H., *A Mathematician's Apology* (Cambridge: Cambridge University Press, 1967).

Hatt, Étienne, 'La praxis d'Alix Cléo Roubaud', *Art Press*, 416 (2014), 54–57.

Heath, Stephen, 'Barthes on Love', *SubStance*, 37–38 (1983), 100–06.

—— 'Difference', *Screen*, 19:3 (1978), 51–112.

Henric, Jacques, 'Comment guérir de l'envie de mourir', *Art Press*, 365 (2010), 73.

Herndl, Diane Price, 'Desire', in *Feminisms: An Anthology of Literary Theory and Criticism*, ed. by Robyn R. Warhol and Diane Price Herndl (Houndmills: Macmillan Press, 1997), pp. 485–88.

Irigaray, Luce, *Ce sexe qui n'en est pas un* (Paris: Minuit, 1977).

——*Être Deux* (Paris: Grasset, 1997).

——*J'aime à toi* (Paris: Grasset, 1992).

——*Passions élémentaires* (Paris: Minuit, 1974).

——*Speculum de l'autre femme* (Paris: Minuit, 1974).

—— *Speculum of the Other Woman*, trans. by Gillian C. Gill (New York: Cornell University Press, 1985).

Jaanus, Maire, 'The *Démontage* of the Drive', in *Reading Seminar XI: Lacan's Four Fundamental Concepts of Psychoanalysis*, ed. by Richard Feldstein, Bruce Fink and Maire Jaanus (New York: SUNY Press, 1995), pp. 119–36.

Jérusalem, Christine, 'Boucles & Spirales: effets de circularité et de déplacements dans l'œuvre de Jacques Roubaud', in *Jacques Roubaud, compositeur de mathématique et de poésie*, ed. by Agnès Disson and Véronique Montémont (Nancy: Absalon, 2010), pp. 111–23.

Jones, Ann Rosalind, 'Writing the Body: Toward an Understanding of "L'Écriture Feminine"', *Feminist Studies*, 7:2 (1981), 247–63.

Jouet, Jacques, *Poèmes de métro* (Paris: P.O.L., 2000).

Kinzer, Greg, 'Possible Worlds: Trans-world Travel, Haecceity and Grief in Jacques Roubaud's *The Plurality of Worlds of Lewis*', *Journal of Modern Literature*, 34 (2011), 162–81.

Klebes, Martin, *Wittgenstein's Novels* (London: Routledge, 2006).

Kristeva, Julia, *Tales of Love*, trans. by Leon S. Roudiez (New York: Columbia University Press, 1987).

Lacan, Jacques, *Le Séminaire, Livre XI: Les Quatre Concepts fondamentaux de la psychanalyse* (Paris: Seuil, 1973).

——*Le Séminaire, Livre XX: Encore* (Paris: Seuil, 1975).

— *On Feminine Sexuality: The Limits of Love and Knowledge (Encore, The Seminar of Jacques Lacan, Book XX)*, ed. by Jacques-Alain Miller, trans. by Bruce Fink (New York: W.W. Norton & Company, 1998).

Landes, Donald A., 'Expression and Speaking-*with* in the Work of Luce Irigaray', in *Luce Irigaray: Teaching*, ed. by Luce Irigaray and Mary Green (London: Continuum, 2008), pp. 169–80.

Laugier, Emmanuel, 'En d[eh]ors: quelques notes depuis *Dors* précédé de *Dire la poésie*', *Cahier Critique de Poésie*, 8 (2004), 45–48.

Leighton, Angela, *On Form: Poetry, Aestheticism, and the Legacy of a Word* (Oxford: Oxford University Press, 2007).

Léon, Paul, 'Eustache, Alix et ses *Photos*: "un futur antérieur sans cesse déchiré"', *Traces photographiques, traces autobiographiques*, ed. by Danièle Méaux and Jean-Bernard Vray (Saint Étienne: Publications de l'Université de Saint-Étienne, 2004), pp. 137–44.

Lerner, Ben, *The Hatred of Poetry* (London: Fitzcarraldo Editions, 2016).

Marsal, Florence, 'Mourning and the Call to Possible Worlds in Jacques Roubaud's Poetry', *Sites: Journal of Twentieth-Century/Contemporary French Studies*, 6 (2002), 357–69.

Mathews, Timothy, *Alberto Giacometti: The Art of Relation* (London: Tauris, 2014).

Metford, John, 'Le Solitaire chez Éluard', *French Review*, 54:5 (1981), 699–707.

Michel, Natacha, 'Roubaud 1978: Les mots de seconde bouche', *Critique*, 35 (1979), 594–609.

Miller, Jacques-Alain, 'On Semblances in the Relation Between the Sexes', in *Sexuation*, ed. by Renata Salecl (London: Duke University Press, 2000), pp. 13–27.

Miner, Earl, *An Introduction to Japanese Court Poetry* (Stanford: Stanford University Press, 1968).

Moncond'huy, Dominique, 'Description d'un projet de lecture de Jacques Roubaud', *La Licorne*, 40 (1997), 115–56.

—— 'Sonnet et entreprise de mémoire', in *Jacques Roubaud, compositeur de mathématique et de poésie*, ed. by Agnès Disson and Véronique Montémont (Nancy: Absalon, 2010), pp. 279–91.

Monte, Michèle, '*Quelque chose noir*: de la critique de l'élégie à la réinvention du rythme', *Babel*, 12 (2005) <http://babel.revues.org/1093> [accessed 15 December 2013].

Montémont, Véronique, 'Ce que l'œil dit au texte: Poésie et photographie chez Jacques Roubaud et Lorand Gaspar', *LittéRéalité*, 14:2 (2002), 17–37.

—— 'Comment (ne pas) représenter le corps malade: Hervé Guibert, Alix Cléo Roubaud, Annie Ernaux', in *Photographie et mises en images de soi*, ed. by Christine Delory-Momberger (La Rochelle: Himeros, 2006), pp. 87–101.

—— *Jacques Roubaud: L'amour du nombre* (Lille: Presses Universitaires du Septentrion, 2004).

—— '"Je t'aime jusque là": (Jacques Roubaud éditeur du *Journal* d'Alix)', in *L'Écrivain éditeur*, ed. by François Bessire, 2 vols (Geneva: Droz, 2002), II, pp. 207–19.

—— 'L'œuvre en souffrance: le Journal 1979–1983 d'Alix Cléo Roubaud', *Texte*, 39–40 (2006), 189–222.

—— 'Parler de nombres: la représentation sémantique du nombre dans le cycle du *grand incendie de londres*', in *Jacques Roubaud, compositeur de mathématique et de poésie*, ed. by Agnès Disson and Véronique Montémont (Nancy: Absalon, 2010), pp. 71–83.

—— 'Photographier, écrire, respirer: Alix Cléo Roubaud, Journal 1979–1983', *La Faute à Rousseau*, 35 (2004), 49–50.

—— 'Roubaud's Number on Numbers', *Journal of Romance Studies*, 7 (2007), 111–21.

Mortimer, Armine Kotin, 'Loving Writing: *Fragments d'un discours amoureux*', *Symposium*, 54:1 (2000), 27–42.

Mourier, Maurice, 'Frontière de la poésie', *La Licorne*, 40 (1997), 21–30.

Mourier-Casile, Pascaline, 'Li(v)re – Cette Pratique – (Fragments d'une lecture inachevée des deux premières Branches du *Grand incendie de Londres*', *La Licorne*, 40 (1997), 77–89.

Muresan, Maria, 'Image-poésie, image-souvenir et *piction*', in *Jacques Roubaud, compositeur de mathématique et de poésie*, ed. by Agnès Disson and Véronique Montémont (Nancy: Absalon, 2010), pp. 333–44.

Nugent, Robert, *Paul Éluard* (New York: Twayne, 1974).

Oseki-Dépré, Inês, 'D'une traduction amnésique (à propos de *Algo: Preto*, de Jacques Roubaud)', *Alea*, 11 (2009), 387–402.

Oulipo, *Oulipo* (Paris: Association pour la diffusion de la pensée française, 2005).

Oxenhandler, Neal, 'Paul Éluard', *Chicago Review*, 2:4 (1948), 128–31.

Perec, Georges, *Beaux présents belles absentes* (Paris: Seuil, 1994).

—— *La Disparition* (Paris: Gallimard, 1969).

—— 'Still life / Style leaf', in *L'Infra-ordinaire* (Paris: Seuil, 1989), pp. 107–19.

Perloff, Marjorie, *Poetry On and Off the Page: Essays for Emergent Occasions* (Evanston: Northwestern University Press, 1998).

Plichon, Charlotte, 'Alix Cléo et Jacques Roubaud: "un dialogue vivant"', *Culture et communication: Le magazine du ministère de la Culture et de la Communication*, 199 (2012), 16–17.

Poucel, Jean-Jacques, 'Introduction: The Challenge of Constraint', *Poetics Today*, 30:4 (2009), 611–34.

—— *Jacques Roubaud and the Invention of Memory* (Chapel Hill: University of North Carolina Press, 2006).

—— 'Jacques Roubaud's Intersections', *Sites: Journal of Twentieth-Century/Contemporary French Studies*, 7:2 (2003), 208–28.

—— 'Quelques remarques sur les tombeaux poétiques de Jacques Roubaud', in *Jacques Roubaud, compositeur de mathématique et de poésie*, ed. by Agnès Disson and Véronique Montémont (Nancy: Absalon, 2010), pp. 293–305.

Pradeau, Christophe, 'R14: portrait de l'artiste en liseur', in *Jacques Roubaud, compositeur de mathématique et de poésie*, ed. by Agnès Disson and Véronique Montémont (Nancy: Absalon, 2010), pp. 185–95.

Puff, Jean-François, 'Le Déploiement du nouveau chez Roubaud', *Formes Poétiques Contemporaines*, 1 (2003), 99–119.

—— 'L'Écriture photographique de *Quelque chose noir*', *Formes Poétiques Contemporaines*, 2 (2004), 313–24.

—— 'Fictions et mode de la détermination dans *Trente et un au cube*', in *Jacques Roubaud, compositeur de mathématique et de poésie*, ed. by Agnès Disson and Véronique Montémont (Nancy: Absalon, 2010), pp. 319–29.

——*Jacques Roubaud: rencontre avec Jean-François Puff* (Paris: Argol, 2008).

——*Mémoire de la mémoire: Jacques Roubaud et la lyrique médiévale* (Paris: Éditions Classiques Garnier, 2009).

—— 'Le modèle des troubadours dans l'œuvre poétique de Jacques Roubaud', *Les Cahiers du Ceracc*, 2 (2003) <http://www.cahiers-ceracc.fr/puff.html> [accessed 5 January 2014].

Purnelle, Gérald, 'Une enquête sur le vers d'aujourd'hui', *Formes poétiques Contemporaines*, 1 (2003), 123–30.

—— 'Formes et métriques contemporaines', *Formes Poétiques Contemporaines*, 1 (2003), 13–24.

Ramazani, Jahan, *Poetry of Mourning: The Modern Elegy from Hardy to Heaney* (London: University of Chicago Press, 1994).

Rannoux, Catherine, 'Nomination et mémoire de la langue dans *le grand incendie de londres*', in *Jacques Roubaud, compositeur de mathématique et de poésie*, ed. by Agnès Disson and Véronique Montémont (Nancy: Absalon, 2010), pp. 173–83.

Reggiani, Christelle, 'Portrait de l'artiste en poète: paradoxes de l'auteur roubaldien', in *Jacques Roubaud, compositeur de mathématique et de poésie*, ed. by Agnès Disson and Véronique Montémont (Nancy: Absalon, 2010), pp. 135–46.

Rhodes, S. A., 'Aspects of Paul Eluard', *French Review*, 30:2 (1956), 115–20.

Rivas, Daniel, 'Eluard's "L'Amoureuse": Mimesis and Semiosis', *French Review*, 55 (1982), 489–96.

Roche, Denis, *Éros énergumène* (Paris: Seuil, 1968).

Rose, Jacqueline, *Sexuality in the Field of Vision* (London: Verso, 2005).

Rosolato, Guy, 'L'Amour fou', in *Du surréalisme et du plaisir*, ed. by Jacqueline Chénieux-Gendron (Paris: José Corti, 1987), pp. 125–36.

Rossignol, Jean-Philippe, 'Notes de lecture, Alix Cléo Roubaud', *Revue des deux mondes*, (2010), 183.

Roubaud, Alix Cléo, *Journal (1979–1983)*, ed. and intro. by Jacques Roubaud, 2nd edn (Paris: Seuil, 2009).
Roubaud, Jacques, 'L'Amour, la poésie: Hypothèses', in *De l'amour*, ed. by École de la cause freudienne (Paris: Flammarion, 1999), pp. 81–104.
—— *Autobiographie, chapitre dix* (Paris: Gallimard, 1977).
—— *La Boucle* (Paris: Seuil, 1993).
—— 'Bourbaki and the Oulipo', *Journal of Romance Studies*, 7 (2007), 123–32.
—— *Cent vingt-huit poèmes composés en langue française de Guillaume Apollinaire à 1968: une anthologie de poésie contemporaine* (Paris: Gallimard, 1995).
—— *Churchill 40* (Paris: Gallimard, 2004).
—— *Ciel et terre et ciel et terre, et ciel* (Paris: Argol, 2009).
—— *Description du projet*, intro. by Jean-Jacques Poucel (Caen: Nous, 2014).
—— *Dors* précédé de *Dire la poésie* (Paris: Gallimard, 1981).
—— *Du noir tombe* (n.p.: Colorature, 1985).
—— *Exchanges on Light*, trans. by Eleni Sikelianos (Iowa City: La Presse/Fence Books, 2009).
—— *La Fleur inverse: Essai sur l'art formel des troubadours* (Paris: Ramsay, 1986).
—— *La forme d'une ville change plus vite, hélas, que le cœur des humains* (Paris: Gallimard, 1999).
—— *Le Grand incendie de Londres* (Paris: Seuil, 1989).
—— *L'Invention du fils de Leoprepes* (Saulxures: Circé, 1993).
—— *Ma vie avec le docteur Lacan* (Bordeaux: Éditions de l'Attente, 2004).
—— 'Mandarin au cube: Entretien avec Pierre Lartigue', *La Licorne*, 40 (1997), 159–62.
—— *Mathématique:* (Paris: Seuil, 1997).
—— *Mono no aware: Le sentiment des choses* (Paris: Gallimard, 1970).
—— *Octogone* (Paris: Gallimard, 2014).
—— 'Les Oiseaux n'ont pas de prose: Réflexions sur *La fin du poème*, de Giorgio Agamben', *Po&sie*, 117–18 (2006), 143–45.
—— 'Poème de présentation composé pour une lecture de *Trente et un au cube* à Shakespeare et C°', *Almanach de Shakespeare and Company*, 1 (1974), 167–71.
—— *Poésie:* (Paris: Seuil, 2000).
—— 'Poésie, et l'extrême contemporain', *Po&sie*, 41 (1987), 40–44.
—— *Poésie, etcetera: ménage* (Paris: Stock, 1995).
—— *Poésies juveniles* (Montpellier: C.G.C., 1944).
—— 'Quatre états de poésie', *Change*, 18 (1974), 85–95.
—— *Quelque chose noir* (Paris: Gallimard, 1986).
—— 'Quelques thèses sur la poétique', *Change*, 6 (1970), 7–21.
—— 'Si quelque chose noir: douze poèmes', *La Licorne*, 40 (1997), 229–33.
—— *Signe d'appartenance* (Paris: Gallimard, 1967).

—— 'Le silence de la mathématique jusqu'au fond de la langue, poésie', *Po&sie*, 10 (1979), 110–24.

—— *Sleep* preceded by *Saying Poetry*, trans. by Matthew B. Smith (Providence: La Presse, 2019).

—— *Some Thing Black*, trans. by Rosmarie Waldrop (Elmwood Park: Dalkey Archive Press, 1990).

—— *Sphère de la mémoire (Pentalogue)* (Saulxures: Circé, 1993).

—— 'Sur le Shinkokinshū, huitième anthologie impériale japonaise', *Change*, 1 (1968), 73–106.

—— 'Traité de la lumière', *La Licorne*, 40 (1997), 235–53.

—— *Trente et un au cube* (Paris: Gallimard, 1973).

—— *Les Troubadours: Anthologie bilingue* (Paris: Seghers, 1971).

—— *La Vieillesse d'Alexandre* (Paris: Ivrea, 2000).

Roubaud, Jacques, and others, 'Entretien presque imaginaire sur le sentiment des langues', *Change*, 29 (1976), 8–14.

—— 'Le Rythme, le formel et le formalisme', *Action Poétique*, 62 (1975), 61–75.

Roudinesco, Elisabeth, 'Écrire d'amour: hommage à *Action poétique*', *Mezura*, 49 (2001), 359–67.

Roy, Claude, *La Conversation des poètes* (Paris: Gallimard, 1993).

Salecl, Renata, 'Love and Sexual Difference: Doubled Partners in Men and Women', in *Sexuation*, ed. by Renata Salecl (London: Duke University Press, 2000), pp. 297–16.

Samoyault, Tiphanie, 'Autobiographie, chapitre trois: Archétypes de la totalité et formes de la totalisation dans *Mathématique:*', *La Licorne*, 40 (1997), 101–14.

Scepi, Henri, 'Éloge de la contrainte ou ce que peut le poème', *La Licorne*, 40 (1997), 31–46.

Scott, Clive, *The Poetics of French Verse: Studies in Reading* (Oxford: Clarendon Press, 1998).

Sheringham, Michael, 'Les Vies anglaises de Jacques Roubaud', in *Jacques Roubaud, compositeur de mathématique et de poésie*, ed. by Agnès Disson and Véronique Montémont (Nancy: Absalon, 2010), pp. 235–47.

Silverman, Kaja, *The Acoustic Mirror: The Female Voice in Psychanalysis and Cinema* (Indianapolis: Indiana University Press, 1988).

Smock, Ann, 'Jacques Roubaud's "Sonnetomania"', *Literary Imagination*, 12:3 (2010), 344–54.

—— *The Play of Light: Jacques Roubaud, Emmanuel Hocquard, and Friends* (New York: SUNY Press, 2021).

Soler, Colette, 'The Subject and the Other (I)', in *Reading Seminar XI: Lacan's Four Fundamental Concepts of Psychoanalysis*, ed. by Richard Feldstein, Bruce Fink and Maire Jaanus (New York: SUNY Press, 1995), pp. 39–44.

— 'The Subject and the Other (II)', in *Reading Seminar XI: Lacan's Four Fundamental Concepts of Psychoanalysis*, ed. by Richard Feldstein, Bruce Fink and Maire Jaanus (New York: SUNY Press, 1995), pp. 45–53.

Stamelman, Richard, 'Paul Éluard, "La courbe de tes yeux"', in *Twentieth-Century French Poetry: A Critical Anthology*, ed. by Hugues Azérad and Peter Collier (Cambridge, Cambridge University Press, 2010), pp. 90–97.

Stein, Gertrude, '*Lifting Belly* (fragment)', *Action Poétique*, 82–83 (1980), 90–97.

Strauss, Jonathan, 'Paul Éluard and the Origins of Visual Subjectivity', *Mosaic*, 33:2 (2000), 25–46.

Tenenbaum, Gérald, 'La quête de structure en mathématiques et littérature: convergences et divergences, au singulier pluriel', in *Jacques Roubaud, compositeur de mathématique et de poésie*, ed. by Agnès Disson and Véronique Montémont (Nancy: Absalon, 2010), pp. 39–44.

Thom, René, *Paraboles et catastrophes* (Paris: Flammarion, 1983).

Thomas, Jean-Jacques, 'Roubaud propose', in *Jacques Roubaud, compositeur de mathématique et de poésie*, ed. by Agnès Disson and Véronique Montémont (Nancy: Absalon, 2010), pp. 147–57.

Thomas, Jean-Jacques and Steven Winspur, *Poeticized Language: The Foundations of Contemporary French Poetry* (University Park: Pennsylvania State University Press, 1999).

Tyers, Meryl, 'Jacques Roubaud, "Dès que je me lève"', in *Twentieth-Century French Poetry: A Critical Anthology*, ed. by Hugues Azérad and Peter Collier (Cambridge: Cambridge University Press, 2010), pp. 230–39.

Vernier, Richard, *'Poésie ininterrompue' et la poétique de Paul Éluard* (Paris: Mouton, 1971).

Vialar, Thierry, *Handbook of Mathematics* (Paris: Books on Demand, 2015).

Viegener, Matias and Christine Wertheim (eds), *The Noulipian Analects* (Los Angeles: Les Figues Press, 2007.

Watrous, Lisa, 'Love's Universal Impetus: Luce Irigaray and Alain Badiou', *L'Ésprit créateur*, 52 (2012), 66–73.

Whiting, Charles G., 'Eluard's Poems for Gala', *French Review*, 41 (1968), 505–17.

Yates, Frances A., *The Art of Memory* (London: Routledge, 1966).

York, R. A., 'Éluard's Female Landscape', *Orbis Litterarum*, 35 (1980), 59–73.

Radio

Roubaud, Jacques, Yves Pagès and Gisèle Fournier, 'Page 124 – Oubli', *Le Carnet d'or*, France Culture, 19 April 2014.

Index

Modern French Identities

Edited by Jean Khalfa

This series aims to publish monographs, editions or collections of papers based on recent research into modern French Literature. It welcomes contributions from academics, researchers and writers worldwide and in British and Irish universities in particular.

Modern French Identities focuses on the French and Francophone writing of the twentieth and twenty-first centuries, whose formal experiments and revisions of genre have combined to create an entirely new set of literary forms, from the thematic autobiographies of Michel Leiris and Bernard Noël to the magic realism of French Caribbean writers.

The idea that identities are constructed rather than found, and that the self is an area to explore rather than a given pretext, runs through much of modern French literature, from Proust, Gide, Apollinaire and Césaire to Barthes, Duras, Kristeva, Glissant, Germain and Roubaud.

This series explores the turmoil in ideas and values expressed in the works of theorists like Lacan, Irigaray, Foucault, Fanon, Deleuze and Bourdieu and traces the impact of current theoretical approaches – such as gender and sexuality studies, de/coloniality, intersectionality, and ecocriticism – on the literary and cultural interpretation of the self.

The series publishes studies of individual authors and artists, comparative studies, and interdisciplinary projects and welcomes research on autobiography, cinema, fiction, poetry and performance art and/or the intersections between them.

Volume 1 Victoria Best & Peter Collier (eds): Powerful Bodies. Performance in French Cultural Studies.
220 pages. 1999. ISBN 3-906762-56-4 / US-ISBN 0-8204-4239-9

Volume 2 Julia Waters: Intersexual Rivalry. A 'Reading in Pairs' of Marguerite Duras and Alain Robbe-Grillet.
228 pages. 2000. ISBN 3-906763-74-9 / US-ISBN 0-8204-4626-2

Volume 3 Sarah Cooper: Relating to Queer Theory. Rereading Sexual Self-Definition with Irigaray, Kristeva, Wittig and Cixous.
231 pages. 2000. ISBN 3-906764-46-X / US-ISBN 0-8204-4636-X

Volume 4 Julia Prest & Hannah Thompson (eds): Corporeal Practices. (Re) figuring the Body in French Studies.
166 pages. 2000. ISBN 3-906764-53-2 / US-ISBN 0-8204-4639-4

Volume 5 Victoria Best: Critical Subjectivities. Identity and Narrative in the Work of Colette and Marguerite Duras.
243 pages. 2000. ISBN 3-906763-89-7 / US-ISBN 0-8204-4631-9

Volume 6 David Houston Jones: The Body Abject: Self and Text in Jean Genet and Samuel Beckett.
213 pages. 2000. ISBN 3-906765-07-5 / US-ISBN 0-8204-5058-8

Volume 7 Robin MacKenzie: The Unconscious in Proust's A la recherche du temps perdu.
270 pages. 2000. ISBN 3-906758-38-9 / US-ISBN 0-8204-5070-7

Volume 8 Rosemary Chapman: Siting the Quebec Novel. The Representation of Space in Francophone Writing in Quebec.
282 pages. 2000. ISBN 3-906758-85-0 / US-ISBN 0-8204-5090-1

Volume 9 Gill Rye: Reading for Change. Interactions between Text Identity in Contemporary French Women's Writing (Baroche, Cixous, Constant).
223 pages. 2001. ISBN 3-906765-97-0 / US-ISBN 0-8204-5315-3

Volume 10 Jonathan Paul Murphy: Proust's Art. Painting, Sculpture and Writing in A la recherche du temps perdu. 248 pages. 2001. ISBN 3-906766-17-9 / US-ISBN 0-8204-5319-6

Volume 11 Julia Dobson: Hélène Cixous and the Theatre. The Scene of Writing.
166 pages. 2002. ISBN 3-906766-20-9 / US-ISBN 0-8204-5322-6

Volume 12 Emily Butterworth & Kathryn Robson (eds): Shifting Borders. Theory and Identity in French Literature.
226 pages. 2001. ISBN 3-906766-86-1 / US-ISBN 0-8204-5602-0

Volume 13 Victoria Korzeniowska: The Heroine as Social Redeemer in the Plays of Jean Giraudoux.
144 pages. 2001. ISBN 3-906766-92-6 / US-ISBN 0-8204-5608-X

Volume 14 Kay Chadwick: Alphonse de Châteaubriant: Catholic Collaborator. 327 pages. 2002. ISBN 3-906766-94-2 / US-ISBN 0-8204-5610-1

Volume 15 Nina Bastin: Queneau's Fictional Worlds.
291 pages. 2002. ISBN 3-906768-32-5 / US-ISBN 0-8204-5620-9

Volume 16 Sarah Fishwick: The Body in the Work of Simone de Beauvoir.
284 pages. 2002. ISBN 3-906768-33-3 / US-ISBN 0-8204-5621-7

Volume 17 Simon Kemp & Libby Saxton (eds): Seeing Things. Vision, Perception and Interpretation in French Studies.
287 pages. 2002. ISBN 3-906768-46-5 / US-ISBN 0-8204-5858-9

Volume 18 Kamal Salhi (ed.): French in and out of France. Language Policies, Intercultural Antagonisms and Dialogue.
487 pages. 2002. ISBN 3-906768-47-3 / US-ISBN 0-8204-5859-7

Volume 19 Genevieve Shepherd: Simone de Beauvoir's Fiction. A Psychoanalytic Rereading.
262 pages. 2003. ISBN 3-906768-55-4 / US-ISBN 0-8204-5867-8

Volume 20 Lucille Cairns (ed.): Gay and Lesbian Cultures in France.
290 pages. 2002. ISBN 3-906769-66-6 / US-ISBN 0-8204-5903-8

Volume 21 Wendy Goolcharan-Kumeta: My Mother, My Country. Reconstructing the Female Self in Guadeloupean Women's Writing. 236 pages. 2003. ISBN 3-906769-76-3 / US-ISBN 0-8204-5913-5

Volume 22 Patricia O'Flaherty: Henry de Montherlant (1895–1972). A Philosophy of Failure.
256 pages. 2003. ISBN 3-03910-013-0 / US-ISBN 0-8204-6282-9

Volume 23 Katherine Ashley (ed.): Prix Goncourt, 1903–2003: essais critiques.
205 pages. 2004. ISBN 3-03910-018-1 / US-ISBN 0-8204-6287-X

Volume 24 Julia Horn & Lynsey Russell-Watts (eds): Possessions. Essays in French Literature, Cinema and Theory.
223 pages. 2003. ISBN 3-03910-005-X / US-ISBN 0-8204-5924-0

Volume 25 Steve Wharton: Screening Reality.
French Documentary Film during the German Occupation.
252 pages. 2006. ISBN 3-03910-066-1 / US-ISBN 0-8204-6882-7

Volume 26 Frédéric Royall (ed.): Contemporary French Cultures and Societies. 421 pages. 2004. ISBN 3-03910-074-2 / US-ISBN 0-8204-6890-8

Volume 27 Tom Genrich: Authentic Fictions.
Cosmopolitan Writing of the Troisième République, 1908–1940.
288 pages. 2004. ISBN 3-03910-285-0 / US-ISBN 0-8204-7212-3

Volume 28 Maeve Conrick & Vera Regan: French in Canada.
Language Issues.
186 pages. 2007. ISBN 978-3-03-910142-9

Volume 29 Kathryn Banks & Joseph Harris (eds): Exposure.
Revealing Bodies, Unveiling Representations.
194 pages. 2004. ISBN 3-03910-163-3 / US-ISBN 0-8204-6973-4

Volume 30 Emma Gilby & Katja Haustein (eds): Space.
New Dimensions in French Studies.
169 pages. 2005. ISBN 3-03910-178-1 / US-ISBN 0-8204-6988-2

Volume 31 Rachel Killick (ed.): Uncertain Relations.
Some Configurations of the 'Third Space' in Francophone Writings of the Americas and of Europe.
258 pages. 2005. ISBN 3-03910-189-7 / US-ISBN 0-8204-6999-8

Volume 32 Sarah F. Donachie & Kim Harrison (eds): Love and Sexuality.
New Approaches in French Studies.
194 pages. 2005. ISBN 3-03910-249-4 / US-ISBN 0-8204-7178-X

Volume 33 Michaël Abecassis: The Representation of Parisian Speech in the Cinema of the 1930s.
409 pages. 2005. ISBN 3-03910-260-5 / US-ISBN 0-8204-7189-5

Volume 34 Benedict O'Donohoe: Sartre's Theatre: Acts for Life.
301 pages. 2005. ISBN 3-03910-250-X / US-ISBN 0-8204-7207-7

Volume 35 Moya Longstaffe: The Fiction of Albert Camus. A Complex Simplicity.
300 pages. 2007. ISBN 3-03910-304-0 / US-ISBN 0-8204-7229-8

Volume 36 Arnaud Beaujeu: Matière et lumière dans le théâtre de Samuel Beckett: Autour des notions de trivialité, de spiritualité et d' « autre-là ».
377 pages. 2010. ISBN 978-3-0343-0206-8

Volume 37 Shirley Ann Jordan: Contemporary French Women's Writing: Women's Visions, Women's Voices, Women's Lives.
308 pages. 2005. ISBN 3-03910-315-6 / US-ISBN 0-8204-7240-9

Volume 38 Neil Foxlee: Albert Camus's 'The New Mediterranean Culture': A Text and its Contexts.
349 pages. 2010. ISBN 978-3-0343-0207-4

Volume 39 Michael O'Dwyer & Michèle Raclot: Le Journal de Julien Green: Miroir d'une âme, miroir d'un siècle.
289 pages. 2005. ISBN 3-03910-319-9

Volume 40 Thomas Baldwin: The Material Object in the Work of Marcel Proust.
188 pages. 2005. ISBN 3-03910-323-7 / US-ISBN 0-8204-7247-6

Volume 41 Charles Forsdick & Andrew Stafford (eds): The Modern Essay in French: Genre, Sociology, Performance.
296 pages. 2005. ISBN 3-03910-514-0 / US-ISBN 0-8204-7520-3

Volume 42 Peter Dunwoodie: Francophone Writing in Transition. Algeria 1900–1945.
339 pages. 2005. ISBN 3-03910-294-X / US-ISBN 0-8204-7220-4

Volume 43 Emma Webb (ed.): Marie Cardinal: New Perspectives.
260 pages. 2006. ISBN 3-03910-544-2 / US-ISBN 0-8204-7547-5

Volume 44 Jérôme Game (ed.): Porous Boundaries: Texts and Images in Twentieth-Century French Culture.
164 pages. 2007. ISBN 978-3-03910-568-7

Volume 45 David Gascoigne: The Games of Fiction: Georges Perec and Modern French Ludic Narrative.
327 pages. 2006. ISBN 3-03910-697-X / US-ISBN 0-8204-7962-4

Volume 46 Derek O'Regan: Postcolonial Echoes and Evocations: The Intertextual Appeal of Maryse Condé.
329 pages. 2006. ISBN 3-03910-578-7

Volume 47 Jennifer Hatte: La langue secrète de Jean Cocteau: la mythologie personnelle du poète et l'histoire cachée des Enfants terribles.
332 pages. 2007. ISBN 978-3-03910-707-0

Volume 48 Loraine Day: Writing Shame and Desire: The Work of Annie Ernaux.
315 pages. 2007. ISBN 978-3-03910-275-4

Volume 49 John Flower (éd.): François Mauriac, journaliste: les vingt premières années, 1905–1925.
352 pages. 2011. ISBN 978-3-0343-0265-4

Volume 50 Miriam Heywood: Modernist Visions: Marcel Proust's A la recherche du temps perdu and Jean-Luc Godard's Histoire(s) du cinéma.
277 pages. 2012. ISBN 978-3-0343-0296-8

Volume 51 Isabelle McNeill & Bradley Stephens (eds): Transmissions: Essays in French Literature, Thought and Cinema.
221 pages. 2007. ISBN 978-3-03910-734-6

Volume 52 Marie-Christine Lala: Georges Bataille, Poète du réel.
178 pages. 2010. ISBN 978-3-03910-738-4

Volume 53 Patrick Crowley: Pierre Michon: The Afterlife of Names.
242 pages. 2007. ISBN 978-3-03910-744-5

Volume 54 Nicole Thatcher & Ethel Tolansky (eds): Six Authors in Captivity. Literary Responses to the Occupation of France during World War II. 205 pages. 2006. ISBN 3-03910-520-5 / US-ISBN 0-8204-7526-2

Volume 55 Catherine Dousteyssier-Khoze & Floriane Place-Verghnes (eds): Poétiques de la parodie et du pastiche de 1850 à nos jours. 361 pages. 2006. ISBN 3-03910-743-7

Volume 56 Thanh-Vân Ton-That: Proust avant la Recherche: jeunesse et genèse d'une écriture au tournant du siècle.
285 pages. 2012. ISBN 978-3-0343-0277-7

Volume 57 Helen Vassallo: Jeanne Hyvrard, Wounded Witness: The Body Politic and the Illness Narrative.
243 pages. 2007. ISBN 978-3-03911-017-9

Volume 58 Marie-Claire Barnet, Eric Robertson and Nigel Saint (eds): Robert Desnos. Surrealism in the Twenty-First Century.
390 pages. 2006. ISBN 3-03911-019-5

Volume 59 Michael O'Dwyer (ed.): Julien Green, Diariste et Essayiste.
259 pages. 2007. ISBN 978-3-03911-016-2

Volume 60 Kate Marsh: Fictions of 1947: Representations of Indian Decolonization 1919–1962.
238 pages. 2007. ISBN 978-3-03911-033-9

Volume 61 Lucy Bolton, Gerri Kimber, Ann Lewis and Michael Seabrook (eds): Framed!: Essays in French Studies.
235 pages. 2007. ISBN 978-3-03911-043-8

Volume 62 Lorna Milne and Mary Orr (eds): Narratives of French Modernity: Themes, Forms and Metamorphoses. Essays in Honour of David Gascoigne.
365 pages. 2011. ISBN 978-3-03911-051-3

Volume 63 Ann Kennedy Smith: Painted Poetry: Colour in Baudelaire's Art Criticism.
253 pages. 2011. ISBN 978-3-03911-094-0

Volume 64 Sam Coombes: The Early Sartre and Marxism.
330 pages. 2008. ISBN 978-3-03911-115-2

Volume 65 Claire Lozier: De l'abject et du sublime: Georges Bataille, Jean Genet, Samuel Beckett.
327 pages. 2012. ISBN 978-3-0343-0724-6

Volume 66 Charles Forsdick and Andy Stafford (eds): La Revue: The Twentieth- Century Periodical in French.
379 pages. 2013. ISBN 978-3-03910-947-0

Volume 67 Alison S. Fell (ed.): French and francophone women facing war / Les femmes face à la guerre.
301 pages. 2009. ISBN 978-3-03911-332-3

Volume 68 Elizabeth Lindley and Laura McMahon (eds): Rhythms: Essays in French Literature, Thought and Culture.
238 pages. 2008. ISBN 978-3-03911-349-1

Volume 69 Georgina Evans and Adam Kay (eds): Threat: Essays in French Literature, Thought and Visual Culture.
248 pages. 2010. ISBN 978-3-03911-357-6

Volume 70 John McCann: Michel Houellebecq: Author of our Times.
229 pages. 2010. ISBN 978-3-03911-373-6

Volume 71 Jenny Murray: Remembering the (Post)Colonial Self: Memory and Identity in the Novels of Assia Djebar.
258 pages. 2008. ISBN 978-3-03911-367-5

Volume 72 Susan Bainbrigge: Culture and Identity in Belgian Francophone Writing: Dialogue, Diversity and Displacement.
230 pages. 2009. ISBN 978-3-03911-382-8

Volume 73 Maggie Allison and Angela Kershaw (eds): Parcours de femmes: Twenty Years of Women in French.
313 pages. 2011. ISBN 978-3-0343-0208-1

Volume 74 Jérôme Game: Poetic Becomings: Studies in Contemporary French Literature.
263 pages. 2011. ISBN 978-3-03911-401-6

Volume 75 Elodie Laügt: L'Orient du signe: Rêves et dérives chez Victor Segalen, Henri Michaux et Emile Cioran.
242 pages. 2008. ISBN 978-3-03911-402-3

Volume 76 Suzanne Dow: Madness in Twentieth-Century French Women's Writing: Leduc, Duras, Beauvoir, Cardinal, Hyvrard.
217 pages. 2009. ISBN 978-3-03911-540-2

Volume 77 Myriem El Maïzi: Marguerite Duras ou l'écriture du devenir.
228 pages. 2009. ISBN 978-3-03911-561-7

Volume 78 Claire Launchbury: Music, Poetry, Propaganda: Constructing French Cultural Soundscapes at the BBC during the Second World War.
223 pages. 2012. ISBN 978-3-0343-0239-5

Volume 79 Jenny Chamarette and Jennifer Higgins (eds): Guilt and Shame: Essays in French Literature, Thought and Visual Culture.
231 pages. 2010. ISBN 978-3-03911-563-1

Volume 80 Vera Regan and Caitríona Ní Chasaide (eds): Language Practices and Identity Construction by Multilingual Speakers of French L2: The Acquisition of Sociostylistic Variation.
189 pages. 2010. ISBN 978-3-03911-569-3

Volume 81 Margaret-Anne Hutton (ed.): Redefining the Real: The Fantastic in Contemporary French and Francophone Women's Writing.
294 pages. 2009. ISBN 978-3-03911-567-9

Volume 82 Elise Hugueny-Léger: Annie Ernaux, une poétique de la transgression.
269 pages. 2009. ISBN 978-3-03911-833-5

Volume 83 Peter Collier, Anna Magdalena Elsner and Olga Smith (eds): Anamnesia: Private and Public Memory in Modern French Culture. 359 pages. 2009. ISBN 978-3-03911-846-5

Volume 84 Adam Watt (ed./éd.): Le Temps retrouvé Eighty Years After/80 ans après: Critical Essays/Essais critiques.
349 pages. 2009. ISBN 978-3-03911-843-4

Volume 85 Louise Hardwick (ed.): New Approaches to Crime in French Literature, Culture and Film.
237 pages. 2009. ISBN 978-3-03911-850-2

Volume 86 Emmanuel Godin and Natalya Vince (eds): France and the Mediterranean: International Relations, Culture and Politics.
372 pages. 2012. ISBN 978-3-0343-0228-9

Volume 87 Amaleena Damlé and Aurélie L'Hostis (eds): The Beautiful and the Monstrous: Essays in French Literature, Thought and Culture.
237 pages. 2010. ISBN 978-3-03911-900-4

Volume 88 Alistair Rolls (ed.): Mostly French: French (in) Detective Fiction.
212 pages. 2009. ISBN 978-3-03911-957-8

Volume 89 Bérénice Bonhomme: Claude Simon: une écriture en cinéma.
359 pages. 2010. ISBN 978-3-03911-983-7

Volume 90 Barbara Lebrun and Jill Lovecy (eds): Une et divisible? Plural Identities in Modern France.
258 pages. 2010. ISBN 978-3-0343-0123-7

Volume 91 Pierre-Alexis Mével & Helen Tattam (eds): Language and its Contexts/ Le Langage et ses contextes: Transposition and Transformation of Meaning?/ Transposition et transformation du sens?
272 pages. 2010. ISBN 978-3-0343-0128-2

Volume 92 Alistair Rolls and Marie-Laure Vuaille-Barcan (eds): Masking Strategies: Unwrapping the French Paratext.
202 pages. 2011. ISBN 978-3-0343-0746-8

Volume 93 Michaël Abecassis et Gudrun Ledegen (éds): Les Voix des Français Volume 1: à travers l'histoire, l'école et la presse.
372 pages. 2010. ISBN 978-3-0343-0170-1

Volume 94 Michaël Abecassis et Gudrun Ledegen (éds): Les Voix des Français Volume 2: en parlant, en écrivant.
481 pages. 2010. ISBN 978-3-0343-0171-8

Volume 95 Manon Mathias, Maria O'Sullivan and Ruth Vorstman (eds): Display and Disguise.
237 pages. 2011. ISBN 978-3-0343-0177-0

Volume 96 Charlotte Baker: Enduring Negativity: Representations of Albinism in the Novels of Didier Destremau, Patrick Grainville and Williams Sassine.
226 pages. 2011. ISBN 978-3-0343-0179-4

Volume 97 Florian Grandena and Cristina Johnston (eds): New Queer Images: Representations of Homosexualities in Contemporary Francophone Visual Cultures.
246 pages. 2011. ISBN 978-3-0343-0182-4

Volume 98 Florian Grandena and Cristina Johnston (eds): Cinematic Queerness: Gay and Lesbian Hypervisibility in Contemporary Francophone Feature Films.
354 pages. 2011. ISBN 978-3-0343-0183-1

Volume 99 Neil Archer and Andreea Weisl-Shaw (eds): Adaptation: Studies in French and Francophone Culture.
234 pages. 2012. ISBN 978-3-0343-0222-7

Volume 100 Peter Collier et Ilda Tomas (éds): Béatrice Bonhomme: le mot, la mort, l'amour.
437 pages. 2013. ISBN 978-3-0343-0780-2

Volume 101 Helena Chadderton: Marie Darrieussecq's Textual Worlds: Self, Society, Language.
170 pages. 2012. ISBN 978-3-0343-0766-6

Volume 102 Manuel Bragança: La crise allemande du roman français, 1945–1949: la représentation des Allemands dans les best-sellers de l'immédiat après-guerre.
220 pages. 2012. ISBN 978-3-0343-0835-9

Volume 103 Bronwen Martin: The Fiction of J. M. G. Le Clézio: A Postcolonial Reading.
199 pages. 2012. ISBN 978-3-0343-0162-6

Volume 104 Hugues Azérad, Michael G. Kelly, Nina Parish et Emma Wagstaff (éds): Chantiers du poème: prémisses et pratiques de la création poétique moderne et contemporaine.
374 pages. 2013. ISBN 978-3-0343-0800-7

Volume 105 Franck Dalmas: Lectures phénoménologiques en littérature française: de Gustave Flaubert à Malika Mokeddem.
253 pages. 2012. ISBN 978-3-0343-0727-7

Volume 106 Béatrice Bonhomme, Aude Préta-de Beaufort et Jacques Moulin (éds): Dans le feuilletage de la terre: sur l'œuvre poétique de Marie- Claire Bancquart.
533 pages. 2013. ISBN 978-3-0343-0721-5

Volume 107 Claire Bisdorff et Marie-Christine Clemente (éds): Le Cœur dans tous ses états: essais sur la littérature et l'art français.
230 pages. 2013. ISBN 978-3-0343-0711-6

Volume 108 Michaël Abecassis et Gudrun Ledegen (éds): Écarts et apports des médias francophones: lexique et grammaire.
300 pages. 2013. ISBN 978-3-0343-0882-3

Volume 109 Allison and Imogen Long (eds): Women Matter / Femmes Matière: French and Francophone Women and the Material World. 273 pages. 2013. ISBN 978-3-0343-0788-8

Volume 110 Fabien Arribert-Narce et Alain Ausoni (éds): L'Autobiographie entre autres: écrire la vie aujourd'hui.
221 pages. 2013. ISBN 978-3-0343-0858-8

Volume 111 Leona Archer and Alex Stuart (eds): Visions of Apocalypse: Representations of the End in French Literature and Culture.
266 pages. 2013. ISBN 978-3-0343-0921-9

Volume 112 Simona Cutcan: Subversion ou conformisme ? La différence des sexes dans l'œuvre d'Agota Kristof.
264 pages. 2014. ISBN 978-3-0343-1713-9

Volume 113 Owen Heathcote: From Bad Boys to New Men ? Masculinity, Sexuality and Violence in the Work of Éric Jourdan.
279 pages. 2014. ISBN 978-3-0343-0736-9

Volume 114 Ilda Tomas: Arc-en-ciel: études sur divers poètes.
234 pages. 2014. ISBN 978-3-0343-0975-2

Volume 115 Lisa Jeschke and Adrian May (eds): Matters of Time: Material Temporalities in Twentieth-Century French Culture.
314 pages. 2014. ISBN 978-3-0343-1796-2

Volume 116 Crispin T. Lee: Haptic Experience in the Writings of Georges Bataille, Maurice Blanchot and Michel Serres.
316 pages. 2014. ISBN 978-3-0343-1791-7

Volume 117 Ashwiny O. Kistnareddy: Locating Hybridity: Creole, Identities and Body Politics in the Novels of Ananda Devi.
208 pages. 2015. ISBN 978-3-0343-1814-3

Volume 118 Michaël Abecassis et Gudrun Ledegen (éds): De la genèse de la langue à Internet: variations dans les formes, les modalités et les langues en contact.
278 pages. 2015. ISBN 978–3-0343-1798-6

Volume 119 Peter D. Tame: Isotopias: Places and Spaces in French War Fiction of the Twentieth and Twenty-First Centuries.
592 pages. 2015. ISBN 978–3-0343-0837-3

Volume 120 Daniel A. Finch-Race et Jeff Barda (éds): Textures: Processus et événements dans la création poétique moderne et contemporaine. 242 pages. 2015. ISBN 978–3-0343-1898-3

Volume 121 Hélène Sicard-Cowan: Vivre ensemble: éthique de l'imitation dans la littérature et le cinéma de l'immigration en France (1986– 2005). 149 pages. 2016. ISBN 978–3-0343-1944-7

Volume 122 Mercedes Montoro Araque et Carmen Alberdi Urquizu (éds): L'entre- deux imaginaire: corps et création interculturels. 216 pages. 2016. ISBN 978–3-0343-1926-3

Volume 123 Maureen A. Ramsden: Crossing Borders: The Interrelation of Fact and Fiction in Historical Works, Travel Tales, Autobiography and Reportage.
191 pages. 2016. ISBN 978–3-0343-1995-9

Volume 124 Jean Khalfa: Poetics of the Antilles: Poetry, History and Philosophy in the Writings of Perse, Césaire, Fanon and Glissant.
388 pages. 2017. ISBN 978–3-0343-0895-3

Volume 125 Mathilde Poizat-Amar: L'Eclat du voyage: Blaise Cendrars, Victor Segalen, Albert Londres.
252 pages. 2017. ISBN 978–1-78707-296-1

Volume 126 Philippe Willemart: L'Univers de la création littéraire: Dans la chambre noire de l'écriture: Hérodias de Flaubert.
160 pages. 2017. ISBN 978–1-78707-458-3

Volume 127 Margaret Atack, Alison S. Fell, Diana Holmes and Imogen Long (eds): French Feminisms 1975 and After: New Readings, New Texts. 276 pages. 2018. ISBN 978-3-0343-2209-6

Volume 128 Matt Phillips and Tomas Weber (eds): Parasites: Exploitation and Interference in French Thought and Culture.
284 pages. 2018. ISBN 978-3-0343-2266-9

Volume 129 Zoe Angelis and Blake Gutt (eds): Stains / Les taches: Communication and Contamination in French and Francophone Literature and Culture.
274 pages. 2019. ISBN 978-1-78707-443-9

Volume 130 Michaël Abecassis avec Marcelline Block, Gudrun Ledegen et Maribel Peñalver Vicea (éds): Le Grain de la voix dans le monde anglophone et francophone.
332 pages. 2019. ISBN 978-1-78874-107-1

Volume 131 Philippe Willemart: L'écriture à l'ère de l'indétermination: Études sur la critique génétique, la psychanalyse et la littérature.
232 pages. 2019. ISBN 978–1-78874-631-1

Volume 132 Augustin Voegele: De l'unanimisme au fantastique: Jules Romains devant l'extraordinaire.
382 pages. 2019. ISBN 978-1-78874-513-0

Volume 133 Maggie Allison, Elliot Evans and Carrie Tarr (eds): Plaisirs de femmes: Women, Pleasure and Transgression in French Literature and Culture.
278 pages. 2019. ISBN 978-1-78874-383-9

Volume 134 Aaron Prevots: Bernard Vargaftig: Gestures toward the Sacred.
144 pages. 2019. ISBN 978-1-78997-357-0

Volume 135 Susie Cronin, Sofia Ropek Hewson and Cillian Ó Fathaigh (eds): #NousSommes: Collectivity and the Digital in French Thought and Culture. 184 pages. 2020. ISBN 978-1-78874-767-7

Volume 136 Anaïs Stampfli: La coprésence de langues dans le roman antillais contemporain. 456 pages. 2020. ISBN 978-1-78874-578-9

Volume 137 Philippe Willemart: Les mécanismes de la création littéraire: Lecture, écriture, génétique et psychanalyse.
214 pages. 2020. ISBN 978-1-78997-737-0

Volume 138 Maureen A. Ramsden: The Evolution of Proust's 'Combray': A Genetic Study.
152 pages. 2020. ISBN 978-1-78997-785-1

Volume 139 Charlène Clonts: Gherasim Luca: Texte, image, son.
454 pages. 2020. ISBN 978-1-78997-916-9

Volume 140	Polly Galis, Maria Tomlinson and Antonia Wimbush (eds): Queer(y)ing Bodily Norms in Francophone Culture. 304 pages. 2021. ISBN 978-1-78997-514-7
Volume 141	Natalie Berkman: OuLiPo and the Mathematics of Literature. 340 pages. 2022. ISBN 978-1-78997-780-6
Volume 142	David Gascoigne and Ana de Medeiros (eds): Marie Nimier: Le Sujet et ses écritures / The Self in the Web of Language. 312 pages. 2021. ISBN 978-1-80079-195-4
Volume 143	Carole Bourne-Taylor and Sara-Louise Cooper (eds): Variations on the Ethics of Mourning in Modern Literature in French. 332 pages. 2022. ISBN 978-1-78997-273-3
Volume 144	Sophie Large et Flora Valadié (éds): Le Fanon des artistes. Perspectives transaméricaines. 288 pages. 2022. ISBN 978-1-80079-630-0
Volume 145	Ashwiny O. Kistnareddy and Alice Roullière (eds): Catching up with Time: Belatedness and Anachronies in Francophone Literature and Culture. 258 pages. 2022. ISBN 978-1-80079-337-8
Volume 146	Alexandra Cătană: Le corps de la lettre: La quête de la totalité dans la poétique d'Isidore Isou 404 pages. 2023. ISBN 978-1-80079-706-2
Volume 147	Bronwen Martin: The Ecological Vision of J.M.G. Le Clézio 170 pages. 2024. ISBN 978-1-80374-067-6
Volume 148	Thea Petrou: Form and Love in the Poetry of Jacques Roubaud 308 pages. 2024. ISBN 978-1-80079-265-4

www.ingramcontent.com/pod-product-compliance
Lightning Source LLC
Chambersburg PA
CBHW071536110726
47908CB00007B/1910

* 9 7 8 1 8 0 0 7 9 2 6 5 4 *